It's summer
sexy Medi
causin

Summer SURRENDER

Three sizzling summer stories from
favourite authors Sarah Morgan,
Susan Stephens and Cathy Williams!

Summer SURRENDER

Sarah MORGAN

Susan STEPHENS

Cathy WILLIAMS

Mills & Boon, an imprint of Harlequin (UK) Limited, Eton House, 18-24 Paradise Road, Richmond, Surrey TW9 1SR

SUMMER SURRENDER
© Harlequin Enterprises II B.V./S.à.r.l. 2012

Capelli's Captive Virgin © Sarah Morgan 2009
Italian Boss, Proud Miss Prim © Susan Stephens 2009
The Italian's One-Night Love-Child © Cathy Williams 2009

ISBN: 978 0 263 89783 8

010-0612

Harlequin (UK) policy is to use papers that are natural, renewable and recyclable products and made from wood grown in sustainable forests. The logging and manufacturing processes conform to the legal environmental regulations of the country of origin.

Printed and bound in Spain
by Blackprint CPI, Barcelona

Capelli's Captive Virgin

Sarah
MORGAN

USA TODAY bestselling author **Sarah Morgan** writes lively, sexy stories for both Modern™ and Medical™ romance.

As a child Sarah dreamed of being a writer and although she took a few interesting detours on the way, she is now living that dream. With her writing career she has successfully combined business with pleasure and she firmly believes that reading romance is one of the most satisfying and fat-free escapist pleasures available. Her stories are unashamedly optimistic and she is always pleased when she receives letters from readers saying that her books have helped them through hard times.

Romantic Times has described her writing as 'action-packed and sexy' and nominated her books for their Reviewer's Choice Awards and their 'Top Pick' slot.

Sarah lives near London with her husband and two children who innocently provide an endless supply of authentic dialogue. When she isn't writing or reading Sarah enjoys music, movies and any activity that takes her outdoors.

Readers can find out more about Sarah and her books from her website www.sarahmorgan.com. She can also be found on Facebook and Twitter.

CHAPTER ONE

'SIGNOR CAPELLI doesn't have an opening in his diary for five months.' The stunning blonde receptionist spoke faultless English and was clearly experienced in providing an impenetrable shield between her sexy billionaire boss and the public. 'You wouldn't believe the demand for divorce lawyers of his calibre. And anyway, his personal clients are all men.'

Lindsay dug her nails into her palms. 'I don't need a divorce lawyer. That isn't why I want to see him.'

And she *knew* his clients were men.

She knew everything about him. She knew that when a man instructed Alessio Capelli to handle his divorce, the wife in question might as well give up. The ruthless Sicilian lawyer had apparently made it his life's mission to ensure that women gained as little as possible from the end of a relationship. She also knew that his various business interests had made him a billionaire in his early thirties, which meant that he now worked purely for entertainment value.

And what sort of man found entertainment in crushing people's fragile marriages?

The girl tapped a perfectly manicured nail on the glass desk. 'I could call one of his team?'

'I need to speak to *him*.' Eaten up by worry, Lindsay tried to think clearly. She hadn't slept for three nights, the adrenaline was surging round her body and she felt physically sick as she contemplated what was unfolding before her. 'Please— I've flown to Rome specially—it's a personal matter. Something between myself and Signor Capelli.' A vision of her sister's pale face tormented her, but Lindsay had no intention of revealing her family secrets to this glacial beauty.

It was an unnerving experience—trying to gain access to the last man in the world she wanted to see. A bit like stepping towards the edge of a very sheer, crumbling cliff face, knowing that there could be only one outcome.

She was going to fall—

The receptionist raised her beautifully shaped eyebrows and it was obvious from her disbelieving gaze that she found it unlikely that someone like Lindsay would ever share anything personal with Alessio Capelli. 'Did he give you his mobile number?'

'No, but—'

'Then clearly he doesn't want you to contact him. Women who have a *special* relationship—' the receptionist paused for emphasis and gave a faintly patronising smile '—always have that number.'

Lindsay wanted to tell her that her taste in men didn't run to arrogant, heartless marriage wreckers, but she sensed that she wouldn't be believed.

Alessio Capelli was a magnet for women. His profession should have acted as a deterrent but instead it seemed to increase his appeal—as if every woman on the planet wanted to prove that they could win over this notorious cynic.

She stepped aside as another beautiful girl sauntered up to the bold curve of glass that formed the ultra-modern reception desk. 'The boss is in the gym, taking out his frustrations on a punchbag. If that file he is waiting for ever arrives, send it straight up to him on the sixteenth floor.'

As she listened in to the conversation Lindsay's gaze slid towards the bank of elevators at the back of the foyer. *Could she?* Her heart skipped a beat at the shear audacity of the idea. No, she couldn't possibly. She didn't break rules—

But somehow her feet were walking—quickly.

Waiting to feel a hand on her shoulder at any moment, Lindsay shot through the open doors and slammed her shaking hand onto the button that said sixteen.

As the doors closed she felt nothing but relief and then realised that her respite was only temporary.

She still had to get to Alessio Capelli.

Her heart was pumping, her palms were clammy and she fumbled with the lock of her bag as she searched frantically through the work she'd brought to do on the plane. *Work she'd been too worried to touch.* Exactly what sort of file was Alessio Capelli waiting for? Something buff-coloured and formal? Thick? Thin? Something in a sealed envelope? Hands shaking, she pulled out a file and tucked it under her arm. It didn't look particularly official, but it would have to do.

Sick with nerves, she checked her appearance in the mirrored wall. Looking back at her was a serious young woman dressed in a crisp white shirt and a straight black skirt that stopped just above the knee. Her pale blonde hair was twisted into a severe knot at the back of her head and her make-up was discreet and professional. She looked—businesslike.

No wonder the receptionist hadn't thought she was the sort of woman likely to have attracted the attention of Alessio Capelli, a man renowned for being seen with *extremely* beautiful women.

Something stirred inside her. A tiny spark of female vanity that she tried almost instantly to suppress.

But she *had* attracted his attention, hadn't she?

Once.

Once, he'd noticed her. In fact he'd more than noticed her. If she hadn't rejected him, they'd have—

Lindsay put her hands on her skirt and slid it slowly up her thighs until it revealed the same amount of leg as the girl downstairs had been showing. She stared at herself for a moment. Then she gave a nervous start and let the skirt drop just as the lift doors opened.

For crying out loud—*what was she thinking?*

Trying to look confident, she approached a set of glass doors manned by a muscular security guard.

Alessio Capelli certainly made sure he was well protected, she thought dryly, wondering whether it was because of his indecent wealth or the number of enemies he'd made in the pursuit of that wealth.

He was hard, cynical and ruthlessly ambitious. Unfortunately he was also sexier than any man had a right to be and Lindsay felt a moment of pure panic as the moment of confrontation grew closer.

She focused her mind on her sister.

Ruby. This was about Ruby, not her.

Ruby was her one and only priority.

'I'm here to see Alessio Capelli.' She smiled at the security guard. *'Sto cercando il Signor Capelli.'*

The man looked at the file under her arm and immediately punched a number into a keypad. The doors opened, revealing a state-of-the-art gym offering an incredible view over the rooftops of Rome.

Despite the breathtaking architecture, it was an all-male domain—the atmosphere thickened by testosterone, the room a melting pot of male ego, pumped muscle and raw aggression.

The security guard took one look at her uncertain expression and gestured towards a man who was throwing hard, rhythmic punches at a bag.

'That's him. That's the boss.'

Lindsay was grateful for his help because, without it, she never would have been able to identify the infamous Sicilian.

It wasn't what she'd expected of a billionaire with a taste for the finer things in life. But perhaps it was symbolic, she thought wryly, that Alessio Capelli had chosen this particular method of keeping his body in top physical condition. Did he run or lift weights like the other men in the room? No. He chose to thump the living daylights out of something.

Which simply confirmed what she already knew—that he was a tough, ruthless, cold-hearted machine who knew nothing about emotion.

Several of the other men glanced in her direction and suddenly she felt as vulnerable as a lone gazelle finding itself in the middle of a pride of lions.

Gritting her teeth, Lindsay kept her own eyes forward and followed the security guard across the room.

Alessio Capelli hadn't seen her. He continued to pound his fists into the bag, the muscles of his arms and shoulders bunched in a display of physical force. His bronzed skin gleamed with sweat and his shorts and vest top displayed a physique honed to perfection by hard, punishing exercise. His shoulders were wide and powerful, his body athletic as he threw punch after punch with ruthless precision and impeccable timing.

Watching this display of brutal male aggression, Lindsay faltered, sure that the security guard had made a mistake.

This was the wrong man. It wasn't him.

It was six months since she'd seen him, but Alessio Capelli's smooth sophistication and startling good looks were still inconveniently lodged in her brain. Not that it had been looks alone that had drawn her attention. For her, the quality that had made him dangerously attractive was his astonishing intellect. He was a man who used his razor-sharp brain to twist legal precedent to his advantage. His weapon was words, and he used them with lethal skill to achieve the outcome he wanted, whether it was winning a case or seducing a woman into his bed. As a lawyer he was, she knew, the very best.

As a human being—

Lindsay flinched as the man in front of her punched his fist hard into the bag. There was nothing smooth or suave about this particular man. On the contrary, he seemed to represent masculinity at its most basic level.

And then the angle of his body shifted and Lindsay drew in a sharp breath because she could now see the tiny scar above his left eye and the slight bump on his nose that blemished an otherwise faultlessly handsome face.

Once seen, never forgotten.

Every inch of his cold, hard features was etched into her memory for ever.

Horrified by the sudden flash of awareness that exploded through her body, Lindsay took a step backwards regretting the circumstances that had forced her into his path again.

Averting her eyes from his spectacular body, she suddenly wished he were dressed in a formal suit and standing on the other side of a very large desk.

How could she possibly have a serious conversation here?

He was half naked, for goodness' sake.

Half naked and *angry*, if the power behind those rhythmic punches was anything to go by.

That missing file had obviously been something important.

He still hadn't noticed her and it crossed her mind that she could still slink away and wait outside the door for him to finish his workout.

And then his gaze shifted and he stilled.

Dark, deep-set eyes connected with hers and in that single moment the world seemed to shrink. Nothing existed outside the square metre that contained the both of them.

They stared at each other in silence, exchanging a long, lingering glance that was wholly sexual. Trapped by the intimate demands of his intense dark gaze, Lindsey felt the blood pound in her head and she ceased to breathe.

He'd had exactly the same effect on her the first time she'd seen him and it was as terrifying now as it had been then.

Even knowing who he was and what he did for a living had done nothing to lessen the sheer physical impact of the man. He was unashamedly and blatantly masculine, his Sicilian roots evident in every bold line and hard angle of his impossibly handsome face. Stripped virtually naked, he was even more breathtaking. Unlike most men, he had no need of clothes as a disguise for physical imperfections. Alessio Capelli looked even better undressed than he did dressed.

His eyes were dark and framed by such thick, long lashes that it was as if nature had decided to emphasise such an unusually striking feature with extra care. Other men might have used those lashes as an effective screen for his emotions, but not Alessio Capelli. His gaze was direct and unflinching and she suspected that the reason he never felt the need to conceal his emotions was because he'd never actually experienced an emotion of any sort in his life.

He dealt with facts and numbers. And they were *big* numbers if the rumours were correct.

Feeling eighteen rather than twenty-eight, Lindsay cleared her throat. 'Hello, Alessio.'

His fists dropped to his sides and his eyes didn't leave hers. Then he slowly removed each of his gloves and dropped them onto a nearby bench.

'You've chosen a romantic venue for a reunion, Lindsay.' He spoke in perfect English, but in every way that mattered he was pure Sicilian. The dark good looks, the arrogance, the simmering volatility barely held in check by the veneer of sophistication that surrounded him like another skin—all products of his ancestry.

A wicked thrill of pleasure that he hadn't forgotten her was immediately replaced by dismay.

Flouting the powerful messages from her brain about not responding to him, her insides tumbled with excitement and her knees weakened. *This* was why she didn't trust herself around him—every second that she was in his company, her life became a battlefield. She was instantly trapped in a vicious conflict between what her body wanted and what her brain wanted.

The layers of protection she'd built around herself melted away in an explosive blast of raw chemistry. Her grip on the present slipped, and her mind twisted the highly charged sexual attraction into the ugly, destructive monster she knew it to be.

Terrified by the sudden glimpse into her own vulnerability, Lindsay reminded herself again that this was about Ruby. *Ruby was the reason she was here.*

'I'm surprised you haven't forgotten me, given the number of blonde women in your life. They must merge after a while.'

Amusement shimmered in his eyes as he reached for a towel. 'The unexpected is always memorable. You walked away from me.'

And she could tell from his tone that no woman had done that before.

'There was never the slightest possibility that I'd become involved with you. Unlike you, I think with my head.'

He laughed at that, and Lindsay frowned slightly because over the months she'd managed to forget that he had a sense of humour. And she knew why—that sense of humour made him seen more human and she didn't want to think of him in that way. It suddenly seemed vitally important to remember that he was cold, ruthless and unemotional. In her head he needed to be as unattractive as possible.

But the smile he gave her was anything but unattractive. 'So why are you standing in front of me now?'

'I'm here because I need to talk to you.' And that was true. But it didn't change the fact that she was painfully aware of him. *And he knew it.*

Alessio Capelli had so much experience with women that it would have been impossible for him *not* to know and the slow lift of his brow confirmed it.

'You have flown all the way from England just to talk to me? I didn't realise you found my conversation so stimulating.'

Lindsay was trying hard to ignore his superior height and the width and power of his shoulders. She hadn't needed a display of his boxing prowess to be aware of his strength. Strength was woven through his very being; an essential part of the man. Everyone who came up against him crumbled. Physically and mentally he was a titan.

And he made his living from using that strength against others.

Against women.

Suddenly she wished desperately that she could wind the clock back. If she could have done so, then she wouldn't have chosen Rome for a city break and she definitely would have paid more attention to where she was walking late at night.

Indirectly this whole situation was her fault.

If she'd never met him he would have remained in her head as a professional adversary instead of a man. When their paths had crossed professionally she would have been wearing her protective cloak, instead of which—

'I tried calling you from England,' she said crisply, 'but no one would put me through to you. I've travelled here purely because you're *impossible* to get hold of. Your staff will never say where you are. How do your clients contact you?'

He wiped his hands on the towel. 'If you were a client,' he said evenly, 'you would have been given a different number to call.'

The same number as his women? Dismissing that thought,

Lindsay bit her lip. 'I told them on the phone that I wanted to talk to you about a personal matter—'

'Then it's hardly surprising that they didn't put you through. They know that I never discuss personal matters.'

'I said it was urgent.'

'Which they would have translated as meaning that you were a journalist working to a tight deadline.' He looped the towel around his neck and Lindsay frowned slightly, wondering what it was like to lead the sort of life where everyone wanted to know everything about you.

'That was why no one would answer my questions? Because they thought I was a journalist?'

'I've trained my staff to be suspicious. A tiresome necessity driven by being in the public eye.' A cynical smile on his face, he stooped to retrieve a bottle of water from the floor. 'I'm intrigued as to what could possibly be important enough to drag you back into my disreputable presence. Hopefully you've finally decided to abandon those principles of yours and explore the endless pleasures of emotionless sex.'

'Alessio—'

'You've no idea how much I'm looking forward to getting you naked, *tesoro*.' His dark drawl connected straight to her nerve endings and she felt a flash of heat low in her pelvis.

He was doing it on purpose, she knew he was. *Trying to unsettle her.*

'You just can't help yourself, can you?' She struggled to keep her voice level. 'You have to embarrass me.'

'*Mi dispiace,*' he purred, his eyes glinting wickedly. 'I'm sorry—unfair of me, I know. It's just that I just love watching you blush. Your cheeks are the same colour they will be after we've had frantic sex.'

'That is never going to happen. Accept it.'

'That shows how little you know me. I have a compulsive

need to change situations that aren't to my liking.' He smiled—a slow, dangerous smile. 'It's called negotiation.'

'Negotiation is when both parties get what they want—it's supposed to be a win-win situation.'

'I understand the winning bit—I'm not so good at accepting half a solution.' His tone was gently apologetic but his dark eyes were as cool and unemotional as ever. 'When I want something, I want all of it. Not part of it.'

Her heart was racing out of control and her thoughts were going in much the same direction. 'You're not my type, Alessio.'

'That's what makes it so exciting, *tesoro*.' He was clearly enjoying teasing her, tying her in knots. 'If your taste in men ran to dangerous divorce lawyers, it would be boring. The chemistry between us must be very inconvenient for you.'

The conversation had taken a dangerous direction.

It's like sailing a ship through a storm, she thought wildly. *Almost impossible to keep it from being blown off course.*

He took her somewhere she didn't want to go.

Somewhere she'd marked as off-limits a very, very long time ago.

'Ruby—' she croaked. 'I'm worried about Ruby.'

'Ah.' His eyes narrowed slightly. 'I should have known that your sudden arrival would have something to do with the disappearance of that racy, naughty little sister of yours.'

'Disappearance? So you don't know where she is, either?' His words successfully dampened the sexual chemistry that had been threatening to eat her alive. Deeply troubled by that piece of unwelcome news, Lindsay sank her teeth into her lower lip, her mind speeding ahead, sifting through the options. 'I thought—I hoped that you'd know what was going on. I thought she might have said something to you.'

'Why would she do that?'

'Because you're her boss! She's been working for you for the last six months.'

'And you think I spend my working day exchanging confidences with my administrative staff?' Alessio lifted the water bottle to his lips and drank deeply and Lindsay watched in dazed, mesmerised silence, momentarily distracted by the bronzed column of his throat and the tangle of dark, male chest hair at the curve of his vest. Intercepting her gaze, he lowered the bottle slowly and a hint of a smile touched his hard, sensuous mouth. 'It's unwise to look at me like that,' he warned silkily, 'if you don't intend to follow through. And we both know that this isn't the time or the place.'

The knowledge that he'd read her so easily was almost as disturbing as the unexpected and unwelcome burst of warmth that erupted low in her pelvis. 'Do you ever think of anything other than sex, Alessio?'

'Yes.' Relaxed and in control, he scanned her flushed cheeks with disturbing intensity. 'Sometimes I think about money.'

Lindsay looked away briefly, furious with herself for giving him the opportunity to increase her discomfort. 'Can we *please* just talk about Ruby?'

'If we must.' His tone shifted from bite to boredom and he glanced at the clock on the wall. 'Obviously you're still trying to exert your authority over her.'

'It isn't about authority. I love her and I care about her.'

'As long as she is living her life the way you think she should live it. I don't claim to be an expert on love, Lindsay, but I think it's something to do with accepting people as they are and not trying to change them. You grip her like an eagle holding its prey.'

Lindsay felt a stab of pain, hurt by his criticism of her relationship with Ruby. He had no idea. *No idea what their lives had been like.* The quicksand of her emotions shifted and she stayed still, not allowing herself to be sucked down by the past. 'As you say, you know nothing about love.' *She wasn't going to let her mind drift backwards.* 'She hasn't phoned me for a week and that's not like her. She isn't answering her phone and when I called your office they said that she hasn't been in but they don't seem to know any more than that. I'm worried. Really worried.'

'Worried that she's slipped out of your grasp? She's twenty-one. Old enough to make her own mistakes without any outside interference.' He adjusted the towel. 'And it appears that she's done just that.'

Lindsay stood still, tortured by a moment of self doubt. *Was* she interfering? No, this was her sister they were talking about. 'Ruby is extremely vulnerable. When we met you and your brother last summer—well, she'd just come out of a very destructive relationship. She was devastated and—' She broke off, reluctant to reveal anything about their past. 'On the surface she seems all bubbly and together but— You may think you know her, but you don't.'

His eyes fastened on her face. 'She's been working for me for the past six months. I suspect that I know a great deal more about your sister than you do.' His tone was dry. 'And now you'll have to excuse me. I'm seeing a client in an hour and I'm flying to the Caribbean after that. Which is where, incidentally, your sister should be. She was supposed to be assisting me with a big case.' He strolled through a pair of swing doors and Lindsay hesitated briefly before following him.

Client—case—

He was obsessed with work; totally focused on generating still more wealth to add to his billions. Why?

Frowning slightly, Lindsay dismissed the question instantly.

She wasn't interested in what had turned Alessio Capelli into a ruthless, money-making machine. All she cared about was her sister. And he'd just revealed a small amount of information. Not much—just a morsel, but at least it was something.

'She knew you were expecting her to go to the Caribbean?'

'Of course. She was in charge of all the logistics both before and during the trip.'

'There's no way Ruby would have just abandoned her responsibilities like that—' Lindsay stopped dead, realising that she'd followed him into the changing room.

Fortunately for her it was empty, but Alessio threw her a challenging glance, a sardonic gleam in his dangerous dark eyes. 'You intend to continue this conversation while I shower?' He pulled the tee shirt over his head, his lack of concern about his semi-naked state in direct contrast to her own growing discomfort.

Faced with a full-on display of breathtaking male physique, Lindsay felt her heart thud hard against her chest. 'Could you just—not do that for a moment—?' Her voice cracked and she tried again. 'All I'm asking for is a few minutes of your time to talk. Please.'

'If all you want is to talk, then the going rate for a minute of my time is about a thousand dollars. Unless you've suddenly won the lottery, you couldn't possibly afford me. However, if you *don't* want to talk then I'll consider a preferential rate.' His gaze raking her flushed cheeks, he gave an unsympathetic laugh. 'What's the matter? If you're shocked, then you have only yourself to blame, *tesoro*. If you follow a man into the shower then you need to accept the consequences. It probably isn't the best action for someone who is trying to deny the sexual side of their nature.'

'I'm not denying anything. Yes, there's chemistry between us—' incurably honest, she stumbled over the words '—but that doesn't mean I have to act on it. Being an adult is about taking responsibility for your choices.' His amused glance set fire to her cheeks and Lindsay lifted her chin. 'You're *not* my choice.'

'No?'

Somehow the conversation had become personal again and Lindsay lifted a hand and rubbed her fingers over her forehead. This wasn't how she'd planned it. She'd been determined not to make it personal. 'Please—can we just talk about Ruby?'

'Of course. You talk. I'll shower. If you're so confident about your "choices", it won't bother you to see me naked.' His hands dropped purposely to his shorts and she inhaled sharply and averted her eyes.

He was trying to unnerve her, she knew that, and the best response would have been to stare boldly at him and say something cutting, but her brain had turned to treacle and her tongue wouldn't move.

'Outside,' she muttered incoherently. 'Perhaps I should wait for you outside—'

'Why would you need to do that?' His voice was silky soft. 'Not having problems with your "choices", are you? Not finding that famous willpower of yours tested? Is that why you're wearing the formal suit and the prim hairstyle? You're hoping that if you're tightly buttoned up on the outside, the inside will follow?'

'I came straight from work.'

'Ah, yes—your work. Lindsay Lockheart, relationship counsellor. How's that all going? The last time we were interviewed by the same radio show you were earnestly urging people to use RAP, your new Relationship Analysis Programme.' He sounded amused. 'I tried it out with my last girlfriend. Unfortunately I finished with her before we reached the end of it.'

Lindsay bit her lip. 'You don't need my programme to identify that your relationships are all shallow and meaningless. The programme isn't designed to factor in the emotional shortcomings of a cynic like you.'

'So perhaps you should release a version called the Cynic's Relationship Analysis Programme.' He smiled. 'Conveniently shortened to CRAP.'

Her face burned. 'I'm not here to rehash our professional differences.'

'I've always been intrigued as to how you've managed to build a reputation as an expert on relationships when your own experience in that area is so limited.'

It was as if he'd stripped off her clothes with the slice of a knife and left her vulnerable and exposed in front of him. Lindsay suppressed a helpless shiver, trying to find the weapons to fight him.

But confrontation wasn't her speciality.

No wonder he was unbeatable as a lawyer—he identified a person's weakness and then he pounced without hesitation or conscience.

If it weren't for Ruby she would have been out the door and back on the plane.

As it was she forced herself to focus on Ruby again.

'I need to know if my sister is involved with your brother.' *Please say no*, she begged silently. *Please say that isn't what's happened here*. 'She was definitely seeing someone, but she was very cagey about it and that isn't like her. Normally she tells me everything.'

'Everything? So that you can enjoy a vicarious sex life?'

Lindsay gritted her teeth. 'Could they be together? Could she be having an affair with Dino?'

'I'm sure she could. They seemed to find each other—entertaining.'

A cold trickle of dread ran through Lindsay's veins. 'And you didn't try to stop them?' Even without looking she was conscious that he'd removed the rest of his clothes and she kept her eyes firmly fixed on the wall. 'It didn't occur to you that they're *totally* unsuited?'

'Unlike you, I don't make it my business to interfere. My control streak doesn't extend to managing other people's relationships. And I am not my brother's keeper.' Arrogantly confident, he strolled towards the showers and she caught a glimpse of hard male muscle, strong thighs and bronzed skin. Then he closed the door and she heard the sudden rush of water.

Momentarily released from his presence, Lindsay sucked in a breath and blinked back tears of frustration and worry. If circumstances had been different she would have walked away because when it came to verbal sparring she was no match for him. He tied her in knots. But his words had left her deeply worried for her sister and frustrated by his lack of support.

As far as she was concerned, this was the worst-case scenario. It appeared that Ruby *was* involved with his brother, to the extent that she no longer even cared about her job.

If Alessio was telling the truth, then her sister had abandoned her responsibilities.

What would have made her do that?

Why would she have behaved in such a reckless, irresponsible fashion?

And why hadn't Alessio put a stop to it when it was obvious that the whole thing was going to crash and burn in the most disastrous way possible?

Couldn't he see? *Couldn't he see that a relationship between Ruby and Dino was an accident waiting to happen?*

Lindsay stared angrily at the shower cubicle.

Yes, of course he could see that. But he didn't care about anyone but himself.

He had no idea what that sort of relationship would do to Ruby.

It crossed her mind to tell him the whole tragic story in the hope that it might appeal to his sense of decency. But she honestly didn't think Alessio Capelli had a decent side.

What had possessed her to come here?

It had been a completely wasted journey.

They were so, so different in their approach to life, their beliefs—everything.

Feeling another rush of concern for her sister, Lindsay tried to think as she might. Where would Ruby have gone? What exactly had she done? *And why had she done it?* 'Did you encourage them?' She raised her voice to be heard above the shower and the sound of water stopped suddenly.

He emerged from the shower, a towel looped around his lean hips, his mouth curved into a cynical smile. 'Even you can't be *that* naïve. Two hormonal adults don't need encouragement, Lindsay. All they need is opportunity.'

'And I've no doubt you created that opportunity.' Rubbing her forehead with the tips of her fingers, Lindsay tried to think clearly. 'You encouraged them, I know you did. You knew how strongly I felt about the two of them becoming involved. When we first met, I told you Ruby was just getting over a broken relationship. She was—incredibly vulnerable. Still is. Your brother is the last thing she needs at the moment.' Lindsay swallowed. 'Did you do this on purpose? To punish me because I refused you? Was this about your ego, Alessio?'

Dark lashes veiled his gaze. 'If you're looking for somewhere to lay blame for your sister's behaviour, perhaps you should look a little closer to home.' His tone several shades cooler, he gave a careless shrug. 'If anyone is to blame for the way your sister lives her life, then it's surely you.'

'Me?' Genuinely shocked by that harsh analysis, Lindsay gaped at him. 'That's ridiculous. I've always warned her against having meaningless affairs and I certainly warned her to stay clear of you and your brother.'

'Precisely. For a relationship counsellor, you clearly know very little about human nature.'

'What's that supposed to mean?'

'That the forbidden and the dangerous is always more exciting than the permitted and the safe,' he said flatly. 'I can guarantee that the day you warned her to stay clear of me was the same day she showed up at my office looking for a job.'

'And you gave her one.' She couldn't keep the reproach out of her voice and he gave a dismissive shrug.

'There was a vacancy in my administrative team. Ruby is decorative, sociable and a relatively competent secretary.'

'Relatively?'

Alessio's mouth curved into a faint smile. 'Well, she's not here, is she? She does have a tendency to become—easily distracted.'

'By your playboy brother, presumably.' Frustration mingled with anxiety and Lindsay shook her head. 'You didn't think that throwing the two of them together might not be a good idea?'

'I allow *my* sibling to lead his own life. And unlike you I don't see anything wrong with animal passion. On the contrary, I endorse animal passion. It's one of the few truly honest human emotions.' With a casual movement Alessio unhooked the towel and threw it carelessly over the nearest bench. 'You ought to try it some time.'

Blinded by a disturbing vision of raw masculine perfection, Lindsay felt her mouth dry and looked away quickly. 'You're doing this on purpose,' she muttered hoarsely, 'trying to unnerve me.'

'Does it unnerve you my being naked?' As relaxed as she was tense, he ripped the packaging from a fresh shirt and thrust his arms into the sleeves. 'That's interesting. Next time you're analysing behaviour, you might want to dwell on that. Deep down, buried underneath that layer of control, is a real woman trying to get out.'

'Ruby.' Her voice hoarse, Lindsay kept her eyes fixed on a point on the wall, trying to erase the shockingly vivid image of dark body hair and substantial manhood. 'We were talking about Ruby. You don't even care that she might have gone off with your brother.'

'On the contrary, I do care. I'm as keen as you are to contact her. You can look. I'm decent.'

'You are? I mean—you want to know where she is, too?' Relief flooded through her. Perhaps she'd misjudged him. He did, after all, have a human side. 'Then what have you done so far? Have you tried to contact your brother?'

He'd pulled on a pair of beautifully cut dark grey trousers, but the white shirt still hung loose, affording a tantalising glimpse of masculine chest hair shading hard muscle. 'Like your sister, he isn't answering his phone. I suspect they're otherwise occupied.'

Lindsay made a distressed sound. 'But *you* can find them. I know you have contacts. It won't take you long to track them down.'

The snowy-white silk shirt seemed to emphasise his masculinity and Alessio threw an amused look in her direction as he fastened the buttons with slow, deliberate movements of his long fingers. 'Your belief in the degree of my influence is quite sweet. Do powerful men turn you on, Lindsay?'

'Please stop it.' A hoarse whisper was all she could manage because her body was in such a turbulent state. 'Please, please stop it. I'm just relieved that you're as keen as I am to intervene before this relationship goes too far.'

'I have no intention of intervening in the relationship.'

Confused, Lindsay frowned. 'But you said—'

'I said that I am as keen as you are to find out where Ruby is—' he reached for his silk tie '—but *not* because I intend to counsel her on her choice of men. I believe in letting people make their own mistakes in life.'

Lindsay just stared at him. 'Then why are you keen to find her?'

'Under the terms of her contract, your sister was obliged to give notice if she intended to terminate her employment. She hasn't.' With skilful grace his fingers produced a perfect knot and he eased the tie up to his bronzed throat. 'If she doesn't turn up for work by four o'clock this afternoon, she loses her job. I thought it only fair to warn her of that fact.'

There was a buzzing in Lindsay's ears. 'You're going to *fire* her?' The words came out as an appalled squeak. 'That's ridiculous.'

'That's business. I employed her to do a job. She's not doing it. Be grateful I'm not suing her for breach of contract.' His tone hardened and she gazed at him in shock.

'Even you can't be that hard-hearted.'

His eyes held hers. 'What would you say if I went back to my office this afternoon and fired someone on the spot?'

'I'd say you were a megalomaniac,' Lindsay said faintly and a smile flickered at the corners of his mouth.

'You'd say I was unfair. Employers and employees have a certain responsibility towards each other. I'm a fair employer but I expect the same degree of fairness in my employees. I expect a certain code of behaviour. Your sister broke that code. I intend to make an example of her.'

Lindsay closed her eyes. If she'd thought things were bad before this conversation, they were fast becoming worse.

'No.' She shook her head in disbelief. '*Please* don't do this—Ruby really likes working for you.' *Although she'd never understood why.* 'Losing her job would be devastating.'

'It will send a clear message to other employees to think twice before they wilfully abandon their contracts.' Showing not a glimmer of remorse or uncertainty, he reached for his jacket. 'Your sister has until four o'clock. If she isn't on my plane, ready to do the job for which she is employed, then her time with my company is over.'

'Alessio, I'm begging you not to do this—'

His gaze lingered on her face. 'Normally I have no problems with a woman begging, but on this occasion you're wasting your time. If she isn't here within the hour, she's fired.'

CHAPTER TWO

LINDSAY stood in stunned silence, wondering how a bad situation had suddenly become so much worse.

Ruby was about to lose *everything*. 'Please don't take her job away from her. When her relationship with your brother crashes, Ruby is going to be devastated.'

'Only if she has unrealistic expectations about relationships, which, being your sister, she undoubtedly will have.'

Reminding herself that an argument on that topic would get her nowhere, Lindsay bit her lip. 'If she loses her job as well, it will finish her.'

'Or perhaps it will teach her an important lesson about loyalties, priorities and the fact that actions have consequences.' His tone was unsympathetic. 'Ruby is employed by me to do a job. If she can't or won't do it, then I don't want her on my team.'

'She's a junior member of your secretarial staff. I'm sure you have literally *hundreds* of people who could easily take her place on this trip of yours.'

'That isn't the point. This is Ruby's responsibility. If she lets me down, she's out.'

'If she lets you down then you should fire your brother!' Lindsay glared at him. 'He's as much to blame for this situation as Ruby. More because he's eight years older than her!'

'My brother runs his own area of the business—his actions are of no interest to me.' Displaying not a whit of sympathy, he slipped his Rolex onto his wrist and fastened it. 'Stop trying to run her life. You can't protect her from everything. This might be just the wake-up call that Ruby needs. I'm sure it will prove to be a useful life experience for her. There's nothing quite like a few knocks to toughen a person up.'

What did someone like him know about knocks? He went through life giving them, not receiving them. Someone with his wealth and confidence knew *nothing* about struggling to survive. *Nothing about uncertainty and insecurity.*

'Ruby *needs* this job. And she's usually very responsible. This isn't like her. I don't understand it.'

'My brother and Ruby couldn't keep their hands off each other. It's called passion,' he said dryly. 'It happens to the best of us.'

'But they didn't have to act on it. They're not children,' Lindsay said tartly. 'They should have known better.'

His gaze dropped to her mouth and lingered there with disturbing intensity. 'You've never been so overwhelmed by passion that you throw caution to the wind?'

Her face burned scarlet. 'I'm an adult, Alessio, not a teenager. And one of the characteristics of adulthood is the ability to exercise self-control when the need arises.'

For some reason he seemed to find that amusing. 'That comment makes me wonder whether that legendary self-control of yours has ever been truly tested.' His gaze lifted to hers, his dark eyes burning with sexual challenge. 'When did you last struggle not to rip a man's clothes off, Lindsay?'

When she'd first met him—

Before she knew who he was and what he did for a living.

Her heart was bumping against her chest. 'We were talking about Ruby.'

He smiled. 'So we were. Well, your sister is either lacking

your iron self-control, or she is a master tactician who has her eye on a higher prize. There's always the possibility that she's hoping that my brother will marry her.'

'Ruby isn't interested in marriage.'

'All women are interested in marriage if the prize is high enough.' His tone was deeply cynical and Lindsay shook her head.

'Ruby knows that your brother isn't the marrying kind any more than you are.' But he'd scattered doubt in her mind. *Did* her sister know that? Or was she deluding herself, as so many women did once they were in the throes of passion? 'We both know that their affair isn't going to last five minutes.'

Alessio raised his eyebrows. 'They did your CRAP test?'

Lindsay flushed. 'We both know that they're not in love. Theirs is a relationship based on casual sex. To be successful, a relationship has to be founded on real intimacy. But that's something I don't for a moment expect you to understand.'

He gave a slow smile. 'I don't have any problems with intimacy, Lindsay. In fact, intimacy is my favourite method of relaxation.'

Her entire body warmed under his lazy scrutiny and she straightened her shoulders, instinctively rejecting her response. 'I'm talking about *emotional* intimacy.'

He leaned his wide shoulders against the wall, a wicked sparkle in his eyes. 'By emotional intimacy I assume you mean a cuddle after sex.' Tilting his glossy dark head to one side, he pretended to consider the point for a moment. 'I'm not totally averse to that, providing the woman in question has pleased me. I can be generous when it suits me.'

She knew he was winding her up and she also knew that she was getting herself deeper and deeper into trouble. The atmosphere was suddenly impossibly tense and she told herself that it was just because they were talking about sex.

'Let's just not even discuss this,' she muttered faintly. 'You and I will *never* agree on what makes a good relationship.'

Under the penetrating force of his dark gaze she felt heat rush through her body.

'A good relationship is one that ends when it is time for it to end,' he said dryly, 'and doesn't struggle along for years in mortal agony.'

'Oh, please.' Determined to ignore everything that was happening to her, Lindsay made an impatient sound. 'Next you'll be telling me that divorce lawyers do the human race a favour.'

'Not the whole human race. Just a select few who I believe to be worthy of my particular skill set.'

'You make money out of people's misery.'

'So do you,' he returned instantly, the glint in his eyes suddenly hard. 'The difference between us is that I've built a successful business based on reality, whereas yours is based on fantasy. You peddle dreams. Fairy tales. Happy ever afters.'

'That isn't true—'

'Expecting a relationship to last in today's society is the stuff of fantasy.'

'That isn't true either—'

'Then why is my phone always ringing? Why am I busier than I've ever been?' Cool and calculating, he watched her. 'Because people are finally accepting that expecting to be hooked to someone for life is totally unrealistic. Better to do what my brother and your sister are currently doing—have wild exciting sex until it is no longer exciting. Then move on.'

Listening to him rip holes in everything she believed in, Lindsay felt her limbs tremble. 'I *completely* disagree with you.'

His eyes lingered on her mouth. 'Well, of course you do. If you didn't, you'd be out of a job. I watched you on television last week, recommending ways in which a certain Hollywood actress could save her marriage. Lindsay Lockheart, relationship expert. You look cute on the screen, by the way.' His voice was dangerously soft. 'Cute and convincing, which is all the more surprising when you bear in mind that Lindsay Lockheart, relationship expert, has never actually had a relationship herself.'

Ignoring the mockery in his eyes, Lindsay defended herself. 'It's true that I've never been married, if that's what you mean.' Her heart pumped hard because he was pressing in close to a subject she avoided.

He studied her in silence, his expression thoughtful. 'It wasn't what I meant. Do your clients know that you're a fraud, Lindsay?' His tone pleasant, he slipped his arms into his jacket and her face flamed.

'I've had relationships, Alessio.'

'I'm not talking about a dinner date or a dignified trip to the opera.' With unconscious grace, he strolled purposefully towards her, suddenly looking every inch the sophisticated, successful lawyer. Gone was the street-fighter image of moments earlier. The transformation from rough and tough to slick and sophisticated was complete. Dressed in a dark grey suit that moulded his powerful shoulders to perfection, he exuded wealth and success. The only thing that hadn't changed was the air of raw power that clung to him like a second skin.

Lindsay felt her heart rate double and fought the impulse to take a step backwards. No way was she going to let him have the upper hand. He'd stop in a moment—he had to.

But he didn't.

He strolled right up to her and backed her against the wall, decisive, masculine and very much the one in control.

Flustered, she lifted her hands and then dropped them again. 'Alessio, for goodness' sake—'

'I'm not talking about a staid exchange of views over a quiet drink in one of your English country pubs. I'm talking about an explosion of passion, real intimacy.' He planted a powerful arm on either side of her head, blocking her escape route. 'I'm talking about *real* intimacy, Lindsay. Hot, sticky, exciting intimacy—intimacy that makes your heart race and makes you forget that you have responsibilities—'

'Alessio—'

'Intimacy that's out of your control. Intimacy that drives you to bad decisions. I'm talking about man-woman stuff.' His eyes glittered, dark and dangerous, and his mouth was suddenly terrifyingly close to hers. 'Animal instinct.'

'Alessio!'

'Ever felt that, Lindsay—' his breath was warm against her mouth '—the sort where logic and self-control don't get a look-in?'

He was going to kiss her.

This time, Alessio Capelli was going to kiss her.

There was a buzzing in her ears, her knees felt like jelly and her stomach burned with wicked sexual excitement. Even as her brain struggled to resist it, she could feel herself going under, submerged by swirling waters of dark, dangerous passion.

The damaged child inside her was screaming at him to go away, but the woman inside her wanted him right where he was.

His gaze held hers for a long moment and then his arms dropped to his sides and he took a step backwards. '*That's* the sort of relationship I'm talking about, little Lindsay.'

Her heart was pounding so hard that for a moment she was terrified that she might actually pass out. She blinked several times to clear her vision and forced herself to breathe slowly. And then humiliation rushed through her veins because she knew she'd been microseconds away from sliding her arms round his strong neck and pressing her mouth against his. 'I don't know what you're talking about.' It wasn't disappointment she was feeling. It absolutely wasn't going to be disappointment.

'I know you don't. And that's the point I'm making. How

the hell has someone like you managed to carve out a career for yourself advising couples on their relationships?'

It wasn't safe to be this close to him. And not because of him.

She just couldn't trust herself— 'Just because I haven't made a mistake—'

'Your idea of a mistake is another person's idea of a life,' he said dryly and she clasped her hands in front of her.

'You're talking about meaningless sex—'

'And you don't think two people can have a relationship based on meaningless sex?' His eyes narrowed. 'Trust me, *tesoro*. A relationship based on meaningless sex is the best sort.'

His remark restored her common sense. 'Which brings us right back to the point I made earlier—' strength ran through her veins and she met his gaze bravely '—that you don't know anything about true intimacy. Intimacy is not a cuddle at the end of sex. Intimacy is about sharing. Real love is about sharing thoughts and feelings, hope and fears.'

Alessio gave a faint smile. 'Then I'm truly relieved that I've managed to avoid your type of "intimacy",' he drawled. 'And people's spurious belief in something they call love is what keeps my phone ringing.'

Lindsay gave an exasperated sigh. 'Love exists. And if you've never experienced that first-hand or witnessed it, then I feel sorry for you. It must be very cold and lonely in your bed.' She regretted the words instantly and, sure enough, his sensual mouth curved into a wicked smile.

'Generating heat in my bed isn't one of my problems,' he drawled softly, 'so any time you need a practical demonstration of alternative energy sources, just bang on my bedroom door, *tesoro*.'

Lindsay lifted her fingers to her forehead and breathed deeply. 'I suppose it's your job that's made you so very cynical—'

'Realistic,' he slotted in helpfully. 'It's made me realistic. Which is why I haven't had to pay out a fortune in alimony.'

'You have no experience whatsoever of sustaining a loving, intimate and accepting relationship.'

His gaze was mocking. 'Of course "loving, intimate and accepting relationship" can be conveniently shorted to LIAR, a word which effectively describes everyone who claims to be happily married.' He glanced at his watch. 'Fascinating and absorbing though this discussion is, I have an anxious client waiting in my office, eager to eradicate the last LIAR in his life, and I'm due to fly to the Caribbean immediately after that.'

Flustered, she tried to marshal her thoughts. 'But Ruby—'

'Console yourself that Ruby is, at this moment, probably having the best sex of her life. If she happens to have the sense to show up at the airport, I'll suggest that she calls you,' he said in a cool tone. 'If not, then next time you do speak to her, you can advise her to start looking for a new job.'

Emotionally shattered by her encounter with Alessio, Lindsay sat alone in the café, her tiny cup of espresso coffee untouched on the table in front of her.

It had been worse than she'd feared. *So much worse than she'd feared.*

Despite all her efforts, just being near the man unsettled her and it had become harder and harder to think of Ruby.

Even now, as she tried to focus on her sister's plight, her mind was haunted by Alessio Capelli's dark, sardonic smile.

Lindsay stared blankly at the dark, pungent coffee in the tiny cup, wishing for the millionth time that her sister had never taken the job.

For Ruby—young, impressionable and so desperately wounded after her last disastrous relationship—the lure of a job in sun-baked Italy, in the employment of a sophisticated billionaire, had proved too tempting to turn down.

A fresh start, she'd called it.

More like 'out of the frying pan into the fire', Lindsay

thought wearily, remembering just how hard she'd tried to persuade Ruby to see sense.

'Alessio is a typical Sicilian male. He might seem very modern and charming, but underneath—' she tried hard to make Ruby see the truth '—underneath he's ruthless, macho and his view of women is firmly stuck in the Stone Age.'

Dark eyes staring into hers, demanding her attention.

'You didn't think he was so unbearable when he saved our necks that night by the Coliseum. If he and his brother hadn't happened to be passing—' Ruby gave an expressive shudder. 'They were amazing. I mean it was like something out of a movie, wasn't it? The two of them taking on that gang of thugs and they beat them easily.'

Lindsay just looked at her sister helplessly, not knowing what to say.

It was all too easy to see how Ruby might have been seduced by the romance of the whole situation, because for a short time she'd felt the same way.

Once Alessio Capelli had dispensed with the gang who had surrounded them, he'd lifted her gently but decisively to her feet, his sexy dark eyes faintly quizzical as he'd studied her in the dim light.

For that one breathlessly exciting moment, she'd forgotten who, and where, she was.

With his broad shoulders and superior height, he'd seemed so powerful and *safe* that she'd actually swayed towards him, driven by the delicious and unfamiliar curl of desire low in her pelvis.

Looking back on it now, she realised that she probably would have been safer with the gang that had attacked them.

Fortunately for her, Alessio had released her before she could make a complete and utter fool of herself, but not before he'd awakened a part of Lindsay that she'd previously refused to recognise.

The two brothers had taken them to the bar of the most expensive hotel in Rome, a venue so exclusive that Lindsay wouldn't have had the courage to put her toe inside the door of such a place if she hadn't been with them.

Overawed by the opulent surroundings, it had been several minutes before she'd noticed the deference of everyone around her and several more minutes to realise that the arrogant, powerful man currently extending a glass of champagne in her direction actually *owned* the hotel. Vastly entertained by the fact that she had no idea who he was, he'd introduced himself properly and it was at that point that everything had fallen apart for her.

Alessio Capelli.

Of all the men who could have come to her rescue, it had been Alessio Capelli, the ruthless divorce lawyer who had a reputation for protecting his male clients from 'gold-digging' women.

The irony was, she knew him. Their paths had crossed professionally. They'd never met in person, but they'd been interviewed on several occasions by reporters keen to publicise their opposing views on relationships. And as she'd familiarised herself with his opinions, Lindsay had gritted her teeth and fumed. When asked to comment on some of her techniques for predicting marital success he'd been scathing and derogatory in his remarks.

And as if that weren't enough, she'd worked with some of his clients on an individual basis. She'd seen first-hand some of the damage he'd wrought.

'Alessio Capelli crushes women,' she told her sister flatly, but Ruby simply shrugged.

'Not all women. Just the greedy ones. You didn't think he was so objectionable when he used his muscle to save you from that lowlife. I bet he's a *fantastic* kisser.' Ruby gave her a wicked look. 'Rumour has it that what Alessio Capelli doesn't know about seducing women isn't worth knowing.

Come on, Linny. I know you always use logic and common sense, but you have to admit he's *gorgeous*. And if you don't like your men dark and intimidating, there's always his cute younger brother...'

Lindsay clamped her lips together, deciding not to point out that only two weeks earlier Ruby had been so devastated over the end of a relationship that she hadn't seen the point of living.

'Ruby—try and be a bit more analytical,' she urged. 'Think beyond the handsome face. Do you have the same views on life? Do you share the same values? Do you have what it takes to sustain a relationship?'

'I'm just having fun, Linny. Not planning a wedding,' Ruby snapped at her. 'You're *so* serious. You should have an affair with Alessio Capelli. It would do you good. A week of sun, sex and hot Sicilian man.'

Closely followed by a lifetime of heartache.

'I'm not interested in a meaningless affair with someone whose values I don't respect. And we're talking about you, not me. I just don't think you should get involved with anyone else for a while,' Lindsay said tactfully and Ruby's eyes clouded slightly.

'Don't worry. I've learned that lesson.'

Lindsay stared at her cold coffee now.

Had she?

Or was Ruby in the middle of yet another wild, crazy affair that would undoubtedly lead to another major emotional crash?

Her thoughts driving her almost demented with worry, Lindsay reached for her phone and called everyone she knew one more time. But still no one had any news of Ruby.

So now what?

Feeling helpless, she glanced at the clock on the wall of the café. Ruby had less than an hour to make the flight.

She tried to think positively.

There was still time for Ruby to turn up. She knew the importance of reliability in the employment market—she wouldn't let Alessio Capelli down…

Suddenly Lindsay felt an ominous stabbing pain above her eye and winced as she recognised the beginnings of a migraine. *Oh, no, not now.* And not here, in a foreign country where nothing was familiar.

Gritting her teeth, she reached into her bag for the packet of tablets she carried with her. But there was no sign of them. With a frown, she emptied the contents of her handbag over the table and rummaged through it. No tablets.

Infuriated with herself for forgetting to replenish the tablets last time she'd used them, Lindsay swept the items back into her handbag and tried to think clearly. Normally she'd take a tablet, lie down for a few hours and emerge revived.

This time she had no tablets and the hands of the clock were relentlessly moving towards four o'clock. She didn't have time for a headache. She knew what Ruby was capable of doing—

Drenched with sudden panic, Lindsay forced herself to breathe slowly—to *think*.

What could she do?

With something approaching desperation, Lindsay pressed her fingers against her temples, searching for alternative options.

The knifelike pain in her head increased and she closed her eyes. But with her eyes closed she had a sudden vision of Ruby's pale lifeless face and she shot to her feet in the grip of an overwhelming panic. It took a moment to wrestle her overactive imagination back under control and remind herself that she had no evidence that anything bad had happened to Ruby.

There was probably a perfectly simple explanation for all this.

Perhaps her phone was broken, or perhaps she'd simply lost track of the time and had every intention of returning to the Capelli offices in time for the Caribbean trip.

Perhaps she was there now, offering an apology for her lateness to Alessio Capelli.

Keeping that thought uppermost in her mind, Lindsay reached for her bag and paid for her coffee.

Perhaps, she thought as she left the café, this whole night-mare would have a swift and happy ending.

CHAPTER THREE

ALESSIO CAPELLI rode the glass elevator down to the ground floor of his office building, ignoring the insistent buzz of the telephone that was tucked in the pocket of his suit.

He should have been rejoicing. In one short meeting he'd gained another high-profile, influential client and, more to the point, he'd ripped him away from a rival law firm. Ruthlessly competitive, Alessio waited for the usual high that came from defeating an adversary, but this time there was nothing.

Instead his brain was dominated by a picture of a pair of troubled blue eyes and blonde hair so tightly secured at the base of her slender neck that not even a strand was likely to escape.

Control, he thought dryly. Lindsay Lockheart was big on control. She controlled her hair, she controlled her emotions, but most especially she controlled her little sister.

For a woman who made her living trying to modify human behaviour, Lindsay was appallingly naïve when it came to understanding the actions of her younger sibling.

He'd never met anyone so serious. She acted as though she were ninety, and yet he knew she was only in her late twenties.

He strode across the polished marble floor of the lobby, through the revolving glass door and out into the street where his car awaited.

As if conjured straight from his thoughts, there was

Lindsay Lockheart. She was standing by his car wearing the same crisp white shirt and slim black skirt that she'd had on earlier, her small overnight bag clutched in her fingers. Her delicate chin was held at a certain angle and there was a hopeful look in her eyes that melted into anxiety as she saw that he was on his own.

His driver shot him a look of nervous apology and Alessio sighed, lifted a brow in sardonic appraisal and focused his gaze on her pale face. 'If you want to spend more time conversing, then I'm going to have to bill you.'

She stepped towards him. 'Has Ruby turned up?'

'You are obsessed with your sister's movements.' He handed his case to his driver, noting the way her cheeks blanched. It was a strange sibling relationship, he mused. Just how far was Lindsay prepared to go for her wayward sister? And, more interestingly, why?

'I love my sister,' she said huskily, 'and I won't apologise for that. Nor do I intend to explain myself to you.'

'A decision that leaves me quite weak with relief,' Alessio confessed in a lazy drawl, his eyes drawn to the tempting thrust of her breasts through her perfect white shirt. 'I can't imagine anything more likely to challenge my attention span than a summary of your family history. So, if you haven't come to bore me, why are you here?'

'I was checking whether you'd heard anything. I thought she might have turned up to do her job.'

'Sadly for Ruby, the answer is no.'

Her slim shoulders sagged slightly as he delivered what was clearly a very unwelcome piece of news. 'Could you give her a few more minutes? Just in case?'

'No,' he said gently, 'I couldn't.'

She closed her eyes briefly and he saw that her lashes were long and thick, the skin on her eyelids as pale as the rest of her face. 'Please—' Her voice cracked and when she opened her eyes again there was desperation there. 'I—I know we don't agree on things, but this is really important to me. Is there anything I can do to stop you firing her?'

The wild and wicked side of him took over. 'Come in her place.'

He made the demand in absolute confidence that she would refuse.

The way they lived their lives was diametrically opposed. On the surface they clashed, conflicted and disagreed.

But perhaps the biggest discordance lay *under* the surface. The powerful pull of sexual attraction disturbed her and he had a strong feeling that the roots of that disturbance were to be found deeper than the obvious restrictions posed by her ridiculously idealistic belief system.

He knew there was no way that Lindsay would ever voluntarily put herself in his path, so when she responded with a shocked 'I can't do that,' he shrugged, reflecting on the fact that being constantly right could border on the tedious.

'Of course you can't.' He couldn't resist goading her a little more. 'To be trapped with me in a romantic Caribbean hideaway would be a completely unfair test of your willpower. I understand.'

'You flatter yourself, Signor Capelli.' Her voice shook and her cheeks had slightly more colour than they had a moment earlier. 'I could lie naked in a bed with you and still have no trouble resisting you because I know you're just not right for me.'

Alessio laughed, thoroughly enjoying himself. 'Now *that's* a challenge no red-blooded Sicilian could refuse.'

'I wasn't issuing a challenge,' she said stiffly. 'I was merely pointing out that the brain does actually play a prominent part in my decisions although I can understand that you, as a "red-blooded Sicilian", might find that hard to comprehend since you obviously think with a very different part of your anatomy.'

And that particular part of his anatomy was currently

making its existence felt in the most predictable way possible, Alessio acknowledged wryly. And given that Lindsay Lockheart had yet to discover the wonders of sex without emotional attachment, the only available solution to this particular attack of animal lust appeared to be a cold shower.

'If you have so much faith in your mental discipline, why would you be afraid to come with me?'

'I'm *not* afraid.' Her chin lifted and suddenly the tension between the two of them reached screaming pitch.

'You're afraid, Lindsay,' Alessio said softly, 'and I'll tell you why. So far, the only thing that has kept me from having sex with you is lack of opportunity.'

She was so deliciously easy to shock, he mused, watching as her eyes widened and hot colour poured into her cheeks.

'That's nonsense. We could have all the opportunity in the world and I still wouldn't have—we wouldn't—' She swallowed. 'The ability to think and use our brains is what separates us from animals. I'm in control of what I do.'

'If you're so confident about that, then come in your sister's place.'

He could see a tiny pulse beating in her creamy throat as she struggled with the challenge he'd thrown into her path. 'I can't just abandon my life.'

'You mean you don't trust yourself to be on a Caribbean island with me and not have sex.' He gave a slow, sure smile. 'Be honest, Lindsay. You know that your logical approach to relationships is going to be worth nothing when we're both naked. And you're afraid to lose.'

'Damn you,' she whispered, her eyes sparking angrily. 'Damn you for making this about us when it should be about my sister.'

'If it was about your sister, then you'd come.'

The lawyer in him interpreted every expression that flickered across her face. Nerves, worry, stress, fear and something else that he couldn't immediately identify—something much, much more complex than all the other emotions put together—

'I can't just drop my life at a moment's notice.'

'You're worried that one of your clients might get divorced when you're not looking and that would be bad for publicity?'

'I don't care about publicity. I don't care about winning and losing. I care about people. *I care about Ruby.* And I'm not coming with you.'

Alessio was astonished by the depth of his disappointment.

Why should it matter to him? It wasn't as if his bed was going to be empty.

There was no shortage of beautiful, sophisticated women desperate for his attention. Women who wouldn't waste time fighting him. Why would he be bothered about Lindsay's refusal?

And then he gave a wry smile, a flash of insight giving him the reason for his reaction.

He *hated* losing.

He absolutely hated losing, but it had been so long since he'd lost at anything that he hadn't immediately recognised the feeling. And if there was one thing designed to send his competitive streak into overdrive, it was the concept of losing.

Lindsay Lockheart represented a challenge. And when had a woman ever been a challenge to him?

Aware that his driver was agitated about the time, he applied analytical skills to the problem. 'Fine. If I hear from her before you do I'll be sure to tell her that you cared about her. But not enough to do her job in her place. Have a good flight back.' And with that carefully orchestrated parting shot he strode towards the car, wondering how long it would take.

Three strides? Maybe four?

'All right.' Her voice stopped him on two and he smiled to himself as he turned because in the end it had been disappointingly easy.

Women were so predictable.

'*Scusi?*' He pretended to be confused, watching as she walked towards him like someone going to the gallows.

'Why would you be surprised? You've won, Alessio. Isn't that what you always do? You find your opponent's weakness and you exploit it.' Without giving him time to answer, she pushed past him and slid into the back of the car.

And clearly she wasn't used to getting into the back of a limousine. Accommodating her sudden movement, her skirt slid up to mid-thigh and Alessio's attention was momentarily diverted. *Fabulous legs,* he thought absently, his libido acting like a break on his thought processes. Who would have thought that Lindsay Lockheart was hiding a body like that under her sober, serious black skirt? Those long, shapely legs appeared to be encased in sheer stockings with a hint of a sheen and Alessio found himself wishing that her skirt were just slightly shorter…

Then she tugged the skirt down and Alessio started to breathe again.

'Let me get this straight—' trying to ignore the vicious ache in his loins, he dragged his gaze away from her slender ankles and leaned an arm on the roof of the car '—you're offering to warm my bed in the Caribbean?'

'No, I'm not.' She turned her head and her blue eyes connected with his. 'You may think you've won, but winning doesn't matter to me. All that matters is protecting Ruby. And if stepping into her shoes protects her job, then fine, I'll work for you.' Her tone was cool and collected, but he saw that her pupils were dilated and her breathing was rapid and shallow. Her fingers clutched her bag tightly and Alessio suddenly had a disconcertingly clear image of her naked and squirming on his silk sheets, those same slender fingers curled around a certain part of him.

How much of a nudge would it take to push her from prim to passionate?

He decided to push her a little further out of her comfort zone. 'My client is recovering from the end of a disastrous marriage. He needs relaxation and legal counsel.' *Was she wearing lipstick?* He didn't think so but there was a tempting sheen to her lips. 'A relationship counsellor would be about as helpful on this trip as a blizzard at a barbecue.'

'I'm not accompanying you in my role as relationship counsellor.' She tucked her bag neatly by her side, but still she didn't look at him. 'I worked for a year in a law firm in London when I left college. You can give me a full brief. Whatever it is you expect of Ruby, I'm sure I'll be able to fulfil it. And I *can* relax, Alessio, if that's what's worrying you.' But every angle of her body shrieked tension. She looked like someone who was on the verge of snapping in two.

The trip was clearly going to be a nightmare for her. 'Are you doing this to save your sister's job or to prove to yourself that your brain is stronger than your body?'

She stilled. 'I don't need to prove anything.'

'So it's all about your sister.' But he didn't believe that for a moment. He sensed that there was much, much more behind her acceptance than a desire to protect her sister's job. He also sensed that his careless challenge had touched something deep inside her. 'You think you can make it through a whole week without lecturing me or my client on love and marriage?'

She bit her lip—*the same lip he couldn't stop staring at.* 'Of course.'

'Or sleeping in my bed?'

'That will be the easy part.'

Alessio studied her profile thoughtfully. What had promised to be a mundane, uneventful business trip suddenly seemed full of interesting possibilities. 'What happens when emotions overcome your rational side, Lindsay?'

'Making decisions based on emotions is always a mistake. I don't let that happen.'

Alessio's eyes dropped to the perfect curve of her mouth and drifted down to the slim column of her neck. 'Are you saying that you've never made an impulsive decision based on an emotion?'

'No.' Her tone was crisp. 'And I'm sure that you haven't, either. Even when you're in bed with a woman I'm wiling to bet that part of you stays detached. You exercise control over your emotions all the time and you're much too cynical to allow yourself to be taken for a ride.'

Surprised by her insight, Alessio laughed. 'You might be right about that. All right, Lindsay Lockheart—' he reached out a hand and took the passport she held out to him '—let's see how an incurable cynic and a relationship counsellor get on when confined in a small space. I have a feeling that the next week is going to be interesting.'

Private jet. *Why did he have to own a private jet?*

She'd been hoping for safety in numbers for their flight to the Caribbean, instead of which it was just her and Alessio and a discreet cabin staff who only materialised when something was needed.

Trying not to be overawed by the sumptuous interior of the plane, Lindsay steadily called her way through her list of clients, relieved to have something to do that didn't involve talking to Alessio Capelli. 'I know, Alison,' she soothed as she listened to the latest round of developments in her client's tempestuous marriage, 'but do you remember what we talked about last time we met? About selective listening?' Catching Alessio's amused gaze, she gritted her teeth. 'I'll be back next week and we can talk about it then.' Lindsay ended the conversation and dialled her next number, determined that he wouldn't unsettle her, but all too aware of his own conversation.

'Let her sweat, Jack,' he drawled, the phone tucked between his cheek and his shoulder as he studied the screen of his laptop. 'She'll be lucky to walk away with the staff flat by the time we've finished with her.'

Lindsay gritted her teeth, kept her own call as brief as possible and tried to ignore the worsening pain in her head.

When he finally hung up, she glared at him. 'Don't you ever feel guilty? That poor woman has probably given the best years of her life bringing up his children and making him a home, while he was off picking a younger model.'

Alessio stretched his legs out in front of him, completely relaxed. 'That "poor woman" abandoned her two young children to pursue her affair with her ski instructor.'

Taken aback, Lindsay frowned. 'Oh—that's terrible. The poor man. Is he doing all right?'

'He will be by the time I've finished.' Alessio gave a deadly smile as he pulled a file out of his briefcase. 'Revenge is sweet. We'll get her where it hurts her most.'

Lindsay ignored that comment. 'How are the children?'

'Better off without her.' Alessio opened the file and scribbled something in the margin of the first page while Lindsay watched him, deeply troubled.

'However deep his own pain, I'm sure he wouldn't want to hurt the mother of his children.'

'Are you?' Alessio reached for a file from the table. 'That's why you're not a divorce lawyer.'

Lindsay put down her appointments diary carefully. 'You can't apply cold, hard facts to people's relationships. It just doesn't work. It's important to delve deeper. I'm immediately asking myself why she would do a thing like that. Why would any mother leave her children? Was she depressed or something?'

Alessio gaze was faintly mocking. 'I think it's fair to say that she was *extremely* depressed once she realised that she'd trashed her chance of receiving a generous settlement.'

Lindsay lifted her fingers to her forehead, telling herself

that his warped humour and lack of sentiment was good. If he kept talking like that it would make it easier to ignore the chemistry that still managed to crackle between them. Chemistry that made it impossible for her to relax.

How was she going to survive a week with him?

It wasn't that she had doubts about her own willpower, because she didn't; it was more that their powerful sexual connection stirred up something dark and ugly in the depths of her brain. *Something that she didn't want to face.*

Feeling a flicker of panic, she concentrated her mind on work. 'People usually have reasons for the way they act, Alessio. If she left her children, then—' her hand dropped to her lap as she pondered the issue '—perhaps she didn't want children in the first place. Did he pressure her? Was he a lot older than her? Was parenthood an issue that they discussed before they married?'

Incredulous dark eyes met hers. '*Accidenti*, how would I know? I'm a lawyer, not a psychiatrist.' With an impatient flick of his long fingers, Alessio flipped through the pages.

'But surely they should try some form of counselling before they just give up. He should let her come back and try again. There are children involved—'

'What makes you think she wants to come back?'

Appalled, Lindsay stared at him. 'Doesn't she?'

He lifted his gaze to hers. 'Lindsay—' his voice held a warning note '—you're doing it already. Ignoring the facts and looking at the emotions.'

'Emotions are *important*.'

'But they're *your* emotions,' he pointed out gently, 'not my client's.'

'But the children—'

'You seem particularly sensitive to this situation. Are you this emotionally involved with every case you deal with? No wonder you're always so tense.'

'I'm not tense.' She was agonisingly aware of him, of his powerful shoulders and his hard, handsome face. *Why is it*, she wondered desperately, *that a person can still be devastatingly attractive even when they are so deficient in other more important qualities?* 'You hate women, don't you?'

He raised an eyebrow. 'Is this my cue to say that some of my best friends are women?'

'That's not friendship.'

His smile was impossibly attractive. 'Friendship means different things to different people.'

And she was in no doubt as to what it meant to him. 'But you seem to make it your life's work to make sure that women don't profit from marriage.'

'Only when the *purpose* of their marriage was profit. I don't believe that marriage should be a source of income.' His long bronzed fingers played idly with his pen and she lifted her own fingers and rubbed her forehead again. The dangerous mix of cool and charismatic was making her head spin.

'It's the source of *your* income,' she pointed out, and his smile widened.

'Touché.' He glanced up as a uniformed girl sashayed down the plane with a tray of refreshments. 'Ah—supper. Are you hungry, Lindsay?'

Her head was getting worse and to make matters worse her stomach was starting to churn. 'Actually, no. But thank you.' She wished once again that she hadn't left her pills at home. This whole situation was going to be difficult enough without having to do it with a headache. 'Perhaps this would be a good time for you to tell me something about the objective of this trip. If I'm to assist you, I'd better know something about the case.'

'My prospective client hasn't yet appointed legal counsel,' Alessio purred. 'He simply wishes to discuss his situation. I've agreed to listen.'

'So he's not even sure he wants a divorce?'

'He knows he wants a divorce—he just hasn't yet decided how to go about it. Or who he wants to represent him.'

'So he might choose you.'

'If he can afford me, he'll choose me.' Alessio suppressed a yawn and Lindsay shot him a bemused glance.

'Why do you do this? You *obviously* don't need the money.'

'I enjoy the mental stimulation. I'm naturally competitive. I enjoy winning.'

'Do you really think it's "winning" to destroy someone's marriage?'

'Marriages come to me ready broken.' His dark eyes flashed a warning. 'And lecturing me isn't in your job description.'

'But has your client even tried to fix what's wrong? Perhaps if he talks to an outsider—someone who isn't involved—' Lindsay broke off and winced as another shaft of pain lanced her head. Her stomach churned horribly and she sat totally still, willing it to settle.

Not now. She didn't need this to happen now.

Alessio frowned, his eyes fixed on her face. 'Is something wrong?'

'Nothing at all.' She could just imagine how a man like him would react to a woman with a migraine. Deciding that it was best to make her escape while she could, she stood up gingerly. 'If you'll excuse me for a moment. I need to use the bathroom.'

His eyes lingered thoughtfully on her face. 'Last door on the left.'

Wishing he weren't studying her quite so intently, Lindsay followed his directions and pushed open a door. Had circumstances been different she would have been amazed by the beautiful bathroom that confronted her, but as it was she felt too ill to react with anything other than relief at the prospect of privacy.

Closing the door carefully behind her, she put her hand on her stomach and took a deep breath. How long was the flight to the Caribbean? She hadn't even asked, but without her medication she knew that she was going to be ill for all of it. And it was going to be horribly embarrassing.

Why now? *Why now, when she really needed to have her wits about her?*

Her head throbbed and she just wanted to lie down, but the thought of doing so in front of Alessio prevented her from returning to the cabin. Instead she sat down on a chair and leaned her head against the cool, marble wall, closing her eyes.

If only the pain would stop—

She didn't know how long she sat there. She was in too much pain to move; so much so that when the bathroom door opened, she barely reacted.

'*Maledizione,*' a rough masculine voice cursed softly, 'how long have you been like this? Are you ill?'

'Migraine. I'll be OK. Just leave me alone for a bit.' Her eyes tightly shut against the light, Lindsay felt a firm masculine hand touch her forehead and then he muttered something under his breath in Italian.

'I thought you were looking pale. Why didn't you say something before?'

'Alessio, please just go away,' she muttered. 'You're difficult enough to deal with in good health. Trust me, you don't want to be in here. I think I might be sick.'

Apparently undeterred by that warning, he scooped her easily into his arms and carried her through a door that led to a bedroom. Then he laid her gently on the enormous king-size bed. The soft pillow was cool against her cheek and it felt so wonderful to lie down that she gave a moan of gratitude.

'Maybe you're not all bad,' she mumbled. 'At this moment in time I almost like you.'

His eyes gleamed. 'Stop talking, Lindsay. You might say something you regret.'

'Sorry. Forgot you don't want women to like you.' She
winced as another bolt of pain shot through her head. 'Well, this
must be a first for you. Tucking a sick woman into your bed.'

'Do you have tablets in your bag?' He sounded cool and efficient and her eyes drifted shut, her teeth gritted against the pain.

'Forgot them. Packed in a hurry.' She snuggled deeper into
the pillow. 'I didn't even know planes came with beds. I guess
it's an essential item for a man like you.'

'Believe it or not, I don't use it for seduction. Being able
to sleep when I need to makes me more efficient,' he said dryly,
pulling a heavy silk cover over her. 'So—what am I going to
do with you?'

The pain was agonising and she winced as a shaft of light
penetrated the window. 'You're going to pass me my phone.
I need to try calling Ruby again—'

'Stop thinking about your sister and think about yourself
for once.' A frown in his eyes, Alessio leaned across and
closed the blinds, shutting out the beams of sunlight. 'Better?'

She never would have believed him capable of being so
thoughtful. But her stomach was still churning and she was
terrified that she was going to be sick over his handmade
shoes. 'I think you'd better leave now—for your sake.'

It seemed as though he was following her advice because
he rose to his feet and left the room. But he returned moments
later with a bowl and placed it by the bed, apparently unfazed
by the situation. 'I'm going to fetch you a doctor.'

If she'd had more energy Lindsay would have laughed.
They were in mid-air, for goodness' sake. Where was he
going to find a doctor?

Perhaps he meant that he was going to talk to a doctor on
the phone, but what good would that do?

The pounding in her head was unbearable, but when she
heard voices next to her she gingerly opened her eyes and saw
a man standing with Alessio.

With a frown, he sat down on the bed, asked her a few questions and then opened his bag.

Dimly in the back of her mind Lindsay was wondering how Alessio had managed to produce a doctor in mid-air, but her head was hurting too much to care and she was almost sobbing with gratitude as the doctor gave her medication and then left the room. Moments later, something deliciously cool was placed gently against her throbbing head.

She opened her eyes a slit and saw Alessio sitting next to her. He'd removed his tie and the sleeves of his white shirt had been rolled back to reveal strong forearms shadowed with dark hairs. As always he looked strong and capable and, surprisingly perhaps, not the slightest bit put out by her sudden illness. 'The doctor thought this might help.'

'Thank you. That feels wonderful. Why are you still here?' But she felt intensely vulnerable and pathetically grateful to him for not walking out and leaving her alone. 'I suppose your ego won't allow a woman to claim a headache when she's in your bed.' Her remark made him smile.

'Be quiet and go to sleep, Lindsay.'

'You really are impossibly good-looking,' she muttered as the medication started to take effect and her eyes drifted shut. 'It's a shame you're such a selfish bastard.'

CHAPTER FOUR

SHE woke to find the pain gone and Alessio sprawled on the bed next to her, his eyes closed.

Still sleepy, Lindsay gazed at his dense lashes and the hard lines of his perfect bone structure.

So this was what it felt like to wake up next to a really, *really* gorgeous man. Like not getting up, she thought dreamily. Like spending all day lying in bed staring at him; counting those incredible eyelashes, studying the blue-black stubble that darkened his jaw, following the sensuous curve of his firm mouth.

Even relaxed and asleep, he looked strong and hotly masculine.

She was still in the process of contemplating his mouth when his eyes opened and he looked at her. His gaze locked with hers and for a sizzling moment they shared something agonisingly intimate. The response of her body was instantaneous and without thinking what she was doing, Lindsay lifted a hand and touched his cheek.

She felt the roughness of his jaw against her sensitive palm— man against woman—and then she saw his eyes narrow slightly.

'I gather you're feeling better?' His voice was roughened by sleep, but it was enough to pierce her dreamy state and return her to full consciousness.

Completely awake now, she snatched her hand away and stared at him in horror.

'Oh—' Skidding away from him, she quickly sat up and her hair slid over her shoulders. Only then did she realise that, not only had someone removed the clips from her hair, but they'd also undressed her down to her underwear. She was horribly embarrassed, and her first impulse was to leap from the bed and lock herself in the bathroom, but without clothes she was trapped. Clutching the satin quilt to her throat, she glared at him. 'What are you doing in my bed?'

'It's *my* bed, *tesoro*.' He closed his eyes again and a slight smile played around his firm mouth. *That gorgeous mouth that she'd been examining in such detail.* 'My plane. My bed.'

'But—' she kept the covers up to her chin '—what I mean is—why are you lying next to me?'

'Sorry to disappoint you, but this plane only comes with one bedroom. I don't generally find that I need guest accommodation.'

'You could have slept on the couch.'

'I could have done, yes.' Eyes still closed, he smiled. 'But that would have made me thoughtful and caring, and I'm a selfish bastard, Lindsay. Remember?'

Lindsay tightened her fingers on the covers. 'That was incredibly rude of me. I shouldn't have said that—I'm sorry. I don't know why I did.'

'You were honest about how you felt,' he said dryly, 'I suspect for the first time in your life.'

Lindsay hesitated. 'But I was wrong,' she said quietly. Yes, he'd obviously sprawled next to her for a few hours' sleep, but only after he'd brought a bowl, fetched a doctor and generally made sure that she was as comfortable as possible. 'Who undressed me?'

'I did. I must say, for a relationship counsellor you choose extremely seductive underwear.' He gave a half smile. 'You're full of surprises.'

'You shouldn't have undressed me.'

'I felt sorry for you strapped up in that starched suit. You couldn't possibly get the rest you needed. Is the headache gone?'

She moved her head slightly to test it and then nodded gingerly. 'Yes. Thank you. Where did you find a doctor in mid-air?'

'In the cockpit of my plane.' In no apparent hurry, Alessio sat up, suppressed a yawn and then sprang from the bed with unconscious grace. He strolled to the far side of the bedroom, yanked open a cupboard and removed a fresh shirt. 'My co-pilot is medically trained.'

It didn't matter what he was doing or what he was wearing, he was unfairly good-looking, Lindsay thought helplessly. Whether he was stripped to the waist and sweaty from exercise, sleek in a suit, or rumpled from a few hours' rest on the bed, he still managed to look gorgeous.

With a moan of frustration, she closed her eyes, reminding herself that his looks concealed an ice-cold temperament and a complete lack of emotional intelligence.

But that wasn't quite true, was it?

He could have walked away and left her to her agony, but he hadn't. Nor had he been remotely fazed by the fact that she'd taken ill on his plane. Remembering the glass of water he'd held to her lips at one point, she turned her head into the pillow, terrified by her feelings.

It didn't change a thing, she told herself desperately. All right, so perhaps he did have a human side. But that didn't alter the fact that he didn't believe in love, had no desire to sustain a relationship and made his living from ripping the guts from people's marriages.

It didn't change who he was.

And it didn't change who she was, either. *Didn't change the way she felt inside.*

She opened her eyes and found him looking at her.

'Are you all right?' He frowned. 'Headache back?'

'No. I'm fine.'

'Good. We'll be landing in another two hours. I'm going to take a shower and then make some calls. Help yourself to the bathroom.'

'Wait.' Scooping her hair away from her face, she raised herself on her elbow. 'You haven't even told me where we're going. You just said it was the Caribbean.'

'We're going to Kingfisher Cay, west of Antigua. One hundred acres of isolated palm-fringed beaches and guaranteed isolation.'

'I've never heard of it.'

'The only people who have ever heard of it are the people who can afford to go there,' he said dryly. 'A holiday on Kingfisher Cay is by personal invitation of the owner.'

'And your prospective client is holidaying there as we speak?'

'He needed a rest from the publicity surrounding his disintegrating marriage. He's treating himself to some rest and relaxation.'

'And you're taking advantage of his vulnerability by turning up and offering him legal counsel?'

Alessio gave a cool smile. 'A good divorce lawyer is what makes him able to relax. Without me protecting his interests, he wouldn't be able to risk turning his back on the scheming hussy he married.'

Lindsay's mouth tightened and she gripped the quilt in her fingers. Clearly the thoughtfulness he'd displayed during the night had just been a blip.

'Don't you think the owner of the island might object to you using his exclusive Caribbean hideaway for your own commercial interests?'

'No.' Alessio looked as though something had amused him and she frowned.

'Does he know you're bringing me?'

'Why does it matter?' A dangerous light in his eyes, he strolled purposefully towards her, his smile widening as she retreated to the far side of the bed.

The closer he came, the harder it was to breathe and she felt as though her body were on fire. 'There might not be enough accommodation.'

'We can always share.'

Lindsay flattened herself against the bed head. 'I'd rather sleep with the sharks.'

He stopped, his expression mocking as he registered her growing agitation. 'Then you'd better hope that your little sister did at least one part of her job correctly and booked two suites.' With that disconcerting observation, he turned and walked through to the bathroom, leaving her with a pounding heart and a guilty conscience.

Ruby.

She hadn't even thought about her sister since she'd woken up and she knew why, of course. There had been no room in her brain for anything or anyone except Alessio Capelli.

She needed to call Ruby. She needed—

With a groan, Lindsay flopped back down onto the pillows. What she really needed was to be back in London living her life. *Not* trapped in a private jet, en route to a billionaire's Caribbean hideaway.

The seaplane soared above a sparkling turquoise sea.

'Oh, my goodness,' Lindsay breathed softly, her gaze drawn to yet another emerald-green island surrounded by deserted sandy beaches. 'It's incredible. So beautiful. I had no idea. I've never before understood everyone's obsession with accumulating wealth, but if wealth means seeing a place like this—'

It was idyllic. If it weren't for her anxiety about Ruby, she might even have been able to relax.

Lindsay frowned, realising how ridiculous that was. If it hadn't been for Ruby, she wouldn't be here! And if she started thinking that this was a holiday, she'd be in trouble. The only way to survive a week with Alessio Capelli was to be businesslike.

Absorbed by the contents of the file on his lap, Alessio appeared unaware of her inner turmoil. 'You've never been to the Caribbean?'

'No, I—' She broke off. She didn't want to reveal anything about herself to this man. What would someone like him make of her disordered, disastrous childhood? He'd laugh or make one of his sharp, lawyerlike comments that always made her shrink. 'I haven't really travelled.' Not wanting to think about her past, she peered down at the surf breaking on a beach below her. 'Is that where we're going?'

'Yes.' Unlike her, he hadn't once glanced out of the window, instead concentrating on working his way through the thick sheaf of documents. Occasionally he scribbled a note in the margin, sometimes he underlined, rarely he frowned and crossed out a chunk of text with big, bold strokes of his black pen.

Did he ever relax? She studied his profile for a moment. He'd showered and shaved and was now dressed in light-weight trousers and a cool shirt.

'Why do you work so hard? Is it all about the money?' She blurted out the question and he lifted his head and looked at her.

'Money is important up to a point. After that, the amount becomes irrelevant.'

Lindsay tried to imagine having so much money that the total became irrelevant. 'Well, you've long passed that point,' she muttered, 'so why do you carry on?'

'Because it entertains me.' He slid his pen into his pocket and closed the file. 'I enjoy the process.'

'You mean you enjoy making people miserable.'

His eyes gleamed. 'On the contrary, I free them from misery to begin a new life.'

'Don't you ever worry that you've taken apart something that could be fixed?'

'Unlike you, I don't feel the need to control everybody else's actions. If someone comes to me seeking legal advice, I give it. I don't try and persuade them that they're wrong.'

'But what if some of those marriages could be saved? Perhaps some of those poor children could be spared the misery of spending their lives shuttling backwards and forwards every other weekend.'

Alessio slipped the file into his briefcase and snapped it shut. 'You're extremely concerned about the children in every relationship.'

Her heart thudded against her chest. It really wouldn't pay to underestimate this man. He was *so* astute. 'Of course. Who wouldn't be?' She gave a humourless laugh. 'Sorry—you're not at all concerned, are you?'

'I think a bad relationship can be every bit as damaging for children as a split family.'

'But what if the bad relationship could be fixed?'

'You're ridiculously sentimental about everything and you take it far too personally.' His gaze was suddenly thoughtful. 'Or maybe it *is* personal. Is it personal, Lindsay? Or do you feel this strongly on every subject?'

Her mouth dried. 'I care, that's all.'

'I know. I'm just wondering why.'

'Because I'm a human being.' Deeply regretting ever starting the conversation, Lindsay concentrated her attention on the Caribbean Sea, which sparkled beneath her in the dazzling sunlight. She'd forgotten that he was a lawyer. With a few simple words he'd turned everything around and suddenly she was the one in the dock.

She needed to be careful.

Really careful.

'So what do you want me to do?' Realising that they'd finally arrived, she turned to him. 'I mean, I expect you were planning to brief me on the flight, but I was ill—do you have something I should read? What's my role?'

He circled a word on the page in front of him and then looked up. 'Your role, Lindsay, is to act as my assistant.' His dark eyes held hers for a moment and she felt everything inside her grow warm.

Appalled by her extremely unwelcome reaction to him, she frowned and dragged her gaze from his. 'I know that I'm your assistant, but I'm just not sure what you expect of me. Some details would be helpful.'

'I expect you to make our client feel comfortable. We need to make him feel that we understand his situation and that we're committed to representing his interests.'

'All right.'

'I don't expect you to ask if he's tried counselling.'

Lindsay swallowed. 'Fine. Are you going to tell me about him?'

'Not yet. His presence on the island is top secret. If his identity was leaked, it could cause a problem. The owner prides himself on guaranteeing the absolute discretion of everyone on the island.'

'But he trusts you?'

'Lindsay—' his voice was gentle '—I *am* the owner. It's my island.'

'Yours?' She looked at him stupidly and then out of the window at the sugar-soft sandy beach that stretched towards a stylish beachfront villa. Another villa was visible farther along the sand. 'You own this? I thought you were a lawyer, not a property magnate.'

'I have several business interests.' He slid the file into his briefcase.

Lindsay arched an eyebrow. 'Worried that the divorce business might not sustain you into your old age, Alessio?'

'It's good business practice to diversify and I find my various business interests complement each other. You'd be surprised how many men are eager to check into remote, five-star luxury in order to escape their marriages.'

'Escape responsibility, you mean.'

Alessio gave a faint smile. 'As I was saying, Kingfisher Cay fits nicely into my business portfolio. The rich and famous are guaranteed an exclusive hideaway in which they can lick their wounds, safe in the knowledge that the world's press aren't watching them.'

'And safe in the knowledge that their exclusive private villa comes with free legal advice.'

'I wouldn't exactly describe it as "free".' Alessio leaned across and unfastened her seat belt, his eyes settling on her black skirt. 'I have a feeling that the first thing you might want to do is rethink your wardrobe. You're going to be extremely hot in that suit.' He was uncomfortably close to her and although she wanted desperately to look away, somehow she couldn't quite manage it. It was as if he were holding her there, trapped. Helpless. Something flickered in the depths of his eyes, something raw and elemental, and her heart started to bump rapidly against her chest.

'I have a change of clothes in my bag,' she said hoarsely, but still he didn't move, the temperature between them rising to intolerable levels as he held her gaze.

Then he released his own seat belt and stood up. 'Good.'

She thought he was smiling, but she couldn't be sure because he was talking to the pilot in rapid Italian and then the door of the plane opened and sunlight and warmth filled the cabin.

Alessio turned, his hair gleaming blue-black under the burning sun, more shockingly handsome than any man had a right to be. 'Welcome to Kingfisher Cay.'

So he was handsome, she'd always known that.

Damn the man.

Feeling hot, sticky and desperately unsettled, Lindsay dumped her small overnight bag on the floor of the villa and burst out laughing. When Alessio had told her she would be staying in a villa she'd imagined that she'd be sharing something relatively modest with several other people. Instead, the smiling staff member who had met their seaplane had led her to a private villa. A villa just for her. And her overnight bag looked as out of place as she felt.

The spacious living room opened directly onto the beach and was decorated in a sophisticated palette of cool colours that created an atmosphere of restful calm. The bedroom was dominated by an enormous teak four-poster bed, draped in acres of light creamy muslin and dressed with piles of silk cushions in elegant, restrained shades.

Lindsay stared around her in disbelief, so distracted by her surroundings that she forgot she was hot, sticky and desperately uncomfortable. She forgot about the hot burn of sexual awareness that had been with her ever since she'd arrived at Alessio's office. She even forgot that she still hadn't managed to contact Ruby. She was so stunned by the sheer luxury of the villa that for a moment she simply stood there.

What was she doing here?

Had this really been Ruby's life? It was hardly surprising she'd loved her job if this was one of the perks.

She strolled through a door and found herself in a lavish marble bathroom that again opened directly onto the beach. Taking in the multispray shower and the array of exclusive toiletries, Lindsay shook her head.

It was possible to lie in the bath and stare at the palm trees swaying on the beach.

If staying here was work, what did Alessio Capelli do for entertainment?

Hearing footsteps behind her, she turned and saw a pretty blonde girl dressed in a white uniform standing in the doorway.

'I'm Natalya. I'm your housekeeper for the duration of your stay at Kingfisher Cay. Anything you want, you have only to ask. I expect you're hot and tired after your journey. Would you like to change while I unpack for you?'

Unpack? Unpack what, exactly?

Lindsay's eyes slid to her bag. It sat forlorn and abandoned in the centre of the polished wooden floor. 'I don't have much luggage. I wasn't expecting— This was a bit of an—impulse trip.'

As if anyone would come to a place like this on impulse. Even for the elite few fortunate enough to be able to afford it, it would be a rare treat. For the rest of the population, the silky sand and turquoise sea of Kingfisher Cay would never be more than a picture to drool over in an exotic travel brochure. Except that this place didn't feature in travel brochures.

Natalya didn't appear to find the absence of luggage at all odd. Obviously accustomed to the odd behaviour of the rich and famous, she simply smiled. 'We pride ourselves in being able to provide anything and everything you need. If you like, you can give me a list. Or I can simply provide you with what I think you'll need for a happy and comfortable stay here.'

Lindsay smiled at that. 'You're even prepared to do my thinking for me?'

'We're used to living here,' Natalya murmured. 'We know what you're likely to need.'

'I don't want to put you to any trouble. I'm sure you have plenty of other guests.' More important guests.

'We have a staff ratio of eight to one.'

'One member of staff for eight guests?' Lindsay was thinking that seemed like a lot when the girl smiled.

'Eight members of staff for each guest.'

Stunned into silence, Lindsay simply gaped at her. 'Oh—'

'Signor Capelli asked that you meet him at the Beach Club for a drink in twenty minutes.'

'Right.' Lindsay looked at her helplessly. 'And where is that, exactly?'

'If you come to the front of your villa when you're ready, I'll direct you.'

Alessio nursed his drink and stared moodily at the smooth turquoise ocean as he contemplated the case. He wasn't surprised that the 'A' list Hollywood star wanted a divorce. What surprised him was that the man had been foolish enough to marry his co-star in the first place.

She had 'opportunist' written all over her particularly stunning face.

What was it about a beautiful woman that turned otherwise sensible men into fools?

A yacht drifted across his line of vision, the sails providing an elaborate splash of colour against the endless blue.

'Alessio?'

Irritated at being disturbed, he turned his head and found himself staring straight into the grave, serious eyes of Lindsay Lockheart.

Hovering awkwardly in her sensible navy skirt and tailored shirt, she looked as out of place as a sparrow suddenly finding itself in the midst of a flock of exotic birds.

Controlling or not, she must really love her sister, Alessio mused as he acknowledged just how uncomfortable she was and how little she evidently wanted to be here.

'I thought you were going to change.'

'I *did* change.' Startled, she glanced down at herself, as if checking that her clothes hadn't suddenly disappeared. 'This is a different outfit.'

Alessio contemplated the formal navy skirt with a mixture of exasperation and amusement. 'Clearly you consider it prudent to always be ready for a funeral.'

Soft colour highlighted her cheekbones. 'I'm dressed for work. I gave a television interview in London just before I flew to see you in Rome. *Obviously* at the time I didn't know I was going to need clothes for a warm climate.'

On the surface she appeared brisk and businesslike, but as she pulled out the chair opposite and sat down Alessio noticed the tremor in her hands. And she wasn't quite meeting his eyes. Instead she placed her notepad on the table in front of her and opened it, clearly relieved to have something to focus on that didn't include him. 'Right. Let's get started.'

Unable to resist the opportunity to tease her, Alessio lounged back in his chair. 'What, no foreplay?'

Her gaze flew to his and a flash of sexual awareness darkened her eyes from blue to indigo.

Watching her reaction, Alessio saw the exact moment that she rejected that response. She took several breaths and her fingers tightened on the pen.

Ignoring his comment, she wrote the date neatly and carefully at the top of the pad. 'I thought it would be sensible to take some notes on what you want me to do.'

She just blocked it out, he mused silently. This sizzling chemistry between them was something that she just tried to ignore.

'Efficient, Lindsay. Always in control. Tell me something—' fascinated by the tiny pulse in her slender neck, he studied her for a long moment '—do you ever do anything on impulse?'

'Coming here was an impulsive action,' she responded instantly. 'I hadn't planned to spend the next week on a Caribbean island with a—' She broke off and he raised an eyebrow.

'You were saying? With a—?'

'I'm here in place of my sister, so that you don't have reason to fire her. Talking of which, have you managed to contact your brother?'

'I haven't tried.' Alessio swivelled his gaze to one of the bar staff, who immediately produced two refreshing cocktails filled with crushed ice and topped with exotic fruit. 'Have a drink. You need to relax.'

She ignored the drink. 'Why?'

'Because too much tension is bad for your health.'

She frowned impatiently. 'I mean, why haven't you tried to contact your brother? You promised that you would.'

'I've already left one message.'

'Then leave another. Keep ringing until he answers!'

'What would be the point of that? He'll respond when he's ready.' Watching her body language, Alessio reached for his drink. 'Are you always this wound up? Your blood pressure must be sky-high.'

'I'm not wound up.' But even the way she was sitting shrieked of tension. She perched on the edge of her chair, her back straight and her hands on the pad in front of her, ready to take notes.

'Do you even know how to relax? Or is it just that you're afraid to relax with me?' It was as if she was watching herself all the time, using iron willpower to make sure that she didn't slip up.

'I relax when the time is appropriate. This isn't that time. So what's happening with your client?' She was brisk and business-like, her blonde hair drawn back from her face, her shirt buttoned almost to the throat. 'What time are we meeting him?'

'I have no idea. He hasn't arrived.'

Exasperation shone in her eyes. 'So, when is he coming?'

'When it suits him.'

'You haven't asked?'

Alessio smiled. 'I'm sure he'll arrive when he's ready.'

'But you've adjusted your working schedule to accommodate him—'

'And he's paying me for the privilege,' Alessio drawled softly. 'How he chooses to use my time is entirely up to him. In the meantime we're free to—relax and get to know each other better.' He saw the movement in her throat as she swallowed.

'I don't want to get to know you better. I already know you well enough.'

'But didn't you say that it was important to delve deeper?'

'You're twisting my words.'

'I'm merely playing your own words back to you.'

She turned her head and looked at the ocean, but he could see the desperation in her eyes and she took several small breaths before turning back to him. 'If you don't need me to work immediately then perhaps you could lend me the file and I'll go back to the villa and make some notes. At least then I'll be prepared when he finally turns up. I can sign a confidentiality agreement if you think it's necessary.'

He wondered what it would take to get her out of that navy skirt and away from her legal pad. 'Do you sail?'

'Sorry?' She looked startled. 'Why are you asking that?'

'Because we need to find a way of passing the time until my client arrives. I have other suggestions, of course...' Alessio allowed his sentence to remain unfinished, enjoying the confusion in her eyes.

'I don't need you to entertain me.' Apparently that last remark was sufficient to make her reach for her drink. Lifting it to her lips, she took a large sip and then put the glass carefully back down on the table. 'If you have no immediate need for me, I'll just stay in my villa and take the odd swim. You carry on and do whatever it is you usually do when you're here.' Her tight voice suggested that she knew exactly what his usual form of entertainment was, and Alessio laughed.

'You're going to swim?'

'Why is that funny?'

'Because I've never seen anyone swimming in a navy skirt before. And you seem determined not to be parted from yours.'

'Don't be ridiculous.'

'I just can't imagine you relaxing enough to strip off.'

'I've already told you—I'm perfectly capable of relaxing, Alessio.'

He studied her for a moment wondering what it was about her that was holding his attention. 'In that case go and change out of those warm winter clothes and have a dip in the sea. I'll pick you up at eight o'clock for dinner.'

'I don't have anything to change into.'

'My staff will have rectified that by now, I'm sure.' He'd given them an exact brief on what he wanted and now he was waiting with interest to see how Lindsay reacted to her new wardrobe. He had a feeling that the clothes she wore were part of her defence.

What would happen to her rigid control when she was no longer protected by the comforting security of navy blue or black?

She was convinced she had the mental strength to resist the chemistry between them.

Alessio suddenly discovered just how much he was looking forward to proving her wrong.

CHAPTER FIVE

LINDSAY stared at her reflection in despair.

When she'd returned to the villa to find the wardrobe stocked with a wide selection of summery clothes, she'd been relieved and grateful.

Reluctant though she'd been to admit as much to Alessio, she was *boiling* and had been finding her skirt scratchy and uncomfortable in the shimmering Caribbean heat.

Relief had turned to amazement as she'd examined the contents of her new wardrobe more closely.

Unaccustomed to such a degree of luxury, she was woman enough to feel a flare of excitement as she'd rifled through the dresses on the rail and sifted her way through beautifully folded tops and cardigans, all separated by tissue paper to minimise creasing. And it hadn't just been clothes. There were shoes, all in her size, bags, accessories and a basket heaped with a selection of exclusive make-up, all new and still in the packaging.

But her laughter had faded as soon as she'd realised that none of the clothes was what she would have chosen. It was true that neither of the two skirts she had with her was suitable for a week on a Caribbean Island. For a start they were just too hot and, yes, she'd be the first to agree that they were also too formal.

But there was informal and then there was—romantic. *Romantic and sexy.* And the entire wardrobe that had been provided for her seemed to fall into that category. She'd spent half an hour rifling through the rail over and over again, searching for something that said 'work in a warm climate'. But everything in front of her just seemed to shriek 'take me, take me'.

The options had either been too short, too fitted, too low cut, or too dressy.

One dress in particular had caught her attention and she'd looked at it in despair, knowing that only an extremely sexually confident woman would dare to wear strapless, scarlet silk.

She certainly wasn't that woman.

Which was why, in the end, she'd opted for the turquoise dress.

It shimmered in the light and had clearly been lovingly created by some top designer with seduction in mind.

It wasn't quite as terrifying as the wicked scarlet dress, but it still made her feel uncomfortable.

How could she possibly join a man like Alessio Capelli for dinner wearing something like this?

It was asking for trouble.

For a start it was semi-transparent, presumably designed to be worn over glamorous underwear on an intimate occasion. Or possibly over a swimsuit, by someone so wealthy that shockingly expensive silk could be regarded as beachwear.

The rest of the wardrobe was much the same. Brightly coloured tops, beach dresses, long floating skirts—everything achingly feminine and designed for an ultra-romantic holiday.

But she wasn't on holiday.

And knowing Alessio Capelli—*knowing his ego and his arrogance*—if she wore these clothes, he'd take it as a sign that she wanted to take their relationship a step further.

It was incredibly generous of him to have provided her with a suitable wardrobe, but—

Her eyes narrowed as a sudden thought struck her.

Generous? Was he being generous? Or was he testing her in some way?

Remembering the way he'd teased her, she suddenly realised that it was far more likely that there was a deeper darker reason for the choice of clothes.

Angry with herself for being so naïve, she glared at her reflection in the mirror.

This wasn't generosity on his part.

He *wanted* her to feel uncomfortable.

He *wanted* her out of her depth.

Apparently he found the unfortunate chemistry between them entertaining and he didn't bother to pretend otherwise. But nor was he allowing her to pretend. He was upfront and straight about the attraction.

And she was honest enough with herself to admit that she was on dangerous ground. Alessio wasn't a man that women could easily ignore. He was, quite simply, the most devastatingly attractive man she'd ever met. Sinfully handsome, he had a way of looking at a woman that made her think of nothing but sex.

And it wasn't just looks. If it had been, perhaps she would have found him easier to resist, but his sharp intelligence made him stimulating company and she was finding it impossible to forget how kind he'd been to her on the plane when she'd been ill.

That kindness had been all the more surprising given his reputation.

If she was honest, the chemistry between them was starting to terrify her.

She, of all people, knew the dangers of that degree of chemistry—*she knew just how easy it was to confuse overwhelming physical attraction with something deeper*. And yet, even knowing that, her body still hummed and simmered and responded to the lazy, suggestive glint in his eyes.

And she didn't want that. Dear God, she really, *really* didn't want that.

She'd seen where that could lead.

Feeling intensely vulnerable and incredibly alone, Lindsay sank down on the edge of the bed and forced herself to do something that she never usually allowed herself to do.

She thought about her childhood.

Instead of blocking out those memories, she allowed them to filter through to her brain. What started as a trickle became a flood, and for a brief, horrible moment she was a little girl again, curled up in her tiny bed with her younger sister asleep in her arms. And she was listening to the sounds through the wall. Those sounds.

The sounds she hated.

The sounds that meant that her father would be coming back home for a while. 'It's all right, Lindsay, we'll be a family again. Everything is going to be different now.'

Breathing rapidly, Lindsay rose to her feet, slamming the lid back down on her thoughts, appalled at how quickly she could regress from competent professional to needy child.

She was well aware of how vulnerable the needy child was. Look at Ruby. There was no doubt in her mind that her mixed up little sister flitted from one relationship to another because she was looking for the love and security she hadn't had as a child.

Impatient with herself, Lindsay paced barefoot into the bathroom.

But she wasn't going to do that.

Sex wasn't love.

Sex wasn't security.

Sex was just—well, sex.

Turning on the taps, she leaned over the washbasin, filled her palms with cold water and splashed her face as if washing her face might also wash away the memories that she'd conjured up.

It had only been a brief glimpse, but it was enough.

Enough to strengthen her resolve.

With the cool water came a feeling of calm and she blotted her face with a towel and stared in the mirror.

It didn't matter what dress she chose to wear. It wasn't going to make a difference to who she was or how she'd chosen to live her life. She was never, ever going to let sexual chemistry cloud her judgment.

Never. It just wasn't going to happen. No matter how sexy the man. No matter what the temptation.

Having seen first-hand the devastation that such a relationship caused, there was no way she was going to make that mistake herself. And wearing a sexy dress and a pair of gorgeous shoes wasn't going to change that.

She made decisions with her head and her brain, not with her body.

It didn't matter that she was in paradise with a dangerously sexy man and a wardrobe to die for.

She was still using her brain. She was still in charge of her decisions.

She could wear any one of those sexy dresses and it wouldn't make a difference to the outcome of the evening.

'Let's see which one of us suffers most, Alessio Capelli,' she murmured under her breath as she selected a lip gloss from the basket of make-up that had been left for her use. Removing it from its packaging, she applied it to her lips and stared at herself with satisfaction.

Clothes and make-up didn't dictate your choices in life.

She could be naked and she'd still be able to resist Alessio Capelli because that was what she wanted to do.

It was all about choices and she knew which choice she was going to make.

Alessio strolled up to the open door of the villa and paused, stunned by the vision that confronted him.

The door was open and he watched transfixed as Lindsay—

a vastly different Lindsay—twisted her hair into a knot and fastened it with a clasp made from a seashell.

Her slender form shimmered in turquoise silk, an exotic vision of femininity. His gaze lingered on the curve of her bottom and he felt an instantaneous surge of lust.

'Well—' without waiting for an invitation, he strolled into the living room '—you clearly didn't have a problem finding something to wear in the wardrobe.'

And he'd expected her to. In fact he'd prepared himself for protests. But there was no protest. Instead she appeared almost serene.

'Why would I have had a problem?' Tilting her head, she checked her reflection in the mirror, as composed and controlled as ever. 'It's incredibly generous of you to lend me so many beautiful things. Thank you, Alessio.' With a smile that appeared genuine, she slid her feet into a pair of sparkling jewelled shoes with heels so high that walking should have been impossible.

Scanning the length of her legs, Alessio was forced to admit that, yet again, Lindsay Lockheart had surprised him. He hadn't expected a positive reaction to the wardrobe he'd provided. He'd instructed the staff to select glamorous clothes, designed to accommodate the needs of a relaxed woman on a beach holiday.

Lindsay wasn't anyone's idea of a relaxed woman.

Knowing what he knew about her desire to control every aspect of her life, he was astonished that she'd apparently embraced someone else's choice of clothes—particularly when those clothes were a dramatic departure from her normal choice of dress. He had a strong suspicion that dressing in a boring and businesslike fashion was all part of her desperate urge to control her surroundings and the way everyone reacted to her. That being the case, he would have expected her to be uncomfortable parted from her crisp white shirt and her safe

navy skirt. Instead she was reacting to her new look with decidedly feminine enjoyment.

Far from rejecting the clothes, she seemed to be revel-
ling in them.

His experienced eye noted the subtle touches of make-up
that drew attention to her soft, lush mouth and her smooth
creamy skin.

And then something in her eyes caught his attention—a
cool unspoken challenge that was at odds with a woman who
was dressing up purely for pleasure.

And he knew then that she wasn't relaxed.

He smiled to himself, deriving a certain satisfaction from
the fact that he'd read her correctly after all. She wasn't at all
relaxed. But she was determined that he wouldn't know it.

So why was she wearing the clothes?

Why wasn't she standing in front of him demanding that
he find her a navy linen suit or something else designed to ex-
tinguish the last burning embers of a man's libido?

'Has your client arrived?' Still focusing on her reflection
she pushed a few wisps of blonde hair away from her face.

'Not yet.'

'Clearly he has money to burn.' Lindsay turned to face him.
'I'm sure you'll charge him for your time, whether he turns
up or not.'

'Of course.'

They were sustaining a conversation and yet an entirely different form of communication was simmering beneath the
surface of cool civility. With his skill at reading women, Alessio
noted the slight flush in her cheeks that had nothing to do with
the application of make-up and the darkening of her eyes.

Dealing with his own burn of lust, he wondered how long
they were going to play this game.

'I still haven't managed to contact Ruby.'

He had a feeling she'd raised the subject of her sister purely to remind him of the reason she was here.

'That doesn't surprise me. If she wanted you to know where she is, she would have told you.'

Alessio felt the vicious tug of lust deep in his loins because she looked truly beautiful and something about the way she was looking at him drove every rational thought from his head.

'Something wrong, Alessio?' She raised an eyebrow and he smiled in response, well aware that she'd won that round.

Suffer, her eyes were saying and he almost laughed because he *was* suffering and he was completely sure that she knew it.

For a brief moment he contemplated backing her against the enormous bed and removing the dress he'd paid for, but he knew that such an unsubtle approach would just give her opportunity to reject him.

So instead he satisfied himself with a long, lazy look at her.

The colour of the dress was perfect for her skin and hair; turquoise shot with strands of blue and green, the dress fell from tiny beaded straps and was cut to display the tempting dip between her breasts. Alessio's appreciative gaze lingered on the hollow cleft and he heard her sharp intake of breath.

'Do you think you could remove your eyes from my cleavage?'

He smiled. 'Why would I want to do that? You look spectacular.'

'Thank you.' She accepted the compliment in a business-like fashion and walked briskly towards the door. Only once she'd created a safe distance between them, did she turn. 'Are you coming?'

Alessio strolled towards her and tucked her hand into the crook of his arm, feeling a flicker of satisfaction as he felt her initial resistance.

He knew that she was nowhere near as cool and indifferent as she was pretending to be.

But instead of withdrawing or arguing, she simply smiled again. 'I'm looking forward to dinner. What are the local delicacies?'

You are, my beauty, Alessio thought, steering her through a lush tropical garden and down onto the silky white sand. *You're going to be my starter, main course and dessert.*

Lindsay sat down at the table, trying not to show how disconcerted she was that they were dining alone on the private beach in front of the villa.

'This is nice,' she lied. Silver cutlery glinted in the late evening sunlight, a bunch of colourful tropical blooms formed the centrepiece of the table and several candles flickered in the gentle breeze. With the soft sound of the sea licking the shore, it was idyllic, romantic and totally inappropriate for their relationship. The clothes had been bad enough, but this—

This was the setting for seduction, not business. For lovers, not colleagues.

Another test?

Was he putting her through this on purpose?

She cast what she hoped was a casual glance in his direction, but he was as cool and controlled as ever, his handsome face revealing absolutely nothing of his thoughts. Instead he watched her with those dark eyes that she suspected saw far too much.

'I would have thought you would have preferred to dine in the restaurant.' Pleased with how relaxed she sounded, she reached for the cocktail.

'We could have dined in the Beach Club, but this is more— intimate…' he paused and the word hung in the air between them, heating the atmosphere and raising the tension '…and I know you're a real fan of intimacy, Lindsay.'

'Absolutely.' But not with him. The last thing she wanted or needed was intimacy with Alessio Capelli.

'You seem a little tense.'

Tense? *Tense?*

Her entire body was being overtaken by a ferocious sexual awareness and the feeling totally unsettled her. She really, really didn't want to feel like this. 'Why would I be tense? Who could possibly be tense in a place like this?' Nervously looking for something to do with her hands, she leaned forward to help herself to a canapé and saw his eyes drift down to her cleavage.

Immediately she sat back in her chair, her skin heating as he gave a soft smile.

'You don't like the look of the canapés? I can instruct the staff to bring a different selection.'

'Not at all. I decided to save myself for the main course.' Hoping desperately that the staff would serve her, Lindsay struggled with the urge to glance down and check she was decent. She badly wanted to haul her dress up to her neck. It was one thing to be full of bravado when she was staring at her reflection in the mirror, and quite another to maintain that feeling when confronted by a man of Alessio's sophistication and experience.

She suspected that he was playing with her and his next action confirmed it.

A faint smile on his hard mouth, he reached forward and selected a canapé for himself. 'I find that the right taste on the palate actually increases the appetite.' With a slow, deliberate flick of his tongue, he devoured the tiny pastry. 'Sort of culinary foreplay.'

Her heart was thumping hard. 'So you even think about sex when you eat.'

'Sex and food are closely related. Each requires the full involvement of the senses and each satisfies a basic human need.'

Lindsay was desperately conscious of the slow build of warmth low in her pelvis and suddenly she was angry with him—*angry with him for making her feel this way.*

Obviously he thought that the clothes and the setting would guarantee the outcome he wanted.

Well, she was about to show him how wrong he was about her.

'Those canapés do look delicious,' she said sweetly. 'Maybe I will try one after all.' She leaned forward again and this time she made no attempt to prevent her dress from offering what she was sure was a generous glimpse of cleavage.

Without once glancing in his direction, she nibbled at the corner of a pastry and then gave a soft moan and licked her lips. 'That,' she murmured softly, 'tastes absolutely sublime.' Closing her eyes, she slowly slid the rest of the morsel between her lips and chewed slowly. Then she opened her eyes and looked straight at him, challenge in her gaze.

His eyes were black and deadly and held hers for a long, disturbing moment. His long, bronzed fingers toyed idly with the stem of his wineglass and she felt a wicked, delicious curl of excitement low in her belly as the tension between them rocketed to the point of explosion.

'You look warm, Alessio.' Her voice calm and steady, she reached for the refreshing cocktail that had been placed by her plate. 'Is something wrong?'

His eyes held hers for a long, pulsing moment and when he finally spoke his voice was husky with the sizzling tension that was bubbling up between them. 'I hope you know what you're doing.'

'What am I doing? Simply enjoying the food and the surroundings.' And proving to herself that she was in control. *That she could resist this man.* 'Presumably that's what you intended when you set this up. Or did you have something else in mind, Alessio?'

'You're playing with fire, *tesoro*,' he warned softly, 'and you're going to be burned.'

'Fire is perfectly safe as long as you know how to handle it.'

His gaze didn't shift from hers. 'Perhaps that depends on the heat of the flame.'

Sure of herself—*proud of herself*—Lindsay smiled. 'You're hot, Alessio,' she said calmly, 'but you're not *that* hot.'

'No? So why can't you stop thinking about sex? Why are you sitting there trying to wipe out images of the two of us together in that enormous canopied bed?'

She gave a tiny gasp, but there was no emotion in his cool gaze, just a glimmer of masculine satisfaction that showed her that, no matter how hard she tried to shift the balance, he still had the upper hand.

'Your misplaced degree of confidence in yourself must mean that you're often disappointed.'

'I'll tell you whether I'm disappointed when you're naked underneath me and I'm deep inside you.'

'I can't believe you just said that.' Lindsay rose to her feet, knocking her drink over in the process.

With supersonic reflexes, a lean, bronzed hand shot out and caught the glass, preventing a spillage.

'What can't you believe? The fact that I thought it? Or the fact that I said it?' Suddenly he had the upper hand again and she lifted a hand to her throat, feeling her pulse racing under the tips of her fingers.

His words had created a vivid image that she couldn't dismiss from her head. An image she'd been trying hard not to look at.

'For a supposedly highly intelligent male, you're extremely narrow-minded.'

'I'm honest. I'm telling you what I'm thinking. Sit down, Lindsay. You've been goading me all evening. You can't expect me not to respond.'

'Not every man is as obsessed with sex as you.'

He lifted an eyebrow. 'Lindsay, I'm a normal, red-blooded male with a healthy sex drive. I've never denied that. You've been sucking your fingers, moaning with pleasure and flashing your gorgeous breasts at me for the last half hour. What did you expect?'

'I expected the reaction I got.' She sat back down, her gaze wary. 'Which just goes to show that despite your intelligence, you think with your hormones and not your brain. Which in turn explains why you've never sustained a relationship outside the bedroom.'

'I've never sustained a relationship outside the bedroom because that's been my choice.'

'What are you afraid of, Alessio?' If she hadn't been watching carefully she might have missed his reaction because it was swiftly controlled.

Controlled, but definitely there.

'Do I look afraid?'

'I think you've *learned* to hide how you feel. You're afraid you won't be able to control your emotions, so you make sure that you don't engage them.' Why, oh, why, had she ever thought she'd be able to cope with this man? 'We're very different, Alessio. Just accept it.'

'I accept that we're different. It's the differences that excite me.' His voice was silky soft and seductive. 'I think we'd be hot in bed. And you think it too, don't you, Lindsay? That's why you're fighting it every step of the way. This chemistry between us is so powerful that you're afraid you're being sucked in. You want to be in control, but even while you're reaching for your drink you're wondering how it's going to feel when I finally kiss you.'

Her mouth was so dry she could barely form the words. 'You're *not* going to kiss me.'

'I am.' He dropped his gaze to her mouth, his tone faintly apologetic. 'When I want something, I have to have it. It's part of my personality.'

Lindsay reached for her drink. 'You could talk to a trained

counsellor about that. You might find that a course of cognitive behavioural therapy might help.'

'I find it's simpler just to take what I want.' He gave a careless shrug of his broad shoulders. 'It's going to happen, Lindsay. Stop fighting it.'

Lindsay carefully put down her drink. Her hand was shaking so much it was that or spill it.

Before she could respond, the several waiters arrived with a tempting platter heaped with fresh seafood, bowls of salad and hot crusty bread.

As the food was served she was aware of Alessio watching her. Could he see? Could he see that her fingers shook when she picked up her fork? Could he see that she was in turmoil?

When they were alone again, she lifted her head and looked him in the eye, banishing visions of his bronzed, naked body covering hers. 'I'm prepared to perform whatever tasks you expected of Ruby. I'm quite sure that providing you with bedroom entertainment wasn't one of them.'

'There has never been any chemistry between us.'

'And that's all it takes to establish a relationship from your point of view? Chemistry?' Her laugh was tinged with derision. 'That's deep, Alessio. I'm sure your past encounters have been extremely—satisfying.'

'I make sure that they are.'

'I'm not talking about sexual satisfaction. I'm talking about something far deeper and more long lasting than that.' There was a cooling breeze from the sea but she still felt desperately hot. 'You're an intelligent man. Surely you demand more from a woman than the ability to simply lie down in your bed.'

'Absolutely.' Alessio didn't shift his eyes from her face. 'I demand a great deal more than that. And I'm sure you'll deliver.'

Was it her or had the temperature on the beach suddenly gone up? 'You shouldn't reduce every relationship to the physical.'

'You shouldn't dismiss sexual satisfaction until you've tried it.'

'What makes you think I haven't?'

'Because you're inexperienced.'

'You know nothing about my private life. Nor do I intend to discuss it with you.'

'Lindsay—' his tone was gentle '—you've been teasing and tempting me since the moment I arrived at your villa this evening. I don't know whether you're trying to prove something to yourself, but only someone *very* inexperienced would play those sorts of games with someone like me.'

'I'm not playing games.'

'I haven't quite worked out if you're a virgin or not,' he murmured, his strong fingers closing around the stem of his glass. 'You're certainly a bit old to be a virgin, but if you've had sex with anyone before, then I'm guessing that it was an instantly forgettable experience. And at this precise moment you're feeling very, very unsettled because you know that sex with me would be a completely *unforgettable* experience.'

Finally she lifted her head and looked at him. 'You're so arrogant.'

'You know we'll be good together, but you're afraid to admit it.'

'That isn't what's happening here at all! I'm not denying that you're attractive, of course you are. Nor am I denying that there's a certain—' she swallowed '—chemistry between us. But the reason I'm not acting on it has nothing to do with fear. It's a choice, Alessio. You and I have nothing in common, nothing on which to base a good relationship. Anything between us would be over in a flash.'

'I generally find that I can maintain my performance for little longer than a "flash",' he purred and she gave a murmur of exasperation.

'Alessio, please.' For some reason it suddenly seemed desperate that she make him understand. 'I will not allow myself to make huge decisions based on something as fleeting as chemistry.'

'It wouldn't be fleeting.' Dark lashes shielded his gaze. 'I'd want you again and again, in every conceivable position.'

Her limbs weak and her heart pounding, Lindsay stood up and dropped her napkin on the table. Why had she ever thought she could beat him at his own game? 'Sex without love is an extremely unsatisfying form of entertainment. I'm not interested.'

'I've never left a woman unsatisfied in my life.'

'All right, you win.' She lifted a hand in a gesture of supplication, so desperately unsettled by their verbal exchange that she knew she needed to escape. 'Enough. I don't want to talk about it anymore. I'm here in place of my sister. If you want me to do any legal work for you, then please knock on my door.'

And, please, don't let it be any time soon.

CHAPTER SIX

LINDSAY stood under the shower, letting the jets of ice-cold water cool her thoroughly overheated body.

Why, oh, why had she thought she'd be able to cope with being alone with Alessio for a week? After barely a few hours in his company she was so tense and wound up that she felt physically sick.

Her body was tormented by a nagging sensation that no amount of cold water could cure. He hadn't even touched her and yet she felt weak and limp and just utterly *drugged* with longing for something that she absolutely shouldn't and couldn't have.

Angry with herself, she thrust the palm of her hand against the shower knob and the flow of water ceased.

Alessio Capelli was arrogant, cold and frighteningly unemotional. Presumably those traits had contributed to his success in his chosen career. How else would he have been able to destroy people's marriages without losing sleep?

But the problem wasn't him, was it? The real problem was *her*. Her feelings; her response to him—

Feeling despair seep into every pore of her body, Lindsay sank onto the floor of the shower and wrapped her arms around her knees. Her hair hung wet down her back and she swept a hand over her face to clear the water from her eyelashes. Yes, he was arrogant, cold and frighteningly unemotional, but what really bothered her was the fact that everything he'd said to her had been correct.

No matter how much she'd tried to focus her mind on something else, she *had* found herself thinking of nothing but sex. One glance at his firm mouth and she'd started wondering how he kissed; a chance glimpse of dark male hair at the neck of his shirt and she'd immediately imagined him naked.

With a murmur of self-disgust, she covered her face with her hands.

She couldn't stop imagining the two of them together and for the first time in her life she was starting to understand how sheer sexual hunger could be so overwhelming that it could drive a person to make *really* bad decisions.

If he were here now, she'd be touching him.

And that would have been a disaster because Alessio Capelli was *totally* wrong for her.

Yes, he would undoubtedly be a skilled and exciting lover, but what else would he give her? The answer to that was *nothing but trouble*.

With a low groan she let her hands drop into her lap and leaned her head back against the wall. It would have been so easy to just knock on the door of his villa and let him take it from there. And she had no doubt that he would have instantly taken control. He was that sort of man, wasn't he?

And then what?

She was only too aware of the dangers of that sort of relationship. She spent her working life counselling people to look deeper.

So why was she struggling with her decision?

Because never in her life before had she wanted a man the way she wanted Alessio Capelli.

Suddenly she felt a burst of uncharacteristic anger towards Ruby. This was her fault. If she hadn't abandoned her job...

Was Ruby experiencing a similar degree of chemistry with Dino Capelli? If so, then it was little wonder she'd vanished without caring about her job or her sister.

And anyway, how could she be angry with Ruby? It wasn't really her sister's fault, was it?

After her uncertain, disordered childhood and then the collapse of a disastrous relationship, it was easy to see how she'd been dazzled by the wealth and charisma of the Capelli brothers.

With a sigh, Lindsay got to her feet and wrapped herself in one of the huge soft towels that were left ready for her use.

It was time to pull herself together. What use would she be to Ruby if she was suffering from a bruised heart herself?

No, sex with Alessio Capelli would undoubtedly have been amazing, but it was too high a price to pay for the mess she'd be in afterwards.

She was glad she'd walked away. In fact she was proud of herself.

Lindsay dried her hair methodically and then slid into a sheer silk nightdress that was nothing like her normal choice of bed wear.

But as she slipped into the large canopied bed she felt suddenly more alone than she'd ever felt in her life.

Without doubt she was the only woman who had ever walked away from him.

Trying to dismiss images of a powerful arrogant Italian stretched out next to her, she pressed her face into the pillows and pulled the soft cover over her shoulders.

Instead of focusing on the nagging throb low in her body she needed to think of his bad points. Of all the logical reasons why they shouldn't be together.

And there were certainly plenty to choose from.

Tired after a sleepless night, Lindsay forced her trembling legs along the smooth stone path that led to the Beach Club.

Given the choice she would have eaten breakfast alone.

She would have locked the door and stayed indoors in the air-conditioned tranquillity of her luxurious villa, but that wasn't an option. She was here to do a job and she was well aware that if she didn't play the part, then Alessio might still fire Ruby.

At least now she was on her guard. She'd let herself become complacent. She'd *totally* underestimated the devastating effect he had on her.

But now she was prepared.

Having been awake for most of the night, she'd had more than enough time to select her outfit for the day, and this time she'd been less cavalier in her choice of dress.

She'd bypassed swimming costumes, shorts and sarongs and instead chosen a white skirt that drifted down to mid-thigh. She'd teamed it with a strap top in a pale shade of lilac, cut high enough on her chest to ensure that no cleavage was revealed. And it fitted perfectly. She was confident that there was no chance that it would gape or reveal anything if she leaned forward. In an impulse of femininity that she didn't want to examine too closely, she'd slipped some delicate silver bangles onto her arm.

It was fine.

Everything was fine.

And everything remained fine until she walked onto the terrace and saw him.

He was seated at a table next to the beautiful swimming pool, a cup of coffee half drunk on the table in front of him.

Every part of his masculine physique emanating power and authority, he was talking to a man in a lightweight suit, but the moment he saw Lindsay his eyes narrowed and he said something that Lindsay couldn't hear.

The other man melted swiftly into the background leaving Lindsay the entire focus of Alessio's attention.

'*Buon giorno.*' He spoke in a low tone that was inaudible to all around, his eyes cool and assessing. 'Did you sleep well?'

'Perfectly, thank you.' She pulled out a chair and sat down opposite him, ignoring his knowing smile. 'Any sign of your client?'

Please say yes, she begged silently. A third person might dilute the tension that seemed to surround them.

'There's been a hurricane warning. He's decided not to fly out until the weather improves.'

Startled, she looked at him. 'A hurricane?'

'Don't worry. Kingfisher Cay hasn't suffered a direct hit once in the past sixty years. It will pass us by.'

Lindsay glanced up at the blue sky, noticing a few wisps of cloud on the horizon. 'Let's hope you're right.'

'Are you afraid of storms?'

'I love storms—' without looking at him, she helped herself to slices of fresh pineapple and mango from a plate in the centre of the table '—so if you're hoping that I'll seek the shelter of your strong arms, you're going to be disappointed.'

Alessio laughed. 'So far I haven't had to rely on the weather to entice a woman into my bed.'

'I'm sure you haven't.' She made a point of examining the deep gold flesh of the mango. 'Where there's money, there will always be women.'

'Ouch, Lindsay, that was cruel.' He was still laughing at her, apparently totally unaffected by her dig.

'No, really—I feel sorry for you—' picking up a fork, she speared a piece of mango '—you must be incredibly lonely. Meaningless sex has to become boring after a while.'

'Obviously you've never had really good sex,' he said dryly and Lindsay concentrated on her plate, taking her time over selecting her next piece of tropical fruit.

'For you it's a sort of sport, isn't it? A type of physical workout. You just don't engage your emotions. Don't you want *more*?'

'"More" being marriage?' He drained his coffee. 'I think you know me better than that.'

'I don't know you at all.'

'That's your choice,' he said silkily, his dark eyes glinting dangerously as he watched her. 'Feel free to take a voyage of discovery at your convenience. You look tired, Lindsay. Did something keep you awake last night? Your thoughts, perhaps?'

'I slept perfectly,' she lied. 'So if you have no client to see today, what are you going to do?'

'I have another difficult case that needs my attention. I intend to go out on the yacht. A change of scene sometimes helps me focus.'

Weak with relief at the news that he wasn't going to be around during the day, Lindsay finished the fruit on her plate and actually managed a smile. 'Of course. Don't worry about me. I quite understand that you need some time to yourself.' Maybe this wasn't going to be so hard after all. She could curl up in her villa with a book. Once she was confident he was nowhere near the island, she might even change into one of those revealing swimming costumes and risk a swim in the sea. 'I'll be fine.'

'I know you'll be fine—' he reached out a hand and helped himself to a piece of exotic fruit from the platter in front of him '—because you'll be with me. You're my assistant, remember? Where I go, you go.'

'When you're working, yes. But if you're simply having a day off on your yacht—'

'I don't take days off. I'll simply be working in a different venue.' His strong fingers dissected the fruit with ruthless precision while Lindsay stared in dismay.

He expected her to go with him? 'You'll be working on a boat?'

'A catamaran, to be precise. She's moored over there on the jetty.'

Lindsay turned her head and stared at the beautiful craft, the hull glistening white in the dazzling Caribbean sunshine. Just the two of them. Trapped. *On that?* Being on an island was bad enough, but being on a boat— 'I know absolutely nothing about boats.'

'I'll handle the boat.' He nodded to one of the waiters who instantly produced more coffee. 'Your duties will involve something else entirely.'

Her stomach lurched. 'What exactly will you want me to do?'

'I'm not sure yet.' He gave a slow smile. 'But when I've decided, you'll be the first to know.'

Despite her reservations, the sail was exhilarating—two hours of glorious sunshine while the boat skimmed joyously across the water, the sails arching against the kiss of the wind.

By the time Alessio finally sailed the boat into a curved, sheltered bay, Lindsay's face was pink from the sun and stinging with the spray of the sea.

And she felt fantastic. Unable to hide her elation, she kneeled on the seat and peered over the side of the catamaran, down into the clear depths of the blue Caribbean sea. It was like looking into an aquarium. The sun sparkled on the water and tropical fish in a rainbow of colours darted beneath her. And ahead of her was a perfect curve of white sand, fringed by palm trees and surprisingly lush vegetation.

She glanced back at him. 'Are we the only people here?'

'You wanted a party?' His movements sure and confident, he secured a rope and lowered the anchor.

'It's like being shipwrecked,' Lindsay murmured, turning her head and staring at the stretch of deserted beach.

'Five-star shipwreck.' Alessio produced a bottle of chilled champagne and deftly removed the cork. Pouring the bubbling liquid into two thin-stemmed flutes, he held one out to her. 'To a productive afternoon.'

Lindsay rose slowly to her feet and took the glass hesitantly. 'I don't drink in the middle of the day.'

'Take a sip.' Alessio raised his own glass in her direction. 'I think you might be about to discover a whole new vice.'

Because of the way he was looking at her, *because of the way he was making her feel*, Lindsay took a tentative sip and the surprisingly light and delicious drink seemed to sparkle in her mouth. She swallowed and smiled. 'It's delicious,' she admitted and took another sip. 'Really refreshing. It doesn't taste alcoholic.'

'Well, believe me, it is.' Putting down his own glass, he leaned behind her and carefully coiled a rope. 'Don't drink too much, especially if you're not used to it. Boats and alcohol don't mix and I don't want to be fishing you out of the water.'

'Then why did you want me to drink it?'

'Because this particular champagne is an experience that everyone should try at least once in their lives.' He gave a slow smile. 'A bit like no-strings sex.'

She took another sip of the delicious champagne, watching as the sun glinted on his glossy hair. 'For me, sex has to be an expression of love.'

'That's because you haven't tried the other sort.'

'I wouldn't want to.'

He turned to face her, a smile softening the hard lines of his mouth. 'Oh, you do want to, *tesoro*.' His voice soft, he stepped forward so that his body was virtually touching hers. 'You do want to. But you're afraid.'

Suddenly dizzy, she put her glass down on the seat next to her. 'Of course I'm afraid. I'm afraid of being hurt.'

'No, that isn't it.' He leaned closer to her and she felt the roughness of his jaw graze the softness of her cheek as he whispered in her ear. 'I think you're afraid that you might actually enjoy it. And then where would you be? A relationship counsellor who has made her name dismissing casual sex, suddenly embroiled in a no-strings affair. You'd have to rethink your career.'

Her eyes closed. He smelt fantastic and her senses swirled dangerously, sucking her down. Telling herself that it was just the champagne, she stepped backwards and would have fallen over the coiled rope if he hadn't reached out and steadied her.

Instinctively she put a hand on his shoulder, feeling rock hard muscle under her fingers. *He's strong*, she thought dizzily—*really strong.*

For a moment she just stood there, her body sending out signals that she was desperate to ignore.

Then, without warning, he released her. 'Are you wearing a swimming costume under that outfit?'

'Yes.' Her mouth was dry, her heart thumping and her mind—her mind was in a mess.

'Then I suggest that a dip in cold water might do us both good.' Without waiting for her response, he stripped off his shirt and shorts, poised for a moment on the edge of the boat before executing a perfect dive into the sun-dappled water.

Suddenly dizzy, Lindsay realised that it had actually been quite a while since she'd taken a breath. To be precise, since the moment he'd stripped off his shirt exposing powerful shoulders and bronzed skin.

No wonder women chased him, she thought weakly, watching as he emerged from the depths of the water, the water streaming from his dark hair as he wiped a hand over his face to clear his vision.

'Come on, Lindsay.'

She looked at him with something close to desperation. Joining him in the water somehow seemed symbolic. If she jumped—if she made that leap— 'The boat might drift.'

'The boat is fine. If you don't come in, I'll come and get you.'

Slowly, she wriggled out of her shorts and tee shirt. It *was* hot, she told herself, and her costume was perfectly decent. It didn't enter her head to follow him into the water head-first. Instead she walked to the end of the boat and gingerly picked her way down the ladder, holding tightly, pausing slightly as she registered the depth of the water beneath her.

'Typical Lindsay,' Alessio drawled, 'never one to jump if she can hold on to a ladder.'

Ignoring the amusement in his tone, she forced herself to let go of the ladder.

The cool, smooth water closed over her heated body and for a moment she felt small and insignificant, with nothing but ocean beneath and around her.

'This feels a bit weird.' Disconcerted, she glanced down and gasped as a shoal of blue fish darted beneath them. 'Oh, my goodness—'

'Blue Tang. The diving in this area is spectacular.'

Feeling a bit foolish, she swam a little closer to him. 'Are there sharks?'

His eyes focused on something over her shoulder and the laughter faded from his face. 'Ah—it seems that there are,' he said softly. 'Don't move, Lindsay, he's probably just being nosy—'

With a horrified gasp, she clutched at his shoulders and, too late, saw the wicked gleam in his eyes. 'Oh—I hate you. *I hate you!* That was an awful thing to do.'

'There are no sharks.' His hand curved around her waist. 'The reef stops them swimming this close to the land.'

'It does feel slightly menacing, having all that water beneath you,' she confessed, not brushing his hand away quite so quickly as she would have done had they been on dry land. 'It's beautiful. And—weird,' she admitted, 'not being able to touch the bottom.'

'You haven't swum off a boat before?'

'I don't generally find the opportunity during my working day.'

He gave a slow smile. 'You need to rethink your working day, *tesoro*. Life is to be lived, not just survived.' His hand was still on her back—large, warm, *strong*.

'I like my life.'

'That's because you don't know what you're missing. Stay there, I'll fetch you a snorkel.' He swam away from her, hauled himself back onto the boat with athletic ease and returned moments later with two masks in his hand. 'Try this.' Ignoring her protests, he adjusted the mask and eased it over her head. 'Put your head in the water and see if it leaks.'

After a moment of hesitation she decided that it would be safer just to follow his orders for once, and dutifully held her breath and put her face in the water.

An amazingly beautiful and varied underwater world stretched out beneath her and when she finally had to lift her head to breathe, she was smiling. 'All right. Just this once I'm willing to concede that you're right about something. I love it.'

He showed her how to breathe through the tube and how to dive down and clear it. Then he swam off and left her to get used to it by herself.

She experimented, becoming more and more adventurous and delighted by the brightly coloured fish she saw darting in shoals beneath her. When she finally stopped swimming and lifted her head, she saw Alessio taking the boat onto the beach.

She swam to the shore, removed her mask and snorkel and walked towards him. The white sand was silky soft under her feet, the sun blazing down on her head and shoulders.

'I've packed us some provisions.' He hauled some baskets out of the boat and handed her one. 'This island is very pretty. Worth exploring.' He dragged the boat farther up the beach, away from the lick of the sea.

Then he pulled out a cool box and a rug and strolled farther up the beach towards the palm trees. 'Your pale English skin will need the shade.'

Unlike him, she thought ruefully, scanning his golden brown shoulders and bronzed back as he casually threw the rug onto the sand. He had the sort of skin that turned brown in an instant.

He lay on his back on the rug and closed his eyes. 'An hour,' he murmured. 'We'll spend an hour here and then we'll sail back to Kingfisher Cay.'

She sat down, leaving a respectable distance between the two of them. 'How did you find this place?'

'I was sailing one day and came across it. I bought it.'

'Retail therapy, Alessio?'

Eyes still closed, he smiled. 'I had a wild idea that I might build a villa for myself on it one day. I like the fact that it's relatively inaccessible. The way the land curves means that it isn't visible from any other island. No photographers with long lenses. I like my privacy.'

'Is that why you don't allow cameras on Kingfisher Cay?'

'Yes. I want the guests to know that they're truly on holiday.'

'So are you going to build yourself a house here?'

'Maybe. At the moment we only use it for privileged guests who want a deserted island experience.'

'How did you find Kingfisher Cay?' Suddenly curious, she frowned down at him. 'I mean, you're Italian.'

'Sicilian.' His tone a shade cooler, he raised himself up on his elbows. 'I'm Sicilian.'

And he looks Sicilian, she thought desperately, *with those strands of blue-black hair flopping over his bronzed forehead.* He looked dark and dangerous and— 'All right, you're Sicilian—' she spoke quickly '—but why the Caribbean? You have your own islands in Italy.'

'No one would sell me Sicily.' His eyes gleamed with sardonic humour and she found herself laughing too, although a tiny part of her wondered whether perhaps he wasn't joking.

'Do you have to *own* everything?'

'If you're asking if I'm a possessive man—' he gave a slow, expressive shrug of his broad shoulders '*Sì*. If I want something, then, yes, I have to own it.' His eyes lingered on her face and she shivered, suddenly agonisingly aware that it was just the two of them on a deserted island.

'Can I ask you something else?'

'Ask.'

'Who was it that put you off marriage?'

For a moment he didn't respond and then he sat up, the muscles in his abdomen tensing as he leaned forward and flipped open the lid of an elegant basket. 'Are you hungry?'

That was it? He was going to ignore her question? 'You said I could ask you something—'

'And you did.' Reaching into the basket, he removed a number of dishes that wouldn't have disgraced a top restaurant.

'But you haven't answered me.'

'I didn't say that I'd answer.' He broke the bread in half and handed her a piece. 'I said you could ask.'

Exasperated, she looked at him. 'Do you ever stop being a lawyer?'

'Am I being a lawyer?'

'You guard every word you say.'

His eyes lingered on her face for a moment and then he smiled. 'In much the same way that you guard everything you do.'

She pulled at the bread with her fingers. 'You should have been a politician. You only ever reveal what you want to reveal. Doesn't matter what the question is, because the only answer you're going to get from Alessio Capelli is the one he wants to give.'

'Spilling my guts has never been my style.'

'And yet you have a really high profile in the press.'

'Their choice, not mine.' He was totally indifferent. 'I give them nothing.'

'Why don't you live in Sicily? Or aren't you prepared to discuss that either?'

'Sicily isn't a good base for an international business. I divide my time between my office in New York and my office in Rome.'

Lindsay finished eating and wiped her fingers. 'Do you ever go back to Sicily? Do you have family there?'

There was an imperceptible change in him. 'Just my brother. And he's with me in Rome.'

'Are your parents alive?'

He moved so swiftly that she didn't stand a chance. One moment she was sitting on the sand, congratulating herself that they were actually managing to sustain a conversation about something other than sex or divorce—*a faltering, fragile conversation maybe, but a conversation nevertheless*—and the next, she was on her back in the sand and his hard, powerful body was pressing down on hers.

'I don't give interviews, *tesoro*.' For a few suspended seconds his mouth hovered tantalisingly close, almost but not quite touching her. And the promise of that touch made her lips tingle and her body ache, and the stab of delicious anticipation was so agonising that she could hardly breathe as she waited for him to kiss her. Her senses were primed, her pulse rate frantic, her nerve endings exploding like fireworks on bonfire night. And just when she'd decided that he wasn't going to do it—*that it wasn't going to happen*—he did.

And it was nothing like she'd imagined it to be.

Alessio Capelli was pure alpha male—arrogant, confident, imposing his will on those around him.

Whenever she'd thought about kissing him, she'd imagined his hand in her hair, his mouth rough and demanding as he took what he wanted. So the slow, seductive pressure of his mouth on hers came as a shock. He was a skilled, expert kisser—a man who knew exactly how to draw the maximum response from a woman. The heat rushed through her body, lighting every nerve ending like a match held against paper. And she melted in the heat of that kiss, her body growing warm and heavy as sizzling excitement concentrated itself low in her pelvis.

With slow, deliberate precision, he coaxed her lips apart and she felt the intimate stroke of his tongue stealing both her breath and her willpower. And she didn't ever want him to stop because it was the most delicious, perfect kiss she could have imagined and if the world had ended right then she wouldn't have cared.

It was as if he'd drugged her, his touch sending every rational thought from her spinning brain.

His body shifted above her and she felt his warm, strong hand slide across her shoulder. She was held immobile by sensual bondage; it was only when his lips moved from her mouth to her breast that she realised he'd somehow removed the strap of her swimsuit.

Control slid away from her and she moaned and lifted herself against the warmth of his mouth, desperate for his touch. Her frantic response obviously met with his approval because he gave a soft, appreciative laugh.

'*Adoro il tuo corpo.*' His voice husky, he concentrated his attention on one dusky pink nipple. 'I love your body.' As if to prove just how much he loved her body, his hand slid slowly down her thigh, the touch of his fingers creating havoc with her senses.

It was exciting, terrifying and utterly, utterly addictive.

Desperately she tried to regain some control over what was happening, but every time she tried to gasp out a protest he'd touch her in a particular way and she'd be sucked back down into a whirlpool of wicked, delicious pleasure from which there was no escape.

It was the heavy thrust of his erection against her thigh that finally shocked her out of her state of dizzy stupor.

'No—Alessio, no—' With a groan of denial, she put her hand on his chest, resisting the impulse to stroke rather than stop. But she had to stop. 'I can't—not like this—'

He was above her, his weight pressing her into the soft sand, powerfully male and unashamedly aroused. 'What's wrong with this? I am too heavy for you?' Suddenly he sounded impossibly Italian, his normally confident English slightly less fluent than usual. Slowly, he trailed a gentle, exploratory finger over her mouth. 'You are feeling shy?'

There was no way she could put into words what she was feeling because she'd never felt it before. She was used to being in control. Normally she thought of herself as assertive and self-reliant, but where were those qualities now? She was lying passive, dominated by a sexually confident male, and that was bad enough, but the thing that really shamed her was that she was enjoying it. A small secret part of her was thrilled by his strength and virility.

Alessio Capelli had never heard the phrase 'politically correct', she thought dizzily, closing her eyes to break the sizzling connection between them. 'We haven't—this is just impulse and it's all wrong. Sex should be a conscious decision, not an impulse. It should be planned.' *Oh, Lindsay, Lindsay, you really shouldn't be doing this. If you eat too much chocolate you put on weight, and if you sleep with men like Alessio Capelli—*

'So far, this is going exactly the way I planned, *tesoro*,' he murmured, amusement in his voice as he lowered his dark head and delivered a lingering kiss to her neck. 'Tell me something, Lindsay—' his voice was a soft, dangerous purr '—if there was no tomorrow, would you do this?'

He dangled temptation in front of her without hesitation

or conscience and she gave a low moan, rejecting the answer
that came into her head.

'There *is* a tomorrow.'

'But sometimes it is good to live your life as though there
isn't,' he murmured, his fingers gently tracing her cheek.
'That is good, no?'

For a moment Lindsay lay there dazed and then gradually
his words sank into her brain. 'Wait a minute.' Her voice was
husky and she cleared her throat. 'Did you just say that you
planned this?'

'We're alone and half-naked on a desert island, *tesoro*.' His
mouth discovered a sensitive spot just under her jawbone and
Lindsay's insides clenched.

'And that makes sex inevitable?'

'I hate to let an opportunity go to waste,' he breathed softly
and she closed her eyes tightly because the shift from
meltdown to misery had happened in the space of a heartbeat.

Dear God, she was a fool.

'I'm a person, Alessio, not an opportunity.' Her voice
breaking slightly, she pushed at his chest and he shifted away
from her, his dark eyes narrowed in question.

'You appeared to be enjoying yourself.'

'I enjoy chocolate—but I know when to say no. Don't you
have any morals?'

'Obviously I do.' His tone cool, Alessio rolled onto his
back. 'You said no. I stopped.'

'Do us both a favour next time—don't start.' Her body felt
warm and alive, as if someone had flicked a switch that could
never again be turned off. 'Don't touch me again, Alessio.'

'*Sì*, you are right—it was good.' He gave a low laugh and
she looked at him fiercely.

'I didn't say it was good—'

'But you don't want me to touch you again—' his eyes

drifted shut, the smile on his hard mouth one of raw male arrogance '—and that says everything there is to be said.'

'It says, I don't want you to touch me again!' Her heart was pumping like an athlete in a sprint. 'Are you having trouble with your English?'

'No, but I think you're having trouble with your "choices",' he said silkily. 'You were sure what you wanted—now, you're not so sure.'

She scrambled to her feet, averting her eyes from the haze of dark hair on his bronzed chest. 'I want to go back to Kingfisher Cay. I want to go back right now.' Before she did something, really, *really* foolish.

'Unfortunately, we can't do that.'

'Yes, we can.' Control was slipping through her fingers. 'You sailed here, you can sail back again.'

'No, I can't.' His tone was suddenly serious. 'You and I have a real problem, Lindsay.'

She lifted her fingers to her forehead, anger fading to despair. 'I know we have a problem.' Her body was still humming with sexual awareness, but she took a deep breath and looked him in the eye. 'It will be fine if we just ignore it. We're both adults and we're perfectly capable of resisting temptation if we choose to do so.'

'We're at cross purposes. I wasn't talking about the chemistry between us. I don't see *that* as a problem.' He turned, a sardonic smile on his face. 'And just so that we're both clear, I have no intention of resisting temptation, so, if that's the route you plan to take, you're on your own. You'll be resisting without my help.'

Still trying to cope with his cool admission that he had no intention of resisting temptation, Lindsay bit her lip. 'Well, if that's not the problem—'

'When did you last look at the sea or the sky, Lindsay?'

His tone deceptively gentle, his eyes flickered behind her. 'Do you remember that storm I mentioned?'

Storm? For a moment she stared at him, her mind refusing to go further back than the kiss.

And then she turned her head and looked at the ocean.

Somehow, at some point during their picnic—and afterwards—the sea had turned from glasslike smooth stillness, to an angry, boiling furnace. Waves lashed the shore and the sky had turned from perfect blue to ominous grey. 'Oh, my goodness—I didn't notice—'

'I think we were both rather distracted,' he drawled, irony in his gaze as he sprang to his feet.

Lindsay felt a flash of panic. 'Call someone. Use your mobile phone.'

'I didn't bring it. There's no signal here. And anyway, no boats will come out in this and the wind is too strong for the seaplane. We'll have to wait it out.'

Lindsay's insides lurched. 'Is it the hurricane?'

'No, but I suspect it must have changed course or we wouldn't be experiencing this weather.' His gaze lingered on the sky for a moment and then he bent down and gathered up their things. 'I'll just secure the boat and then we'll go and find shelter. There's an old abandoned cottage on the other side of the island. It will be more protected there. We'll shelter until the storm passes.'

Horrified, she stared at him. 'And how long will that be?'

'I have absolutely no idea.'

'You're suggesting that we stay here alone?' She licked her lips and her eyes slid to the angry sea. 'You did this on purpose.'

'I'm flattered by your assessment of my powers,' he said dryly, 'but even I can't change the course of a hurricane. With luck it will just graze the island and lose power over the sea. Come on. If it doesn't blow itself out, you'll have plenty of time to blame me for the sins of the world over the next few days. Pick up the picnic blanket and the rest of the food. I need to see to the boat.'

'But it's already on the beach—'

'Trust me, in a few hours, this won't be beach.'

And they were going to be trapped together. She looked at him in horror, expecting to see signs of worry on his face, but his eyes gleamed with something that looked like anticipation. 'You're actually enjoying this, aren't you?'

'It's something out of the ordinary and, yes, that's exciting in its own way. Unlike you, I don't like life to be too predictable. Where's the challenge in that? Come on. We need to find ourselves some shelter.'

CHAPTER SEVEN

'You're shivering. Are you cold?' His tone sharp, Alessio hauled the rest of their things into the single-storey cottage and immediately the sound of the building wind was muffled.

'I'm not cold,' Lindsay lied, resisting the temptation to rub her hands down her bare arms. Why, oh, why was fate so cruel? Why couldn't she at least have had something with her that could have covered her up? She wished now that she'd returned to the boat to pick up more provisions, but Alessio had insisted that they move as fast as possible.

And it had been the right decision. By the time they'd walked for twenty minutes along the beach, the wind had risen dramatically.

She'd been relieved when she'd spotted the cottage on the far side of the tiny island. It was slightly protected by the curve of the land and Lindsay could see that they'd be safer there than in the little bay where they'd landed.

'What is this place?' The cottage was obviously old and she hesitated on the doorstep, wary of trespassing. 'Who owns it?'

'I suppose I do, technically. Before me it belonged to an eccentric millionaire who didn't much like people.' Alessio was prowling around the deserted rooms, as if he were looking for something. Occasionally he'd pause and put his hand against a window. 'We'll shelter in here. Stay away from the window in case the glass is blown in. We have rugs, plenty of water and some food. We'll be fine for a few days, if necessary.'

'A few *days*?' Appalled, Lindsay gaped at him. 'I can't stay here for a few days! I need to contact Ruby.'

He spread the rug on the floor. 'It doesn't make much difference whether you're on Kingfisher Cay, or here. Ruby isn't answering your calls.'

'But what if she tries to contact me?' Lindsay paced the floor, desperately worried. 'What if she rings in a panic? What if she needs my advice? I won't be answering my phone and *what will she do then*?'

'She might have to make a decision on her own. Believe me, that would do her the world of good.' Watching her pace the room, he frowned suddenly. 'You're stranded in a storm and still you're thinking about your sister. When exactly do you worry about yourself? You should be asking me if we're going to get out of here, or if the cottage is likely to be blown away.'

'We'll be fine, I'm sure.' Barely registering those possibilities, Lindsay started to bite one of her nails and then let her hand drop. 'But if Ruby needs to contact me—what if she hears about this storm?'

'She doesn't know you're with me, so she won't understand its relevance. And anyway, you're safe here.'

Suddenly realising just how isolated they were, Lindsay felt her stomach flip. She didn't feel safe. She didn't feel safe at all, and her growing tension had nothing to do with the threatening weather. Outside, the wind was starting to whistle and howl, buffeting the cottage and rattling the windows. But the real threat to her well-being was on the inside.

Dressed only in his swimming shorts, Alessio was now sprawled on the rug watching her.

'Are you going to pace all night?'

'I can't relax—'

'When are you going to let your sister lead her own life?

You try and control her every movement—it's no wonder she's rebelled and vanished into the sunset. You created this situation by behaving more like a mother than a sister.'

It was as if he'd punched her.

Appalled, Lindsay stared at him. 'No.' She shook her head in furious denial. 'I *don't* control her. I just offer her support.'

'Support is "I'm here if you need me",' Alessio drawled. 'Support isn't "you're not doing what I think you should do".'

Lindsay's head was filled with images of a vulnerable toddler clinging to her in bed, night after night. 'You don't understand—'

'*Maledizione*, why do you think she hasn't called?' His tone was brutally direct. 'Because she knows you're going to disapprove of what she's doing. She knows that when you pick up that phone, all she's going to get from you is a lecture.'

'No.' Lindsay's lips felt dry. 'No, that isn't—'

'Have you ever tried to understand her? Did you ever ask yourself why she wanted to stay in Rome? I'll tell you why—because it was the only way she could possibly run her life without your constant interference.'

Frozen to the spot, Lindsay could barely breathe. 'That isn't true.' Her stomach heaved and for a moment she actually felt physically sick. 'And you have no right to say those things to me. What does someone like you know about love? Or relationships?'

She turned and paced back across the room, her arms wrapped around her body as she struggled to hold herself together.

It wasn't true. None of the horrid things he was saying was true.

Yes, she was protective of Ruby. But she was the older sister. It was her responsibility to look after Ruby. She'd always done it, ever since they were children.

'Will you let me sleep in your bed, Linny?'

She'd smothered Ruby with love, compensating for the

lack of care and affection they'd received from their parents. She'd been the sister *and* the mother.

Lindsay dug her hands into her hair as she forced herself to examine the facts.

Of course she was going to support her sister and offer advice. She'd been the very best sister she could be. Hadn't she?

Tormented by a tiny seed of doubt, Lindsay felt as though her entire world were unravelling.

She'd been so sure of herself. So certain. And suddenly she just didn't feel certain anymore.

She needed space to think—

She needed to get out of this confined space—

Somehow she managed to make her lips move. 'I need some air.' Tugging open the door, she staggered as a powerful gust almost dragged it out of her hand, the wind howling like a choir of a thousand ghosts, daring her to venture outside.

But Lindsay didn't care—

Whatever lay outside, it had to be better than being trapped with Alessio.

Wincing as the door was almost taken off its hinges, Alessio spent a few seconds cursing the whole female race and their tendency to the dramatic, before springing to his feet.

Hurricane-force winds were blowing outside and she'd decided that she *needed some air*?

Was she crazy?

But even as he asked himself that question, something slightly uncomfortable twisted inside him. No, she wasn't crazy. She was just upset. Very, very upset.

And he was the cause of that upset.

Unaccustomed to experiencing feelings of guilt, Alessio strode towards the door, reminding himself that he'd merely told her the truth. And if it had been a painful truth, well, that was because she'd been deluding herself.

In the long term, he'd done her a favour.

She'd probably thank him.

So why was he wishing he could wind the clock back and been given an opportunity to keep his mouth shut?

Trying to dismiss the image of her white face and the distressed look in her eyes, Alessio strode to the door.

If she didn't have the sense to know it was dangerous out there, then he was going to have to go and fetch her.

Immediately the strength of the wind stole the breath from his lungs and he wondered how someone as slight as Lindsay had managed to stay upright in the path of such a powerful force.

As he secured the door behind him he found himself wondering why she hadn't turned back.

But he knew the answer to that. She hadn't turned back because of him. She was either so angry with him she couldn't bear to be within the same four walls, or else she was so upset by what he'd said that she needed to think.

Either way, she was putting herself in physical danger.

Black, deadly clouds had replaced perfect blue sky and Alessio glanced along the beach, searching for a solitary figure.

And then he saw her. Her arms were wrapped around her body and she was staring out to sea, apparently oblivious to the anger of the storm that was building. Her pale hair had broken loose from the clasp and for once she hadn't bothered to pin it up again. As if to taunt her with that fact, the wind caught it and blew it wildly around her face and shoulders. She looked like a mermaid, contemplating a return to the sea. She also looked—fragile.

Alessio frowned. *Fragile?* He always thought of Lindsay Lockheart as composed and controlled. Even the night she'd been attacked on the streets of Rome, she'd been remarkably collected, more concerned about her sister than herself.

But she didn't look composed or controlled. She looked—broken.

Swearing fluently in two different languages, he strode across to her, ready to blast her for taking such a stupid risk.

But as he drew closer he saw that her cheeks were wet and her eyes were glistening.

Maledizione—

Alessio executed an emergency stop, his natural inclination to retreat in the face of female emotion acting as a break. Given the choice, he would have preferred to do battle with ten storms than mop up tears.

He took a step backwards.

Obviously she wanted to be alone, he reasoned. If she'd wanted his company, she would have stayed in the cottage.

Convincing himself that what she needed most was some space and time to herself—*after all, hadn't she chosen to come out here alone?*—he was about to retreat when another powerful gust of wind slammed into them and she lost her balance.

In one stride, Alessio was next to her. He closed his arms around her and braced his strong legs to support them both against the force of the wind. 'Do you have a death wish? It isn't safe out here!' She felt impossibly fragile and he wondered why she hadn't already been blown over.

He glared down at her, but his feelings of anger and exasperation dissolved in an instant as he registered her tortured expression. '*Why* are you looking at me like that?'

This was a different Lindsay. A desperately unsure, insecure Lindsay. There was no sign of the competent exterior that she presented to the world. She even *looked* different, for once oblivious to the fact that her hair was blowing loose around her face and the fact that she was dressed only in a swimming costume. She looked incredibly young.

Incredibly beautiful...

Engulfed by a sudden explosion of lust that was almost more powerful than the storm, Alessio contemplated slinging her over his shoulder and taking her back to the cottage for the type of one-on-one comfort he knew he was capable of delivering.

He was responsible for her upset and he was confident that he could fix it.

But then she lifted her eyes to his and she looked so vulnerable that for once he decided not to say what was on his mind.

Instead he dragged his gaze from the trembling curve of her soft mouth and tried to focus on something non sexual. *Like the fact that they were both about to be blown to the outer reaches of the Caribbean.* Torn between concern for her safety and guilt that he was the cause of her distress, he tried to haul her back up the path, but she refused to move. 'We have to go inside.'

She looked at him blankly and exasperation mingled with concern because she was the most decisive woman he'd ever met and yet she was clearly incapable of making any sort of decision.

Tears glistened on her lashes and shadows flickered across her eyes. 'What if you're right?' She had to raise her voice to be heard above the howl of the wind and he gritted his teeth.

There was a storm blowing and she wanted to *talk*?

'I *am* right,' Alessio assured her, confident that it was the right response regardless of the question. He slid his arm around her shoulders and urged her up the path. 'We need to get inside. Now. *Pronto.* Before we find ourselves transported to the next island.'

'No. I mean about Ruby.' She stopped, her hand in her hair to prevent it from blowing wildly around her face. 'What if you're right about Ruby? What if the reason Ruby isn't ringing me is because she thinks I'll judge her? What if it is my fault? What if I've driven her away?' Another powerful gust of wind almost knocked her off her feet and Alessio made a unilateral decision and scooped her into his arms.

She'll thank me later, he thought as he strode back up the narrow, sandy path to the comparative safety of the cottage. Shouldering the door shut against the raging, angry storm, he lowered her gently to the floor.

'*Don't* leave the cottage again.' His tone was sharper than
e'd intended and when he saw the sheen in her eyes he cursed
imself for not being more sympathetic. If he didn't tread
arefully she was going to dissolve in a sodden heap and that
vas the last thing he wanted or needed.

Resigned to the inevitable, Alessio waited for her to collapse
obbing against his chest, but instead she turned away.

'Just give me a minute.'

On unfamiliar territory, Alessio stared at her rigid shoul-
ers, trying to work out what he was supposed to do next.
lthough he had plentiful experience of tearful women, he'd
ever been with one who didn't want him to see her crying.
nd everything about her body language told him that Lindsay
ockheart was trying very hard not to let him see her crying.

Alessio hesitated, torn between the options of steering the
onversation onto neutral ground and just dealing with the
ssue straight out.

Never one to avoid a problem, he tackled it head-on.

'Apologies aren't my speciality,' he gritted, 'but I think I
we you one. I was unsympathetic and my comments were
ar too personal—'

'You don't owe me an apology.' She sounded stiff. Formal.
nd she still didn't look at him. 'You don't have to apologise
or being honest. I'm the one who was deluding myself.' The
nly indication that she was still crying was the way she dis-
reetly lifted her hand to wipe her face, but somehow that
ninimal gesture increased his feelings of guilt.

'You obviously thought you were acting in the best inter-
sts of your sister—' He broke off as he saw her flinch and
ift a slender hand to silence him.

'Alessio, please don't say any more. There's only so much
onesty I can take in one go.'

He'd been trying to help. But softening the truth wasn't his
orte.

Alessio raked his fingers through his hair, stunned by realisation that for once he was *totally* unsure what he sho say next. He was a lawyer. He *always* knew what to say n 'What I'm trying to say is that you probably—definitely,' corrected himself swiftly, 'you *definitely* know better tha do what works for Ruby.'

'Apparently not.'

'You're a *great* sister.' Alessio delivered that statem with what he hoped was an appropriate degree of convicti 'Ruby is lucky to have someone like you watching over h

For a moment she didn't answer. Then she wiped her f with her fingers once more, and turned to face him. 'N Everything you've said is true. I *have* been too controlli I thought I was protecting her, but I've handled her in worst way possible. I've done all the wrong things at all wrong times.'

His hands tightened on her arms. 'For all the right reaso

'I've let her down. She's my responsibility, but I've ma it impossible for her to turn to me because she knows I'll upset and worried, and—I've missed the fact that she's gro up…' Her voice wobbled and for a moment she stopp speaking and just breathed.

Waiting for her to finish her sentence, Alessio discove that her determination not to lose control in front of him v a thousand times more moving than a cascade of tears.

'Lindsay—'

'Don't say anything,' she muttered. 'This is—a bit di cult—' she lifted a hand to her mouth and then let it fall ag '—and the reason it's difficult is because everything you is true. I've failed her.' For some reason the brave smile v a greater attack on his conscience than her tears and Ales swore softly.

'*Why* do you feel she's your responsibility?'

Lindsay looked at him for a moment. 'Because she's

little sister,' she whispered, 'and it doesn't matter what she does, she'll always be my little sister.'

'Precisely.' Feeling as though he were drowning, Alessio ran a hand over the back of his neck. 'You're her sister, not her mother.'

'I've always looked after her.' She gave a twisted smile. 'Or, at least, that's what I was trying to do. But it seems I haven't been helping her as much as I thought.'

Alessio inhaled sharply. 'Take no notice of anything I say. As you rightly point out, I know nothing about relationships. Relationships are always complicated, Lindsay—' his tone was harsher than he'd intended '—that's why I avoid them.'

'Do you mind if we don't talk about this anymore right now?' Clearly hanging on to control by a thread, she turned away from him and walked over to the huge blanket. 'It's very dark.'

'It's the storm. It will pass, but probably not before nightfall. We'll be spending the night here.'

He waited for her to have hysterics or make some sharp remark about him having engineered the situation, but she did neither. Instead she simply dropped to her knees onto the blanket and curled up with her back to him.

'If you don't mind, I think I might sleep. I haven't had much sleep since Ruby went missing…' Her voice tailed off and for a moment she hesitated. 'But of course she isn't actually missing, is she? She just doesn't want me to know where she is.'

Lying there, trying to make herself as small as possible, she reminded him of a lost child.

'You must be very angry with her.'

'Angry?' Her voice was thickened with tears. 'How could I possibly be angry with her when it's all my fault? You're quite right. I've driven her away. My behaviour has driven her away.'

Nowhere near as forgiving, Alessio found his own anger

towards Ruby flaring to life. She should have known how much her sister would worry. *She should have picked up the bloody phone.*

It was obvious that Lindsay, however misguided, had genuinely been acting for her sister's benefit and, sensing the depth of her hurt, Alessio gritted his teeth, taking her pain as yet another example of why love was the utter pits. Why did anyone bother? *Who wanted to put themselves through that.* Much better to build a barrier around one's emotions.

And that was what he'd done, of course.

From a very early age.

He sat down next to her. His eyes rested on the smooth skin of her bare shoulder and then followed the line of her red swimsuit. It dipped temptingly into her tiny waist and then rose again to accommodate the feminine swell of her hips. Instinctively he lifted a hand to trace that all too tempting curve, but there was something in the way she held herself that stopped him. Instead, he rolled onto his back and stared up at the ceiling, practising restraint for the first time in his life.

Reminding himself not to express his opinion of her sister ever again, he closed his eyes.

It was going to be a long night.

Lindsay lay in the depths of misery, drowning in self-blame.

This was *all* her fault. She could see that now.

If she'd been more approachable and less judgmental, Ruby would have felt able to confide in her—she would have *called.*

How could she have been so horribly wrong? She spent her working life helping couples see that there were always two points of view, and yet had she ever listened to what Ruby wanted? No, she hadn't. She'd been so afraid that Ruby would choose the wrong path in life that every time her sister had opened her mouth, she'd lectured and dictated. Don't do this—don't do that.

And who was to say that Ruby's choices would have been the wrong ones?

Alessio was right. The wrong path for one person was the right path for another.

Ridden with guilt, Lindsay squeezed her eyes tightly shut. She loved her sister so much. So much. And had she helped her? No.

She was a stupid idiot.

The thought of how badly she'd handled everything was like a physical pain.

She'd been so convinced that her approach was the right one. After what she'd seen as a child, she'd been determined not to follow the same route. And determined not to let her sister follow the same route. But she'd attached such a strong belief to her own strict code that it had prevented her from understanding how others felt. Since when had she become so pompous and set in her ways that she'd decided there was only one right way to do things?

Perhaps Ruby was, at this moment, having the time of her life with Dino Capelli.

Perhaps she wanted to share that happiness and excitement, and the reason she wasn't calling Ruby was because she knew she wouldn't approve.

Would Ruby ever turn to her again?

Tears slid down her face and this time she didn't bother trying to stop them because it was dark and Alessio was asleep.

Convinced that she was alone with her misery, she gave a start of shock as a strong male hand curved over her shoulder.

'*Stop* crying.'

Appalled that he knew she was crying, Lindsay froze. 'I'm not crying.'

He muttered something in Italian. 'I tell you now,' he said roughly, 'I have absolutely *no* experience in comforting women. It isn't something I excel at. Ask anyone.' He hesitated. 'Normally I'm the one making them cry.'

Lindsey gave a choked laugh. 'I can believe that. But for once you're not to blame. Everything you said is right. I might even get round to thanking you at some point. And you don't need to worry—I don't want comfort.' She sniffed and scrubbed a hand over her face, relieved that it was dark. 'Anyway, I thought you had to be the best at everything.'

'Only the things that interest me. Strangely enough I have no ambitions to excel at drying women's tears,' he drawled softly, 'but on this one occasion, given that I'm the cause of your upset, I'm prepared to make an exception.'

Realising just how great a sacrifice that was on his part, she almost managed to smile. This must be almost as bad for him as it was for her. 'You're not the cause. Go to sleep, Alessio.'

But his strong, warm hand didn't move from her shoulder. 'This rug is the only dry thing in the place and I'd like to keep it that way. *Stop* feeling guilty about your sister.'

'Why?' She mumbled the words, wondering why she was discussing it with him. Alessio Capelli wasn't anyone's idea of a perfect confidant. 'It's *all* my fault.'

'It isn't your fault. I keep telling you, Ruby is responsible for what she does.'

'I've stopped her talking to me.'

'And what if she *had* talked to you? You would have been given a running commentary on all her wild behaviour and it would have driven you crazy with stress. You wouldn't have said anything, but you still would have felt it. You're much better off not knowing.' His tone rang with exasperation and she almost laughed.

'You make it sound so easy.'

'It *is* easy. It's time to toughen up, Lindsay,' he said gruffly. 'How have you managed to get through the past two decades when you worry so much about everything?'

'I don't really worry—'

'You're avoiding life because you're afraid of it.'

Lindsay stilled. 'That isn't true.'

'You're worried that your sister will be hurt and maybe she will—' his voice was low and male in the darkness '—but maybe she will have an affair that she will remember for ever. Memories of real passion that will last long after the hurt has faded. What will you have, Lindsay? The memory of dangerously exciting moments that you successfully resisted?'

He was right, she realised painfully. She *was* afraid. Afraid of falling into the same trap as the couples she counselled, afraid of being drawn into the wrong decision, *afraid of being like her mother*....

She wiped her tears with the back of her hand. 'You live dangerously all the time. So how do you manage never to be hurt?'

'I don't let people get close.'

'But what sort of life is that?'

There was a moment of silence and then he gave a hollow laugh. 'I'm not the one lying on the rug crying, Lindsay.'

'Caring for people and having people care about you is the only really important thing in life.' It was just because it was dark, she told herself, that it was easy to talk to him.

'And is it worth caring even when you get hurt?'

'Even then. It's what makes us human.'

'Ah—but you told me only a few days ago that I'm not human, so that explains why we think differently.'

She could hear the trace of humour in his voice. 'I thought life was straightforward. But everything suddenly seems so complicated.'

'Relationships always are. That's why I avoid them.'

'But you can't just go through life avoiding relationships. Relationships—love—well, that's what makes life bearable, isn't it?'

'Relationships—maybe. Love? Definitely not. In fact I'd go as far as to say that love is probably one of the things that often makes life *un*bearable. Believe me, I see it all the time.'

'But the people you see aren't in love anymore. Perhaps they never were.'

'There are other types of relationships.'

'I know. And that's where I've let Ruby down,' Lindsay admitted, relieved that it was dark so that he couldn't see her face. Somehow the dark made it easier to talk. 'We're very different like that. I was always worried that she would confuse chemistry with love and I've seen so many relationships fall apart because all the couple shared was chemistry. I've never contemplated being in a relationship that was just about sex.'

It was a moment before he answered and when he finally spoke his voice was soft in the darkness.

'Haven't you?'

A shiver of awareness ripped through her whole body and she didn't pretend to misunderstand him.

'Well—maybe I have. Once.' Her heart was thumping and bumping against her chest, as if it were trying to escape while there was still a chance.

His fingers tightened on her shoulder. 'You have willpower that most people would envy.'

'If you're talking about us, then we would have been a nightmare together, you know we would.'

He gave a low laugh and rolled her gently onto her back. 'It would have been explosive, *tesoro*. And you know it. Which is why you've been holding back. What's wrong with sexual attraction, Lindsay?'

'Nothing, as long as both parties recognise it for what it is. Ruby doesn't.'

This was the time that she should push him away. This was the time she should tell him that, although she'd realised she'd handled Ruby all wrong, she didn't want to change the way she lived herself. She wasn't about to hurl herself from a place of safety into the dangerous unknown of raw sexual excitement.

She should tell him that. She should tell him that *right now*.

But she couldn't manage to form the words. Instead her hand slid over his shoulder, feeling the hard curve of male muscle under her seeking fingers.

This level of chemistry wasn't something she'd ever experienced before—and probably never would again.

If she let it pass, would she regret it?

Would she look back in her old age and think, *If only?*

Or would she smile and tell her grandchildren that passion wasn't always dangerous, as long as you recognised it for what it was?

There would be no 'happy ever after' with Alessio Capelli, but she knew that, didn't she? It wasn't a mistake. It was a choice.

'Lindsay—' The husky, questioning note in his voice made her realise that her hand had curved around his neck.

She sensed that he was holding back—*that this was all up to her*—but she had no more time to agonise over her decision because her hands were drawing his head towards hers.

Apparently it was all the encouragement he needed because he instantly took control, his hands not quite steady as he rolled her onto her back and covered her body with his.

It seemed that her senses still remembered how he'd kissed her on the beach, and a pool of heat coiled itself in her pelvis and she waited in an agony of anticipation for the slow, skilled assault of his mouth.

Only this time he didn't give her slow.

This time he brought his mouth down on hers with a driven sense of purpose that propelled her from a state of simmering anticipation to explosive excitement. Hot with longing, she felt him cup her face with lean, strong hands and then part her lips with his tongue. He took her mouth with devastating expertise, his demanding and intimate exploration creating erotic curls of heat low in her pelvis.

It was like being drugged and her last coherent thought

was, *How did he learn to kiss like this?* Before she slid dow
and down into a sensual world that was beyond her control

Her senses connected like an electric circuit, sending
sparks to every part of her and she was lost, totally lost.

She pressed herself against his hard, powerful body, felt th
roughness of his thigh graze against the softness of hers, fel
the scrape of stubble against her cheek as he dragged hi
mouth from hers only to bury it in her neck.

'Alessio—I can't wait—don't wait—' She writhed, lost in
the sensation he was creating. 'Please—' But her plea turned
to a moan as she felt his mouth fasten over the pink, throbbing tip of her breast. Up until that moment she hadn't ever
realised that he'd removed her costume and suddenly she wa
aware that she was naked. But the feeling that engulfed he
wasn't embarrassment, but desperation.

It seemed that the more he touched her, the more she
wanted, and when she felt his hand reach down between her
thighs she gave a low moan of encouragement that changed
to a gasp as she felt the skilled slide of his fingers.

She felt wild, desperate and totally unlike herself, writh-
ing against him as she tried to relieve the unbearable ache in
her pelvis.

'You feel *so* good, *tesoro*,' Alessio groaned and then gently
moved his hand, cupped her bottom and positioned her to his
satisfaction.

For a breathless moment she felt the hot, silken tip of his
erection against her, and then he brought his mouth down on
hers again and entered her with a series of controlled thrusts
that drove the breath from her body. He was big, *so big* that
for a moment she tensed, and he must have sensed her sudden
apprehension because he paused for a moment and lifted his
mouth from hers just enough to speak.

'I'm hurting you?'

'No, I—no—'

'Then relax, *tesoro*,' he instructed huskily, 'and let your body do what it is desperate to do.' But he lowered his mouth to hers again and kissed her until the explicit movement of his tongue in her mouth made her rake her fingers over the smooth muscle of his shoulders.

She whimpered deep in her throat and he lifted her hips and sank himself deep inside her, his eyes half-open as he watched her abandoned response. And then he withdrew slightly and did it again, creating waves of pure pulsing pleasure that consumed her entire body.

Completely out of control, she clung to him, her cries smothered by his mouth, her body hovering on the edge of ecstasy as he drove her higher and higher. And then finally, when she thought she couldn't possibly go on any longer, her body exploded around him and the rhythmic pulse of her moist flesh drove him to his own completion.

Alessio held her firmly as he surged into her over and over again and his rhythmic thrusts prolonged her own sensual ecstasy until the whole experience became one long shower of intolerable excitement.

He woke to sunshine and silence and even before he turned his head to glance around the room, he knew he was alone.

The storm had blown itself out and bright shards of sunlight shone like spotlights through the windows of the cottage.

But there was no Lindsay.

Experienced in the art of shifting reluctant women from his bed, Alessio found it something of a surprise to realise that at some point Lindsay had actually left without disturbing him.

The fact that she hadn't waited around for soft words or even a repeat performance, astonished him. He waited to feel relieved but instead he felt a thud of—

What, exactly?

Disappointment?

Well, of course, disappointment. Just as he'd predicted, i had been the most explosive sexual encounter of his life and he'd had no intention of restricting himself to one night.

Slightly irritated that they couldn't have started the day the way they'd ended it, Alessio sprang to his feet, retrieved hi swimming shorts and glanced around the cottage.

Exactly when had she left? And why?

It wasn't as if she hadn't enjoyed the experience. Remembering her soft cries and passionate response, he gave a slow smile. She'd definitely enjoyed the experience—which made her absence all the more strange.

Yanking open the door, he strode out onto the beach that had been the venue for her trauma the night before. A few pieces of driftwood had been washed up in the storm but the sea was now idyllically calm. And there was no sign of Lindsay.

A faint frown touching his brows, Alessio strode across the soft sand and followed the curve of the bay back towards the cove where he'd secured the boat. The sky was a perfect blue the sun dazzling, it was as if the storm of the night before had never happened.

A splash drew his attention and Alessio saw a flash of blonde hair and creamy female skin. It was Lindsay, and she was swimming far out in the bay. As he watched she dived under the surface again and vanished.

In the grip of a serious attack of lust, Alessio strode purposefully into the waves, plunged under the water and powered his way over to where she was snorkelling.

'Oh—' She surfaced with a gasp, her hair sleek and wet against her head, a bright smile on her face. 'You made me jump! It's such a beautiful day.'

That was it? *That was all she was going to say?*

'*Buon giorno.*' He watched with masculine satisfaction as the colour bloomed in her cheeks, but still she made no reference to what had happened the previous night.

Instead she dragged her gaze from his and concentrated on staring down into the water. 'It's *so* clear—I've never seen anything like this. I just couldn't resist having another go before we leave. Snorkelling is just the *best* thing.'

Not quite the best thing, Alessio thought to himself idly, his attention suddenly captured by the droplets of water on her soft mouth. Her lower lip was a full, generous curve. Remembering just how good she tasted, he was about to kiss her when she dived under the water again.

Simmering with frustration and tormented by the nagging throb of his body, Alessio cursed softly and wondered why it was that Lindsay continually surprised him.

During his walk from the cottage to the beach, he'd prepared himself to handle various different emotions from her—embarrassment, affection, *regret*?

The one thing that he hadn't expected was that she'd make no reference to what they'd shared. At the very least, he'd resigned himself to a conversation about what had happened between them.

There were women, of course, who could enjoy the passionate encounter they'd experienced the night before and move on without a word.

But Lindsay wasn't that sort of woman.

Frowning slightly, he watched as she surfaced again.

'I saw a shoal of clownfish next to the reef! Honestly, Alessio, this is just the best thing I've ever done.' Wiping the water from her face, she smiled at him. 'Aren't you going to swim?'

Swim?

Simmering with suppressed sexual tension, Alessio searched her wide blue eyes for signs that she was creating this torture on purpose. But there was no flirtatious twinkle or wicked gleam, and in the end he was forced to admit that she *obviously* had absolutely no idea of the effect she was having on him.

Which gave him a whole new problem. Usually at this point in a relationship, the woman in question was snuggled against him, already planning a future that wasn't going to happen. *Usually* his problem was extracting himself, so it came as something of a shock to discover that he had no desire whatsoever to extricate himself from Lindsay.

Distinctly unsettled by just how badly he wanted to drag her back to the cottage, Alessio dipped down under the surface of the water, consoling himself with the fact that it was perfectly natural to want her again. While it was true that he didn't exactly embrace long relationships, neither did he indulge in one-night stands. So everything he was feeling was entirely normal.

He just needed to get her back in his bed until—well, until he no longer wanted her in his bed.

Simple.

CHAPTER EIGHT

EXHAUSTED from the lack of sleep, a night of rampant sex and the stress of acting a part, Lindsay sat in the bow of the yacht, facing forwards. The energy required to behave in a bright, happy mood had completely sapped the last of her reserves.

She barely even remembered the storm. For her, the hurricane had been inside her, a wind of change, blowing aside her all her old beliefs and leaving them wrecked and in pieces.

She felt—*she felt*—

Lindsay lifted her chin and turned her face to the sun. She wasn't going to ask herself how she felt. She didn't *dare* ask herself how she felt because she didn't want to know the answer.

And what difference did it make, anyway?

He wasn't going to be interested in her feelings. Alessio Capelli didn't do feelings. She knew that. He was famous for it, wasn't he? No ties. No emotions.

And she wasn't going to allow herself to mind that he hadn't once mentioned what had happened the previous night—*hadn't even kissed her*.

For a brief, disturbing moment her mind flickered back to the intensity of what they'd shared and she clutched the rail more tightly.

'Lindsay, come here.' His cool command sent shivers of awareness down her spine and for a moment she hesitated.

She wasn't actually sure that she had the energy to keep up the pretence of normality. But if she didn't go—

Forcing herself to think neutral thoughts, she turned and strolled to the back of the boat.

He handled the boat with confidence and a sure touch, dark glasses shading his eyes from the harsh rays of the sun. 'You need to wear a hat. You'll burn.' Reaching down, he picked up a hat and slipped it onto her head in a decisive gesture. 'You're very fair. You need to be careful.'

Careful?

Lindsay swallowed back the hysterical laugh that almost burst from her throat. *Careful?* If she'd wanted to be careful, then she wouldn't have spent the night the way she had. What they'd shared hadn't been remotely careful. It had been reckless, wild and totally abandoned. 'I thought you were encouraging me to take more risks.'

'Sunburn is a certainty,' he drawled, 'not a risk. And it's painful.'

Suddenly she was grateful for the hat. She pulled at the wide brim, shading her features and, hopefully, her facial expression. And she wondered what had made her naïvely think that she'd be able to share one incredible night with him and then walk away as if nothing had happened.

Unable to stop herself, Lindsay risked a sideways glance at him and immediately her eyes collided with his penetrating dark gaze. Her insides tumbled, flames licked through her body and she turned away quickly, knowing that she'd embarrass herself if she looked at him any longer.

No clinging, no sighing and no long, desperate looks, she reminded herself desperately. She'd known it was just for one night.

But when they'd finally connected in the most intimate way possible, she'd wanted it to be for always.

And she knew it was because she was in love with him

She'd known it the moment she awoke and found herself in his arms. For her, it had always been so much more than chemistry. Perhaps she'd always been a little bit in love with him, ever since that evening when he'd come to her rescue.

So in the end, she'd been true to herself, hadn't she?

Her choice had been sex with love, even though that love wasn't returned.

Love.

Horrified that he'd see something in her expression, Lindsay kept her eyes fixed on the horizon, desperately hoping that his expertise with women didn't run to reading minds.

'Are we going to talk about this?' His voice was a deep, dark drawl and she kept her eyes on the water, trying to forget the way he'd sounded when he'd breathed soft words of encouragement to her during the night.

'Talk about what?'

'Oh, well, let's see—perhaps because you spent the night having wild sex with a wicked divorce lawyer who you don't approve of. That might give most women pause for thought.'

'I made my choice.'

'You made your choice when you were in an extremely emotional state. Those circumstances frequently lead to regret.'

'I don't regret anything.' And it was true. She would have done the same thing again. Yes, she'd been upset. Confused. Emotional. But for that one night she'd also been—curious. She'd wanted to give in to the amazing chemistry between them and see where it led.

She'd wanted to have that one moment. And now, for the first time, she understood what made other people act in a reckless fashion.

She *really* understood.

Was this how her mother had felt?

Lindsay stood still, thinking about her mother as a woman for the first time. A sexual woman.

'Lindsay?'

She dragged her mind back from the confusing mists of he childhood and realised that Alessio was watching her intently And she knew that even if nothing but pain was to follow, she would have done exactly the same thing again if she'd been given the choice. 'I'm not blaming you, if that's what you're worried about.'

Suddenly she was relieved that she'd made the decision to get up before he awoke. It had removed the temptation to snuggle against him and initiate the type of intimacy that she knew he hated.

It had also removed the utter embarrassment of having to face him for the first time in the revealing spotlight of the morning sunshine.

'Lindsay—'

'Can we talk about something else?' She interrupted him quickly, adjusting the hat again simply because she needed to do something with her hands. *Something other than sliding them round his neck.* 'I completely understand that being trapped on a boat with the woman you spent the night before with must be your idea of a nightmare. But you *really* needn't worry. I don't want to talk about it either.'

She waited for him to give some indication that he was grateful for her sensitivity, but he simply studied her in brooding silence until the longing inside her became so acute that she knew that if she didn't move away she'd do something that would embarrass both of them.

Alessio Capelli has taught me everything about passion, she thought desperately, *but what he hasn't taught me is how to walk away afterwards.*

Three hours later Lindsay lay in a luxuriously scented bath, staring at an unbroken view of smooth white sand and palm trees

She felt drained after the emotional battering she'd

received over the past twenty-four hours, but, strangely enough, she also felt calmer than she'd felt in years.

For the first time ever her heart rate stayed steady when she thought about her mother.

And when she thought of Ruby it was with resignation rather than desperation.

And as for herself—

On the bed next door was her dress, laid out ready for the evening. It was the simplest dress in her new wardrobe. Powder-blue and summery rather than sexy. And that suited her.

The last thing she wanted was Alessio thinking she was trying to engender a repeat performance.

She was painfully aware that if they hadn't been trapped on an island, she wouldn't be seeing him again. And clearly he was finding their continued proximity a major cause of irritation.

They'd arrived back at Kingfisher Cay just before lunch. Alessio had immediately leaped from the boat onto the narrow wooden jetty, paused to exchange a few words with the staff member hovering ready to take the boat, and then strode off to his villa without so much as a single smouldering glance in her direction.

It was obvious from his body language that he had no desire to spend another moment in her company.

And had that hurt?

Yes. It had been agony, because no matter how many times she told herself that this was what she'd expected, she'd still *wanted* something entirely different.

Lindsay sniffed and slowly rubbed the bubbles over her skin. Even though she knew exactly who he was and the rules he played by, she was still human enough—*female enough*—to have wished that he'd swept her into his arms, carried her to the nearest private place and demanded a repeat performance.

But Alessio Capelli didn't do repeat performances, did he?

She slid farther under the bubbles, trying to ignore the recurrent buzz of electricity coursing through her body. It was as if he'd flicked a switch, but hadn't bothered to turn it off again afterwards.

And now she had to live with the consequences.

The next time she chose to have a wild fling, she was going to make sure that she'd planned her escape route. Instead of both being able to go their own ways, pretending that nothing had happened, they were both trapped here in paradise— forced to confront each other. And everything about the setting was designed to make that as hard as possible.

Kingfisher Cay was designed for romance. From its curved soft beaches, to the privacy of its coves, it was a place for lovers.

Exasperated with herself, Lindsay stepped out of the bath and reached for one of the large, soft towels that had been laid out ready for her use.

Stupid, stupid, stupid.

She'd *known* what he was like.

She wasn't going to turn into one of those sad, deluded women who thought they'd be the one to make a bad boy change his wicked ways.

Wrapping the towel around her body, she sat on the edge of the bath, staring blindly at the smooth, tiled floor.

So that, she thought numbly, was that.

One night with Alessio Capelli.

And now she had to play the game until she could escape from Kingfisher Cay and back to her old life.

A tap on the door made her heart rate double, but it was just Natalya, smiling an apology for having disturbed her.

'Signor Capelli requests your presence for drinks at the Beach Club at seven.'

Lindsay's heart performed a series of leaps, but she somehow managed to nod. Horrified by the sudden flash of excitement that came from the realisation that she was going to spend an evening in his company, Lindsay watched Natalya go and gave herself a sharp talking-to.

But despite her best efforts to rein it in, her mind was racing ahead.

He couldn't be that anxious to remove her from his presence, could he? Not if he was inviting her to join him at the Beach Club for the evening?

The Beach Club at night was the most romantic setting. Built on stilts, the glass floor extended over the shallow water of the cove, allowing guests to feel as though they were walking on the clear, illuminated water. During the day, guests swam up to the bar for a drink; at night it was transformed by flickering candles, soft music, food designed to take the palate on a roller-coaster ride of gastronomic bliss. It was a lovers' paradise.

And he wanted her to join him there.

She was going to have another night with him.

All right, so another night wasn't a lifetime, but it was something and it was *now*.

Lindsay dried her hair and walked past the powder-blue dress on the bed. Heart thumping, she reached into the wardrobe and pulled out the sexy red silk dress that she'd fingered in awe on the first day.

The old Lindsay would never have worn that dress. But she wasn't the old Lindsay anymore, was she?

She felt—different.

She felt like seizing the moment. Even if it was only one more night, she wanted to make the most of it.

Her hands shaking, she slid it over her scented skin, smoothed it over her hips and then looked at herself in the mirror.

Yes. Oh, yes.

The dress was *desperately* sexy. Feminine, confident—totally unlike anything she'd ever worn before.

And that was fine. Because she didn't feel the way she'd ever felt before.

She was going to spend an evening at the Kingfisher Cay
Beach Club with Alessio Capelli. It was right that she should
look glamorous.

Lindsay applied her make-up, slid her feet into a pair of
amazing red silk shoes and took a last look in the mirror.

She barely recognised herself.

On impulse she leaned forward and removed one of the
scarlet flowers from the vase on the table. Snapping off the
stem, she slid it into her hair and secured it with a pin.

Feeling confident, sexy and excited, she picked up her bag
and walked along the path that wound its way towards the
Beach Club, smiling as she anticipated Alessio's reaction to
her transformation.

Her excitement lasted right up until the moment she saw him.

He was leaning on the bar looking every inch the billionaire
tycoon. Broad-shouldered and powerful, he was deep in conversation with a tall, handsome man who looked extremely familiar.

Lindsay's heart lurched.

Oh, no—

She knew instinctively that this man must be Alessio's
mysterious and elusive client and the reason he looked
familiar was because he was a major Hollywood film star
whose films she'd seen on many occasions.

And it was immediately obvious to her that Alessio hadn't
invited her for a romantic evening at all.

He'd invited her because his client had arrived.

Lindsay stopped dead, wanting to slink back to her villa,
but knowing that if she moved they'd see her.

What was she supposed to do?

It felt surreal, seeing such a famous man in person, when
she was used to seeing him on the big screen. Remembering
that guaranteed privacy was one of the many benefits of
Kingfisher Cay, Lindsay felt a flash of panic and wondered
whether she'd better leave.

The rich and famous obviously had a silent pact not to betray
the whereabouts of their set, but she wasn't one of them, was she?

Uncertain and uncomfortable, she was just about to retreat
when Alessio lifted his dark head and saw her.

For a moment his eyes locked on hers, then they slid slowly
down over her bare shoulders and down over the dips and curves
of her body accentuated so lovingly by the bold red dress.

Heart thumping, Lindsay waited in breathless anticipation
for his reaction, but when he finally lifted his eyes back to hers
they were blank of expression.

Nothing.

Instead he lifted a hand and beckoned her over and she
went, of course, because the delicious red dress was already
drawing attention that she didn't want, and because he wasn't
the sort of man you said 'no' to.

It was ironic, she thought miserably, that the only man
she'd wanted to notice her didn't appear to be noticing her.

She'd got it so, so wrong.

He hadn't invited her to spend a romantic evening with him.
He was expecting her to join in a meeting with his client. But
what was still *more* embarrassing was the undeniable fact that
he was aware of her mistake. That one single glance had told
him that she was dressed for sex and passion, which accounted
for the tightening of his hard mouth and the sudden cooling
of his gaze.

Alessio knew.

In her mind she could hear him saying, 'You should be so
lucky, *tesoro*. You had your one night. That was it.'

Mortified, Lindsay was too busy wishing she could crawl
back to her villa and hide to feel remotely star struck by
meeting the famous actor.

Telling herself that the presence of another person would
make the whole difficult evening a great deal easier, Lindsay
joined them, noticing that if anything this huge star was even

more handsome in real life than he was on the screen. His eyes were bluer and shone with a hint of humour that was usually absent in the roles he played.

Lindsay glanced around her, expecting the other guests to be staring, but then she realised that the people who came here were all similarly famous. She recognised the lead singer from an extremely famous rock band, a supermodel and a billionaire industrialist who was never out of the news.

In this company, the 'A' list actor blended comfortably.

She was the odd one out.

It felt surreal, sipping her drink next to a man whose love life had been played out across the pages of the world's gossip magazines.

Desperately miserable, Lindsay glanced briefly at Alessio and then wished she hadn't because once her eyes rested on the sharp lines of his profile it was impossible to look away.

The actor was outlining his personal situation and Alessio angled his dark head, his gaze sharp and acute as he sifted through the facts. *You can almost see his brain working,* Lindsay thought helplessly, watching his unwavering focus on his client. His astonishing intelligence was evident, not only in the observations that he made, but also in the sharp glitter of his eyes and in every line of his hard, handsome features. He was clever. Clever and strong.

Lindsay's eyes drifted to the dark shadow of his jaw. He was a man to whom decision-making came easily. Not for him the agonies of 'shall I shan't I' suffered by lesser mortals. No wonder people trusted him with their darkest secrets and their biggest problems. He was coldly analytical and decisive, which explained why he wasn't remotely impressed or intimidated by the presence of Hollywood's favourite film star.

Most men would have faded into the background.

Not Alessio.

Lindsay smiled politely as Alessio introduced them

fighting down a spurt of panic as she realised that, although she was with one of America's biggest film stars, the only man she wanted to stare at was Alessio.

The Sicilian lawyer was actually more startlingly handsome than the man whose presence on the screen had made him the object of fantasy for millions of women worldwide.

Deciding that the only way she was going to make it through the evening was to not look at him, or think about him, Lindsay focused all her attention on the actor and his situation.

So *he* was the one contemplating divorce—

Does his wife know? she wondered. Or was this just an exploratory meeting to ascertain how much a divorce was going to cost him?

'I should have listened to the old saying—marry in haste, repent at leisure.' He drained his glass of champagne. 'Good sex is never a reason to get married.'

'You sound uncannily like Lindsay,' Alessio said in a cool tone, a sardonic gleam in his eyes as he glanced at her. 'She doesn't approve of relationships based on sex.'

'On the contrary—' she lifted her head and smiled '—I have no problem with relationships based on sex, providing the parties involved understand that physical chemistry alone isn't a good basis for marriage. If sex is all you have in common, then fine. Just don't get married.'

'That's the best advice anyone has ever given me. I only wish I'd met you a couple of years ago. You would have saved me a fortune.' Draining his glass, the actor looked at her thoughtfully. 'I take it you're not married?'

'No.'

'And you have no problem with relationships based on sex.'

Was it her imagination or was this gorgeous man who was famed for his liaisons with equally gorgeous women actually smiling at her? *Flirting with her?*

'I think it's important to be realistic.'

'Where have you been all my life?' The actor was laughing now, a look of sexy invitation in those famous blue eyes. 'How long are you here for? Come and spend some time with me in Los Angeles after you leave. I'll show you the sights.'

'I might just do that.' Desperately miserable about Alessio and feeling suddenly reckless, Lindsay smiled back at him. Reckless? Since when had reckless been an adjective that applied to her? A week ago she'd never done anything reckless in her life. Now she seemed to be doing nothing but reckless things.

And on top of that it suddenly seemed desperately important to show Alessio that she wasn't pining. He'd barely glanced in her direction and the message he was sending her had come across loud and clear.

Not interested.

Unlike the actor who barely seemed able to drag his eyes away from her face and body, Alessio seemed hardly to notice her presence. He didn't address her directly, his gaze didn't once linger on her bare shoulder or her cleavage and he seemed totally relaxed.

Clearly whatever wild chemistry had possessed him before last night had been extinguished by the heat of that one single encounter.

For him, there was nothing left.

Suddenly it seemed incredibly important for her pride and self-esteem that he didn't realise just how bad she felt.

And to be fair, it wasn't exactly his fault that she felt bad, was it?

He hadn't once lied to her. He hadn't promised her anything.

He'd been completely true to his nature, which was to keep relationships light and easy.

She was the one who'd broken the rules—by expecting something she couldn't have.

The actor was gazing at her mouth with ill-concealed fascination. 'Have you ever been to Hollywood?'

'Perhaps we ought to dispense with your current wife before you contemplate a replacement,' Alessio drawled in a soft tone, putting his empty glass on the bar and gesturing towards a table that had been reserved for them in the most secluded area of the Beach Club. 'Shall we eat?'

Sensing his black mood, Lindsay glanced at him nervously. Was he still annoyed that she'd misinterpreted the whole situation and dressed for a romantic evening?

His client didn't seem bothered.

In fact he continued to flirt outrageously.

As the staff served them discreetly Alessio turned the conversation to the issue of divorce and asked a number of blunt, specific questions about the actor's marriage. Very much the lawyer, he was brief and businesslike, reducing the relationship to a series of cold facts.

Lindsay concentrated on her food, listening while Alessio dealt with the actor's questions and then summarised his options.

She didn't feel the slightest inclination to intervene or even urge him to reconsider. What did she know about relationships? After last night, she'd decided that she knew nothing.

And that, Lindsay thought bleakly, *was that.*

Another celebrity marriage bit the dust.

The actor sat back in his chair, his eyes on the gentle curve and dip of Lindsay's cleavage. 'Well, if we're done, Alessio, I feel like relaxing. You've no idea how amazing it feels to be able to chill out, knowing that for once your evening is not going to be replayed in the morning papers. Can you spare your assistant for the rest of the evening?'

'I'm afraid not. She has work to do.' Alessio's tone was smooth and his eyes blank of expression, but something in his manner delivered his message loud and clear because the actor gave a frown and then shrugged.

'OK. Some other time.' His eyes lingered on Lindsay's mouth. 'Don't leave without taking my number.'

'Your number is in the file.' Very much the one in control, Alessio rose to his feet and extended a hand. 'My team will contact you when you're back in L.A. Enjoy your stay. And try not to marry your next co-star.'

Feeling increasingly awkward, Lindsay stood up as well and stammered a goodnight.

And finally, Alessio looked at her. 'My villa.' It was a cool command. 'I want to work on this straight away.'

And it was obvious that he was annoyed with her, Lindsay thought miserably as she followed him up a path that led to a villa out of sight of the rest of the exclusive resort.

He was going to remind her that it had been just the one night.

He didn't want to see glamorous red dresses or flowers in her hair.

Too tense even to react to the luxurious villa or the stunning setting, she flinched as he yanked open the sliding doors that led from beach to living room.

'Nice,' she muttered timidly and then felt suddenly angry with herself because she'd never allowed herself to be intimidated by him before and she just *hated* the fact that she felt like that now. By nature honest, she decided that it was best to come clean, however awkward that might be. 'Look—it was a misunderstanding, all right? When I received your message I thought—' She broke off and he lifted a brow.

'You thought what? That this was your chance to join the ranks of Hollywood?'

Taken aback by this unexpected verbal attack, Lindsay just stared at him. 'What are you talking about?'

Dark colour accentuated his cheekbones and he prowled across to her, his eyes stormy. 'I'm talking about you flirting with my client. I'm talking about the flower in your hair, the sexy red dress and the killer heels. *That's* what I'm talking about, Lindsay.'

Her gaze locked with his, she suddenly couldn't breathe.

He thought the dress was sexy?

Even though she could feel the atmosphere sparking dangerously, she felt a wild thrill of pleasure.

'Alessio—'

His hands were on her shoulders, tight bands of steel. 'I'm talking about the fact that you're a relationship counsellor, but you didn't once try and talk him out of his divorce. Not once.' His handsome face hard and unyielding, he powered her back against the enormous bed that dominated the room until she tumbled backwards onto the silken cover.

'Alessio—'

He came down on top of her, bronzed, muscular and very much the dominant male. '*Why* didn't you try and talk him out of divorce?' One strong hand buried itself in her hair and he kept his gaze locked with hers. 'Why was that, *tesoro*? Was it because you were hoping that you might be the next candidate?'

'Don't be ridiculous—' Lindsay stared up at him with huge, shocked eyes. Her heart thudding out of control, explosions of excitement turning her body into a simmering cauldron of dangerous sensation. '*You* were the one who told me that you didn't want me here in my role as relationship counsellor—'

'You dressed for sex. What happened to those principles of yours?' With a decisive movement, he slid a hand under her bottom and hauled her against the thickened ridge of his arousal. 'What happened, *tesoro*? You meet a film star and suddenly a relationship based on sex seems like a good idea?'

All she could feel was heat. The heat of his body. The heat of his mouth next to hers. *The heat of her own desperate need—*

'Alessio—' Her words were smothered by the force of his kiss, his mouth taking hers in a punishing, demanding, volcanic assault that tipped her into a sensual world that was entirely new to her.

The hot slide of his tongue in her mouth sent a shaft of excitement shooting from brain to belly and her hands clutched at his shirt, tugging it free from his trousers.

She wasn't thinking. She was no longer *able* to think. It was all about instinct. Primal, animal instinct.

Swearing in Italian, Alessio shifted his weight so that he had full access to her body. Then he pushed her dress up to her waist in a rough, impatient movement that drew a gasp of shocked excitement from her parted lips.

With no concession to modesty, he slid a demanding hand over her bared body and then pushed her thighs apart and buried his mouth against the most private part of her.

Lindsay choked out a protest, but he held her with firm, confident hands, his mouth warm against the dampened silk of her panties. Then his fingers curled into the flimsy material and he gave a forceful yank, removing that final barrier with determined fingers before focusing all his attention on that one single part of her that he'd exposed specifically for his pleasure.

She felt as though she were back in the storm, the entire force of nature directing its power onto her.

His fingers gentled as he parted her and then she felt the warm, moist flick of his tongue caressing her *there* and it felt so wickedly good, *so maddeningly, impossibly exciting*, that for a moment the world went black.

And then her body exploded into a climax so intense that her hands clutched frantically at the sheets and her body arched against his skilful mouth.

Weakened and dizzy, she barely had time to catch her breath before he shifted again, this time so that he was over her, once again in a position of domination. His shirt was hanging loose where she'd torn at it and he reached down and dealt with the zip of his trousers with an impatient hand.

There was a breathless moment of anticipation when she felt the hard silken promise of his masculinity and then he entered her with such a possessive, powerful thrust that her body immediately spun out of control again. Her second climax was as powerful as the first and she heard him groan in disbelief as the rhythmic contractions of her body added to the delicious friction created by his own thrusts. It was blisteringly hot, terrifying and thrilling all at the same time, her body controlled by the primal rhythm he'd set.

And for Lindsay the pleasure didn't just peak, it went on and on in a glorious shower of ecstasy that was heightened by the warm, silken thickness of his arousal deep inside her.

She wanted to cry out, but she was robbed of breath and she felt his arm slide under her hips, lifting her, demanding still more from her quivering, helplessly aroused body. He surged into her again and then again, each thrust increasing the incredible intimacy and she was so overwhelmed by the power and strength of him, so utterly dominated by his aggressive sexuality and devastating masculinity that she had no choice but to go where he led her.

'You're incredible and you feel *so* good—' He growled the words against her mouth, his voice unsteady as he drove himself deeper. Groaning something in Italian, he slid a hand up her thigh, encouraging her to wrap her legs around him. 'Sexy, sexy woman—'

Was she?

Maybe she was. All she knew was that her body didn't feel like her own anymore.

The excitement was so intense that she was almost blind with it, her body meeting the urgent demands of his with the same desperate compulsion that he obviously felt.

It went on and on, explosion after explosion until she was wild with it, until she could do nothing but rake her nails over the smooth muscle of his powerful shoulders, holding on to the one thing that seemed solid. Again and again she lost control and finally he lost control right along with her, thrusting deeply, filling her with the explosive force of his climax.

For endless moments neither of them spoke or moved.

Lindsay lay there stunned, eyes closed, her heart so full of emotion that it stole her breath.

His head was still buried against her shoulder and his breathing was harsh and uneven. Suddenly her fingers ached to stroke that thick, glossy hair. She desperately wanted to lean her face into his shoulder and kiss him, not with passion, but with love.

There were things she wanted to whisper to him.

She wanted to tell him how she felt.

But that wasn't allowed, was it?

That wasn't part of the deal.

So she squeezed her eyes tightly shut and forced herself to swallow back all the words that wanted to spill out of her mouth.

And what was there to say anyway? What could words possibly add to what they'd just shared? Their connection had been total. Their intimacy complete. She'd expressed her feelings through her body. She'd given *everything* and he'd taken and given right back. Everything.

So in the end she hadn't been able to have sex without love.

She hadn't been capable of that.

Alessio lifted his head. She could feel him looking at her, but she didn't dare open her eyes because of what she might reveal.

Then he rolled onto his back and pulled her firmly into his arms, his vastly superior strength giving her no opportunity to resist.

Her head was nestled against his shoulder and her hand lingered on the hard muscle of his abdomen. 'I should go back to my villa—'

'You're not moving.' His grip tightened on her. 'Except perhaps to stand up and remove that dress. From now on when you're in my bed, I want you naked.'

'Alessio—'

'I don't understand you,' he confessed in a raw tone. 'You spend your whole life preaching about how sex should be par f a committed relationship and every time we make love, you ry to dash off.'

'We're not in a committed relationship,' she muttered, her eart thumping crazily. 'You don't do relationships.'

'Neither do I do one-night stands.' He turned onto his side nd cupped her cheek with his hand, forcing her to look at im. 'And you're not doing them, either.'

She stilled. 'I—I thought that was what you wanted.'

His eyes narrowed. 'That's why you were leaving? Because you thought it was what I wanted?'

'Of course. I didn't want to embarrass you by still being round in the morning.'

He gave a slow, devilish smile. 'Do I look embarrassed?'

'You hate morning-after conversation.'

'Who said anything about conversation?' he drawled oftly, rolling her onto her back again and bringing his mouth lown on hers.

This time she woke in his arms, feeling warm, safe and exually sated. If it had been possible to stop time, then she vould have picked that moment, because she couldn't magine ever wanting to be anywhere else.

Watching him sleep, her eyes drifted to the firm contours f his mouth and instantly she felt her body stir. Despite the hysical demands of the previous night, she still wanted him.

Again and again—

Perhaps she was more like her mother than she'd thought.

Driven by an impulse that she didn't even try and under-tand, Lindsay slid a hand over his bare chest, dislodging the heet so that his body was exposed. Then she pressed her lips gainst his shoulder blade, slid lower and trailed her mouth ver his nipple and down to his hard abdomen. For a moment he lingered in that dangerous, tantalising spot and then she noved lower and found him semi-erect.

Without thinking what she was doing, she took him gently in her mouth and felt him harden instantly. She heard his soft groan and felt the bite of his fingers in her hair as she explored his velvet thickness with her lips and tongue, totally addicted to his body.

The harshness of his breathing told her exactly how he felt about her bold exploration, and then he lifted her and she straddled him, her hair falling forward as she bent to kiss his mouth.

'*Maledizione*—you're incredible,' he groaned and he captured her face in his hands, holding her mouth against his as he kissed her with explicit intent.

Her body was burning and she shifted her pelvis and lowered herself slowly onto his straining shaft, her eyes closing as he filled her. Then his hands dropped to her hips and he held her, guiding her into an erotic rhythm that sent them both rocketing towards another orgasm.

Lindsay flopped onto his chest and he locked his arms around her and kissed the top of her head. His skin was warm against her cheek, the dark hairs of his chest tickling her sensitised flesh.

'*Buon giorno*—good morning.' His voice was huskily amused and his hold on her tightened. 'That was an incredibly good way to be woken up.'

Slightly shocked by how uninhibited she was with him Lindsay kept her face buried in his neck. She just adored his body and as for what he did to *her* body—

'I could stay on Kingfisher Cay for ever.' *He smells fantastic*, she thought dizzily, pressing her mouth against the bronzed skin of his shoulder.

'You're enjoying the watersports, *tesoro*?' He was still teasing her and this time she lifted her head and looked at him.

'Not just the watersports.' It was her turn to tease. 'Soft sand, turquoise ocean, rainbow fish—'

'And what about the sex?' Supremely confident, he flashed

her a smile that melted the flesh to her bones. 'I thought you
didn't want a relationship based on sex—'

Did he know how she felt?

Something shifted inside her, a tiny warning of danger, like
a wispy white cloud suddenly appearing in an otherwise perfectly blue sky.

'We don't have a relationship, Alessio,' she breathed,
kissing him again before he could say anything else. 'We're
just having sex.'

And she wasn't going to think about that now.

Wasn't going to think what the future held for her.

'I can't believe you just said that.' He sank his hands into
her tangled blonde hair and kissed her mouth again. 'I could
play that back to the television networks and make a fortune.
Lindsay Lockheart, relationship counsellor, just having sex.'

'I never said that there was anything wrong with sex,' she
protested lightly, gasping as his warm skilled hand curved
over her bottom. 'Just that it was important not to confuse sex
with love and use it as a basis for marriage—Alessio, please—
I can't think when you do that—'

'I don't need you to think.' With a powerful movement he
rolled her underneath him and looked at her with raw masculine appreciation. 'I've never wanted a woman as much as
I want you.'

And that, she thought to herself, her eyes closing as he
lowered his head and started to perform yet another miracle
on her body, was as big a compliment as any woman was ever
likely to hear from the lips of Alessio Capelli.

CHAPTER NINE

'SO HAVE you called your sister?' Alessio passed Lindsay [a] plate of fruit and some tiny pastries.

It was late morning and they were enjoying a leisurel[y] breakfast on the wooden deck that stretched over the wate[r.] Exotic fish darted beneath them, sending flashes of dazzlin[g] colour through the clear blue water. The only sound was th[e] occasional muted splash as a hummingbird skimmed the wate[r.]

'I haven't called her. I haven't switched my phone on sinc[e] yesterday.' Lindsay hesitated for a moment and then glance[d] up at him. 'I've done a lot of thinking about what you sai[d.] And you were right.'

'About what, exactly?'

Lindsay lowered her gaze and poked at the food on he[r] plate. 'About a lot of things. I *am* too controlling. I've bee[n] treating her like a little girl and she isn't a little girl anymore[.] She gave a twisted smile. 'To me she's still the vulnerable tod[-] dler that used to crawl into bed with me and sleep with he[r] thumb in her mouth. I haven't noticed that she's grown u[p.] Or maybe I did notice and I just didn't want to see it.'

'Stop analysing everything.'

'It's hard not to when you know you've done everythin[g] wrong. I've made it difficult for her to turn to me.' She felt [a] lump in her throat and a sense of helpless frustration becaus[e] she'd tried so hard to get it right—*to give Ruby the love she hadn't had from their mother.* 'In fact, I've made a real mess of things.'

Alessio didn't respond immediately. When he did, his voice was gruff. 'Lindsay, if this is about what I said to you during the storm—I'm the first to admit that I know nothing about emotions. You shouldn't listen to me. I was probably wrong.'

She couldn't hold back the smile. 'Wrong? You think you might have been wrong? Wow. That's quite an admission coming from you. Shall I tell the press?'

His eyes gleamed. 'You want to tell the press how well you know me?'

Lindsay blushed. 'Maybe not. And anyway, you weren't wrong. You were right about everything you said.' She gave a tiny shrug and a painful smile. 'You were honest. Was that difficult to hear? Yes, it was. But it was also important. You've made me see things more clearly.' She was thinking not only of Ruby, but her mother. 'I need to do things differently. And one of those things is not calling Ruby every five minutes. My hands are itching to pick up that phone and just keep dialling until eventually she picks up, but I know I've got to let go. She'll phone me when she's ready. And when she does, I'll just listen.'

'Why don't you try encouraging your sister and see if that helps?'

'You mean tell her that it's fine to have an affair with Dino? I'm not sure I can go that far—'

'She's having one anyway,' Alessio said dryly, 'with or without your consent. I'm no expert on human behaviour, but it seems to me that the more you try and rein her in, the more she rebels.'

'You're probably right,' Lindsay said humbly. 'I'm just worried about her. Worried that she'll be hurt. I don't want that to happen.'

'Being hurt is part of growing up,' Alessio said unsympathetically. 'She'll be hurt—then she'll toughen up.'

Lindsay hesitated, wondering how much to tell him. 'Not everyone is as strong as you.'

'She won't discover how strong she is with you protecting her all the time. Learning how to get yourself out of the trouble you've created is part of growing up. Why do you feel so responsible for her?'

Lindsay picked at her fruit. 'I'm older than her.' *And she knew what Ruby was capable of doing.*

'And being older than her means that you have to act like her mother?'

'Not just because I'm older.' Lindsay picked up her coffee cup and took a sip, too confused in her head to try and articulate her feelings about her parents. 'Ruby—trusts me. She talks to me. Or she used to. And I've seen her in this situation before. I've seen her so head over heels in love with someone that she can't think straight—that the whole of the rest of her life just seems to go out of the window.'

'That's also part of growing up.'

'Maybe. But last time—' Lindsay broke off, her instinctive discretion warring with a strange desire to confide in him.

Why? Why was she finding it so easy to talk to him? It wasn't as if he were pushing her for information. On the contrary, he was lounging in his chair, totally relaxed, just contributing the odd remark.

The odd, extremely astute remark.

He was a good listener—

'She took pills,' Lindsay said flatly, her hand shaking suddenly as she returned her cup to the saucer. 'Ruby swallowed the contents of a bottle of tablets that a doctor had given her to help her sleep after the break up. And she took them while she was staying in the flat with me. That's how I managed to find her and act so quickly.'

'And you're worried that if it happens again, you won't be around to bail her out.'

'Yes.' It was the intimacy they'd shared, she decided, that made it so easy to talk to him.

'So what are you going to do?' His voice was level. 'Live your life glued to her side so that you can grab her wrist before she opens another bottle?'

Lindsay flinched. 'That's a very lawyer-like response. Hard and factual.'

'Pragmatic,' he drawled softly. 'And you need to stop feeling responsible for her. You can offer support, but you can't live her life. If you try and do that you're just going to be hurt, over and over again.'

'I just hate to see her walking into trouble.'

'How do you know she's in trouble?'

Lindsay glanced at him helplessly. 'Because she didn't turn up to work. Because she's with your brother and it's *obviously* just about sex and—' She broke off, realising that she could just as easily be describing her relationship with Alessio and clearly he was thinking it too because suddenly the tension in the atmosphere snapped tight. 'That sort of relationship is asking for trouble.'

'Is it?' The soft emphasis left her in no doubt that they were no longer talking about Ruby.

The breath caught in her throat. Trouble? *Oh, yes, she was in big trouble* and she knew it. Those ominous clouds that were currently just a shadow on the horizon of her mind would build and build. Sooner or later she was going to have to confront them, but it wasn't going to be now. For now, she was still in the sunshine.

'I'm not the same person as Ruby. I can separate sex from love.' She hoped she sounded convincing, but she was horribly aware of his thoughtful gaze lingering on her face.

Agitated, she stared out across the bay and he watched her

for a long moment and then poured himself another cup of coffee.

'Tell me more about what happened with Ruby the first time.'

'The guy she was seeing—well, he suddenly announced that he was marrying someone else and the end of that relationship was nearly the end of her. Ruby always expects too much of relationships. As soon as a guy looks at her she starts imagining weddings and—' Lindsay broke off and folded her arms around her body, horribly conscious of his penetrative gaze. 'It's my fault. I should have tried harder to persuade her to come back to London.'

Alessio was silent for a moment and then he stirred. 'It sounds as though my brother might have his hands full,' he said dryly, an ironic gleam in his eyes. 'It will do both of them good. And now I don't want to talk about them anymore. I'm tired of my brother and I'm tired of your sister. You've barely eaten anything—are you feeling ill?'

'No.' She flashed him a quick smile and shook her head. 'It's all delicious, I'm just not that hungry.'

'With the amount of physical activity we indulged in last night and this morning,' he drawled softly, 'you should be starving, *tesoro*.'

No one had ever spoken to her in such an intimate way before and she felt herself colour.

'I'm fine. So will you take on the actor as a client?'

'I haven't decided yet.' He stretched his legs out in front of him, staring at the clear ocean.

'Well, he's worth a lot so it would be lucrative.'

'I don't do it for the money.'

'No.' Lindsay spoke quietly. 'I know you don't. You do it for other reasons.'

He turned his head and looked at her, his expression suddenly thoughtful. 'And you think you know those reasons?'

'Well, you obviously don't need the money.' Lindsay

glanced round their island paradise with a faint smile. 'You're a very intelligent man and you obviously find being a lawyer intellectually stimulating. But there's more to it than that, isn't there?'

'Is there?'

'Alessio, you could have chosen to specialise in any number of different areas, but you chose to be a divorce lawyer. And you only act for men. Never women.'

His eyes held hers. 'Clients approach me.'

'But you're very selective about who you act for. Sometimes it seems as though you're trying to get revenge on the whole female sex. And yet I know you don't hate women. I think you just hate women who try and benefit from marriage.' She hesitated. 'Were your parents divorced?' Seeing the sudden tension in his shoulders, she cursed herself softly. 'Sorry,' she muttered. 'None of my business.'

'I come from a tiny village in Sicily, which is still living in another time,' he said evenly. 'Divorce doesn't happen. They handle marital disharmony in an entirely different way.'

'You mean they have affairs.'

'Two people are not meant to be locked together for ever. The best that anyone can hope for is serial monogamy.'

'If your father had lots of affairs, then I can understand why you might come to that conclusion.'

He dragged his gaze from hers and concentrated his attention on a yacht that skimmed past them, the wind inflating the sails. It was a full minute before he responded.

'It wasn't my father who had the affairs,' he said flatly. 'It was my mother. And I can't imagine for a moment why I'm telling you this.'

Lindsay stared at his hard profile, feeling incredibly stupid and exasperated with herself. 'Yes,' she said simply. 'Of course. It would have been your mother.'

'Of course?' He turned then, his eyes glittering dangerously, his face more impossibly handsome than ever. 'Why "of course"?' His tone was brittle and she knew that they'd sailed into dangerous waters, but she still felt warm inside because he *had* confided in her and she knew enough about him to realise the significance of that.

He trusted her.

'How do I know it was your mother? Because you refuse to create an emotional bond with women. Because you rescue men from bad marriages to women who aren't in love with them.'

'You've clearly spent a lot of time analysing me,' he drawled and Lindsay shook her head, sensing his immediate withdrawal.

'Of course I haven't. But we've been together these last few days so it would have been impossible for me to not notice certain things about you—'

'Then you've probably also noticed that I'm not into talking about myself—' he rose to his feet, walked round the table and scooped her into his arms '—and that I have a limitless appetite for sex where you are concerned.'

'Alessio—' Breathless, she wrapped her arms round his neck, but he was already striding back into the bedroom and she gave a low moan as his mouth came down on hers.

Alessio lay staring up at the ceiling, his arms locked around Lindsay's sleeping form. Her body was pressed against his, her head nestled in his shoulder and her silken hair tumbling over his chest.

He hadn't thought about his mother for years—*hadn't allowed himself to go there.*

And before today, he'd never discussed his childhood with another person. He'd never revealed intimate secrets to another person.

And yet, for some reason, he'd told Lindsay Lockheart.

Lindsay, with her deeply ingrained sense of responsibility and her unshakeable belief in the existence of love.

And what had that confession achieved?

It had left him feeling naked and bare, and it had left her feeling as though their relationship had turned a corner.

And it had, he thought grimly. *Just not in the direction she was expecting.*

As far as he was concerned, it was time to make an exit.

His mounting tension must have transmitted itself to her because she stirred, her thigh sliding against his as she shifted slightly in the bed.

Lifting her head, she looked at him, her eyes sleepy. Then she lifted a hand and touched his face. 'I love you,' she murmured and he felt every muscle in his body tense.

'I know you do.'

And he felt a stab of guilt because he knew he should never have let it get this far. A woman like Lindsay, who believed in relationships, who believed in marriage—he should have avoided her like the plague.

'It's late,' he said in a cool tone, extracting himself from the affectionate circle of her arms and springing from the bed like a tiger who had spotted a trap. 'I need to have another meeting with my client. Why don't you have a bath or something? Relax.'

Her blue eyes went from sleepy, to wary, to hurt and she slowly pulled the sheet up over her body, covering herself. 'Fine. I'll do that.'

Her quiet dignity dug into his conscience like a thousand knives and he turned and strolled into his dressing room, anxious to escape. But the guilt followed him and he gritted his teeth and cursed himself for breaking his one unbreakable rule. Never confide in a woman. Never make it personal.

And what had he done?

He'd made it personal.

And now he was paying the price.

* * *

Lindsay slipped into the navy skirt, pulling a face as she zipped it up and realised just how hot and uncomfortable she was going to be in such an unsuitable piece of clothing.

A few days ago this outfit had seemed perfectly comfortable. It had suited the way she felt. The way she approached life.

Now it just felt—well, wrong.

But what choice did she have?

Once again, her tiny overnight bag was in the centre of the floor and when Natalya appeared in the doorway, she looked surprised to find Lindsay packed and ready.

'Oh—I came to tell you that you have an hour to pack because Signor Capelli is flying back to Rome this afternoon. But clearly someone has already given you the message.'

Oh yes, someone had given her the message.

He'd given her the message loud and clear.

And she'd been blaming herself ever since because it was *all* her fault. What had possessed her to think he might like to talk to her about his past? What arrogance had made her think that she could be different?

And what had possessed her to tell him that she loved him?

The moment she'd said those words, Alessio had removed himself from danger faster than a fighter pilot hitting the eject button on a doomed plane.

'Thanks, Natalya.' She managed a smile. 'I'll be at the jetty in an hour.'

An hour.

Alessio Capelli didn't hang around, did he?

But what had she expected?

She'd said, 'I love you.' Half asleep and softened by the intimacies they'd shared, she'd said, 'I love you.' And from that point she'd watched their relationship unravel with supersonic speed and hideous inevitability, like dropping a ball of wool from the top of the Empire State building.

And that was what happened when you indulged in a wild, crazy affair with no future.

That was what happened when you let physical chemistry dictate choices.

It would have been very easy to wish she hadn't delved into his background, or said those three little words—but she knew that it wouldn't have changed anything. The ending had always been coming.

And she would have done the whole thing again.

She'd made that choice.

Lindsay relaxed in the soft leather seat, pretending to be absorbed in the file on her lap. To add authenticity to the pretence, she occasionally scribbled something in the margin. But she was scribbling nonsense and her mind wasn't on the contents of the file—it was on the man seated opposite her.

Gone was the sexy lover. Alessio Capelli was once more the ruthless divorce lawyer. Since boarding his private jet, he'd been on the telephone, speaking in rapid Italian to a non-stop stream of people who were clearly desperate for his advice.

After one such call he glanced up at her, his handsome face blank of expression. 'There's a message on my phone from Dino. It seems that he and your sister are back in Rome.'

'Oh. Right.'

'He says they're engaged.'

Lindsay wondered why she felt so numb. 'I'm so pleased for them.'

'Pleased?' His dark brows locked in a dangerous frown. 'How can you be pleased? I would have thought it was the last thing you wanted for her.'

'One thing you taught me was that you can't live someone else's life for them,' she murmured, turning her head and looking out of the window. He'd taught her other things too, things she was never going to forget. Like the fact that sometimes the right choice wasn't obvious. 'I hope they'll be happy.'

'They'll probably drive each other up the wall.' He gave a faint smile. 'And I suppose you'll end up counselling them.'

'And if I fail, you'll end up doing their divorce.'

'Stay with me in Rome.' His blunt command was so unexpected that for a moment she simply stared at him.

'Pardon?'

'This doesn't have to be over, Lindsay.'

His words were so unexpected that for a moment she didn't breathe.

He was offering her more.

He wanted to extend their relationship into the future. Sexually, intellectually they would be good together—

Willing to agree to anything that would give them a little more time together, Lindsay opened her mouth to say yes. But she couldn't do it.

How could she say yes, knowing that he didn't feel anything for her? For him, it was all about the sex and she knew that marriages based on sex didn't last.

She wasn't like her mother. For her, the price was too high.

'You're offering me that coveted position as your mistress?' Somehow, she managed to make a joke of it. 'Well, I can certainly see some advantages. For a start I'd be given *that* phone number. At least I'd be able to contact you when I wanted to without having to doorstep you in your office.'

'So is that a yes?'

She blinked several times, frustrated that tears should threaten now. 'No, Alessio, it isn't a yes. How can it be a yes?'

'Because it's what you want.'

'No,' Lindsay said quietly. 'It isn't. I don't want a relationship that's based on sex. This morning I slipped and said "I love you" and that's something that you just don't want to hear.'

'You're probably more comfortable with those words than

I am. I expect you heard "I love you" when you were growing up,' he said gruffly. 'I didn't.'

Lindsay was silent for a moment. 'Let me tell you the truth about my parents' relationship.' She took a deep breath and plunged. 'They weren't happily married at all. In fact, I don't have a single memory that involves them being happy. I didn't hear "I love you". They shared a powerful chemistry and very little else.' She gave a painful smile. 'That chemistry seemed to stop them from acting sensibly. They'd separate and then get back together and then separate again—they couldn't stop having sex, but they couldn't bear each other's company outside the bedroom.' She broke off and glanced at him, but his handsome face was expressionless as he listened.

'Go on.'

She shrugged. 'Even at the age of seven I used to think to myself, *"Why don't the two of you try* talking *to each other?"* But they just never did. It was hideous. For five minutes it would be delirious happiness because Daddy was home— then they'd vanish to the bedroom and a few hours later the rows would start again.'

'And you witnessed the rows.'

'Rows, sex—my parents didn't seem to think we needed protecting from what was going on. I think they were little more than children themselves.' Lindsay sighed. 'I don't know which was worse—their rows or their divorce. Ruby was the result of one of my parents' many abortive attempts at reconciliation. It didn't work. In fact, having Ruby made things worse. The responsibility of a young baby made it harder for my mother to have a relationship with Dad, so she just abdicated responsibility.'

'So who looked after her?'

Lindsay brushed a speck of dust from her skirt. 'I did.'

Alessio frowned. 'You were seven years old. How could you possibly look after a baby?'

'I'd been looking after myself for several years,' Lindsay told him quietly. 'I just included Ruby in everything I did. I did our washing. I cooked our meals. I hugged her when she cried. Fortunately my school was round the corner so I used to nip home in between lessons and at lunchtime.'

'That explains why you worry about her so much. I often thought you behaved more like a mother than a sister.'

Lindsay rubbed the tips of her fingers over her forehead. 'She actually started to call me Mum when she was about two, but I didn't let her. I wanted her to know that I was her sister, not her Mum. I was too young to understand it all myself, but I think I knew instinctively that she had enough emotional problems without growing up thinking I was her mother.' She looked at him and shrugged. 'It was a mess. I probably didn't handle it right—'

'I think you are incredible,' he said softly and Lindsay faltered, touched by his praise.

'I don't know. Ruby was left very traumatised by the whole thing and I was too young to know how to deal with that. My solution was to smother her in love, but that didn't compensate for the damage done to her confidence and feeling of security. The divorce almost finished her off because Mum blamed her for the whole thing. If she hadn't had Ruby—oh, you can imagine the sort of things she said.'

'I don't think I want to. And what about you, Lindsay? You've talked a lot about your sister and the effect it had on her.' His voice was low. 'What about the effect it had on you?'

For a moment she didn't answer. Then she stirred. 'Well, it made me interested in psychology. And it has taught me that passion isn't a good basis for a marriage. But you already know that. You see that every day in your work.'

'So you want a marriage without passion?' His incredulous tone made her laugh.

'No. No, I don't want that. I'm far too greedy to settle for that.' She met his gaze. 'Which is why I'm turning down your invitation. But thank you.' She smiled. 'Thank you for asking.'

'Greedy? What is it that you want?'

'Oh—' she leaned her head back against her seat, her expression wistful '—the whole dream. I want the passion, yes. But I also want a man who excites me in other ways—a man who is going to love me for who I am, who'll stick with me when things get difficult and who will genuinely care about me.' She glanced at him and shrugged, trying to laugh at herself. 'And that, I suppose, is why I'm still single and likely to stay that way.'

'Lindsay—'

She held up a hand because the whole thing was hard enough without him trying to persuade her. 'Don't say anything else. I don't regret what happened between us, if that's what you want to know. In the end you won, Alessio. I couldn't resist you. But I'd do the whole thing again in a moment. You've changed the way I look at the past—made me understand things about myself that I didn't really understand before.' She frowned. 'I can't forgive Mum for the way she treated Ruby, but at least now I understand a little bit more about how passion can take over.' She blinked several times. 'I can see the runway lights. We're about to land.'

It was over.

CHAPTER TEN

Two weeks later, driven to the point of combustion by yet another wealthy, demanding client, Alessio strode out of the glass meeting room towards the lift.

What the hell was the matter with him?

He used to relish the mental stimulation of his job, but since his return from the Caribbean it had been nothing but a source of irritation.

His mobile phone buzzed and he lunged into his pocket and retrieved it, swiftly scanning the caller's number. Realising that the call was from a Russian supermodel he'd been dating a few months earlier, he gritted his teeth, rejected the call and dropped the phone back in his pocket, appalled by the depth of his own disappointment.

What had he expected?

Lindsay Lockheart telling him she'd changed her mind about having an affair with him?

She didn't want that, did she?

Clearly she wasn't feeling anywhere near the depth of frustration that *he* was.

Loosening his tie with an impatient yank of his fingers, Alessio scowled as one of his team called his name and hurried up behind him.

Now what?

Hadn't he made it clear that he wanted to be on his own?

Visibly nervous, the man stepped into the lift with him. 'I assume from the questions you asked, that you're not prepared to take the case?'

'What case?' His mind still on Lindsay Lockheart, Alessio snapped out the words and his junior colleague blinked in confusion, glancing back towards the meeting room as if checking there hadn't been some mistake.

'Well—*that* case,' he muttered awkwardly. 'He was hoping you'd take it on—at the moment his wife is so angry about his affair that she's threatening to take him to the cleaners.'

'Good for her.'

'I beg your pardon?' Unable to hide his astonishment, his colleague fumbled with the file in his hands. 'You—I don't— he wants your advice.'

'Enrico,' Alessio's voice was cool. 'How old are those children?'

Clearly startled by the question, the man checked the file. 'The older girl is eight, the other one is a baby. Two little girls.'

Two little girls. Two little girls, whose lives were being smashed to pieces.

His mind on Lindsay Lockheart, Alessio took a deep breath. 'She deserves every penny she can get. And my advice is that he should start thinking about his children and his responsibilities, instead of his own investments.'

Gaping at him, his junior colleague ran a finger around his collar as if it were strangling him. 'So you want me to tell him—what exactly?'

Alessio couldn't dispel the image of wide blue eyes and soft blonde hair.

'Tell him to try couples counselling.' His tone biting and sharp, he strode out of the lift and into his office, his body aching so badly it was almost a physical pain.

His personal assistant was hovering, looking harassed. 'Your three o'clock meeting has been rescheduled.'

'Why?'

'Because there are too many journalists outside the building. You don't want to go out there right now—it's being dealt with.'

With an impatient frown, Alessio strode across to the window and stared down at the street below. Even from this height he could see the pack of photographers surrounding the front door of the Capelli offices.

'For the past two weeks I've lived the life of a monk,' he breathed. 'What exactly are they after this time?'

'Nothing new. Still the Lindsay Lockheart thing.' His assistant put a neat pile of papers on his desk. 'You asked for these—'

'*What* Lindsay Lockheart thing?'

'She's been in the papers every day for the past two weeks.'

There was a brief, deadly silence while Alessio digested that information. 'And you didn't think it worth mentioning?' His tone silky soft, he watched as the woman paled.

'You're not normally interested in what the tabloids have to say about your love life—'

'You have precisely two minutes in which to produce a copy of every paper that has mentioned Lindsay Lockheart's name in the last two weeks. You then have a further minute to get the head of PR into my office.' Struggling to contain the volcanic eruption of his temper, Alessio strode to his desk and punched the number of Lindsay's flat into his phone. Her ansaphone clicked on and he cut the connection angrily just as his secretary returned with the papers.

Was she screening calls?

He scanned each paper in grim silence, his temper rising with each line of newsprint he read. Then dropped them onto his desk and strode towards the door.

* * *

Why couldn't they leave her alone?

Lindsay slammed the pillow over her head to shut out the insistent noise of the buzzer. Ever since she'd returned from the Caribbean, she'd had photographers camped on her doorstep. Trapped in her flat, she'd been unable to leave even to buy milk, but it didn't matter because she couldn't face food. She couldn't summon the energy to move.

Every now and then her ansaphone clicked and her heart raced because she couldn't stop hoping that it was *him*. But it never was. Every time the phone rang it was just another client cancelling an appointment.

Her business was ruined. Everything she was—everything she believed—had collapsed around her. It should have been a terrible blow but the awful thing was she didn't even care.

It seemed that *nothing* hurt as much as the fact that Alessio hadn't called.

Sooner or later she was going to have to pull herself together and work out what she was going to do with the rest of her life, but for now she didn't have the energy to move.

And there was no point in moving because her every action was caught on camera for the public to see and comment on.

But could it be any worse?

Did she really care if they took pictures of her without make-up, in rumpled clothes? Could they hurt her any more than they already had?

The thing that had upset her most had been the photographs taken on Kingfisher Cay. *Someone* had snapped them having dinner and the accompanying stories were all about the fact that she'd spent a whole night in his villa. And the stories were sensationalist and tasteless, embellished to sell more copies to a public always hungry for mindless gossip and the humiliation of others.

They'd made her relationship with Alessio sound like some seedy little fling.

And it hadn't been like that.

And it hurt really, really badly. But nowhere near as much as the fact that Alessio hadn't called.

On the plus side, she'd spoken to Ruby, who was very happy and living in Rome with Dino Capelli. And somehow her happiness made Lindsay feel even worse. She'd been so sure about her choices, but now—

Now she wasn't sure about anything.

With a sniff, she pulled the duvet over her head to block out the sound of the buzzer.

Why didn't they go away and leave her alone?

Guilt permeating every fibre of his being, Alessio elbowed his way through the banks of paparazzi crowding outside Lindsay's flat.

'Hey, Alessio—have you come back for seconds?'

With a low growl, Alessio picked the photographer up by his collar and backed him against the wall. 'Clear off,' he muttered thickly, 'and do something about your own life instead of prying into other people's.'

Flashes erupted around him and he knew that he'd just given the press still more fodder for the next day's salacious headlines.

'You'd better watch that temper of yours, Alessio,' the man spluttered and Alessio gave a slow, dangerous smile.

'I'm completely in control.' He didn't slacken his grip. 'Trust me, when I lose my temper, you'll be the first to know.'

'This is assault—'

'No—' Alessio's voice was icy cold as he released the man '—what *you* do is assault. Remember that, because you're starting to annoy me.' His handsome face a mask of disdain, he flicked some dirt from the sleeve of his perfectly cut designer suit. 'And I'm not at my best when I'm annoyed.'

'You can't threaten me.' Blustering and glancing towards

his colleagues for support, the photographer cast a wary glance at the hard set of Alessio's features. 'You can't touch me.'

Alessio's mouth curved into a smile. 'No?'

'I suppose you think I should be scared because you're some hotshot lawyer.' The man was sweating now and Alessio studied him with cool contempt.

'No,' he said softly, 'not because of that.' He reached forward and straightened the man's collar carefully. 'Because I'm Sicilian.'

The man swallowed. 'Are you threatening me?'

Alessio smiled. 'Certainly not.' His eyes lingered on the man's face until the photographer paled and started to shift uncomfortably.

'That's coercion,' he muttered and Alessio lifted an eyebrow. 'What is?'

The man backed off. 'If you ask me that girl's crazy to have anything to do with you. You're bloody lethal.' But the pack of paparazzi all withdrew slightly as Alessio slowly reached into the inside pocket of his suit.

'You want a story?' Laughing at their complete lack of spine, Alessio withdrew a piece of paper and toyed with it for a moment. 'This story should give you a comfortable retirement.' And with that he flicked the paper carelessly towards the banks of photographers, smiling at the resulting mayhem.

Let them take pieces out of each other. He had better things to do.

Turning his back on them, he took the steps to the front door two at a time and buzzed Lindsay's flat.

The crash of her front door opening roused her from her inertia and Lindsay sat upright in bed, clutching the duvet to her chest, frozen in horror.

They'd broken her door down—

Fumbling for her phone, she was about to call the police

when Alessio strode into her bedroom, his eyes glinting dark as anthracite, his mouth a grim line.

Her first emotion was one of unutterable joy.

And then she realised that he wasn't here because of her. He was here because of *him*. Because of the newspapers.

It only took a glance for her to realise that he was positively vibrating with anger.

'Y-you broke my door down.' He looked so impossibly handsome that it was all she could do not to fling her arms round him.

'What was I supposed to do? You didn't answer the doorbell.' He made it sound like a perfectly logical action given the circumstances, and for the first time in days she almost laughed.

'I didn't answer the door because I didn't want to see anyone. And you've let the press in—'

'There are eight security guards planted outside your door,' he growled. 'The press won't be bothering you again.'

Lindsay gave a strangled laugh. 'Eight? You don't think that's overkill?'

'No, I do not. And you should have more concern for your own privacy.'

'What was I supposed to do? I'm not a billionaire, Alessio, I'm just—me.'

The phone rang again and she tensed, bracing herself for the usual. The ansaphone clicked on and yet another client left a message cancelling their next appointment. Wishing he hadn't witnessed that, Lindsay gave a fatalistic smile. 'You see? I can't afford security guards even if I wanted them. I no longer have a job.'

He was glaring at the ansaphone as if it had slighted him personally. 'Your clients are cancelling?'

'Yes.' What was the point of lying? Lindsay shrugged. 'It seems you're not the only one who thinks I'm not qualified

advise anyone on how to maintain a relationship. I suppose
ou've come so that you can say "I told you so" in person.'

'*Why* are they cancelling?'

'I suppose they no longer trust my judgment,' Lindsay
humbled, suddenly weary. *What was he doing here?* 'And I
an hardly blame them for that. It's fine, Alessio. I'm fine. Just
o. Savour your victory.'

'I'm *not* leaving.' He strode across to her window and
losed the blinds.

'What are you doing?'

'Reducing the opportunities for the pack of wolves outside
o take photographs. You really need to learn to protect
ourself—you're *shockingly* naïve.'

She blinked. 'This is a fourth-floor flat, Alessio. You think
hey're going to climb up the drainpipe?'

'Have you noticed the scaffolding being erected opposite?'

'I haven't looked out of the window for two days—' Real-
ing what she'd just admitted, Lindsay looked away. 'It's
een a bit—difficult.'

'You've let the press trap you in your flat?'

'Well, yes, I suppose I have.'

'*Maledizione*, why didn't you call me?'

'Because that number you gave me is reserved for your
overs, and I'm not your lover anymore.' Her voice was croaky
nd black, stormy eyes connected with hers.

'You should have called—*I had no idea*—'

'You have an entire press department—'

'A press department who know I don't usually waste my
me reading the sort of trash written by those sharks outside
our door!'

Lindsay swallowed. *He hadn't known?* 'Right. So you're
lling me—'

'I'm telling you that I found out what was happening le[s] than four hours ago.'

'And if you'd known?'

'Well, for a start you wouldn't have been trapped in yo[u] flat for two weeks. But we can rectify that.' Removing h[er] phone, he made one brief call, speaking in low, rapid Italia[n.] Then he pulled open the door of her wardrobe, pulled out a pa[ir] of trousers and a shirt and flung it on the bed. 'Get dressed.'

'Why?'

Prowling round her bedroom, he found her shoes. 'Call m[e] fussy, but I don't want naked pictures of my future wife pla[s-] tered all over the newspapers.'

'Your—' Lindsay gaped at him. 'What did you just say[?]'

Vibrating with tension, Alessio paced across her bedroo[m] and grabbed her handbag. 'You're going to marry me. Is yo[ur] passport in here?'

'Alessio—'

'We'll leave everything else here.' He glanced around h[er] flat impatiently. 'We can clear it out another time. Are y[ou] going to get dressed?'

'Alessio, you just said—' She broke off as her phone ra[ng] again and yet another client called to cancel.

Swearing first in Italian and then in English, Aless[io] yanked the phone cable out of the wall. 'I've had enough [of] hearing that. They are all idiots—' He gave up on English a[nd] let out a stream of Italian, none of which she understood.

'Alessio!' Lindsay slid out of the bed. 'Stop ranting and ra[v-] ing and *talk* to me for a minute! You're not making any sens[e.]'

'I'm making perfect sense. Is your passport in your handbag[?]'

'Yes, but—Alessio, you just said you were going to mar[ry] me!'

'I *am* going to marry you. But first I want to get you ba[ck] to Rome.' His tone raw, he sank his long fingers into his glossy dark hair in a gesture of frustration. 'I can't protect you here.'

Her legs failing to hold her, Lindsay plopped back onto the bed. 'You can't be serious—'

'It's just too exposed. I own a villa outside Rome. I'm taking you there.'

'No, I mean—about marrying me.' She gave a disbelieving laugh and tried to sort out her muddled head. 'What is this? A sudden rush of chivalry? You think because our affair is all over the newspapers, you have to marry me?'

'It has nothing to do with the newspapers.' He crossed the room and hauled her to her feet again. 'You're going to marry me because I want you with me. Always.'

'Alessio—'

'*Have you any idea what the last two weeks have been like for me?*'

'I thought you said you hadn't seen the newspapers—'

'I'm not talking about the newspapers.' He cupped her face in his hands, his eyes fierce as he looked down at her. 'I'm talking about just not being with you. I—missed you.'

The words were so unexpected that for a moment she didn't reply. 'You missed me in your bed.'

'Well, yes, obviously—' he gave a brief frown '—but not just that. I missed having you around. I like what you have to say—'

'You disagree with me—'

'Invariably—' his eyes gleamed with sardonic humour '—but *always* I find you interesting.'

'You do? You find me interesting?' Her heart was thudding hard against her chest and he gave a groan and lowered his mouth to hers.

'Yes. You're the only woman who has ever been truly honest with me and the sex is amazing. I've missed doing this.' He kissed her slowly and surely and Lindsay sagged against him, her head spinning and her heart so full she felt as though it might burst through her chest.

'You've missed the sex.' She muttered the words against his mouth and he lifted his head and gave a slow, dangerous smile.

'Of course.' And then the smile faded and he stroked her cheeks with his thumbs. 'But most of all I missed *you*. I missed the way you talk and the way you listen. I missed your honesty and your sweetness.'

'Alessio—'

'I want you with me permanently.'

Everything inside her softened and emotion rushed through her. 'You're blaming yourself—'

'*Sì*, I am. This whole situation is *my* fault. But I'll make it up to you.'

She reminded herself that it was just his guilty conscience talking. 'Alessio, I don't want to build my business again. What do I know about relationships? Nothing. I was so convinced that if I could just help people talk to each other, they could sort things out. But all I was really doing was trying to compensate for not being able to sort my parents' marriage out.' Having admitted that, she pulled away from him, finding the whole thing really difficult. 'The truth is that relationships come in all shapes and sizes, and what works for some won't work for others. And sometimes passion on its own can be enough. Marriage isn't everything.'

'You don't believe that.' Alessio picked up the clothes and stuffed them into her hands. 'If you're not dressed in the next two minutes then I'll dress you myself.'

Wondering what had got into him, Lindsay pulled on her trousers, fastened her shirt and pinned her hair into a neat coil. 'There. Satisfied?'

'I won't be satisfied until you're wearing my ring every day and lying in my bed every night,' Alessio breathed and her heart skipped a beat as she looked into his eyes.

'That's a pretty big gesture,' she said shakily, 'even for a guy with a guilty conscience.'

'It isn't a gesture.'

'Oh, Alessio, this isn't fair.' She covered her face with her hands. 'Please, for once, see it from my point of view. This gorgeous, sexy guy who I— This gorgeous sexy guy offers me marriage, but I know it's never going to work so I have to turn him down.'

'Why would you turn me down?'

Her hands dropped to her sides and she looked at him with frustration, breaking up inside because he'd offered her what she wanted, knowing that she'd never take it. 'Because guilt isn't a good basis for a long-term relationship. And it's cruel of you, Alessio—' Her voice broke. 'It's cruel of you to stand there saying these things when you know I have to refuse.'

His eyes glittered hard. 'I'm not letting you refuse. Why would I let you refuse when I know you're desperate to be with me?'

She caught her breath. 'Well, it's nice to know your ego hasn't suffered a blow.'

He swore under his breath. 'We've always been honest with each other, but you're not being honest with me now.'

'Of course I am.'

Alessio raised an eyebrow. 'So finish your sentence, *tesoro*. What was it you said? This gorgeous, sexy guy who I—who you what?'

Lindsay swallowed and looked away. 'Just go away, Alessio,' she muttered. 'On balance it's easier to deal with the paparazzi than you.'

'You were going to say, *this gorgeous, sexy guy who I love*.' His tone soft, he pulled her back into his arms. 'I *know* you love me, Lindsay. You told me.'

'And you ran away so fast you almost tripped.'

'Running away was a reflex action. A lot of women have

used those words and you have to understand that it's instinctive for me to back off.' He gave a driven sigh. 'And it's true that it took me a while to get used to the idea that you love me. But I have done that, and it's fine.'

Lindsay gaped at him in disbelief. 'What?' She gave a tiny laugh. 'You're saying that it's OK for me to love you? That you're going to *let* me? You're so arrogant, Alessio!'

'No, I'm not saying that. Let me finish.' He ran a hand over the back of his neck. 'This is so hard.'

'It isn't hard, Alessio.' She looked at him wearily, all the fight draining out of her. 'I fell in love with you, yes. But as you rightly point out, I'm not the first woman to do that. You've walked away before, you can walk away again. And you don't need to feel guilty about any of this.' She waved a hand vaguely towards the window. 'I honestly don't care. They've probably done me a favour. I needed a change.'

'How much of a change?' His voice hoarse, he took her face in his hands again, tilting her chin so that she was forced to look at him. 'Would it be too much of a change to be married to a wicked Sicilian divorce lawyer?'

'You don't believe in marriage, Alessio.'

'I think expecting two people to stay together is asking a lot,' he admitted, 'unless they truly love each other.'

She stilled. 'What you feel is passion. And passion is no better a basis for a marriage than guilt.'

'That's true, and I understand *why* you believe that after what you told me about your parents. But you're missing one important fact and that's that you can have passion *and* love,' he murmured, taking her face in his hands. 'And that's what we have.'

'No, we don't.'

'I know I'm not saying the right things, but I'm not good at this! I've never told a woman that I love her, before! I'm probably saying it all wrong.'

Lindsay stilled. 'You haven't said it at all.'

'*Sì*, I told you.' His tone was impatient. 'I told you that
I love you.'

'No.' She covered her mouth with her hand and shook her
head. 'No, you didn't say that to me.' Her legs turned to jelly.

'Well, I'm saying it now,' he growled, removing her hand so
that he could crush his mouth against hers. 'I love you, *tesoro*.'

She felt light-headed and terrified at the same time.
Terrified of believing him. 'You've never loved anyone—'

'No.' He folded her in his arms. 'I haven't. I saw how much
pain loving my mother caused my father. In the small village
in Sicily where I grew up, divorce just wasn't an option. And
frankly, I don't know whether he would have divorced her even
if he'd been given the chance. But I lived with his misery and I
felt—helpless. I suppose that's why I saw divorce as a good
thing. He should have moved on—maybe met someone else.'

Lindsay looked up at him, understanding. 'It's so hard
when you're a child—you want to help, and you can't. And
they think it's just about them, but it affects you, too.'

Alessio nodded. 'I've never talked to anyone about it before.'

'You don't have to tell me—'

'I want to. You need to know what you're marrying.' His
gaze was wary. 'I'm not exactly experienced when it comes
to relationships, but I know you are so I'm relying on you to
teach me what I need to know.'

Lindsay gazed at him, tears blurring her vision. 'You really
think you love me?'

'I *know* I love you.' He gave a wry smile. 'And if you knew
how much I'd changed over the past two weeks, you wouldn't
even question me. Twice I've suggested to prospective clients
that they try counselling and just this morning—' He broke
off and Lindsay looked at him quizzically.

'What happened this morning?'

Alessio's face hardened. 'He had two little girls,' he muttered, 'and I couldn't stop thinking of you and Ruby.'

'You didn't take the case?'

He hesitated. 'We're going to act for the wife.'

Lindsay gave a soft gasp and then laughed. 'You're kidding?'

'I want to make sure those two little girls suffer as little as possible. You see what you've done to me?' A gleam in his eyes, Alessio dragged her back into his arms. 'I'm going to be a magnet for every gold-digger in the Western hemisphere.'

'Just as long as they're only interested in your professional skills,' Lindsay murmured, standing on tiptoe and pressing her mouth against his. 'I'm proud of you. And I *do* love you. Very, very much.'

'Just keep saying it.' Alessio hugged her tightly. 'And now I need to give the press something to photograph.' He took her left hand and slipped an enormous diamond solitaire onto her finger.

'Oh, Alessio—' tears blurred her vision '—it's beautiful. But the most beautiful thing was the fact that he loved her. 'I can't believe this is happening.'

'Well, it is. And now stop crying or the press will think I've been doing unspeakable things to you. Are you ready to face the world?'

Still staring at the ring, Lindsay gave a weak laugh. 'Every woman with a pulse is going to want to know how I persuaded you to marry me.'

'Well, they're just going to have to work it out for themselves,' Alessio drawled, leading her towards the door. 'From now on I'm not sharing you with anyone.'

As they walked out onto the pavement flashbulbs exploded in their faces and a voice called out, 'Hey, Lindsay, you're wearing a ring! Care to tell everyone your secret?'

Turning to face the bank of cameras, Lindsay smiled. She couldn't *stop* smiling. 'You'd better listen carefully because this is the last piece of relationship advice I'm ever going to give.' Almost bursting with happiness, she clutched Alessio's hand and smiled up at him, her eyes misting. But when she spoke, the words were intended for him. 'The secret,' she said softly, 'was love.'

* * * * *

Italian Boss,
Proud Miss Prim

Susan
STEPHENS

Susan Stephens was a professional singer before meeting her husband on the tiny Mediterranean island of Malta. In true Modern™ romance style they met on Monday, became engaged on Friday and were married three months after that. Almost thirty years and three children later, they are still in love. (Susan does not advise her children to return home one day with a similar story, as she may not take the news with the same fortitude as her own mother!)

Susan had written several non-fiction books when fate took a hand. At a charity costume ball there was an after-dinner auction. One of the lots, 'Spend a Day with an Author', had been donated by Mills & Boon® author Penny Jordan. Susan's husband bought this lot, and Penny was to become not just a great friend but a wonderful mentor, who encouraged Susan to write romance.

Susan loves her family, her pets, her friends and her writing. She enjoys entertaining, travel, and going to the theatre. She reads, cooks, and plays the piano to relax, and can occasionally be found throwing herself off mountains on a pair of skis or galloping through the countryside. Visit Susan's website: www.susanstephens.net—she loves to hear from her readers all around the world!

For Jenny,
who is both inspired and inspiring.

CHAPTER ONE

Six hours, fifteen minutes in the same hard chair at the same desk, in the same cold office, in the same northern town...

She'd lost the will to live.

Almost...

Arranging a telephone conference with Signor Rigo Ruggiero in Rome was a pain, even for a young lawyer as tenacious as Katie Bannister, because first she had to get past Ruggiero's army of snooty retainers.

Let me speak to him in person, screeched inner Katie, whilst outwardly Katie was calm. Well, she had to be—she was a respected professional.

With no inner life at all.

No inner life? Hmm, wouldn't that make things easy? Unfortunately, Katie was blessed with a vivid imagination and an active fantasy life, and it was always getting her into trouble. Dumpy, plain and unprepossessing became sharp and confident in the blink of an eye—especially over the phone.

In her junior position at the small solicitor's firm, Katie wouldn't normally be expected to deal with such a high-profile client, but this was a trivial matter, according to the senior partner, and if she wanted to work her way up the profession it would be good for Katie to cut her teeth on—

'Pronto...'

At last. *At last!* 'Signor Ruggiero?'

'*Sì…?*'

The deep-pitched voice speared a shiver down her spine. But gut instinct wasn't enough. Did it prove the identity of the speaker? Spoken Italian was sexy; distractingly so. Quickly gathering her thoughts, Katie picked up her notes and went through the security checks she had drawn up.

To his credit, Signor Ruggiero answered them all accurately and politely. To her dismay her imagination insisted on working overtime as she nursed the phone—tall, dark and handsome didn't begin to cover it. Still, this was going better than she had expected after her run-in with his staff. Now it was simply a matter of informing the Italian tycoon that he was the chief beneficiary in his late brother's will.

'My late *step*brother's will,' he corrected her.

The honey-rich baritone had acquired an edge of steel. He sounded stern, cold, uninterested.

A man who was so hard to contact would hardly want chit chat, Katie reminded herself, moving up a gear. 'My apologies, Signor Ruggiero, your late *step*brother's will…'

As the conversation continued Katie picked up more clues. If there was one thing she was good at it was reading people's voices. Time spent training to be an opera singer at one of the world's foremost music conservatoires had allowed her well-tuned ear to instantly evaluate a voice, and this one had both practised charm and a killer edge.

'Can we cut to the chase, Signorina Bannister?'

And cut out print yards of legalese? 'Certainly…'

Katie's reputation at the firm was founded on dogged persistence along with her ability to calm even the most fractious of clients, but after a long day in a cheap suit in a cold office she was at the end of her tether. It wasn't as if she was trying to serve a writ, for goodness' sake; rather she was trying to inform Signor Ruggiero that he had come into money.

More money, Katie qualified, glancing at the magazine the girls in the office had so helpfully placed on her desk. It featured a devastatingly handsome Rigo Ruggiero on the front cover. Not that she was interested. Firming her jaw, she continued to explain to one of the richest men in Italy why she must come to see him in person. To Rome, where she had thought of going as a singer, once…

'Well, I haven't got the time to come over there—'

Katie snapped back to the present. 'Your stepbrother anticipated this…' Her heart picked up pace as she went on to read out the letter of instruction that came with the will. She was normally unflappable, but office tittle-tattle had unsettled her where Rigo Ruggiero was concerned. He was not just a successful tycoon, but a high-profile playboy who lived life in the fast lane. To say that Katie Bannister and Rigo Ruggiero were worlds apart was a massive understatement.

Everyone in the office had thought it highly amusing that the official office virgin had been appointed to deal with Italy's most notorious playboy. Katie's public face had remained unmoved through all this teasing banter, but her imagination had run riot. After her initial trepidation, she had thought, bring it on. What did she have to worry about? Rigo Ruggiero would take one look at dull little Katie Bannister and she'd be safe.

'No, I'm sorry,' she said. 'I'm afraid your late stepbrother's personal effects cannot be sent to you through the post, Signor Ruggiero.'

'Why not?'

'Because…' She took a deep, steadying breath. Forget the letter of intentions—shouldn't he care a little more? And did he have to snap like that? His stepbrother had just died, for goodness' sake. Surely he was curious to learn what he'd been left in the will? 'Your stepbrother's instructions are *most* specific, Signor Ruggiero. He appointed the firm I represent,

Flintock, Gough and Coverdale, as executors to his will, and Mr Flintock has asked me to carry out the requirements therein to the letter—'

'Therein?'

Mockery now?

'Do you always speak legalese to your clients, Signorina Bannister? That must be very confusing for them.' His voice was dry and amused. 'I recommend plain-speaking myself…'

No one had ever criticised her dedication to the letter of the law before and it was becoming increasingly clear that Rigo Ruggiero couldn't care a fig for his stepbrother. She could see him now, lolling back on some easy chair as he took the call— all preposterously white teeth, inky black hair and dark, mocking eyes. Closing her eyes, she willed herself to remain calm. 'What I'm trying to explain, Signor Ruggiero—'

'Don't patronise me.'

The tone of voice both stung and acted as a warning. 'I apologise. That was not my intention.'

'Then I forgive you…'

In a voice like a caress. Was he flirting with her? Unlikely as that seemed, it appeared so, and her body definitely agreed. 'So could we fix an appointment?' she suggested, returning determinedly to the point of the call.

There was silence at the other end of the line, but somehow worldly amusement managed to travel down it anyway. 'Whenever you like,' he murmured.

The throaty drawl was enough to make her body quiver with anticipation. Katie stared out of the window at the cold, autumnal Yorkshire rain. That was the swiftest return to reality she could imagine. Beneath her conventional, even plain exterior, lurked a seam of wanderlust. She had dreamed at one time that it would be the opera houses of the world she'd be visiting. Did she have the courage to make this trip to Rome in her new guise as solicitor, or would the loss of her singing voice be a reminder that was too painful to bear?

'Well,' the deep male voice demanded, 'I don't have all day, Signorina Bannister. When would you like to meet?'

She longed for a break, and she could be in Rome tomorrow. Before she could stop herself the words tumbled out. 'What about tomorrow, Signor Ruggiero? If that's convenient for you…?'

'I'll make it so,' he said.

'Thank you for your cooperation.' She could hardly breathe her heart was thundering so fast. Talking over the phone was easy, but when Signor Ruggiero saw how plain and boring she was in person… And when she saw Rome…

'I look forward to meeting you,' he said. 'You have a lovely voice, by the way.'

A lovely voice… 'Thank you…' Playboys were expected to flirt, and Signor Ruggiero couldn't be expected to know that her voice had been reduced to husky ashes after a fire in her student lodgings. She had been overjoyed in the hospital when she found out all her friends had escaped uninjured, and devastated to discover that after inhaling too much smoke her voice had been reduced for good to a croak. Oddly enough, people who didn't know her history found that husky sound attractive. But that wasn't her only legacy from the fire. She would never sing again and had enough scars on her back to ensure no one would ever see her naked. When her singing career had crashed to a close, she had set about forging a new life as a lawyer. This was a life in the shadows rather than the spotlight, but she wasn't interested in the spotlight; it was the music she missed.

'Signorina Bannister? Are you still there?'

'I beg your pardon, Signor Ruggiero. I just knocked something off my desk.'

Or wished she had, Katie thought, staring at the magazine.

A towering powerhouse of hard, tanned muscle, dressed in a sharp designer suit, stared back at her from the front cover. Rigo Ruggiero couldn't even be accused of having a smooth, rich boy's face. His verged on piratical, complete with sharp black stubble and a dangerous gleam in night-dark, emerald eyes. Add to that a shock of thick black hair and a jaw even firmer than her own—

'You haven't changed your mind about our meeting, I hope?'

There was a faint edge of challenge to his voice that her body responded to with enthusiasm. 'Not at all,' she reassured him firmly. Reaching across the desk, she was about to send the magazine flying to the floor when she paused. The cynical curve of his mouth set her teeth on edge, but she had to admit it was the perfect frame for his arrogant voice. And, as if there wasn't enough perfection in his life, the image showed him with his arm draped around the shoulders of a blonde girl so achingly lovely she looked like a doll rather than a living, breathing woman.

It would be fine, Katie told herself, straightening up. She could do this. The trip to Rome was business and no one could distract her from that.

'I have a question for you, Signorina Bannister.'

'Yes?' Tightening her grip on the phone, Katie realised she was still transfixed by the image of the girl's unblemished skin.

'Why you?' he rapped.

This was no playboy, but a merciless tycoon questioning the wisdom of sending such a young and inexperienced lawyer to meet with him. But he had a point. Why were they sending her? Because she spoke fluent Italian, thanks to her opera training, Katie reasoned, because she was plain, safe and unattached, and, as the newest recruit to the firm, she had little or no say when it came to apportioning work.

Better not let on she was so junior. 'I'm the only solicitor in the firm who could spare the time to come to Rome—'

'You're not much good, then?'

'Signor Ruggiero—'

'Piano, piano, bella...'

Piano, bella? He was telling her to calm down—and in a voice he might use with a lover.

Italian was sexy, Katie reminded herself. The language itself had a lyrical music all its own. And when you added Rigo Ruggiero to the mix—

'So,' he said, 'I'll see you in Rome tomorrow—*sì?*'

See him tomorrow...

He was quicksilver to her caution, one moment stern, the next amused. But he was right to be suspicious about her credentials. She wasn't a great lawyer. She never would be a great lawyer because she didn't have the hunger for it. She sometimes wondered if the passion she'd felt for her operatic career would ever transfer to anything else. But the firm she had worked for since she had retrained as a solicitor had been good to her when her life had gone up in flames, and now she was scarred a role in the background suited her.

'I'll expect you tomorrow.'

Tomorrow...

This was exactly what she'd asked for. But since she'd suggested tomorrow her confidence had been slowly seeping away. The whole idea was ridiculous. How could she go to Rome, the city where she had dreamed of being part of the musical life, only as a second-rate lawyer to deal with one of the most acute minds around?

The only reason Katie could think of was hard, economic reality. The senior partner at her firm was talking redundancies, thanks to the economic downturn, and as last into the firm she was most likely to be first out. There was no question this trip to Rome and her meeting with someone as high-profile as Rigo Ruggiero would add some much-needed colour to her CV.

It made sense—well, to everything except her self-confidence. How could Katie Bannister, dressed by the cheapest store in town, the girl who wouldn't know a fashion must-have if she fell over it, meet with the world's most notorious playboy and come out of that meeting unscathed?

The plain and simple truth was, she had to.

'I'll book a flight,' she said, thinking out loud.

'I'd recommend it,' the man in question interrupted dryly. 'Mail me with the details and I'll make sure someone is at Fiumicino Airport to meet you—'

'That's very—'

Katie stared at the dead receiver in her hands. How rude. Or look at it another way, she persuaded herself; this was a challenge, and she was hardly a stranger to that.

She had laughed when the other girls at the firm had insisted that Katie Bannister had hidden fire and would master the maverick playboy in less time than it took to say hold my briefs—maybe she had possessed that fire once, but not now—and the girls in the office hadn't spoken to him, a man so cold and heartless he could discuss a close relative's bequest without so much as a play of regret. And end a conversation without any of the usual niceties. Rigo Ruggiero was clearly an indulged and arrogant monster and the sooner her business with him was concluded the better she would like it.

It was just a shame her body disagreed.

She'd cope with that too. Palming her mouse, Katie brought up flight schedules to Rome. Could she make it there and back in one day? She would try her very best to do so.

Having replaced the receiver in its nest, Rigo settled back in his leather swivel chair. In spite of the unwelcome message Katie Bannister had delivered from a man he'd hoped never to hear from again, the young lawyer had made him smile.

Because he liked her voice?

It had certainly scored highly in several categories: it was female; it was young; it was husky; it was sexy. Very sexy. And intelligent. And…sexy. He already had an image of her in his mind.

So, he reflected, returning to the purpose of Signorina Bannister's call, his stepbrother had left him something in his will. A poisoned chalice? Shares in a crime syndicate? What? He stood up and started pacing. Why should the man who had shown him nothing but contempt and hatred since the day he had walked into his life leave him anything at all in his will? And what was it about these personal effects that made them so precious only a representative from a solicitor's firm in England could hand-deliver them?

He knew Carlo had been living in the north of England for some years, thanks to the headlines in the papers detailing his stepbrother's countless misdemeanours, and could confidently predict that if these personal effects were gold bars they'd be stolen—likewise jewellery, antiques or art. What else would Carlo care enough about not to chance it going astray? It had to be something incriminating—something that gave Carlo one last stab at him before the gates of hell closed on his stepbrother for ever.

Rigo had been just fourteen when his father married again and seventeen when he had left home for good. He had left home after a couple of years of Carlo's vicious tricks, when home became a cruel misnomer for somewhere Rigo was no longer welcome. How he had longed for his father's love, but that love had found another home. So he conquered his regret and left the countryside to pursue his dreams in Rome. He hadn't heard from Carlo, his elder by eleven years, from that day to this.

But he had a lot to thank Carlo for, Rigo reflected, standing by the floor-to-ceiling windows in his luxurious penthouse overlooking Rome. He lived in the most exclusive part of the city and this was only one of his many properties. Leaving the country all those years ago had led to success, wealth and, more important in his eyes, the chance to live life the way he believed it should be led.

These thoughts brought him back full circle to the girl from England he must somehow fit into his busy schedule tomorrow. Crossing to his desk, he scanned his diary. He'd just sacked the latest in a long line of hopeless PAs. Finding a reliable replacement was proving harder than he had anticipated.

Which left a vacancy on his staff…

If she was half as intriguing as her husky voice suggested, he would gladly clear his diary for Signorina Bannister. He would make the whole of tomorrow free just for her.

CHAPTER TWO

KATIE was having second thoughts. Just packing a few essentials for the trip in her shabby bag proved she wasn't the right person for this job. She might have the heart to handle Rigo Ruggiero, but she lacked the panache. The firm should be sending someone sharp and polished to Rome, someone sophisticated, who spoke the same sophisticated language as him. Two new packets of tights and a clean white blouse did not a sophisticate make, but it was the best she could do. There was nothing in her wardrobe suitable for spending time in Rome with a man renowned for his sartorial elegance.

A few calming breaths later Katie had worked out that, as she couldn't compete, she shouldn't try. She should look at what she was—a competent young lawyer from a small firm in the north of England, which meant a brown suit and low-heeled brown court shoes were the perfect choice.

This wasn't a holiday, Katie reminded herself sternly, though as an afterthought she added a pair of comfortable trousers and a sweater. With the tight schedule she had planned it was unlikely there would be any off-duty time, but if there was she could dress for that too.

But everything was brown, even her bag, Katie noticed as she prepared to close the door on her small terraced house. A life in the shadows was one thing, but she hadn't noticed the colour seeping from it. Perhaps it had gone with the music...

She shook herself round determinedly. She was going to Rome—not as a singer as she had always hoped, but as a representative of a respectable legal firm. How many people got a second chance like that?

Locking the door, she tested the handle and picked up her bag. Tipping her chin at a confident angle, she walked briskly down the path. She was going to Italy to meet one of the most exciting men of his day. She didn't expect to be part of Rigo Ruggiero's life but, for a few short and hopefully thrilling hours, she would be an observer. At the very least she could report back to the girls in the office and brighten up their coffee breaks for the foreseeable future.

Signor Ruggiero had lied. Clutching her sensible bag like a comfort blanket, Katie stood bewildered amongst the crowds on the pavement outside Fiumicino Airport in Rome. The sun was beating down like an unrelenting spotlight and the heat was overpowering. She stared this way and that, but it only confirmed what she already knew, which was, no one had come to meet her. Plus everyone else seemed to know where they were going. She was the only country bumpkin who appeared to be cast adrift in the big city.

And was fervently wishing she'd handled her own transport arrangements into Rome.

What was wrong with her? She had the address...

Having found it in her bag, she looked for a taxi. Was she going to be defeated before she even started this adventure? But each time she stepped forward to claim an empty cab someone taller, slicker and more confident than Katie stepped in front of her—

'Signorina Bannister?'

The voice reached into her chest and squeezed her heart

ight before she even had chance to look around, and when she did she almost stumbled into the arms of a man who put his photographs to shame. Her heart drummed an immediate tattoo. Rigo Ruggiero in the hard, tanned flesh was infinitely better-looking than his air-brushed images—so hot you wouldn't touch him without protective clothing. He was the type of man Katie had spent her whole life dreaming about and wishing would notice her, but who, of course, never would—other than today, when he had no alternative.

'Sorry…sorry.' She righted herself quickly before he was brought into contact with her cheap polyester suit. 'Signorina Bannister? That's me.'

'Are you sure?'

Her cheeks flamed. 'Of course I'm sure…'

Thrusting her serviceable bag beneath her arm, she held out her free hand in greeting. 'This is very good of you, sir—' She braced herself for contact.

Contact there was none.

Startlingly green and uncomfortably shrewd eyes refused to share Signor Ruggiero's practised smile. He was not the man in the magazine photograph. That man was a playboy with pleasure on his mind. The man in front of her was a realist, a thinker, a business tycoon, and he took no prisoners. The hand she had extended dropped back to her side. 'I didn't think you would come to meet me in person—'

'It is my pleasure to do so.'

He even bowed slightly, but his tone suggested it was anything but a pleasure for him.

Katie's worst fears were confirmed. Rigo Ruggiero was hiding disappointment. Having heard her husky voice over the phone, he had imagined he had come to the airport to meet a siren. They had both been misled, Katie reflected wryly. Now this was not business for her; it had become personal. Rigo Ruggiero had shadows behind his eyes she couldn't resist and wanted to understand, and he was so handsome he made her heart ache.

'You had a good journey, I hope.'

'Very good, thank you.' She registered the fact that he had spoken to her in a tone of voice she imagined he might use with a maiden aunt. He was so much taller, bigger and had a more powerful aura than her imagination had allowed and was far more rugged. He was the type of man who could look dangerous even in tailored clothes. The dark trousers complemented his athletic figure and the crisp blue shirt was open a couple of buttons at the neck, revealing a hard, tanned chest, shaded with black hair. The sight of this gave parts of her that were largely unused a vigorous workout. If this wasn't lust at first sight, it was the closest Katie Bannister had ever come to it.

But what she needed now, Katie reasoned with her sensible head on, was some form of identification to prove to Rigo Ruggiero she was who she said she was. On plundering her bag she managed to spill the contents all over his designer-clad feet.

'Allow me, Signorina Bannister…'

To his credit, he immediately dipped to rescue her passport, tickets, toffees, tissues and all the other embarrassing detritus she had accumulated during the flight.

'Why don't I take your bag?' he suggested, staring her straight in the eyes as he straightened up.

My shabby, disreputable-looking bag? 'That's very kind of you. And here's my passport for purposes of identification.'

'I don't think we'll need that,' he said, lips pressing down in an unfeasibly attractive way. And then, in a final cataclysmic put-down, he suggested, 'Why don't you put your passport somewhere safe before you lose it?'

So she wasn't a maiden aunt, she was a child.

She'd made a great first impression. He even held the bag steady for her as she stuffed her possessions back inside. She glanced at him apologetically. He had no need to flag it up

Her clothes, her gaucheness, her red cheeks and clumsiness, all told a story Rigo Ruggiero had no interest in reading.

'And my stepbrother's personal effects?' he pressed, gazing past her.

She wondered if he expected a packing case to be following on. 'Your stepbrother's effects are right here.' She patted the breast pocket of her jacket to reassure him.

'That doesn't look like very much.'

'Well, it is a very small package.' She blushed violently to see him conceal a smile.

'OK,' he said, neither agreeing nor disagreeing, 'I'll get the car.'

'Honestly, I'm quite happy to take a cab—'

'So we arrive at my penthouse in convoy?' he suggested, shooting her a look.

How much better could this get? 'See your point,' she murmured with a nervous laugh.

How much better? A lot better, Katie realised as a blood-red sports car drew up at the kerb. She didn't need to remember the blonde in the magazine to know she was hardly in this class. A sick, heavy feeling was building in her stomach as an admiring crowd gathered around the high-performance vehicle and its elegant driver. They had recognised Rigo, of course, and now they were eager to find out who he was meeting at the airport.

That was what she had to walk through to get to the car.

'I don't bite, Signorina Bannister.'

The throaty drawl drew her attention to the man leaning over the roof of the low-slung sex-machine.

A laugh rippled through the crowd as she locked gazes with him. Everyone was staring at her and she could feel their disappointment. She was not some famous beauty or a super-model. She was about the furthest thing from that you could get. Steeling herself, she took the half-dozen steps required to close the distance between herself and the car. Signor Ruggiero had already stowed her bag, and so all she had to do was get in—but that meant she had to slot herself into an impossibly narrow-looking opening.

'When you're ready,' he drawled.

She had already anticipated that folding her inelegant body into such an elegant car was a skill she didn't possess. She was right and, to her horror, she got stuck.

What made it worse was that Signor Ruggiero came to help her, and all but lifted her into the formed seat, which she now discovered had been moulded around a fairy's bottom.

But at least she was out of sight of the crowd, Katie reasoned as he slid into the driver's seat beside her.

'Comfortable?' He glanced at her to check.

'Perfectly.' On edge.

Now she had to convince herself that you couldn't die from the shock of meeting a man like this in person, and that the air in the confined cabin hadn't changed with an overload of ions and his delicious scent. But it had. And it was charged with something else...sex, Katie realised, primly tugging down her skirt. Rigo Ruggiero radiated sex.

'You can understand my impatience, I'm sure,' he said.

She gripped the seat as the engine roared like a jet.

'This bequest from such an unexpected quarter has intrigued me,' he went on.

This was business, she told herself in a silent shout, but that reassurance was growing a little thin.

'I ask myself,' he said, 'what can be so important that only a personal delivery of the documents would do?'

As he glanced at her, Katie thought: And by a girl like this? She shrank beneath a gaze that took in every stitch of man-made fibre until finally it came to rest on her sensible, low-heeled shoes. She quickly tucked her feet away, out of sight. 'I'm sorry if I kept you waiting.'

He shrugged. 'I must have missed you, somehow.'

Searching for that husky-voiced siren would do it every time.

'But never mind,' he added dryly, flashing that wolf smile of his. 'I've got you now.'

'Indeed you do.'

He shrugged as he released the brake and pulled away. The adventure begins, Katie thought, hoping she was up to it. She didn't need Signor Ruggiero to spell it out. Katie Bannister was hardly the type of woman he would normally put himself out for.

She held on tightly to the seat as he steered smoothly away from the kerb. 'Ten kilometres an hour OK for you?' he murmured as they joined a crawling stream of traffic.

'Sorry, I'm just not used to…'

How many people were used to driving in a sports car? Katie asked herself sensibly. She had entered a world that was completely alien to her, and it would take a while to adjust. Closing her eyes and wishing herself a million miles away wouldn't work this time, because this time she really was living the fantasy.

She didn't realise how tense she had become until she heard Signor Ruggiero say, 'Don't worry, Signorina Bannister. I shall strive to achieve a balance between my impatience and your obvious lack of confidence in my driving ability—'

'Oh, I'm not—' Her mouth slammed shut when she realised too late he was mocking her. And now the set of his jaw did nothing to encourage conversation.

He was hardly her typical client, but this sort of impatience was universal. The reading of a will was notoriously full of surprises and, whether those surprises turned out to be bad or good, human nature demanded answers fast.

Katie's hand crept to the breast pocket of her suit, where she wished fervently for some last small legacy of love for him contained within the envelope she was carrying—though, if past experience was any guide, she was wasting her time.

OK, so meeting Katie Bannister had been a shock, but he was growing used to her unique vibe. She was as different from the women he was used to mixing with as it was possible to imagine, but that wasn't necessarily a bad thing, only different. He didn't need false breasts and false smiles—but neither did he need complications. Signorina Bannister was a quiet little mouse and awkward, which meant he would have to spend more time with her than he had anticipated, but how could he throw her to the wolves in Rome? She was out of her comfort zone and had anticipated more time to prepare before meeting him. She found herself in a much bigger, faster world than her comfortable country cocoon and would have to adapt quickly. Meanwhile they had a forty-five minute journey ahead of them and he couldn't stand this uncomfortable silence. 'I'd like you to call me Rigo.'

She bit her lip. Her pale cheeks blazed. She said precisely nothing.

Ducking his head, he checked the road before steering north-east to Rome. It gave him an excuse to flash a glance at her. 'Try it,' he said, thinking she looked like a rabbit trapped in headlights. 'Rrr…igo…'

She pressed back in her seat. He felt instinctively that this was someone to whom life had not always been kind. Did he have time to be a social worker? OK, so she brought out his protective instinct, but he was no bleeding heart. Perhaps it would help if he let her know he was no threat to her—absolutely no threat at all. 'You don't even have to say my name in Italian,' he said dryly. 'English will do.'

She said his name—a little reluctantly, he thought. '*Bene,*' he said. 'That was very good.'

'And you can call me Signorina Bannister,' she said.

He laughed. And for the first time that day, he relaxed. 'Very well, Signorina Bannister,' he agreed. 'Your wish is my command...' At least on the subject of names.

CHAPTER THREE

MAYBE the client was always right, but she was going to keep this formal. She would never get used to a man like Rigo Ruggiero in the short time available as he seemed to think she could, and so it was better not to try.

But that didn't mean she couldn't enjoy this quietly. This tasty slice of *la dolce vita* was her first real adventure. Rigo Ruggiero—Roma, Italia—a real-life Italian playboy driving a blood-red sports car with Katie Bannister sitting next to him. The closest she had ever come to this before was in her fantasy world.

The view from the tinted window was extraordinary. They had cleared the boring industrial places and were driving into Rome. It was like entering the pages of a living history book—if one with a serious traffic problem, traffic Rigo Ruggiero had no problem negotiating. Her confidence had grown, Katie realised, noting how relaxed she had become. She could get used to this—the Colosseum here…Trajan's Market there. The only place she dared not look was to her left, in case Signor Ruggiero thought she was staring at him. But she didn't need to stare to know he was built like a gladiator and had the commanding face of a Roman general. She could feel that in every part of her.

'Trajan's Market has recently been reopened to the public.'

She refocused as he spoke. This conversational tone was not what she expected from the gladiator in her head, but then she hadn't expected him to speak at all. Signor Ruggiero was being kind by entering into conversation with her—and at least it gave her an excuse to stare at him. 'Really?'

She knew her eager gaze was gauche, but he was perfection, which made it hard not to stare. If she could have designed a man, this would be him. Even her imagination couldn't have mapped a face so perfect or a body made for uninterrupted sin—

'Even in AD 113,' he went on, 'these large shopping malls were in demand.'

As he smiled, a flash of strong white teeth against his tan made her think even more wicked thoughts. She could think of a better use for those firm, mobile lips and those wolf teeth, and when he angled that rough, stubble-shaded chin towards the remarkably well-preserved Roman buildings she felt a pulse begin to throb where it had absolutely no business doing so. Did he know the effect he was having on her? Katie wondered, blushing when he looked at her for her opinion. Hopefully not.

'I read somewhere that Trajan's Market was the experiment in bringing shops together under one roof,' she said, trying to seem gripped by Roman history when the only thing she wanted to be gripped by was him.

His face creased in an attractive smile. 'It was the first— unless you know of one dating from earlier times, of course?'

She shook her head. Obviously he knew more than she did about his own city, but she remained silent, because she thought it was safer to keep things formal rather than to chat. And she had only visited one shopping mall in her whole life. The girls from the office had persuaded her to accompany them and she had vowed, never again! The lights, the crowds jostling her, the shops full of things she didn't need or want. Give her the wide open spaces in the country any day...

'I think Rome is going to be quite an eye-opener for you.'

You could say that again, Katie thought as Rigo steered the sports car down a fashionable shopping street with more glitz and glamour than her poor fantasies could hope to conjure up.

Katie's head was still spinning with all the lavish things she'd seen when she sat down in Rigo's vast, ultra-modern study. Light flooded in, revealing every flaw—or would have done had there been any, but, as she might have imagined, Rigo lived in unimaginable luxury. His penthouse was immaculate, and his study boasted every conceivable high-tech man-toy. She found it starkly beautiful, with its colour scheme of steel and white. There was glass everywhere and vibrant modern art on the walls. Incredibly, the roof could be open to the sky, which it was. Her jaw dropped as she stared up to watch birds wheeling overhead in a flawless cobalt sky. So this was how the rich lived. After the chaos and bustle of the city streets, Rigo's eyrie at the very top of an ancient *palazzo* was a haven of quiet. She could even hear the birds singing if she held her breath.

Katie forced her attention away from the aerial display as Rigo came to sit across the desk from her. He sprawled in such a relaxed fashion, while she was anxiously perching on the very edge of one of his divine cream leather chairs. It was showroom-new, like the huge glass desk in front of her—and that was another concern. What if she left a smudge on its pristine surface?

'Do you like the view?' he prompted.

'I love it.' There were windows to three sides overlooking the rooftops of Rome, but Rigo's husky baritone attracted her more. Her heart squeezed tight as he looked out of the window and she looked at him. He was so perfect. And she would never know him, not properly. But she would never forget today, or how attractive he was, or how polite to her—though how that would affect her future when it came to men remained to be seen. They would all fall short if she compared them to Rigo.

For his part, Rigo seemed to have got over the shock of meeting her and was treating her with indulgence like a young relative recently arrived from the country.

'There's the Colosseum,' he said, pointing it out. 'Can you see it?'

And was that St Peter's Basilica? She wanted to ask, but realised he would only think her more gauche and awkward than ever. Signor Ruggiero's home in Rome was in one of the most fashionable squares and had a panoramic view of so much of the beautiful city.

'I'll draw the blinds,' he said, when she impulsively shaded her eyes to take another look. He pressed a button and it was done. He pressed another button and a tinted glass roof closed over their heads. 'Thank you,' she murmured, glad to be in the shadows again.

And now it was down to business—no more time wasted on wishing Signor Ruggiero could look at her and see her differently, someone with more class and polish than she possessed…and no flaws.

'Are you cold, Signorina Bannister?'

Try frigid.

'You're trembling,' he said.

'Just travel-weary, I expect.' By then he had pressed yet another button on the console on his desk, activating some invisible heat source.

'Travel-weary?' he murmured, and there was a faintly amused look in his eyes. 'I forgot—you've had such a long flight.'

And it would be the same short flight home, Katie thought, knowing she would have to sharpen up with this man or be made a complete fool of. She started by putting a professional smile on her lips. 'Shall we begin?'

'Whenever you're ready,' he said, still looking at her with faint amusement.

Reaching for the thick manila envelope she had put in front of her on the desk, Katie opened it. But concern for its contents washed over her and she stopped. She had heard so many unkind things expressed in wills, and was well aware they could be used like a weapon to hurt those left behind. She hoped she wasn't the bearer of some last bitter note from Rigo Ruggiero's stepbrother.

'What are you waiting for, Signorina Bannister?'

Yes, why should she care what was in the will? She fumbled the sheets and finally managed to spread the document out in front of her. 'This is the last will and testament of—'

'Cut to the chase—we both know whose will this is.'

Rigo Ruggiero's charm had evaporated. He could change in an instant, she had discovered. It would be a foolish person who underestimated him. He had charm only when he chose to have charm.

'My time is short, Signorina Bannister.'

And you are handling this badly, his expression clearly said. She wasn't supposed to get involved. She had received this same criticism at work. It was her only failing, the senior partner had told her at her annual assessment. Deal with the facts, Ms Bannister. We are not employed to dole out tea and sympathy—and make sure you keep an accurate time sheet of every moment you spend with the client.

Even at times like these when she could be revealing anything to Signor Ruggiero? Was she supposed to close her heart and send the bill? She had never managed to do so before, and now she stood less chance than ever. Her clock wasn't running. They should have sent a more experienced member of the firm if they wanted her to account for every second of compassion in her.

'Please move on.'

She did so with a dry throat. Even her so-called sexy voice sounded strained. There was clearly no love lost between Rigo and his stepbrother. Didn't he feel any nostalgia for his childhood? His darkening expression suggested not. She was out of place, out of step here…

Reminding herself she was merely a servant of the firm, she pulled herself together and got on with it, only to have Rigo explode with, *'Tcha!'* as the phone rang. He made her jump as he banged the table. Obviously he didn't want to be interrupted at a time like this, and as he reached for the telephone she spoke up.

'If I answer it I can put them off for you. I can say I'm your PA…'

Briefly, she thought she saw something light in his eyes, and then with a curt nod of agreement he withdrew his hand, leaving her to pick up the phone.

'Pronto?' She shot Rigo a glance. People had different ways of expressing emotion when someone close to them died. Carlo Ruggiero had been part of Rigo Ruggiero's life once—he must be feeling something, though he was hiding it well.

Refocusing on the call, Katie continued to talk in fluent Italian, and only slowly realised that Rigo was staring at her in astonishment.

'Why didn't you tell me you spoke Italian?' he said accusingly as she ended the call.

'I didn't realise it would be of any interest to you.'

He looked taken aback, but quickly recovered. 'No, you're right. Well?' he said impatiently. 'Are you going to tell me who it was?'

She managed her feelings. This was none of her business. 'It appears you have forgotten a rather important engagement…'

He jumped up immediately when she explained. Extracting a phone from his pocket, he placed a call and began to pace.

* * *

He would only break off this meeting before he found out everything for one reason and this was it. The scheme he had set up to fulfil children's dreams came ahead of his personal concerns. If taking a child around the track in his sports car was being brought forward then there must be a very good reason for it. 'Of course he can come right away,' he told his friend.

Moving out of earshot so Katie Bannister couldn't hear, he explained his schedule for the day had been thrown thanks to missing the solicitor he was due to meet at the airport—and, yes, he had found the young woman, eventually.

'A young woman?' his friend murmured with a knowing air.

'A very quiet and respectable young woman,' he emphasised, staring at the back of Katie Bannister's head. She had thick, glossy hair the same shade of honey as her eyes, but she wore it scraped back cruelly in a way that did her no favours. He refocused on his conversation and shut her out. His friend brought her back in again.

'What a disappointment for you, Rigo,' he drawled, 'but no doubt you have a plan in mind to change this young woman's way of thinking?'

Actually, no, he had no plan, and his friend's comment had left him feeling vaguely irritated. 'I'm leaving now.' He ended the call. This was not the moment to be discussing such things, and something about Signorina Bannister called for the role of protector, rather than seducer. She was far too young for him, and almost certainly a virgin—or at least incredibly inexperienced; ergo, she was not his type at all. He stowed the phone in his shirt pocket and turned back to her. 'You'll have to keep this reading on hold. I've been called away. We'll reschedule—'

'But my flight home…' she said anxiously.

'I can only apologise.'

Katie frowned. It wasn't up to her to judge the client, but this was unforgivable. Rigo Ruggiero intended to leave something as important as the reading of his stepbrother's will to race his sports car around a track. Couldn't he do that some other time? His equally arrogant friend hadn't been prepared to tell her much more, but she gathered that was the plan. 'There's no need to apologise,' she said coldly, remembering the senior partner's words. 'After all, you're paying for my time—'

'Plus ça change,' he interrupted and his expression registered nothing more than resigned acceptance of the way of things.

Now she was insulted. Her motive in coming to Rome had not been money. The fact that she had come here to fulfil his stepbrother's last request didn't matter to him at all, apparently.

He saw this change in her and emphasized, 'This is something I cannot miss—'

'And I cannot miss my flight,' she said, standing up.

'You can change it—'

'I'm not sure I can—'

'Why not?'

Because she would have to buy a new ticket—an expense that would mean nothing to this man and that in their present parlous state her firm probably wouldn't reimburse. She had bills to pay—and the prospect of no job to return to ahead of her.

She had tried so hard to strike the right tone and be professional, but she was growing increasingly agitated as she faced Rigo Ruggiero across the desk. Like it or not, they were in conflict now. 'Couldn't you change your appointment?' she suggested hesitantly.

'No.'

'But you are eager to get this over with?' she reminded him. And not put off by a drive around the racetrack with the boys.

'I assure you I am every bit as eager as I was before, but now I must go—'

'Shall I wait for you?'

Already halfway to the door, he spun around. 'Make yourself at home.'

Tension had propelled her to breaking point. She might be

a small-town solicitor, and dull as ditchwater if you compared her to the blistering glamour of a man like this, but she wasn't anyone's doormat. 'Signor Ruggiero, please,' she called, chasing after him. 'This just can't wait—'

'And neither can my appointment,' he called back to her from the door. 'You must be content—'

Content?

As he spoke one strong, tanned hand flexed impatiently on the door handle. 'I will return as quickly as I can—'

'But my flight—'

'Book another flight.'

The next sound she heard was the sound of the door slamming on his private quarters.

Great, Katie thought, subsiding. She was going to miss her flight.

So what would she do? She would have to stay in Rome. But since the fire privacy was all-important. She'd never stayed away from home since the fire. She had never risked anyone seeing her scars. What if a hotel maid or a porter walked in on her by accident? The thought of it made her blood run cold.

She wasn't ready for this—maybe she never would be. And where would she stay? Could she even afford to stay in a city as expensive as Rome on her limited budget?

'Ciao, bella.'

On the point of tears, she swung around clumsily, almost crashing into the fabulous desk as Rigo Ruggiero stormed out of the apartment in a cloud of testosterone and expensive cologne. *Ciao, bella?* He must have mistaken her for someone else.

But her nipples were impressed, Katie realised with astonishment. Well, she could dream, couldn't she? *Ciao, bella...*

Her sensible self lost no time telling her she should be concerned at these unmistakeable signs of arousal, because Rigo Ruggiero roused more than awe inside her, he roused lust.

And frustration.

And anger.

He inspired that too, because this just wasn't fair. How long did it take to race around a track? Was she supposed to sit here waiting indefinitely for him?

She would go and find a cheap hotel, Katie concluded, putting the will back in its envelope. Wandering to the window, she took a last look out, debating whether to book a flight today, tomorrow—or next week, maybe? Who the hell knew? She was of no importance to Signor Ruggiero and had been dismissed. Far from being impatient to know the contents of his stepbrother's will, as he had told her, he had proved himself all too easily distracted. The words *play* and *boy* had never made more sense to her. Rigo Ruggiero was like a film star—all top show. He was a man with too much money and not enough to occupy his time.

Staring down at the road a dizzying distance below, she watched his sleek red car pull out smoothly into the chaos of Roman traffic. Everyone gave way for him, of course. But not her, Katie determined, firming her jaw. Not that she'd ever get the chance. But then her dreamy self came to the fore and she wondered, if she had looked different—more glamorous, more appealing—would Rigo have taken her to the track with him?

And why should she care? It was time to stop daydreaming and start making plans.

An open ticket home was the best thing, Katie decided, and then the moment this business was concluded she could fly home. Rigo Ruggiero might have consigned her to the pigeon-hole marked miscellaneous, along with all the other women who, for reasons of age, or inferior looks, had failed to meet his exacting standards, but even in her dreams she didn't want to spend any more time than she had to with a man so self-absorbed he'd put a drive around a racetrack ahead of the reading of his stepbrother's will.

Which naturally accounted for her heart trying to beat its way out of her chest. Who was she trying to fool? Katie wondered as the phone rang again. She looked across the room. Where were the snooty staff she'd had to get past at his office? Had he sacked them all? Surely a man like Rigo Ruggiero had a PA who could sort out his appointments and answer his phone? But if he had, there was no sign of him or her.

The phone continued to peal until finally she gave in and picked it up. *'Pronto?'*

'Signorina Bannister?'

No. A Hollywood film star, she felt like telling Rigo Ruggiero at that moment. *'Sì,'* she said instead, forcing an agreeable note into her voice.

'I feel bad.'

Oh, no! She pulled a face and somehow managed to sound pleasantly surprised at the same time. 'Oh…?'

'You should make the most of your time in Rome.'

Really? 'But I'll be leaving shortly,' she pointed out, waiting in vain for the surge of relief those words should bring.

'Have you booked another flight yet?'

Ah, so he couldn't wait to get rid of her. 'I was about to—'

'Well, don't. Not until I get back.'

Commands now? Did she work for him? 'But, Signor Ruggiero, I'm not equipped to stay over—'

'Not equipped? What's your problem? Buy whatever you need and charge it to me.'

What? 'I couldn't possibly!' Katie exclaimed with affront—though she did allow her imagination a five-second trolley dash through Rome's most expensive store with Rigo Ruggiero's credit card clutched tightly in her hand. 'I don't have a hotel.'

'A hotel? Don't be ridiculous. I have seven bedrooms.'

Now she really was too shocked to speak.

'Signorina Bannister? Are you still there?'

'Yes,' Katie managed hoarsely.

'Don't forget we still have business to conclude, you and I. I expect you there on my return. How hard can it be?' he added in a more soothing tone. 'My penthouse has a roof garden accessed through the staircase in the hallway, as well as an outdoor pool with the finest views over Rome you'll ever see. There's a resident chef on call at the press of a button, and an entertainment centre with a gym attached to the spa. Use the place like your own. And don't forget—be there when I return. Oh, and in the meantime—answer any incoming calls and make a note of them, would you?'

Katie was still choking out words of protest when Rigo cut the line.

CHAPTER FOUR

THE telephone receiver was in serious danger of connecting with the plate-glass window. And she thought she knew everything there was to know about controlling feelings? Did Rigo seriously expect her to remain on standby at his command? He must think everyone lived the same racy billionaire lifestyle he did. Some people had work to do.

Yes…like answering his phone, Katie concluded as it rang again. Glaring at the receiver, she walked over to the cradle, pressed a few buttons and switched it to record. Now she could take stock. She could fret all she liked, but she *was* going to miss her plane, meaning she *would* have to stay another night in Rome. But not here. Not with Rigo Ruggiero. Not in a million years.

She didn't want to panic anyone, so her first call must be to the office. She would give them a carefully edited version of events. That done, she would book into a reasonably priced hotel—if she could find such a thing in Rome. Then she must do some shopping—toiletries and nightclothes, if nothing else. And if Rigo Ruggiero wanted to hear the reading of his stepbrother's will and receive the package she had brought with her, he could damn well come and find her.

* * *

Katie booked into a respectable hotel, taking a compact room on the fourth floor with a view of the air-conditioning units. But she had everything she needed: a clean bed and a functioning bathroom, as well as a desk, an easy chair and a television. Best of all, there were quiet spaces in the lobby where she could meet up with Rigo when he found her. She was confident he would find her; that was what men like him were good at.

And now what?

She had paced the three strides by six it took to mark out the floor of her room, and was left facing the fact that she was alone in the raciest and most fashionable city on earth...a city she longed to explore. So, she could sit here in her hotel room, or be really adventurous and sit in the lobby.

She could always watch TV...

In Rome?

What about her shopping? There had to be a chain store close to the hotel.

Katie asked the concierge, who directed her to the Via del Corso, which he said was one of the busiest shopping streets in town. It certainly was, she discovered, though it bore no resemblance to any shopping street back home. It was so glamorous and buzzy she just stood and stared when she found it, until people jostled her and she was forced to move along.

So now what? Now she was a tourist, and she was enjoying every minute of it. Work seemed a million miles away...

After a moment's hesitation, she took a deep breath and plunged right in.

To Katie's surprise she loved every moment of the chaotic bustle, and hearing the lyrical Italian language being spoken all around her more than made up for the mayhem of the crowded streets. She had learned to love Italian at the music conservatoire she had attended, in what seemed to her like another lifetime now. Determined to brush all melancholy thoughts away, she told herself that she would never get another opportunity like this and should be savouring every moment so she could store away the memories to share with the girls in the office.

She began with some serious window shopping, which involved frantically trying to work out how many fantasy purchases she could fit into her fantasy wardrobe, not to mention how much fantasy designer luggage would be required to transport all these fantasy purchases home. But there was one adventure she could afford, Katie realised as she walked along, and that was drinking coffee at a pavement café like a real Roman.

She would be mad not to enjoy the shade of late afternoon, Katie convinced herself, feeling a little nervous as she eyed up a likely café. There were a few free seats, and, with all the new scents and sounds around her and the clear blue sky like an umbrella overhead, the temptation to linger and soak it all in was irresistible.

If she didn't do it now she never would. Everyone had their shoulders thrown back in the warmth of the sun, and were talking loudly—as much with gestures as with their voices. This way of life intrigued her. It was so different from seeing people with their backs hunched against an icy wind and she wanted to be part of it, even if it was only for an afternoon. She wanted to let her hair down and be as uninhibited as all the other girls her age, who looked so fashionable and sassy in their street clothes.

Let her hair down? Yes. She might even unbutton her jacket, Katie decided in a wry moment of abandon. Spotting an empty table in a prime position, she targeted it. Why not? Shouldn't she make the most of this short trip and live a little while she had the chance?

The handsome, dark-eyed waiter who brought Katie the menu was quite a flirt. He repeated the old cliché that while she was in Rome she must do as the Romans did—though

he look in his eyes suggested that might be a step too far
or her. When her cheeks pinked up he pursued a different
ine, suggesting *gelato alla vaniglia* as an alternative—
naking vanilla ice cream sound like the most decadent
ood on earth. He advised that this should be accompanied
y a strong black coffee and some iced water to help the
weetness down.

Katie thanked him in Italian. *'Ringrazie molto, signore.'*

'Ah, you speak Italian…!' Elaborate gestures accompa-
ied this exclamation, and then he continued to stare at her
/ith deep pools of longing in his puppy-dog eyes. 'Are you
uite sure that's *all* I can help you with, *signorina*?' he
nurmured passionately.

'Quite sure, thank you.'

Katie smiled. She knew the waiter was only joking but,
ooking around, she had gathered that was the Roman way—
very man was duty-bound to flirt. 'However,' she said, decid-
ng to play the waiter at his own game, 'there is one thing…'

'Sì…?' Hope revived, the man dipped lower.

'May I have my coffee now, please?'

'Certamente, signorina,' he said, affecting disappointment,
ut as he left he gave Katie a wink as if to say he'd recognised
fellow tease.

She was really beginning to enjoy herself, Katie realised,
yes sparkling with fun as the waiter walked away. She hadn't
irted with a man since before the accident and then never
eriously. In fact, this was the most excitement she'd ever had.
:ome was proving to be everything it was reputed to be—
nagical, romantic, awe-inspiring…a city of adventure, and it
ad unleashed something in her.

Let's just hope it wasn't her reckless, inner self, Katie
iused, because that fantasy Katie was far safer locked away.
'hinking of Rigo—which she was doing rather a lot lately—

it wouldn't be wise to push the boundaries too far on this fir
attempt to live her dream.

A shadow fell over her table. A ripple of awareness ra
down her spine.

No.

It couldn't be—

'Signorina Bannister.'

'Rigo!' Lurching to her feet, she quickly sat down agaii
Why should she feel so guilty? But she did. 'You're the la
person I expected to see—'

'Clearly.'

Tipping designer shades down his nose, he shot a glanc
at the waiter. Had he heard something of their conversatior
Well, if he had he'd got the wrong idea. Rigo's hackles wer
so far up he was practically snarling. 'So, this is what you g
up to while I'm away?' he demanded when the waiter disap
peared inside the café.

'Did you enjoy your drive around the track?' she countere
pleasantly.

'I thought I asked you to wait for me at the penthouse?'

'I didn't know how long you would be—'

'I also thought you had a plane to catch,' he interrupte
'You were in a tearing hurry to leave, as I remember—'

'But how can I before I've read the will? And I missed n
plane.' She resisted the temptation to add, thanks to yo
Leaning on her hand, she stared up and from somewhe
found the courage to hold his stare.

Rigo visibly bridled again as the waiter returned with he
coffee. What was the poor waiter supposed to do? She
ordered coffee and he was perfectly within his rights t
bring it. And how dared Rigo question her actions when h
had left her on the flimsiest of pretexts and for an unspec
fied length of time?

But as they still had business to complete her reasonab

self conceded that it might be better to build bridges. 'Would you like to join me?' She pointed to an empty chair.

Rigo pulled out two chairs. 'As you can see, I am not alone...'

Now she noticed his companion was the beautiful young blonde in the magazine. The girl had been shopping and was making her way towards them, weighed down by countless carrier bags. The café was obviously a prearranged meeting place.

Every man turned to watch as the young girl threaded her way through the tables. Katie couldn't blame them, the girl was gorgeous—especially when she lifted the carrier bags on high to avoid hitting anyone with them, revealing even more perfectly toned thigh.

Composing her face, Katie determined to love this young woman for the short time she would have to know her—if only so as not to appear small-minded and deadly jealous, though this resolution took a nosedive when the girl draped herself over Rigo.

'Rigo, il mio amore,' she pouted, tugging at his resistant arm, 'sì sara lunga?'

Having asked whether he would be much longer, she turned her luminous stare on Katie.

Katie smiled, or tried her very hardest to.

After taking full inventory of Katie, Rigo's companion appeared satisfied and risked a sultry smile.

No doubt having concluded I'm no threat, Katie reasoned.

'Antonia,' Rigo protested in a weary voice, 'please try to remember that Signorina Bannister is here in Rome on business.'

Rigo was defending her? She had gone up in the world, Katie thought wryly, trying not to mind when Rigo settled his young companion into the chair next to her own.

'Don't worry, I know when I'm not wanted,' Antonia responded sulkily, refusing to sit down now she had deposited her bags. 'I don't want to be here while you're talking business—'

'Oh, please, don't go on account of me…' Katie seized the opportunity to stand up. 'I was just going anyway—'

'No, you weren't,' Rigo argued. 'You've barely started your coffee.'

Katie's instinctive reaction was to look down at Rigo's hand on her arm. Could he feel her trembling beneath his touch?

'And you sit down too,' he instructed Antonia, lifting his hand away from Katie. 'What's wrong with you both?'

Where to begin? Katie thought, feeling like the poor relation. But Rigo had made it impossible for her to leave without appearing rude, and so reluctantly she sat down again.

Only Rigo appeared relaxed as silence stretched between them. With Antonia sulking and Rigo paying neither of them much attention, this was uncomfortable. 'So…you found me?' Katie mumbled self-consciously. She wasn't the best conversationalist at the best of times—and this was hardly that. As Rigo turned to her she was vaguely aware that the waiter was serving more coffee, as well as a soda and a piece of delicious ice-cream cake known as *semifredo* for Antonia.

'Found you?' Rigo's sexy lips pressed down. 'It appears so,' he agreed, lowering a fringe of jet-black lashes over his emerald eyes. 'I guess it must be fate.'

His direct stare made her hand shake and she quickly replaced her coffee-cup in the saucer before she spilled it.

'Of course,' he added, 'if you will choose to walk down the most popular shopping street in Rome…'

His wry look plus Antonia's raspberry and vanilla scent was a lethal combination, Katie realised, finding her gaze drawn to his sexy mouth. 'Er—yes…'

'And here was I, thinking you were back at the penthouse answering my calls—' his lips pressed down '—while all the time you were out shopping.'

By now her cheeks must be luminous crimson, Katie realised, glancing at Antonia, who, having decided to stay, was wolfing down cake as if calories never stuck to her thighs. 'I awarded myself a break—'

'I applaud your initiative, Signorina Bannister.'

A bone-melting stare over the rim of his coffee-cup accompanied this assurance.

Play with fire and you are likely to get burned, Katie reminded herself, managing to slop her own coffee over the table.

She reached for a wad of paper napkins, but Signor Ruggiero got there first.

'Allow me,' he insisted. 'Tell me, Signorina Bannister,' he said, angling his stubble-shaded chin to slant a stare directly into her eyes, 'should I want to employ you, do you think I could trust you to resist the lure of shopping in Rome?'

Was he serious? Did he think she could endure this level of tension every day? '*If* you wanted to employ me, Signor Ruggiero, I should have to warn you, I'm not free—'

'Rigo,' he reminded her. 'Ah, well,' he murmured, lips pressing down in mock-regret, 'I shall just have to find a way to live with the disappointment.' He glanced at his watch. 'We should be getting back to finish our business. What have you done about your flight?'

'I've bought an open ticket.'

'Ah, good,' he said, relaxing back. 'In that case we're in no hurry, and you have no excuse not to join me and Antonia for dinner tonight.'

Dinner? Tonight? With Antonia and Rigo? It would take too long to list all her objections. To give herself time to come up with a watertight excuse, she smiled as she pretended to consider the offer. While she was doing that, and with exquisitely bad timing, the same testosterone-fuelled waiter placed an enormous dish of ice cream in front of her.

'Or perhaps you would prefer to eat something less wholesome tonight?' Rigo challenged, flashing a vicious stare on the hapless man. 'Ice cream, for instance?'

This was ridiculous, Katie concluded. Men were ridiculous. The waiter was still pulling those funny faces at her, while Rigo was taking the man's interest in her for real. And now both men were glaring at each other.

Because of her?

How preposterous!

CHAPTER FIVE

THIS could only happen in Rome, Katie concluded. She knew the waiter would run a mile if she so much as showed the slightest interest in him. As far as Rigo was concerned, it was slightly different. He was the leader of the pack and brooked no competition, whether false or genuine. No one looked at a woman when Rigo Ruggiero was with her; that was Rigo's law. But he had to understand she wasn't his possession. She was an independent woman of independent means—even if those means were somewhat slim compared to his—and she was trying to enjoy her short time in Rome...or she had been up to a few minutes ago. 'Thank you for the offer of dinner,' she said, standing up, 'but I have decided to have a lazy evening by myself at the hotel—'

'The Russie?' Rigo frowned as he mentioned arguably the most exclusive hotel in Rome and probably the only one that registered on his radar.

Katie had to curb her smile when she mentioned the name of the hotel where she was actually staying. 'I can assure you, it's perfectly respectable,' she said, seeing Rigo's and Antonia's reaction to the name.

'I have no doubt,' Rigo said, looking less than convinced.

When Antonia yawned and said she might as well go home f Rigo was going to ignore her Katie seized the opportunity to suggest they reschedule their meeting for the following morning at nine. There was still plenty of sightseeing she wanted to do. 'If nine isn't too early for you?' She tried very hard not to look at Antonia.

'Nine o'clock is perfect for me,' Rigo assured her, 'but at my penthouse, not your hotel.'

As he stared at her she found the way he had seized back control arousing. But as she had never experienced this sort of power play before...

Slipping on the designer shades, he stood up so that now he was towering over her. 'And this time you shall have my undivided attention.'

Why did that sound like such a threat?

It took her entirely by surprise when he brought her hand to his lips and kissed the back of it. The touch of those warm, firm lips was an incendiary device sending streams of sensation to invade her body and blank her mind.

'Before you go, Signorina Bannister—'

She snatched her hand away. 'Yes?' She tried prim. She tried haughty. And failed miserably with both. Haughty was so foreign to her and, with those wicked eyes staring deep into her own eyes, how on earth was she supposed to fake prim?

'This is most remiss of me,' Rigo said, turning to Antonia and indicating that she should stand up too.

'What is?' Katie tensed, immediately on guard.

'I should have introduced you two to each other—'

'Which I made impossible,' Antonia cut across him to Katie's surprise, 'because I had to guzzle that delicious cake before I did another thing.'

Cake she could understand, but introductions?

'Indeed,' Rigo agreed patiently, brushing a strand of errant blonde hair out of Antonia's eyes. 'Signorina Bannister, I would like to introduce you to my spoiled little sister, Antonia...'

Losing her pout, the girl bounded round the table to give

Katie a hug. 'Welcome to Rome, Signorina Bannister.' And then she found her pout again. 'Rigo never lets me meet anyone interesting.'

Interesting? Katie was so shocked she remained unresponsive for a moment. Well, this was something to report back to the girls in the office, as was the hug, and the kiss on both cheeks from Antonia. Having hugged the young girl back, she thought this had to be the perfect example of the attraction of opposites. Katie couldn't imagine there were many quiet, country secretaries in the world Antonia inhabited, and there certainly weren't any vivacious little pop-star lookalikes in hers.

Now that the barrier of believing Antonia was Rigo's girlfriend had been removed, Katie was surprised to find that conversation between them flowed easily and Antonia soon persuaded her to sit down again. Being a willowy blonde, Antonia didn't look a bit like her tough, dark-haired brother, which meant she must be the child born when Rigo's father had married Carlo's mother. He had no trouble with this relationship, so why did he hate his stepbrother? She really should pay more attention to the editorial in gossip magazines.

'So, do you really have everything you need?' Antonia prompted, giving Katie a meaningful look. 'Now that my wicked brother has kept you here in Rome, you must need to go shopping. It never occurs to you, Rigo,' she added, turning to him, 'that other people don't have a home in every city.' And when he shrugged carelessly, Antonia added, 'I bet poor Katie doesn't even have a decent toothbrush with her—'

'Well, as it happens,' Katie interrupted wryly, getting the gist of this conversation, 'I do need to do some shopping for…essentials.'

'Lucky for you, then, that you have an expert on hand!' Antonia exclaimed, satisfied that her ruse had worked. 'You'll definitely need toothpaste and a hairbrush, and all sorts of boring stuff…'

Katie was relieved Rigo hadn't seen Antonia's theatrical wink.

'Are you offering to take Katie shopping?' he said, frowning.

'Could you spare your sister?' Katie suggested, thinking what fun it could be.

'Anyone who can keep Antonia entertained for an hour or two…' His voice faded when he noticed Antonia looking at him and Katie thought Antonia's smile had faded too. 'I'd love to go shopping with you,' she said, taking pity on the young girl, at which point Antonia quickly brightened.

'But don't forget—dinner at eight,' Rigo reminded them as the two girls collected up their things.

'Really, I'm perfectly happy eating in my room at the hotel,' Katie assured him, sending an apologetic smile Antonia's way.

'I wouldn't hear of it,' Rigo insisted with a decisive shake of his head. 'Antonia is right. You must allow me to make up for leaving you so abruptly this afternoon—'

'I *must*?' The challenge flew from Katie's blunt mouth before she could stop it, which made Antonia laugh.

'It seems to me, you have met your match, Rigo,' she told her brother in Italian.

Rigo didn't look nearly so pleased and Katie took note of the cold look in his eyes. Fortunately, she had the perfect excuse. 'It's very kind of you, but I don't have anything to wear.'

'Antonia is taking you shopping.'

'Yes, for a toothbrush.'

And now Antonia was looking at her as if she had gone completely mad.

'I really don't need anything special to wear for a night in a my hotel…' Seeing Antonia's disappointment, Katie knew she had to backtrack. 'But I do need a really good toothbrush…'

'And I know every toothbrush shop in Rome,' Antonia assured her, smiling again now she had got her shopping companion back onto the right track.

It was easy to see why Antonia was spoiled, Katie con

cluded. Antonia had her brother's charm, only with Antonia that charm didn't have an off switch. But there was another look in Antonia's eyes—a defensive look, almost as if the young girl was used to being let down.

'And if we should see some lovely dresses on the way?' Antonia pressed, glancing anxiously at her brother.

Katie tensed. Shopping for clothes was an absolute no. What if Antonia saw her scars? What if, in her enthusiasm, Antonia burst into the changing room and screamed? She couldn't do that to such a vulnerable young girl. She couldn't risk it. She had to renege on her promise, even with Antonia smiling hopefully at her.

She would have to tread very carefully here, Katie realised with concern.

She was barely given time to worry before Rigo offered her a way out. 'Buy something nice for both of you,' he said, glancing at Katie as he pressed a pile of money into Antonia's hand.

'Oh, no.' Katie held up her hands. This was something she drew the line at. 'I couldn't possibly accept your money—'

'But I can,' Antonia said, quickly securing the wad in her super-sized handbag.

'Please,' Rigo insisted. 'It's the very least I can do after treating you so badly, Signorina Bannister—'

'The very least,' Antonia assured him with a frown.

'So…dinner at eight?' he said, turning to Katie. 'Don't forget—I'll pick you up at your hotel.'

This was a man to whom no one had ever dared to say no, Katie concluded. 'I'll be eating in my room tonight,' she reminded him pleasantly.

'After you go shopping with me,' Antonia insisted.

'Of course,' Katie reassured Antonia with a smile. She was beginning to feel like the bland filling in a particularly glamorous sandwich. 'I can't wait to go shopping…for a really good toothbrush,' she added for Rigo's benefit, 'and I look forward to concluding our business tomorrow morning,' she finished with absolute honesty. How much more of this high-octane challenge could she take? To make the point that she wasn't the type to take advantage, as the waiter threaded nimbly past she picked up their bill from his tray.

Which Rigo stole from her hand with a warning glance.

The shopping trip with Antonia exceeded Katie's wildest expectations.

Did it come any wilder? She had no idea how to rein in Antonia's enthusiasm—this was shopping on a heroic scale. Just as she had anticipated, Antonia ignored her insistence that Katie only needed a toothbrush and, as everything in the shops was so stylishly arranged...

But Katie knew she'd reached her boundary when Antonia called her over to look in one particular window. Katie had never seen so many exclusive boutiques in one place and had been lagging behind. The specialist shops they were browsing now sold everything under the sun and more besides—things that should only come out at night, like garments of a frilly nature, for example...

Katie stood awestruck, taking in the breathtaking display. Cobweb-fine lace and slinky satin vied with cotton so delicate you could see through it—and many of the items were trimmed with eye-catching diamanté and pearl. 'Oh, no, I couldn't,' she said when Antonia tried to persuade her to go with her into the shop. 'You go in if you want to,' Katie said, hanging back.

'Not without you,' Antonia insisted, taking hold of Katie's arm. And before Katie knew what was happening Antonia had marched her into the shop, announcing, 'It's time you spoiled yourself.'

Antonia immediately summoned assistants over to help

them. 'Not with Rigo's money,' Katie said, determined to resist Antonia's enthusiasm.

'But you've got your own money, haven't you?'

How to say, yes, but I need it for bills? Though she could do with some pyjamas for tonight, Katie conceded, mouth agape as she stared around. Did people wear these things?

'Well, that's a start,' Antonia approved when Katie suggested that perhaps pyjama trousers and a vest to sleep in that night might be a good idea.

What the assistants brought them was the furthest thing from Katie's mind, but as she handled the delicate garments her longing for them grew. They were in such glorious colours—turquoise, cerise, lemon and lavender trimmed with baby-pink. It went without saying that she would never find anything like this at home.

Did she have to wear winceyette all the time? Katie wondered, staring at her plain face in the mirror. As no one else was going to see the satin shorts and revealing strappy top she liked, surely it wouldn't hurt to buy a set...or two?

Giving herself the excuse she wouldn't risk offending Antonia, she asked the assistant to wrap them up.

'And what about these?' Antonia cut in, pointing out some racy underwear.

'Oh, no...' Shaking her head, Katie blushed furiously, knowing she would never have the opportunity to wear it. She had only seen underwear like that in magazines before.

'You can't wear white cotton all your life,' Antonia observed, staring frankly into Katie's eyes.

'How do you...' Katie's words froze on her lips. Was she that obvious?

'They are expensive,' Antonia continued thoughtfully as she studied the set, 'so you really should try them on before you buy them.'

Alarm bells rang in Katie's head. She had pushed all her

hang-ups to the back of her mind, she realised as Antonia waited for her to do the obvious and ask to use the changing room. 'No,' she said firmly, knowing she had to get out of this somehow. She'd say she'd changed her mind. 'There's no need...'

'Oh, well, if you're sure,' Antonia said, completely mis-understanding her. 'We'll take these too, please—'

Katie didn't speak up quickly enough and as she watched Antonia handing the racy garments to the assistant they were being wrapped up before she knew it.

She could have stopped this at any time, Katie admitted to herself, but the bare truth was, she didn't want to stop it. She wanted to take the underwear back to her hotel where she could try it on with no one seeing her scars, and pretend.

To make matters worse, the assistant, having secured Katie's purchases in fuchsia-pink tissue paper, was lowering them reverently into a pale pink carrier bag decorated with the logo of a naked woman seated in a champagne glass. 'Very subtle,' Katie commented wryly as the two girls left the shop. She loved the bag, but part of her wished the logo didn't have to be on both sides.

Linking arms with her, Antonia gave Katie a squeeze. 'We're going to buy a few more things for you, and then I'm under strict instructions from Rigo to put you in a taxi back to your hotel— Oh, look,' she broke off excitedly, 'there he is now...'

Katie gasped to see Rigo coming out of a menswear shop across the street. He was just pushing his sunglasses back on his nose and spotted them right away. He came over. How could she hide the carrier bag?

He stood in front of them, making every part of her sing with awareness. But worst of all he was staring at the brazen proof that her latest purchase had not been a toothbrush.

'I trust you girls found everything you needed in the shops?' he said, straight-faced.

She could read the subtext and blushed violently. 'Yes,

thank you,' she said, raising her head to meet his gaze. 'And, as you can see, I'm carrying some of Antonia's bags for her.'

Rigo's amused stare called her a liar.

CHAPTER SIX

WHEN Rigo left them Katie and Antonia continued their shopping, but there was a *frisson* of understanding between them now. Neither girl commented on the change Rigo had made to their day, but they were aware of how profoundly he affected them, each in their own way. It brought them closer, though it took a little time when he'd gone to recapture the rhythm of easy friendship they had established. When they did Katie almost forgot to buy her toothbrush.

The fun of being with someone as non-judgemental and as warm as Antonia was so unexpected Katie threw herself into the expedition with enthusiasm, and by the time she returned to her small hotel room there were lots more packages. Antonia had shown Katie the best shopping in Rome—small boutiques hidden in side-streets around the Piazza Novona and Campo di Fiori, and other places that were well off the regular tourist beat, and when they both finally admitted defeat, they had more coffee and ice cream at a café on Via Acaia, where Katie thought the lemon cream or *crema al limone* and the scrunchy chocolate *stracciatella* were to die for. She insisted before they parted on buying Antonia a special little gift to say thank you to Rigo's sister for being so kind to her.

It was obvious Antonia adored her brother. To hear Antonia

talk you would think Rigo was a saint—but, as Antonia appeared to be the chief recipient of Rigo's generosity, Antonia could hardly be called impartial.

Katie smiled, remembering Antonia's pleasure when Katie bought her a small aqua leather-backed journal. To prove the point, Antonia had started scribbling in it right away, and when she secured the small gilt lock she had exclaimed, 'Thank you so much for today, Katie…'

And when it was she who had everything to thank Antonia for…

Katie's heart went out to the teenager, who on the face of it appeared to have everything a girl of Antonia's age could possibly want, but she suspected all Antonia really wanted was a little of her brother's time.

Time. That was what so many rich and successful people lacked, Katie mused, moving the faded curtain back to stare out of the window. They had none to spare when it came to those closest to them.

'We are friends, aren't we?' Antonia had demanded fiercely when they parted. Whatever she thought of Antonia's brother Katie had put to one side, promising Antonia they would be friends for ever.

After a rocky start it had been a good day, Katie reflected, turning back to look at her purchases spread out on the bed. Now her smile was one of disbelief. What on earth had possessed her? Antonia was the simple answer. Thanks to Rigo's sister, it was goodbye brown, hello colour! And in the open-air market Katie had spotted a silk dress swinging on its hanger in the breeze. In a bright gypsy-rose print, it had long sleeves and a short, flirty skirt, and there was a sexy cut-out panel at the midriff—one of the few places where she could afford to show some skin. With the option of trying it on taken away from her, she hadn't been able to resist. She had added a couple of tops and a shawl to her haul, as well as a pair of jeans—something she had never owned before.

'And trainers,' Antonia had insisted, determined that Katie should update her image. 'For someone who is only twenty-five, you dress too old,' she had commented with all the blunt assurance of a teenager.

And that was me told, Katie reflected, smiling as she left the bedroom to enter her small *ensuite* bathroom. She had treated herself to some foam bath too. It was a cheap way to turn even the most basic of bathrooms into a better place. And now there was nothing more for her to do but soak and dream until she felt like ringing downstairs for Room Service.

Bliss.

Now he remembered why it was so long since he had treated Antonia to dinner. Nothing was quite right for his teenage sister. Their table could have been better—it was too near the door. Their fellow diners were too stuffy—meaning most of them were over twenty-five and had brushed their hair before coming out. She sniffed everything that arrived at their table with suspicion as if three Michelin stars was no guarantee at all, and to top it off she ordered chips with ketchup on the side, leaving everything else on her plate.

But his worst crime, apparently, was *abandoning* Katie in Rome on her first night in the eternal city.

'Katie?'

'Signorina Bannister insisted I call her Katie,' his sister informed him smugly as he raised a brow.

'May I remind you that Signorina Bannister is on a business trip and will shortly be returning home? She was invited to join us tonight, but she refused. And that's an end of it, Antonia.'

And might well have been, had he not felt his conscience prick.

His sister lost no time in turning that scratch into an open wound. 'Do you know where she's staying?' Antonia demanded with her customary dramatic emphasis. '*How* can you leave Katie in a place like that? Can you *imagine* what the restaurant is *like*?'

Yes, he could, unfortunately.

And so the rant went on until he couldn't face another mouthful. Laying down his cutlery, he demanded, 'What do you suggest I do, Antonia?'

Antonia appeared to be studying the menu, and he imagined she was choosing a pudding until she exclaimed, 'A picnic!'

Before he could stop her she called a waiter over.

'Take it to Katie—deliver it,' she begged him, clutching his wrist in her excitement as the waiter hurried away with the order.

'Don't be so ridiculous—'

'You don't even have to see her—'

'I have no time for this nonsense, Antonia,' he snapped impatiently, shaking her off.

'You never have time,' she flared. 'Katie gave me a whole afternoon of her time, which is more than you ever do.' Her voice was rising and people were staring at the small drama as it unfolded. 'Why can't you do something different, for once?'

'I do something different every day, Antonia. It's called business. It's what keeps you in the style to which you're accustomed.'

Thrusting back her chair, his sister took her performance to its ultimate conclusion: The Dramatic Exit. 'Well, if you won't take the picnic to Katie, I will,' she declared, storming off.

They had the attention of the whole restaurant now. As Antonia stalked away he stood up, politely murmuring an apology to those people closest to him. They should be glad of the free entertainment, he concluded as strangers exchanged knowing looks.

He caught up with Antonia at the door. 'Stop this, Antonia. You're drawing attention to yourself—'

'Oh, no!' she gasped theatrically, clutching her chest.

'I will not allow you to walk the streets of Rome alone at night—'

'That's why you must take the picnic to Katie.'

The waiter chose this moment to bring out the hamper—to a touching soundtrack of Antonia's inconsolable sobs. 'Have you no shame?' Rigo murmured, realising this was a ploy Antonia had contrived to get her own way.

'None,' his sister whispered back triumphantly.

Pressing money into the man's hand, he thanked him for his trouble. Then he escorted Antonia outside. Bringing out a handkerchief, he mopped her eyes. 'Stop crying immediately,' he insisted. 'Acting or not, you know I cannot bear to see you cry. If you're so concerned about Signorina Bannister's diet, I *will* deliver this hamper. But not before I see you safely home.'

He thought his voice had been quite stern, but he could have sworn there was a smile on Antonia's face as he helped her into the car.

Katie had put on her new dress, and after examining it from every angle in the full-length mirror had reassured herself that everything she might want to hide was hidden. It was the perfect dress for the perfect night out in Rome. Not that she was going anywhere, but there was no limit to her dream. In fact the dream was so real she had put her shawl and bag on the bed, as if all she had to do was snatch them up last minute before leaving the room.

In reality her skin prickled with apprehension just at the thought. She might be wearing her new dress, but she was frightened to leave the room wearing it.

She performed an experimental twirl, loving the way the silk felt against her skin. There wasn't room for much of a twirl, because the hotel room was very small. She had no complaints—it was functional and clean, which was all she needed.

But Rome was waiting for her outside—and tomorrow she was going home…

Moving back to the window, she stood a little to one side, staring out at the busy street scene far below. There was an open-topped tour bus that stopped right outside the hotel, and she could see people chatting to each other as they waited to board. Across the road was a family-oriented pizzeria with a neon sign. That looked fun too. Perhaps they would have room for one later…

Stop, Katie told herself firmly, pressing back against the wall. It was one thing buying into the pretence of going out and something else when she started to believe it might happen. But pretending had been fun. She had even styled her hair a number of different ways—up and down—but she had forgotten how thick and glossy even boring brown hair could be when it was washed, conditioned and blown dry with more than her usual care and even for a fantasy night out she wouldn't want to look too obvious. Her everyday style was safest, she had concluded. Over the years she had perfected the technique of brushing her hair straight back before twisting it tightly and securing it with a single tortoiseshell pin.

But she wouldn't change a thing about the dress, Katie mused, smoothing her palms over the cool silk. She eased her neck, imagining Rigo at her side…or perhaps behind her with his hands resting on her shoulders. She would lean against him…relax against him, until he dipped his head and kissed her neck as he murmured that he loved her…

She held the image in her heart for a moment, before opening her eyes and facing reality. Rigo was eating dinner with Antonia, after which he would go home to bed.

Antonia had so much to give, Katie reflected, but her brother had no time to take anything from anyone, because Rigo was too busy driving forward…

Rigo…

Leaning back against the wall again, she closed her eyes. He would look like a god tonight. She imagined him wearing a dark tailored suit with crisp white shirt and discreet gold cuff-links. The elegant look would show off his tan, his rugged strength and the power of his commanding personality. His hair would be freshly washed with thick, inky black waves lapping his brow and his cheekbones. He had the thickest, strongest hair she had ever seen, and though Rigo's grooming would be impeccable he would still carry that air of danger that made him irresistible, and like a magnet he would draw the gaze of every person in the room.

And she still wasn't going out, Katie told herself bluntly, opening her eyes as she pulled away from the wall. And whichever way she looked at it dreams could never compete with the reality of Rigo.

No, but dreams were safe, Katie's sensible self reminded her. With dreams there were no complications, no embarrassing moments, no…

Nothing.

But…

The mini-bar was full of chocolate, so it wasn't all bad.

He'd taken Antonia home and then gone back to the penthouse to change into jeans and a casual shirt before setting off again to Katie Bannister's hotel. He felt tense. Wishing-he-didn't-have-to-do-this tense? Expectant tense? He couldn't tell. He only knew they hadn't got off to the best of starts and Katie Bannister was alone in Rome. He wanted her to relax. He wanted to relax.

No, he didn't, Rigo conceded as he shouldered open the door of the small, dingy hotel. Relaxing was the last thing on his mind. He didn't have anything half so worthy in mind for Katie Bannister. His hunting instincts had brought him here. He couldn't get her out of his head, the contradictions—the primness, weighed against the logo on a shopping bag from one of the sexiest lingerie stores in Rome. Her excuse that it belonged to Antonia was a lie. He'd driven Antonia home and unless his little sister had eaten the bag she certainly didn't have it with her. Since then his imagination had dressed Signorina Bannister in lace and silk—which, bearing in mind he'd only seen her in an ugly brown suit before, had been quite a startling revelation.

He approached the reception desk with his package and made his request.

'*Mi dispiace*, I'm sorry, Signor Ruggiero, but there is no reply from Signorina Bannister's room.' The man behind the desk shrugged as he replaced the telephone receiver.

He should have known he would be recognised. It couldn't be helped. 'Could Signorina Bannister be in your restaurant?' He stared across into an uninviting and markedly empty dining room.

'We have no reservations tonight, Signor Ruggiero.'

No surprise there. 'Her room number?'

The man barely paused a beat—something to do with the money he had just pressed into his hand, no doubt, before telling him, 'Room one hundred and ten, Signor Ruggiero.'

There was no answer when he knocked on the door. He used the house phone to ring the hotel kitchen and ask them to put Antonia's picnic in their cold room. Someone would be up right away to collect it, he was told. He waited until the porter arrived, and then he returned to room one hundred and ten. Where would Katie Bannister go this time of night?

He knocked and waited. He heard sounds from the room and knocked again.

She answered the door cautiously, leaving the security lever in place.

'How many times do I have to tell you I don't bite?'

'Rigo?' Her voice rose at least an octave when she gasped his name.

'Unless I have a double…' He leaned back against the wall. The corridor was narrow and they were agreeably close. Signorina Prim's sexy voice had done it again, he registered, enjoying the sensation.

'What do you want?' she whispered nervously through the gap.

Admittedly this wasn't the type of reception he had anticipated, or was used to, but then Katie Bannister wasn't his usual type of date. 'We had a dinner engagement, if you remember?'

'I told you I'd be eating dinner in my room.'

And he had chosen to ignore that. 'You haven't eaten yet?' he said with surprise. 'It's nine o' clock.' As if anyone in Rome ate before nine.

'I didn't say I haven't eaten.' She opened the door a little wider and bit her lip.

She looked cute. 'You didn't say you have eaten,' he pointed out. 'Open the door, Katie. I can't stand here all night.'

The bar slid back and the door opened, but instead of standing to one side to let him in, she retreated into the shadows at the far end of the room.

CHAPTER SEVEN

'GOOD evening, Signorina Bannister. I trust I find you well?'

'Good evening, Rigo,' she said shyly, remaining pressed back against the wall.

'You look nice.' He closed the door softly behind him. Nice? She looked beautiful, which raised a number of questions. But taking things at face value to begin with, he knew her taste in lingerie and had already dallied with erotic images, but seeing this new, softer side had unexpectedly brought out the best in him. Until his suspicions raced to the fore. 'I beg your pardon for calling so late.'

She glanced at her wristwatch.

'And it seems you were going out?' After refusing his dinner invitation, was it possible the waiter won her over?

'I wasn't going anywhere.'

Was that a wistful note in her voice? 'But the dress?'

'I was just trying it on.' Raising her chin, she looked at him steadily. 'I bought it today. I don't know what I was thinking—'

'That it suited you?' he suggested.

'Do you really think so?'

In that moment she was like a child, and as pleasure flashed across her face she touched his heart, something that hadn't happened in a long time. 'Yes, I do. You look great.' Fragile, proud and womanly he didn't say. Even her profile with her hair scraped back so tightly was delicately appealing.

'I was going to return it—'

'Don't you dare—I mean, do as you like,' he said casually as she looked at him in surprise. She wasn't the only one to be surprised by the force of his reaction. 'So…you're not going out, but you'd like to?'

'Not really…' She made a little hand gesture. 'I'm fine right here—'

'But a dress like that is meant to be worn by a beautiful woman on a warm evening in Rome.'

She all but said, that rules me out.

'An evening just like this…'

She laughed nervously as he gestured towards the mean little window. 'It's very kind of you, Rigo—'

'I don't do kind. I'm hungry.'

'But you just ate with Antonia—'

'Fiddly food?' He dismissed the gourmet feast he'd enjoyed with an airy gesture. 'And, as you can see—' he ran a hand down his casual shirt and jeans '—I'm off-duty now.'

She risked a laugh.

'I'm thinking pizza—though Antonia sent a picnic for you, if you prefer?'

'I love your sister!' she exclaimed impulsively. 'Only Antonia would think of a picnic.'

He gave her a wry look. He couldn't deny Antonia held the record for delivering the unexpected, and doing it well. 'The hotel has it in their cold room—but I'm thinking rea Roman pizza.'

He could see she was tempted.

'I'd have to get changed.'

'Into what?'

Her warning look told him not to make light of this becaus she hadn't made up her mind yet.

'You'd have to leave the room while I get changed.'

'I'm not going anywhere. And you're not getting changed. You're fine as you are. Here, grab this.' Snatching up a shawl from the bed, he tossed it to her.

She caught it.

'Now throw it round your shoulders and let's get out of here.'

He gave her no chance to change her mind. Opening the door, he ushered her through.

This wasn't a walk on the wild side—it was absolute lunacy. The moment they left the hotel she felt naked. She never went out in a flimsy summer dress. To do so with Rigo made her feel more vulnerable than ever.

And to think of all the things she could have done to get out of this—she could have played the tiredness card, the headache, the work to finish, the phone call to make, but instead she had fallen under Rigo's spell. It didn't help that he looked like a man from the pages of myth and legend. In casual clothes he was more aggressively virile than she had ever seen him and fitted perfectly into the template of ancient Rome. With his stern features and rugged, fighting form, he could have been a gladiator; the best.

As Rigo eased his pace to accommodate her shorter stride Katie wondered how safe her heart was. As he glanced at her with eyes like back-lit emerald that promised all the danger she could take, she concluded it was her chastity she should be concerned about. Could she trust herself to behave?

Did she want to behave?

If she was ever going to experience lovemaking, wouldn't it be better to do so under the tutelage of an expert?

'I'm not moving too fast for you, am I?'

Her cheeks flushed pink with guilty thoughts. 'Not at all...' Not as fast as my fantasies would have you move.

The dangerous smile creased his cheeks and fired every

nerve in her body. She was transfixed by lips that curved in a firm and knowing smile. He knew how to walk close but not touching. He must know how that made her long to touch him—

And right on cue her scars shouted a stinging hello. They might be covered by the prettiest silk fabric, but they hadn't gone away and were as ugly as ever. And now the doubts crept in. What if Rigo put his arm round her shoulders? What if his hand strayed down her back? What if he pressed those long, lean fingers against her? He couldn't help but feel the ridges. And her final thought? What if he was repulsed by them?

Breathe deeply and stay calm, Katie's sensible self advised. Rigo hadn't made any attempt to touch her and was unlikely to do so. She might be dressed up by her own small-town standards, but she was hardly a femme fatale. This outing was merely a courtesy Signor Rigo Ruggiero was extending to a representative of the legal firm handling his brother's will.

To prove it, they were walking alongside each other like a couple of friends—

Friends?

Friends looked at each other's crotch, did they?

Katie wished her inner voice would shut up and stop acting as her conscience. Rigo's gaze might never stray, but she hadn't perfected the technique of not looking at something so prominently displayed.

What else was he supposed to do with it? her inner voice piped up again.

OK, so he was blessed in every department, but she didn't have to fixate, did she? Hadn't she worked out yet how acute his senses were? Did she want him to know she had a crush?

They had reached a crossing and he stared down at her. 'Are you OK?'

'Perfectly.' But she flinched when he put his hand in the small of her back to steer her across the road.

'Relax.'

Yes, relax. What did she think? That he had X-ray vision now?

'You really are tense…'

She gasped as he caught hold of her hand and quickly concealed it in a cough. Was this supposed to help?

'What are you doing?' he said as she broke free. 'The traffic is dangerous and unpredictable—'

Like Rigo. 'Sorry—I promise to be more careful.'

'I'll make sure of it.' He locked his arm around her shoulder.

For a moment she didn't breathe. Surely he must feel her trembling? And then he walked her straight past the pizza place.

'That's for tourists,' he said as she turned her head.

She had to scurry along to keep up with his easy, loping stride. That wasn't easy on legs that felt like jelly. For the first time in her life she longed for her cheap suit. It might be ugly, but both the fabric and the shape were concealing. 'So where *are* we going?'

'First, we take a bus—'

'A bus?' He really was the master of surprises, she registered silently.

'Unless a tour bus isn't grand enough for you, Signorina Bannister?'

'It's fine by me.' And was what she had wanted to do all along. 'I'm just surprised you take buses…'

'You mean, a man like me?' he said. Rigo's face creased in a smile. 'I know every way there is to get around Rome.' He helped her onto the running board. 'I haven't always travelled by private jet.' He broke off to dig in the pocket of his jeans for some money to pay their fare.

A curtain lifted. She saw him clearly as the youth who had come to Rome with nothing and had made his fortune here. She only realised she was still frowning as she thought about it when Rigo dipped his head to stare her in the eyes. Her heart thundered a warning. 'It's only a bus trip costing a few euros,' he said. 'You can deduct it from your fee, if that makes you feel better?'

Better he misunderstood than read every thought in her head too clearly. 'I'm good—'

'Please allow me to reassure you that I have no intention of compromising your professional duties in any way, Signorina Bannister.'

He made her laugh. His humour was more dangerous than she knew.

And then the self-doubt crept in. Was that what he thought of her? She was all duty and no fun? That equalled dull in any language.

He chivvied her up the stairs. 'The view is better up here.'

He persuaded her to take a seat at the front. She checked her skirt was pulled down as she sat. No wonder Rigo thought her dull. He was easygoing, charming and, even in denim jeans and a fitted casual shirt clinging tenaciously to every hard-wired inch of his impressive torso, he was sex on two strong muscled legs. While she was—

'Dolcezza.'

'What?' He was paying her a compliment. Why couldn't she just accept it?

Maybe because, having sprawled across the seat next to her, Rigo was looking at her in a way that made her cheeks burn.

'I like the new look, Katie; keep it.'

Before she could reprimand him for using her first name he draped an arm around her shoulder and drew her close. 'Though I think you should be tempted to let your hair down.'

The murmured words sent her senses haywire as his warm breath connected with her ear. That must be why it took her a moment to realise what he meant to do, and by then it was too late. As he removed the single tortoiseshell pin from her hair it cascaded around her shoulders.

'Bene,' he said, sitting back.

'My hair ornament, please.' She held out her hand.

'You can have it back later,' he said, putting it in his pocket. 'Now concentrate on the view.'

As he spoke, what might well be his ancestral home hove into view. The Colosseum—the ancient amphitheatre with its pitted archways glowing eerily with honeyed light.

But as Rigo related the history of the building she was gripped. Discovering the man beneath the public face was a non-stop revelation. His depth aroused her to the point where it was no longer possible to concentrate. She had to shift position to ease the ache inside her. She wanted to remain immune to him and soon realised what a pointless exercise that was. What she really wanted was for Rigo to touch her intimately. All this she accepted whilst maintaining a serious conversation about ancient Rome.

CHAPTER EIGHT

EXPANDING her fantasies as the tour bus drove on into the night allowed for Rigo touching her skilfully and persistently, rhythmically and expertly, until she found release. It didn't stop there. They might experiment in the Colosseum—before a concert, maybe. As her gaze slipped to his lips while he talked she indulged in another image—one that stirred her more than most: she was being held down by Rigo while he subjected her to a lengthy feast of pleasure. She wanted sex with him. Which meant it was time to put a stop to such a dangerous fantasy.

Thankfully, Rigo provided the exit she had been looking for, when he thanked her for giving Antonia such a good day.

'It was my pleasure. Your sister is wonderful—and in fairness, it was Antonia who went out of her way to give me a good time.'

'Well, my little sister sees it another way. Come on, we get off here,' he said, standing up.

'But we're not back at the hotel.' She looked in vain for a landmark she recognised.

'Pizza?' Rigo reminded her.

But they seemed to be in the middle of nowhere. Katie frowned.

'I asked the bus driver to drop us here. Come on.' Rigo indicated that she must go ahead of him.

She disembarked onto a dimly lit street. Could this be right? Her skin prickled with apprehension.

'I don't have a clue where I am,' Rigo murmured.

But when she glanced at him in alarm, he smiled.

'You're teasing me—'

'Would I?'

She refused to hold that gaze, and stared instead at the bus as it drove away.

'I haven't always lived in the best part of Rome.'

She couldn't resist the hook and followed him.

'When I left my home in Tuscany and came to Rome I found myself in the Monti—all narrow lanes and steep inclines. It's where craftsmen ply their trade and there was always plenty of casual work for a strong boy from the country.'

By now she was consumed with curiosity. To learn about this other side of Rigo was irresistible.

'Is this our destination?' she said when he stopped walking on the high point of a bridge spanning the River Tiber. As she stared into Rigo's dazzlingly handsome face, waiting for his reply, she got another feeling—he enjoyed showing off his city to someone who wouldn't mock him for how poor he'd been. He still liked these offbeat trails to places that held no appeal for the fashionistas.

He was resting his hands on the stone balustrade, staring out across the river. Her heart picked up pace as he turned to look at her. Suddenly it didn't matter where they were going, and as crazy as it might seem they had reached at least one erotic destination, which was enough for her.

He broke the spell. 'Come on.' Straightening up, he reached for her hand and this time she didn't resist him. She even managed to persuade herself that it made perfect sense for Rigo to take her hand if they had to cross a busy main road. What did she know about Roman traffic? What did anyone

know? Even the Romans didn't know. No one on earth coul
predict the unpredictable.

She shrank against him, glad of his protection as cars an
scooters buzzed around them like angry bees. This contac
with Rigo was the most foreplay she'd ever had. On that shor
journey to safety on the other side tiny darts of pleasure race
up her arm and spread...everywhere.

Rigo led her way up some stone steps that curved steepl
around the outside of an ancient lookout tower. A pair of thes
towers marked either end of the bridge. 'This is the best plac
in Rome to watch the fireworks,' he explained, 'and it's free.

She saw the boy he must have been—a boy who hadn'
wasted time wailing about his fate, but who had squeezed th
last drop of enjoyment out of his new life. And the way he
heart swelled in admiration was a very worrying develop
ment indeed.

At the top of the tower she had to stop to catch her breath
and, resting her arms on the warm stone, she leaned over th
battlements.

'Since when can you fly?' Rigo demanded, pulling her back

Having someone look out for her felt so good and as he
stared down even breathing was difficult. He was clos
enough now for her to feel his body heat warming her.

She turned away. She wasn't sure how to deal with he
feelings or this situation. She was going home tomorrow
They were complete opposites. This was one casual night i
Rigo's life, but her life could be changed for good—

'Open your eyes, Katie, or you'll miss the fireworks.'

There was so much sensation dancing through her vein
she barely registered the first fantastic plumes of sparklin
colour. And then Rigo reached over her shoulder to point ou
some more, and as he did so he brushed her cheek. It made
her turn and now their faces were only millimetres apart. She
looked away, but not quickly enough. A darkly amused stare

was her reward. He must know how strongly she was attracted to him. Did he also know how frustrated she was? Or what agony it was for her to be this close to him? Or that he made her body ache with need and longing?

He pulled back when the fireworks were over, allowing her to breathe freely again. She gulped in air enough to say, 'Thank you for bringing me here.'

'It isn't finished yet.' Spanning her waist with his hands, Rigo turned her to face the river.

There was no way to express her feelings towards what she could see, or what she could sense. Fireworks were falling from the sky, replacing the streamers of moonlight on the river with a dancing veil of fire. And there was fire in her heart.

Leaving the bridge, they walked deeper into the old part of the city. 'Ancient palaces!' Katie exclaimed with pleasure, staring about.

'Once this was a very grand area indeed,' Rigo confirmed, 'and now I have another surprise for you.' As he spoke he opened a street door and a blaze of light and heat burst out.

And good cooking smells, Katie registered, inhaling appreciatively as Rigo held the door open for her. He had brought her to a small, packed pizzeria where the noise of people enjoying themselves was all-enveloping.

'Don't worry,' he said, dipping his head to speak to her when he saw her hesitation, 'you'll be safe with me.'

He had also guessed correctly that she rarely went out, Katie thought wryly. She was glad of Rigo's encouragement.

There was a tiny dance floor on which a number of couples were entwined and a small group of musicians tucked away in a corner. Surrounding this, tables with bright red gingham cloths were lit by dripping candles rammed into old wine bottles.

'Do you like it?' Rigo shouted to her above the noise.

'I love it.' And she loved the feel of his arm around her shoulders.

The party atmosphere was infectious, but she was shy. Without Rigo she would never have ventured into a place like this. But when she took a proper look around and realised that all the other customers were as down-to-earth as she was, she relaxed. This certainly wasn't the type of nightlife she had imagined Rigo would indulge in. And she liked him all the better for it.

'Will you stop trying to tuck your hair behind your ears?' he said as they waited for a seat.

'I'm just not used to it hanging loose—'

'Then you should be. You have lovely hair. Leave it alone,' he insisted. 'You look fine. Ah—' he stepped forward as a portly man dressed in chefs trousers bustled over to them '—I'd like you to meet my friend Gino.'

Katie gathered Gino was the patron.

'Rigo! Brigante!' he exclaimed, clapping the much taller man on the back. 'Why is it I can't get rid of you?'

Katie suspected that both men knew the answer to that, judging from the warmth in their eyes as they stared at each other.

'And who is this?' Gino demanded, turning his shrewd, raisin-black stare Katie's way.

'This is Signorina Bannister…an associate of mine.'

'An associate?' Gino gave Katie an appreciative once-over before shaking hands with her. 'You must think a lot of your associate to bring Signorina Bannister to meet me?' He looked at Rigo questioningly, but Rigo's shrug admitted nothing.

'Signorina Bannister is in need of real Italian pizza before she leaves Rome. Where else would I take her, Gino?'

'Where else indeed?' Gino agreed. 'And for such a beautiful *signorina* I have reserved the best table in the house.'

'But you're full,' Katie observed worriedly. She didn't want to cause anyone any trouble. 'And how could you know we were coming?'

'I don't need to know,' Gino informed her, touching his

finger to his nose. 'I keep my own special table ready at all times for my *speciale* guests…'

Before she could stop him Gino had whisked away her shawl. 'Oh, no!' Katie exclaimed, reaching for it, feeling suddenly naked again.

'You won't need a shawl here,' Gino assured her. 'It's always too hot in my restaurant—'

'But I…'

Feeling exposed and self-conscious beneath Rigo's amused gaze, Katie could only stand and watch helplessly as the burly restaurateur disappeared into the cloakroom with her prized piece of camouflage equipment.

'Don't worry,' Rigo soothed. 'Gino will keep your shawl safe.'

Rigo saw her comfortably settled and then took the seat opposite, while Katie sat demurely, taking stock of her fellow diners. Every other woman around them had stripped down to bare arms and shoulders.

But they all had flawless skin—

'Do you mind if I roll back my sleeves?' Rigo said, misinterpreting her look.

He was halfway through the process and hardly needed her permission. 'Go ahead.' She tried very hard not to stare at his massively powerful forearms and concentrated instead on a formidable steel watch that could probably pinpoint their position in relation to the moon. One thing was sure—Gino was right: it was hot in here. Steaming.

'Ten o'clock.'

'I beg your pardon?' Katie swiftly refocused as Rigo spoke.

'I said it's ten o'clock. I noticed you looking at my watch.'

'I was—'

'Not because you want to go home, I hope?'

Gino saved her further embarrassment, bringing them the pizzas they had ordered. They were delicious. A thin, crispy crust baked just the way she liked it was loaded with succulent vegetables and slicked with chilli oil. Beneath that a yummy layer of zesty tomato sauce was crowned with fat globs of melted cheese. She only realised how hungry she was when she took her first bite—and there was no polite way to eat pizza when you were this hungry.

'Now you see why Gino and I became such good friends,' Rigo said, leaning forward to mop her chin. 'There was always something he needed doing—and I always needed feeding after a hard day of manual labour.'

She could understand how their friendship had been forged. 'You found a mutual need,' she said. And could have bitten off her tongue as Rigo's gaze lingered. 'Indeed,' he agreed, sitting back. 'Napkin?' he suggested.

'Good idea…' Drool was not a good look. She returned her attention determinedly to her food.

'This is only the first course, to whet your appetite.'

'Oh, no. I really couldn't eat another thing…'

'If you lived in Italy you would soon develop a healthy appetite.'

She had no doubt. But was that wise?

Katie sensibly avoided Rigo's gaze, reminding herself she was going home tomorrow.

So? Didn't that mean she should make the most of today?

There was such a festival air in the small bistro Katie was soon tapping her foot in time to the music. Gino had insisted she must try his home-made wine—how right he was. Picking up her glass, she drank the delicious ruby-red liquid down. It was so moreish. Who needed brand names when the house wine tasted like this? She immediately craved more and held out her glass for a refill. 'It tastes just like cranberry juice—'

'And packs a kick like a mule,' Rigo warned. 'So drink it slowly…'

He really did think of her as a kid sister—that, or an ancient aunt. Of course she would drink it slowly.

Well, she had meant to, but it tasted so fruity and innocent, and one more glass couldn't hurt her surely?

'And now you must dance,' Gino insisted, waltzing past with an armful of plates.

'I don't dance.' She announced this to Rigo, who didn't seem to care whether she danced or not.

'Do what you like,' he said, leaning back in his chair.

It seemed to Katie that the young women at the pizzeria had no inhibitions at all, and that their sole reason for being here was to shimmy into Rigo's eye line. Something tight curled in her stomach as she watched them flash lascivious glances at him.

'Well, *signorina*,' Gino said on his return, 'will you make an old man happy?'

It took longer than Katie had expected to focus her eyes on Gino's face, and even longer to register surprise that he was serious. Gino did want to dance with her. Suddenly Rigo's warning about the wine made sense. Her head was on straight, but the room was tilting—and now Gino was opening his arms to her.

'Go ahead,' Rigo said helpfully as the band launched into a wild tarantella.

Having stumbled to her feet, she barely had chance to exclaim, as Gino, quite literally, whisked her off her feet.

CHAPTER NINE

RIGO cut in.

By the time he cut in Katie was happy to forget her reservations and fall into his arms.

Gino melted away.

Had she been set up? Katie wondered. A bleary glance into Rigo's totally sober face told her precisely nothing—at least, not in her present state. This was great. She couldn't dance. She could barely stand up. And Signor Superior had been proven right. The wine had gone to her head. And now she was in danger of making a complete fool of herself.

There was nothing for it, Katie concluded. Before she fell over she had to appeal to Rigo's better nature—that was, supposing he had one. 'If you could just get me back to our table...' When cast adrift in a storm of flying heels and elbows, it didn't do to stand on your pride.

But Rigo didn't lead her off the dance floor. Couldn't he understand? Hadn't he heard her? 'I don't dance,' she complained.

She got a reaction this time. One inky brow rose in elegant disbelief but, rather than leading her to safety, he tightened his grip on her arms. 'Everyone can dance, Signorina Bannister.'

'I absolutely don't dance.' And, taking that as her cue, she broke free and attempted to totter back to their table unaided.

Thankfully, Rigo caught her in his arms just as she was on the point of lurching into a waiter. 'I'm fine.' She flapped her arms around to demonstrate this.

'Well, clearly, you're not.' So saying, he banded her arms firmly to her body.

'Let me go.' Her breath caught in her throat as she stared into Rigo's amused gaze. 'I did warn you about the wine,' he pointed out, keeping a firm hold of her.

Right now the wine was the least of her worries.

And then at Rigo's signal the music changed abruptly. From jigging up and down like frantic monkeys the couples all around them eased effortlessly into the sinuous rhythm of the rumba.

'What did I tell you?' he soothed, murmuring in her ear. 'You dance beautifully…'

How could she not when Rigo had somehow managed to mould her clumsy body to his? And Rigo could dance.

Oh, yes, he could…

By some miracle she stopped wobbling, and began to move her feet in some sort of recognisable pattern. As long as he didn't hold her too close she'd be all right. As long as his hands didn't wander to the scars on her back she could do this.

And now she was even beginning to relax, it felt so safe and good…

Not so her fantasies. They weren't safe at all. Dancing close to Rigo with all the other couples masking them gave Katie's imagination all the excuse it needed. She had everything to learn about a man's body and this was her opportunity.

As the music filled her, her senses grew ever more acute. Her body was like molten honey curling round him until Rigo changed position and her fantasies flew away.

'What's wrong?' he said as she grew tense.

'Nothing…' She took a deep breath and tried to relax, but the magic had vanished. Rigo's hand had slipped into the hollow in the small of her back as they danced and then his fingers had eased a little higher. Good manners for him not to touch her anywhere remotely intimate, but a danger signal for her, and her head had cleared at once. There was no possibility she could relax now. Even her deepest longings stood no chance against her greatest fear. She wanted Rigo to hold her—she also wanted to be perfect. She wanted to rest unresisting in his arms, and dance and dream, and enjoy herself, but how could she with her scars?

'Katie?' Dipping his head, Rigo stared into her troubled eyes. 'If you concentrate on dancing the rest will follow.'

He couldn't know how wrong he was. But as he drew her to him there was something reassuring about him. The power of his command and the fact that she didn't want to make a scene...

His hands slipped lower. Theoretically she should be hearing more warning signals—and this time they wouldn't be connected with her scars, but her body was clamouring and she didn't want to fight it. This was like skirting the fringes of a hurricane and, instead of running as fast as she should in the opposite direction, hoping to be swept away by it.

'Let go,' Rigo murmured, encouraging her to relax.

But the damage was done and now she could think of nothing but securing her mate in the most primitive way possible. 'I'm trying to.'

If only she dared.

He was enjoying this far more than he had expected. His initial impulse had been to rescue Katie from the risk of being trampled by Gino's enthusiasm, but that was before he discovered how she felt beneath his hands. Timid, yet eager, she had everything to learn, and that in itself was irresistible.

He had to remind himself that she was going home tomorrow and there was no time for the style of initiation he had in mind. Resting his chin on her hair, he smiled as he dragged in her light, wild-flower scent. It was a revelation to him to feel how Katie trembled beneath his intentionally light touch. He knew she wanted more. She proved it by moving closer, seeking contact, seeking pressure between their bodies, seeking sex.

So was Signorina Prim strait-laced and just a little drunk, or was she a dam waiting to burst? Perhaps Katie Bannister was the best actress he had ever met. She was certainly a storm loosely contained in a cage of inexperience. He knew that he should take her back to the table and call for the bill, prior to taking her back to sleep alone in her chaste, maidenly bed.

And he would...soon.

If Rigo's hands should slip lower...

Katie gulped. She was relieved that he was nowhere near her scars, of course, but he was almost cupping her bottom, which had set off a chain reaction in parts of her she mustn't know about. But how could she hide her response to him? She didn't have the experience to know. She arched her back. She couldn't help herself. She wanted to feel those big, strong hands holding her. She wanted to read all the subliminal messages that could pass between a man and a woman through the merest adjustment of a finger...

As the sultry beat of the slow, Latin American dance thrilled through her Katie found herself angling her buttocks ever more towards Rigo's controlling hands. It was a signal as old as time and one he couldn't help but read.

She exhaled raggedly as he confirmed this by adjusting the position of his hands once again. His fingertips were dangerously close now and, rather than feeling alarm, she felt small and safe, and violently aroused. She had never done anything as bold as this before, but here in the wholesome surroundings of the simple pizzeria, hidden in a mass of dancing couples, she felt free from the usual constraints. Gazing up, she met with eyes as dark and watchful as the night. Lower still she saw the sardonic smile playing around the corners of Rigo's mouth, and realised he knew.

He knew.

She closed her eyes and tried to steady her breathing, when what she really wanted to do was whisper, make love to me. But, other than in her wildest and most erotic fantasy, she would never find the courage to do that.

His senses were on fire. For the first time in his life he didn't want a dance to end. The sexual chemistry between them had surprised him. He had enjoyed teasing Katie Bannister, the girl he thought of as Signorina Prim, but now his thoughts were taking the direct route to seduction. He wasn't alone in feeling the power of this erotic spell. The other couples on the dance floor were drawn to them like moths to immolate on erotic flame. Even the musicians were swept up in this inferno of desire and, with a key change like a sigh, had reinforced the mood.

But he didn't do one-night stands, or complications. Usually.

'You're quite a surprise to me,' he murmured, feeling her tremble as his breath brushed her ear.

'I wasn't always so dull...'

He wasn't going to argue about Katie's interpretation of dull. Sensing there was more to come, he remained silent.

'I trained to be an opera singer once.'

'Did you?' He couldn't have been more surprised and pulled back to stare into her eyes. 'What went wrong?'

He knew at once he shouldn't have asked. He hadn't meant to spoil the evening for her. Drawing her back into his arms, he held her gently and securely until she relaxed.

She'd tell him if she wanted to tell him, he reasoned. But the revelation had intrigued him. There was obviously so much more to uncover in this woman who favoured dull brown suits—perhaps an artistic diva waiting to break out. But as far as he was concerned, she must remain a shy, brown mouse who was under his protection while she was in Rome. Katie Bannister might be many things, but she was not a seductress—and even if in this sultry setting she appeared to be, it was up to him to keep things light between them and send her home as innocent as the day she had arrived in Italy.' Reluctantly he disentangled himself from her arms. '*Andiamo, piccolo topo—*'

'I am not your little mouse,' she slurred.

And then he realised that three glasses of wine was probably her annual quota back home and she had drunk Gino's firewater as if it were cordial—which almost certainly accounted for her openness about her opera training too.

'You must learn to call me Signorina Bannister,' she insisted, drawing her taupe brows together in her approximation of a fierce stare.

'*Bene,*' he said, happy to indulge her—at least on that one point.

'It's much better if we keep it...' She frowned as she searched for the right word.

'Formal between us?' he suggested. 'I think it's time I took you home now,' he said firmly, holding her away from him at arm's length.

Rigo's sudden change of mood from sexy to serious was so unexpected Katie blanked for a moment. Only when she finally managed to refocus did she wonder how she had ever wasted a moment thinking Rigo Ruggiero uncomplicated and fun. He was a playboy who lived every moment for the pleasure it brought him before moving on to the next distraction. Gino's genuine warmth and the restaurateur's homely restaurant must have clouded her thinking.

OK, that and the wine.

Common sense should have warned her Rigo was not the youth who had pitched up in Rome hoping to make his fortune. Rigo enjoyed these nostalgic visits but that didn't mean he was the same uncomplicated youth he'd been then.

As he frogmarched her back to the table she faced the ugly truth. She was as naïve as she had ever been and Rigo was the same playboy for whom the main attraction on tonight's menu of amusement had been an impressionable out-of-towner. He'd played the game for a while, but had soon tired of her lack of sophistication. She felt bad, because she never put herself in the way of rejection, knowing the outcome was a foregone conclusion. And the one time she had…

Katie smiled as she thanked Gino for her shawl. Rigo was already standing by the door, waiting for her. He couldn't wait to bring the evening to a close. It was up to her to pull herself together and leave with enough pride to be able to deal with him on a professional level tomorrow morning.

Taking a shower in cold reality was the swiftest antidote to male pride he knew. As he held the restaurant door for Katie her cool gaze assured him—don't worry, you won't get the chance. Tipping her chin, she walked proudly past him into the night. Even that amused him. Most women with one eye on his fortune tried harder. Katie wasn't that sort. In her eyes he was a man who preferred racing his sports car to keeping an appointment. Shallow? He was barely puddle-deep. Yes, all this he could see in Katie Bannister's cool, topaz-coloured gaze.

He only had to raise his hand and a limousine drew up in front of them at the kerb. 'Your chariot awaits, *signorina*. I plan ahead,' he said when she looked at him in surprise. 'Don't worry,' he added when her gaze flickered with alarm. 'I'll see you safely back to your hotel.'

He let his driver help her into the car, which appeared to reassure her. He took his seat in the back, ensuring he kept a good space between them. She didn't risk further conversation; neither did he. It seemed the most sensible course of action after the fire they'd ignited at Gino's. He glanced at his wristwatch and was surprised by the way time had flown. 'If you'd like to make our meeting a little later—'

'Not at all,' she interrupted in a way that drew his attention to her lips. She had beautifully formed plump pink lips. The thought of pressing his mouth against them while his tongue teased them apart stirred him. He could imagine how she would taste, and how it would feel when she wound her arms around his neck. 'In that case, I suggest we have lunch immediately afterwards—'

'Immediately after our meeting tomorrow I'll be on a plane home, Signor Ruggiero.'

He awarded her more than one brownie point for that swift riposte. 'I thought we'd agreed you'd call me Rigo?'

She didn't answer, and as she turned away to stare out of the window he found the chill between them erotic. He liked a challenge. And, even if he had decided to take her home and treat her chastity with the respect it deserved, he was a man.

She spoiled the mood by asking for her hair clip.

He shrugged and gave it to her, and then had to watch as she scraped her hair back as tightly and as primly as it would go. She only relaxed when she had completed the transformation from lovely young woman to maiden aunt.

But the obvious had always bored him, which was why Katie Bannister intrigued him. So much passion so tightly controlled could only end one way. And remembering her visit to his favourite shop—what a contrast that style of underwear would be to her precisely ordered hair. When did she intend on wearing it? Was she wearing it? What had provoked Signorina Prim into that walk on the wild side? And what would persuade her to take another walk on the wild side with him?

As if sensing the path his thoughts were taking, she looked at him shyly, but, shy or not, that look plainly said he shouldn't imagine everything had been put on this earth for his amusement.

'In another thirty-six hours,' she said, and with rather too much relish, he thought, 'I'll be back at my desk in Yorkshire—'

'In that case we'll have to work quickly,' he said.

She flashed him a concerned glance.

'I'll take you to the airport immediately after the reading of the will.'

He felt sure she would refuse this offer, but instead she said, 'Thank you, Signor Ruggiero, that will save me taking a cab.'

Katie was on tenterhooks until they reached the hotel. She couldn't wait to bury her head under a pillow and wish the night away so it could be morning and she could gabble out the contents of the will and go home to her dull, quiet, *safe* life. To her disappointment, for the remainder of the journey home Rigo had no trouble keeping things on a business footing and didn't speak to her at all. By the time they reached the hotel she was tied up in knots.

He escorted her across the lobby and even insisted on pressing the elevator button. When the lift doors slid open he kept his finger on that button as he said, 'Goodnight, Signorina Bannister. I hope you sleep well. And don't worry about calling a cab in the morning—I will send a car for you.'

She said thank you for the evening and then got into the lift. She wished, hoped, prayed, Rigo would step in after her. Of course, he didn't. Something she had every cause to be grateful for, Katie reasoned sensibly as the elevator door closed.

After that everything felt flat and a restless night followed. There was only one face in her dreams, which explained why her eyes were red the next morning. Her face was washed-out too, and as for her hair…

Better not to dwell on that disaster, she decided, scraping it back neatly into the customary bun before securing the severe style with the whole of a packet of hair grips.

Job done, she stared at her reflection in the mirror.

Unfortunately, the image hadn't changed. She was the same ordinary person. The next task was automatic. Angling her head to stare at her naked back in the mirror, she checked her scars. Nothing had changed there either. They were still as vivid, the sight of them just as stomach-churning.

What had she expected? Did she think she could wish them away?

Impatient with herself for this moment of weakness, she turned away to dress in modest brown. There was only one thing out of sync in this neat brown package, she concluded after slipping on her sensible brown court shoes, and that was some rather striking underwear, purchased from a luxury boutique in Rome. Well, if she waited for a suitable opportunity to wear it the moths would have a feast.

Before leaving the room she slicked on some lip gloss. Mashing her lips together experimentally, she decided to wipe it off again. Did she want to draw attention? As no other delaying tactics sprang to mind, she drew in a deep, steadying breath and picked up her bag.

CHAPTER TEN

HE SETTLED his shades in place. Zapping the lock, he swung into the car. Resting the phone in its nest, he was still talking, grim-faced and tight-lipped as he pulled away from the kerb outside the imposing hospital building. 'Yes, of course, do everything you can—whatever it takes—and please keep me informed.'

He stopped and drew breath as he cut the line. Now it was business as usual. This was his life—swinging from the charity that meant so much to him to the business that sustained it. The only difference today was that he was going to be late again for a meeting with Katie Bannister.

It couldn't be helped and he wouldn't explain the delay. He didn't want the world knowing what he did in his private time, and only a very few individuals knew he was behind the charitable foundation. His only concern was ensuring confidentiality for anyone helped by the foundation. Today it had provided life-saving surgery; tomorrow he might be taking a teenager around the track in his sports car. Whatever was required he made time for—and sometimes Antonia suffered; he knew that and felt bad about it, but there were never enough hours in a day.

Antonia knew nothing about this other life. She was too young. He would never put the burden of silence on her shoulders.

Resting his unshaven chin on his arm, he waited for a gap in the traffic. Before he could placate Antonia he must meet with Signorina Prim, and learn what last thought Carlo had sent his way. Katie Bannister would be cooling her sensible heels at the penthouse, feeling justly affronted because he was late by more than an hour.

In spite of the rush-hour traffic he made it back in record time. Leaving the sports car where it was sure to be clamped and in all probability towed away, he raced into the building. He stabbed impatiently at the elevator button and barged inside the steel cage before the doors were properly open. Throwing himself back against the wall, he watched the floor numbers changing—more slowly, surely, than they had ever changed before.

Edgy didn't even begin to describe his condition. Impatience steaming out of every pore. He used the few seconds remaining to compartmentalise his thinking. He couldn't take so much anger and concern into this meeting—it wasn't fair to Katie. She didn't know about his day, or the fact that Carlo was trying to stab him one last time from the grave—how could she?

He liked her. She was a quiet little mouse, but the way she stood up to him suggested there was a spine of steel in there somewhere—who wouldn't like that? Maybe if things had been different...

But things weren't different and the elevator had just reached his floor.

She found it hard to believe Rigo would be late again. Surely, not even he could be this inconsiderate—this rude? It proved how little he thought of her professionally; in every way. She was an inconvenience and nothing more. Staring down at the busy main road framed by exquisite palaces and gardens, Katie tried to make herself believe it didn't matter Rigo was late again. Why should she care? This was business. Lots of clients were late for business meetings—some even forgot about them entirely. Why should this be any different?

Because this appointment was with Rigo.

Because of the ache in her heart.

Because she wanted him to treat her better than the average client would treat her, and because she had allowed herself to commit the cardinal sin of becoming emotionally involved with a client—a one-sided arrangement that left her feeling daft and stupid. As she continued to beat herself up her attention was drawn to one of the large Roman car-towing vehicles. No doubt someone else's day was about to be spoiled—

'Katie.'

She whirled around as Rigo's husky voice broke the silence.

'I'm so sorry.' He strode towards her. Having burst in like a whirlwind, he spread his arms wide in a gesture of regret. 'Please accept my apologies.'

She took him in at a glance—the unshaven face, the rumpled clothes, the less than brilliant eyes. A horrible thought occurred to her, making her feel sick inside. Had he come here straight from someone's bed?

And why should she care? Was his sex life her business now?

But she did care. She cared a great deal too much. 'Rigo,' she said, extending a cool hand in greeting. 'I had almost given you up.'

'You've been well looked after, I hope?' He glanced around and relaxed when he saw her coffee.

'I've been looked after very well, thank you, and while I was waiting—'

'Yes?'

His eyes were warmer now. 'I took down some messages for you.'

'*Bene*...good.'

She crossed to the desk to pick up the notes she had made. 'One was from the PA you just sacked,' she said, turning

'Signorina Partilora was most disappointed that you weren't here for her to deliver her message to you in person. Perhaps you'd like me to read it to you—'

'No,' he interrupted. 'That's OK. I can imagine...'

'If you're sure?' Her eyes glinted.

'Signorina Bannister,' Rigo growled, 'if I am any judge, I cannot imagine that such words would ever cross your lips.'

Then I might surprise you, Katie thought, flashing her innocent look. 'I think it's safe to say Signorina Partilora will not be working for you again,' she told him mildly.

Rigo laughed. 'What a relief. I have your cast-iron guarantee on that, do I?'

He was close enough to touch and her senses were ignited by his delicious man scent. If she could bottle that warm, clean, spicy aroma she'd make a fortune, Katie concluded. And then she would be able to walk away from a job she had no passion for.

'The will?' Rigo prompted.

'Yes, of course.' Her eyes stung with tears as she walked to the desk.

Because this was the end, Katie realised. It was the end of her Roman fantasy and the end of her fantasy life with Rigo—except she had no life with Rigo and she'd be going home after this.

Instead of sitting across from her Rigo came up behind her and put his hands on her shoulders. His touch was electric. Had he seen her eyes fill with tears? She couldn't bear the humiliation.

'I understand why you are upset and short tempered,' he said, keeping his hands in place, 'and you have every right to be angry with me. Please be assured my delay was necessary.'

She let her breath out slowly as he lifted his hands away and walked to the other side of the desk. She found it even harder to control her feelings when Rigo was nice to her,

and now her nose was having a seizure, while her throat fel
as if someone was standing on it. 'Shall we start?' sh
managed hoarsely.

'Of course,' he said.

She focused her attention on the legal documents in front o
her, but the imprint of Rigo's fingers on her shoulders remained
She had to remind herself Rigo was Italian and caresses cam
easily to him. Such shows of emotion were practically unhear
of in Katie's world—except perhaps under the office mistleto
at Christmas, when the ancient caretaker made sure she wasn'
left out and always gave her a peck on the cheek.

Rigo made a sign for her to begin.

Must he sprawl across the seat? Must he look quite so sex
even in repose?

In the best acting scene of her life, she began.

Grim-faced, he listened. Carlo had left him everything? Hi
mouth curved with distaste. He couldn't wait to find out wha
'everything' entailed. He guessed debt would play some par
in it. Katie caught sight of his expression and gave him
troubled glance.

Getting up from the desk, he turned his back on her. Toda
he could have used her soothing presence and common sense
Today he wanted nothing more than to have this sordi
business over with so he could ring the hospital. *If they didn
ring him first...*

'There's also a private letter from your stepbrother, Rigo
as well as a small package.'

Katie's soft voice cut through his thoughts and he hear
her push back her chair, get up and walk across the roor
towards him.

'*Grazie.*' He turned.

'I'll leave you, shall I?' she offered, hovering uncertainly

'No.' He held out his hand, palm up. 'Stay. Please,' h

added, when her steady gaze called him to account for his brusque manner.

He walked some distance away before opening Carlo's letter. Katie could have no idea of the depths of depravity to which his stepbrother had sunk and the disgrace Carlo had brought on the family. He didn't want her to know. Why give her that as a parting gift to take home? Like his visit to the hospital earlier, none of this was Katie's responsibility. Let her return to England with her presumptions about his glittering life intact. Just so long as she left Rome as carefree as she arrived he was fine with that.

After years of practice he thought he was immune to feeling, but the sight of Carlo's familiar hand gave him a punch in the gut he hadn't expected. He glanced at Katie, who discreetly looked away. He had shut himself off emotionally years back when his father had chosen a woman and that woman's son over him. The same loneliness and isolation he'd felt then swept over him now.

He tensed, hearing Katie ask him softly, 'Are you all right?'

He nodded curtly and turned back to Carlo's letter. His heart was closed.

Wasn't it?

Dragging the usual mental armour round him, he began to read.

Rigo—
There is nothing I can say to make up for the years I stole from you, but I want to make my peace with you before I die. I'm not giving you anything that isn't rightfully yours.
Carlo.

Cryptic to the end, he thought, ripping open the small package.

The keys of the family *palazzo* in Tuscany tumbled into his hands, followed by his father's ring. He slipped on the ring and felt both the weight of responsibility it carried and an agonising longing. He had waited so long for contact with his father, and that it should come like this...

And to see his home again...his beautiful home...

He lowered the letter to his side as a well of emotion threatened to drown him.

The here and now fell away as his mind travelled back to the past. He had lived a blissful country existence at the *palazzo*, ignorant of pomp and pretension until his father fell in love and brought Carlo and his stepmother home. He had welcomed Carlo with open arms, thinking he would have a brother to share things with, only to have his youthful naïvety thrown back in his face. Carlo hadn't had time to spare for a boy much younger than him, and one who stood in the way of easy money.

'Shall I get you a drink?'

He glanced up, still a little disorientated as Katie spoke to him. 'No. Yes...a glass of water...please.'

'I'll go and get it for you.'

Her expression told him she understood something of what he was going through, and for the briefest of moments there was a real connection between them.

Everything had come full circle, he realised as Katie left him to pace. She was going home. He was going home. He could hardly take it in. He would have liked a bit longer to get used to the idea, but there was no time.

Katie returned a little later with a tray of coffee, hot and strong. She brought him some iced water too. He guessed she had wanted to leave him alone with his thoughts for a while.

'That's very good of you, Signorina Bannister,' he said as she laid everything out for him, 'but I should take you to the airport now.' He glanced at his watch, feeling his head must explode from everything he'd learned.

'There's time enough for that.' She busied herself making sure his coffee was poured the way he liked it.

'I thought you were in a hurry to get back to England.'

'I can't leave you like this—'

'Like what?' he demanded sharply. He didn't need her pity. What business was it of hers how he felt?

She raised her steady gaze to his and as if a veil had lifted a torrent of impassioned words poured out. 'I do this all the time, Rigo—I see this all the time. I can't stand it. I can't stand how cruel people can be to each other.'

'Then you should toughen up.'

'Or get out of the job,' she said thoughtfully.

'There is that,' he agreed, watching her as he sipped the hot, aromatic liquid.

She calmed him. Against all the odds, Katie Bannister calmed him. Dread at what the contents of the will might reveal had been replaced by shock when he'd learned that Carlo had left him the only place he cared about. The *palazzo* had been in the Ruggiero family for centuries and Carlo must have recognised this at the end, so there was some good in him after all. The question now was, could he live with the guilt of knowing the past could never be mended?

Turning away from Katie, he passed a hand over his eyes.

Too much emotion.

But he was going home…

Home…

Growing elation was threatening to leave him on the biggest high he'd ever known. He wanted someone to share that feeling with. He wanted Katie to share it with him, but she was already packing up her things, a little hesitantly, he thought. 'What's on your mind?' She looked as if she was struggling with a decision.

'Oh…you know…' She flapped her hand, dismissing his concern.

'No, I don't know. I want you to tell me. What's wrong?' He was feeling increasing concern for this quiet girl who made everyone else's problems her own and yet seemed so isolated, somehow.

'You have your own problems.'

As always she made light of her own concerns. 'I just inherited an estate and a *palazzo* in Tuscany,' he pointed out. 'How bad can it be?'

'That must mean a lot to you.' All her focus was on him now.

'My birthright? Oh, you know…' He dismissed the home of his dreams, his childhood and his heart with an airy gesture.

'Don't, Rigo. You make it sound so flippant, when anyone with half an ounce of sense can see how much this means to you.'

'You can tell, maybe…' It was a turning point. He wanted the moment to last, but the best thing for Katie was for him to let his driver take her to the airport. A more unworthy part of him was reacting in the age-old way in the face of death. He wanted sex. The urge to make new life was an imperative inborn command. He wanted to have sex with Katie Bannister.

CHAPTER ELEVEN

WHAT was wrong with him? After years of emotional absti-
nence, why this sudden roller-coaster ride? He'd had huge and
fantastic coups in business many times and hadn't felt a thing.
He'd learned long ago to turn his back on an inheritance he
thought he'd never see again. So it wasn't the just the *palazzo*
in Tuscany gnawing at his gut. Was it possible this shy,
innocent girl was slowly melting his resolve and bringing
emotion into his life?

He watched Katie cross the room to the desk in her neat,
precise way. Her feelings were bound up tight just like his.
He would like to see her respond to life and all its opportunities, and with abandon.

'Before I go, here is the list of phone messages I took for
you,' she said in her strait-laced way. 'And don't be offended,
but while I was waiting for you I tidied up that pile of documents by your chair on the floor—'

'I meant to get round to that.'

'How many PAs have you sacked?' she asked him bluntly.

Many, but did he want to frighten her off with an idea
being born in his head? 'I'm not the easiest man to work for,'
he admitted with monumental understatement. 'I need
someone who can use their initiative and do more than answer
the phone—'

'Well, lucky for you,' she cut in dryly, 'I made a list of all the written messages I found lying around.'

'Most of them written on the back of envelopes,' he said, remembering his latest PA's failure to grasp the simple fact that a desk diary could be quite a useful office tool if she remembered to use it.

'Your diary is in quite a mess,' Katie added, levelling a stare on him.

'And has been for some time,' he agreed.

'And the staff at your office…'

Could be called obnoxious; he'd admit that. 'Go on,' he prompted, feeling there was something more to come.

'Have no manners at all,' she told him frankly. 'And that's not good for your image.'

'What image?'

'Exactly.'

He missed a beat. 'Why, Signorina Bannister, I think you just revealed another side to your character.'

'Really?'

'PA—'

'Oh, no.' Shaking her head, she laughed at the thought of him offering her a job.

'Pain in the ass?'

She stared at him and then laughed again. 'For a moment there I thought you were offering me a job—'

'Do you think I'm mad?' he teased her, watching closely for a reaction. Then he told himself the idea of employing her was mad; a momentary lapse of judgement. Did he want a woman who cared so much around him?

His phone rang, bringing these thoughts to an end.

He had a brief conversation before cutting the line.

He swung around, elated. 'Now I could kiss you—'

'Let's not get carried away,' she said awkwardly, losing no time putting the desk between them. 'I don't like to rush you.

but my flight leaves at four o' clock. You've had good news,
I take it?'

'The best—'

It must have been one heck of a deal, Katie concluded.
'Congratulations—'

'Congratulate the doctors, not me—'

'The doctors?'

'A friend of mine has had an operation,' Rigo told her
vaguely, ruffling his thick black hair. His glance was evasive
and he gave her the impression that he thought he'd said too
much already.

'I hope your friend's okay?'

'The operation went really well, apparently.'

'Then that's the best news you could have.'

'And it frees me to go to Tuscany right away.'

'Don't let me keep you. I can take a cab—'

'I wouldn't hear of it. I'll arrange a driver—'

And that would be the end of everything.

Katie froze as Rigo continued chatting about flight schedules. He'd been equally matter-of-fact when they had returned
from their amazing evening together, when she'd felt anything
but matter-of-fact. She'd been frightened by the strength of her
feelings for him—out of her depth and bewildered that feelings
could be so one-sided. She had longed to return to her safe,
quiet life in Yorkshire, but now the opportunity to do so had
arrived she didn't want the adventure to end. She wanted to stay
until she knew the secret of Carlo's will, because something
told her the contents would hurt Rigo. She had to be there for
him, because she cared for him, she cared for him desperately.

There was an alternative, Katie's inner voice suggested—
if she was brave enough.

'I could go back now,' she blurted, clumsily interrupting him, 'or...'

'Or?' Rigo echoed.

Would her mind re-engage in time to speak with clarity when all this man had to do to melt every bone in her body was to turn and give her that look? 'Or I could come with you…' By now she was hyperventilating to the point where she thought she might faint.

'Come with me? I thought you couldn't wait to leave Rome?'

She would have to share at least part of her reason for wanting this, Katie realised. 'Can I tell you the truth?'

'I would expect nothing less of a lawyer,' Rigo responded dryly.

'I'm not even sure I'll have a job when I get home. You see my firm's cutting back—'

'A failing firm doesn't mean you can't get a job elsewhere.'

'I'd take my chances,' she agreed, 'but I'm not sure I ever want to be a lawyer.'

Rigo's brows shot up.

'I get too involved,' she explained. 'Everyone has to constantly remind me I'm not a social worker and should concentrate on the facts—'

'But you still care.'

'Yes, I do.'

'Is that something to be ashamed of?'

'No, but it might mean I'm in the wrong job.'

He laughed. It was a short, very masculine sound. 'And you think you'd be happier working for me? I don't think so, Signorina Bannister.'

'Oh, well…' Raising her arms a little, she dropped them to her sides. Of course Rigo didn't want her working for him. He wanted someone slick and polished at his side. But a longing inside her stirred—a longing so strong she couldn't ignore it. This might be her one chance to embrace change and adventure and, yes, see him sometimes. She drew a deep breath. 'You can't keep a PA—'

'That's true.'

'I might not have the makings of a good lawyer, but I am incredibly organized.'

'And you care too much about people—'

'Not you,' she quickly assured him.

Pressing his hand against his chest, he gave her a mock-serious look. 'Of course not.'

'How about you take me on for a trial period?'

'Are you serious?'

'Absolutely.' She held his gaze. 'Your stepbrother has left you the family estate in Tuscany, but you haven't been there since you were a boy and you don't know what to expect when you get there. I could come with you and take notes—make suggestions. I have a passion for historical design—only a hobby,' she added quickly, cheeks flushing, knowing she was the last person on earth Rigo would turn to for advice. 'And I speak fluent Italian.' Her trump card.

'OK, OK,' he said, halting the flow of her enthusiasm with raised hands. 'Let's stop this fantasy right now. Do you have any idea what the drop-out rate is for my staff?'

'No, but I can imagine. Maybe you need an office manager too.'

'Are you creating a role for yourself, Signorina Bannister?'

'No, I'm identifying a need,' Katie argued. 'A mutual need.' She bit her lip as she came to the crux of it all. 'I need a change and you need a second string.'

'A second string?' Rigo's face creased in his trademark smile, but his eyes were steadily assessing her. 'Do you really think you can walk in here and, after five minutes' exposure to my world, be ready to work alongside me and understand my business? I don't think so—'

'No, of course I don't think that, but we'd both be new to this project—'

'Tuscany is not a project,' Rigo cut across her. 'The Palazzo

Farnese is the past and, though I loved it once, I intend to sell it on. There are too many unhappy memories—'

'Good ones too—'

'Leave it,' he warned. 'You don't know me that well.'

Katie braced herself. 'But you are going to see it before you sell it on?'

'I said so, didn't I?'

'That's good.' She believed it was crucial he did. She'd seen the mixture of emotions pass behind Rigo's eyes when he realised Carlo had left him the *palazzo*—elation being one of them. 'Remedial work might be necessary before the *palazzo* goes on the market. You should make time—'

'Oh, should I?' His gaze turned cold. 'You're an expert, suddenly?'

No, but she knew one thing—Rigo mustn't treat this bequest like a cold-blooded business deal or he would regret it all his life. She knew it would be a difficult pilgrimage for him to make and his look warned her to drop it, but she couldn't; she'd gone too far. 'I wouldn't get in your way. I'd just be there to take notes—act as your go-between. I could even help you source people to handle any necessary restoration work. You wouldn't have time for all that with all your other interests.'

'You seem to know a lot about me, Signorina Bannister.'

'I know you don't have a PA right now.'

Everything inside her tensed as Rigo went silent. The road out of her small town in Yorkshire was littered with returnees who had tried the big city and hurried back to the safety of home. Perhaps she should be doing that too, but she'd tried the big city—admittedly Rome with Rigo Ruggiero in it—and was in no hurry to return home.

'And you're telling me you can start immediately—without giving notice to anyone?'

Yes, she was burning her bridges. 'I have called the office and warned them I might not be back right away.'

'That's not a very good recommendation to a prospective employer, is it?' The look in Rigo's eyes told her how crazy this idea was, but then he added, 'I guess neither of us comes highly recommended where longevity of employment is concerned.'

He appeared to be battling with a decision, while her hands had balled into fists, Katie realised, slowly releasing them. Where had this crazy idea sprung from? She had never come across anyone like Rigo Ruggiero before, she reminded herself. He was still thinking. She had to interpret that as a maybe and, having taken the first step, found the second was much easier. Better to get things out in the open now. 'I do have one condition.'

'You're making conditions?'

Rigo's look pierced her confidence, but this was an all-important step in rebuilding her life. Yes, she was a small-town girl who was scarred comprehensively inside and out—and she should know her place—but retiring into the shadows would be a step back into the dark place she'd inhabited after the fire.

'Go on,' Rigo prompted impatiently.

'If we stay over in Tuscany—'

'I haven't agreed to you coming with me yet.'

'But you will,' she said, crossing her fingers behind her back.

'*If* we stay over?' he prompted.

'I'll need a place to stay.'

'Of course you will.'

'A separate place to stay…' Her face was growing hotter every second.

'Separate from me, do you mean?'

She heard the faint derision in his voice. 'That is correct,' she said tightly, feeling like that certain someone had come back to stand on her throat.

Rigo barked a laugh. 'Why?' he demanded. 'Don't you trust yourself alone with me, Signorina Prim?'

He was a busy man. Why was he making this hard for her? He needed a PA. And as he stared into Katie's pale, passionate face, he knew he wanted her to go with him. 'Well? What are you waiting for?' he snapped, frowning impatiently. 'Grab your bag, and let's go.'

Katie hadn't realised Rigo's idea of a trip to Tuscany would include a sleek white executive jet, which he piloted into Pisa Airport. Scurrying alongside him as he strolled through the terminal building without any of the usual formalities was another eye-opener. Next he introduced her to what seemed like an acre of cream calfskin in the back of a limousine. His chauffeur did the rest, driving them seamlessly through the exquisite Tuscan countryside, while she felt her thigh ping with the proximity of Rigo's thigh and fretted about sleeping arrangements.

Was she mad suggesting this? Dull little Katie Bannister off on a jolly with her drop-dead-gorgeous boss? What surprised her even more was that Rigo had accepted her offer to work for him—temporarily, of course. And now he was sending her senses haywire. She risked a glance his way as the car swept round a bend.

'Look, Katie...that palace on the hill is the Palazzo Farnese.'

Katie looked, but what she saw did not match Rigo's tone of voice. One of the ice-cream-cone-shaped towers looked as if it had been attacked with a battering ram, and to her eyes Rigo's inheritance looked more like a fat toad squatting on the top of the hill than a fairy-tale *palazzo*.

'It's a jewel, isn't it?' he breathed.

Katie hummed, trying not to sound too noncommittal. True, the hill the *palazzo* stood upon was lush and green, and had it been in good order the *palazzo* would indeed be set on the brow of that hill like a jewel. She set her imagination to work. It wasn't so hard. In some places where the passage of time had been kind the ancient stone glowed a soft rose-pink in the late-afternoon sunlight, and there were tiny salt-white houses clustered around the crumbling walls. Yes, it could be called beautiful—if you squinted up your eyes and tried to picture how the *palazzo* might look after a world of renovation—but oh, my goodness, how would Rigo react when they finally arrived?

'My family home…' Rigo's voice betrayed his excitement. 'I haven't been back for years…'

And years and years, Katie thought, trying not to imagine Rigo's disappointment when he moved past this nostalgia for a childhood that had ended with Carlo's arrival on the scene. Strangely, though she had no emotional involvement with the *palazzo*, it called to her too. She was bewitched and could already picture the rooms, which she imagined to have high vaulted ceilings, when they were loved and cared for. She knew instinctively the *palazzo* was worth saving. Monuments to another time were rare and precious and she could never dismiss one out of hand. How she would love to take a hand in restoring it…

And with her sensible head on she had an open ticket home if the job didn't work out.

Having driven up to the grounds, they entered through some ornate gates. A little shabby perhaps but that only added to their charm. They would need checking, of course, to make sure they were safe. She made a note. A gracious drive lay ahead of them, lined with stately sentinels of blue-green cypress. Well, at least those wouldn't need trimming, she thought, noting the overgrown flower beds and thinking of the work needed there. As the limousine swept on she could see it was all very grand—or had been at one time. Crenellated battlements scraped a cloudless cobalt sky and each conical tower, damaged or not, wore a coronet of cloud. 'It's magical,' she murmured.

'Let's hope so.'

Rigo's tone of voice suggested he had ditched the rose-coloured spectacles, and for that she was glad. And the setting was perfect. A limpid silver lake lay behind the *palazzo*, while the ghost of a formal garden could still be seen at the front amongst the weeds. To reach the main entrance they crossed a vast cobbled courtyard, which fortunately had survived intact, and as they passed beneath a stone arch she noticed a royal crest carved into the stone. Her heart juddered to see the same rampant lion engraved on Rigo's father's ring. That royal seal only put another wedge between them.

Rigo saw her interest and dismissed it. 'Everyone's son's a prince in Italy,' he said. 'Look on it as a benefit,' he added dryly. 'You can have a whole royal apartment to yourself.'

She smiled thinly and gave a little laugh. That was what she'd wanted, wasn't it?

CHAPTER TWELVE

ONCE upon a time she had believed in fairy tales, but that was before the fire. She knew Rigo only wanted her for her organised mind with the same certainty she knew this visit would be a disappointment for him. She was in serious danger of falling in love with him, Katie realised as the chauffeur slowed the car.

A group of uniformed staff was waiting for them at the top of the steps. They looked a little anxious, Katie thought, hoping Rigo would reassure them. Her heart was thundering as the limousine slowed to a halt. This was awful. She couldn't bear to think of Rigo disappointed or the staff let down. From start to finish this whole business was proving more disturbing than she could possibly have dreamed.

But Rigo seemed to have come to terms with the damage to the palazzo and put his disappointment behind him. 'I'm home,' he said, seizing hold of her hands.

He quickly let them go.

She followed him out of the car, registering more alarm now she could see how many twinkling windows were broken. She was still calculating the damage when she heard Rigo groan. Following his gaze, she felt like groaning too. A crowd of squealing fashionistas had started pouring out of the doors, pushing the hapless staff aside as they fought to be the first to greet Carlo's brother. These must be Carlo's friends,

Katie realised, only now they were anxious to transfer their affections to Rigo.

'Hold this, will you?'

Thrusting a suitcase-sized handbag into Katie's arms, one of the older, immaculately groomed women elbowed her way through the scrum to reach Rigo, who was handling everyone with charm and patience, but as the woman reached his side and launched herself at him he frowned and turned around to look for Katie.

'You should have waited for me,' he said, coming immediately to her side. 'And whose is this?' he demanded. Removing the handbag from Katie's grasp, he dumped it on the ground. Putting his arm around Katie's shoulders, he shepherded her up the steps.

It didn't mean a thing, Katie told herself as her heart raced. Rigo was a very physical man for whom touching and embracing were second nature—a man who radiated command. Seeing her on the outside of the group had simply stirred his protective instincts.

She stood by his side at the top of the steps as he gave an ultimatum. His Press office would issue a further statement, he said, and in the meantime he was sure everyone would respect his grief and go home.

Smiles faded rapidly. People looked at each other. Then they looked at Katie and a buzz of comment swept through the group. Katie's cheeks reddened as she imagined what everyone must be saying—it ran along the lines of, what was a man like Rigo Ruggiero doing with a woman like her? She didn't have a clue either, if that helped them.

Rigo didn't appear to care what anyone thought, and chose to neither explain nor to excuse her presence.

Everyone saw a different side of him, Katie realised, from the Press, who loved to photograph him, to the hangers-on, who hoped to gain something by being here. She had seen his fun side and wondered how many people had seen that. Right now he was all steel and unforgiving. And if she'd only stopped to think—if these people had only stopped to think—they would all have known that a playboy could never have built up the empire Rigo had. She was as guilty as they were of being distracted by his dazzling good looks and his charm, but she had learned that to underestimate him was a very dangerous pastime indeed.

He went straight from this announcement to introduce himself to the staff and to reassure them. He insisted Katie accompany him for this and he introduced her as his assistant. No one seemed to think this the slightest bit odd and she received some friendly smiles.

Rigo looked magnificent, Katie thought as he returned to the top of the steps to be sure his orders were being carried out to his satisfaction. A Roman general couldn't have had better effect. Hope was already blossoming on the faces of his staff, and a very different look had come over the faces of Carlo's friends.

'We have to be a little patient,' Rigo confided in her, leaning close. 'Everyone has yet to learn that I am a very different man from my brother.'

'I think they may have guessed that,' Katie ventured.

'Your luggage and belongings will be packed and brought out to you,' Rigo announced to those who still refused to believe the gravy train had reached the station. 'Meanwhile, please feel free to enjoy the beauty of the grounds.'

But not the *palazzo*, Katie guessed as a groan went up.

'Come—' his face was set and hard as he turned to her '—we have work to do.'

The power emanating from Rigo was both thrilling and concerning. Even as Katie's hand strayed to trace the pattern of Rigo's breath on her cheek she could not shake the feeling that the inside of the *palazzo* was going to be worse than the outside. Wouldn't he need time alone to deal with his feelings? 'Maybe you'd like space?' she suggested.

'Space?' He looked at her as if she were mad.

'Some time alone? I'm sure I'll have no trouble finding somewhere to stay in town—'

'I thought you worked for me?'

'Of course—'

'Then why would you stay in town? This isn't a holiday, Signorina Bannister.'

'I didn't—'

'Did you bring a notebook?'

This was another side of Rigo—ruthless and without the playboy mask. He walked straight in while she hesitated on the threshold. Beneath her boxy jacket the tight skin on her back had begun stinging with apprehension, but for the first time in a long time she ignored it and started jotting notes: 'Replace damaged architrave...sand down and re-polish entrance doors...replace broken tile just inside the door. Replace all floor tiles,' Katie amended, feeling a chill grow inside her. At her side Rigo had gone quite still.

He swore in Italian. 'This is bad. And if you're still worrying about sleeping arrangements, don't.'

Rigo was in a furious temper, Katie realised, as well he might be, considering the abuse of his ancestral home.

'Whatever the state of this building,' he assured her in a snarl, 'you'll have a lock on your door and at least a mile of corridor between us.' And I wouldn't touch you with a barge-pole, his expression added viciously.

She held her ground and Rigo's stare. She had to believe his anger wasn't directed at her. So her precious chastity would remain intact—that was what she wanted, wasn't it?

Yes, but not like this, not with Rigo treating her like the enemy.

Standing in the centre of what must once have been a

gracious vaulted hall was heartbreaking, even for Katie. They had moved from the seductive heat of Tuscany, from air drenched in sunlight and laced with the heady scent of honeysuckle and roses, into a dank, dark space that reeked of decay. Spilled wine marked what must have once been an elegant marble floor and there were even cigarette butts trodden carelessly into the tiles.

'*Dio,*' Rigo murmured softly at her side.

If he had been anyone else, she would have reached out and grasped his hand to show her support, but she knew he didn't want that. His rigid form forbade all human contact. How would she feel if the beautiful home she remembered from her childhood and had longed to see again turned out to be a crumbling ruin that Carlo's friends had treated like an ashtray?

But a lot of the damage was superficial, Katie concluded as she stared around. She guessed there must have been one heck of a party in anticipation of Rigo's arrival, which made everything look so much worse. But there was some structural work to do as well… She made a note.

Rigo's face reflected both his anger and his agony. He looked on the point of walking out. She could sympathise with that. There had been many times when she had wanted to give up after the fire, and here in the *palazzo* it must seem as if the last remnants of Rigo's childhood had gone up in flames.

'*Vero*…I knew it was too good to be true,' he murmured. 'Now you can see my stepbrother's true nature and his legacy to me.'

As he raked his hair with stiff, angry fingers she could no longer resist the impulse to reach out. 'Rigo, I'm so sorry—'

'I don't need your pity,' he snapped. 'We're going back to Rome. I'm going to put the *palazzo* on the market—'

'And turn your back on it?' She was acutely aware that members of staff were hovering uncertainly in the background.

'I'll do what I have to do.'

'Rigo.' She chased him to the door. 'Don't you think you should—?'

'What?' he demanded furiously. 'Why can't you leave me alone?' He lifted his arm, shunning her concern, but the murmur of a worried staff was still ringing in her ears. 'No—wait,' she said, seizing his arm.

Rigo stared coldly at her hand on his arm. She slowly removed it. Here in this derelict *palazzo*, surrounded by old memories and faded glory with a battalion of servants watching them, she was more out of place than she had ever been, but someone had to try and reach Rigo. 'So Carlo wins—'

'He's already won.' Slamming his fist against the ruined door, Rigo leaned his face on his arm and fought to control his feelings. A long moment passed before he raised his head again. 'Call a meeting of the staff.' He sucked in a steadying breath before adding, 'Tell them I'll meet them here in the hall in two hours' time. And please reassure them,' he continued in a voice that was devoid of all expression, 'that before I go back to Rome they will all be taken care of.'

But who would take care of Rigo? Katie wondered. Seeing his childhood home reduced to a ruin had ripped his heart out. She knew how that felt too. 'Where will you go now?' she said, unconsciously clutching her throat.

'To find my driver. To make certain he has some rest and refreshment before we return to Pisa—'

'To fly to Rome?'

'Yes.' Distractedly he wiped a hand across his face.

'Don't you have to draw up a flight plan?' He needed time to get over this shock before he piloted a plane—before he decided what to do. She was looking for something, anything that would give him time to think.

Rigo shook his head as if to say, don't concern yourself with such things, and his next words proved to be the final nail in the coffin of her dreams. 'There's no job for you here, as

I'm sure you've worked out. Please accept my apologies for a wasted journey,' he added stiffly. 'My driver will, of course, take you to the airport so you can catch the next flight home.'

Home...

The sound of the battered door slamming heavily into place behind him brought more plaster off the walls, but even as Katie turned to look around and saw the group of people waiting for her to reassure them she experienced something she couldn't put a name to. It was uncanny, almost like a sixth sense, but she felt as if she was already home.

CHAPTER THIRTEEN

THE servants were whispering and casting anxious glances Katie's way. Tears stung her eyes when she realised many of them were armed with sweeping brushes, buckets and mops. She crossed the hall, intending only to deliver Rigo's instructions about the meeting, but seeing all those worried faces triggered something inside her. 'Do you have a spare brush?' she said instead to the housekeeper. 'If we all pitch in,' she explained in Italian, 'this won't take so long…'

There was no need for words—no time for conversation from that moment on. There was just concentrated effort from a small team of people including Katie, all of whom were determined to give the grand old *palazzo* a second chance. The Palazzo Farnese might have been brought to its knees by Carlo Ruggiero's lack of investment and care and his friends' rough treatment of it, but everyone sensed this could be a turning point if they worked hard enough.

When the old hall smelled fresh and clean Katie made some discreet enquiries about where Rigo had gone.

'After speaking to his driver he went to the leisure suite,' the housekeeper told her. 'I took the precaution of locking it,' the older woman added, touching her finger to her nose as Gino had. This brought the first smile of the day to Katie's face. 'Very sensible,' she agreed.

Rigo's concern for his driver had obviously delayed their departure, so this was her chance.

'I would not allow those people near the swimming pools,' the housekeeper confided in Katie, 'and the new master has chosen to swim in the indoor pool today.'

The new master? Katie thought of the crest on the arch and on the ring. Here, Rigo wasn't Signor Ruggiero, the infamous international playboy, but someone else entirely. 'The new master?' she prompted.

'*Sì,*' the housekeeper said with pride. '*Principe Ruggiero. Principe Arrigo Ruggiero.*'

Arrigo? Prince Arrigo? 'Ah, yes, of course,' she said. The housekeeper might think her a little slow on the uptake, but it was better to be sure of her facts. And never mind that he was a prince, it was Rigo's state of mind Katie was most concerned about.

Thanking the housekeeper and the rest of the staff for all their help, she left the hall in search of him. She had to know he was all right. She had to let Rigo know he wasn't alone and that she'd stay by his side until he sorted this mess out.

Katie stood in the shadows, watching Rigo power down the length of the pool. He had dropped his clothes on the side and hadn't even stopped to turn on the light, though there was lighting in the pool. The luminous ice-blue water was a perfect frame for the dark shape slicing through it and she was fascinated by Rigo's strength and by his magnificent body. His powerful legs pounded the water into foam, while his sculpted shoulders gleamed bronze as they broke the surface. They were the powerhouse for his punishing freestyle stroke, though every part of him was involved.

And every part of him was naked.

She should turn and walk away, but she couldn't; she didn't

want to. She remained motionless, watching, until Rigo finally cruised to the end of the pool.

Now she really must go…

But the moment came and went and she still hadn't moved.

Rigo sprang out. Water fell away from his hard-muscled frame. Every inch of him was in gleaming, spectacular focus. She remained riveted, staring, learning more about a man's body than she could have imagined. Rigo naked was even more perfect than Rigo clothed…so perfect Katie's scars tingled a reminder that she was not.

'Signorina Bannister?'

His husky voice surrounded her. She shrank as he padded towards her. She couldn't move. She was trapped in the beam of his stare.

'What are you doing here?' he demanded.

She lacked the guile to lie. 'Watching you.' She was careful to stare straight into his eyes, but she could feel his sexual energy invading her. She wasn't afraid. If he had caught her without her clothes she would have been terrified, Katie realised. But shouldn't Rigo be making some attempt to cover up? Was it possible to lack all inhibition? Her body thrilled to think all things were possible for him. But not for her, the scars on her back gave her a stinging reminder.

'Forgive me,' he mocked softly as he came to stand in front of her. 'I would have worn swimming shorts had I expected a visitor.'

'I'm sorry to intrude…'

She was about as sincere as he was. She would never forget these few minutes at the side of an unlit swimming pool. Every craving nerve she had was on fire. She would try to store that feeling. Before this she hadn't understood that such levels of arousal were even possible. The pool lights were reflected in Rigo's eyes, casting forbidding shadows on his rugged face. 'I was worried about you,' she confessed awkwardly.

'Worried about me?'

He sounded amused. Heat grew inside her as he continued to stare at her. Why didn't he walk away? Why didn't she?

Because her bones had turned to honey...

She was slow to react when he moved and her heart drummed a warning, but all he wanted was the towel he'd left on a chair. Relief coursed through her when he snatched it up, but he only used it to wipe his face and left his naked body on full view.

Having dried his face, he drew the towel back over his hair and rubbed it with fluid, lazy strokes. Water-heavy hair caught on his stubble and meshed with his eyelashes, and it seemed forever before he looped the towel around his waist.

'You were watching me for quite some time, worried *signorina*,' he murmured. 'Did you learn anything?'

His eyes were challenging and amused. It came home to her then how much older Rigo was, and how much more experienced and sophisticated. She was little more than a trembling wreck, and had no idea how to behave in these circumstances. 'You swim well,' she ventured.

His short laugh displayed strong white teeth and one inky black brow peaked, but his mouth remained hard and his eyes were watchful. He was fresh from the shock of discovering what had happened to his childhood home, she reminded herself, and had been swimming to exorcise those demons.

But he still had energy to burn...

'You're blushing,' he said.

'How can you see in this light?'

Reaching out, he traced the line of her cheek. 'I can feel the heat coming off you...'

Her swift intake of breath sounded unnaturally loud. 'It is very warm in here...' She gazed about in a pathetic attempt to distract him.

Rigo's low voice pulsed with intent. 'I don't think it's that sort of heat I can feel. Well, *signorina*?' he pressed. 'There must be something other than my swimming technique that kept you fascinated…'

Mutely, she shook her head. It was blood heat in the leisure suite and almost dark. Just the pool lights shimmering behind her like dots of moonlight on a lake. She felt cornered by a powerful predator, a predator she had sought out, and now her reward was to be wrapped in a cloak of arousal as she waited to see what would happen next.

The darkness concealed her flaws, and with Rigo's powerful body changed to shadowy imprecision in that darkness they could almost be two equals meeting here. It was a compelling fantasy in which she longed to lose herself, and as the pool room shrank around them she swayed towards him.

'Careful,' he murmured, putting warm palms on her upper arms, but only in a steadying gesture, 'you're very close to the edge of the pool…'

Still the child. Ever the innocent. Would he never see her any other way?

And shouldn't she be relieved about that?

She made light of it. 'Sorry…I didn't realise—I can hardly see anything in this light.'

Lies. All of it. She had seen every part of him, including the tattoo on his hip. 'I only came because I'm worried about you,' she said again. 'I called the meeting.'

'Good,' Rigo murmured.

His concentration on her hadn't wavered and his watchful eyes bathed her in heat. As he eased onto one hip she was consumed by the longing to touch him.

'Why don't you—?'

'Why don't I what?' she blurted guiltily.

'Why don't you tell me the real reason you came here?'

She heard the faint amusement in his voice. If only he

would stop staring down at her. 'I already said—you had a shock...the will—'

'My brother and I were practically strangers.'

Katie's mouth felt dry as Rigo continued to stare down at her. 'The *palazzo*...' She was grasping at straws, they both knew it. She gasped as Rigo coiled a long hank of her hair around his finger. It must have escaped her bun while she was cleaning.

'The only distress I feel,' he assured her, 'is knowing my stepbrother wasted his life—'

'It doesn't have to be a wasted life.' She gazed up. 'You could change that.'

He laughed and let her go. 'You will learn that it is pointless looking back and wishing things might have been different. They are as they are.'

She had not expected him to move so fast, or to slip his hand into her hair again, and to make the next move cupping her head. 'The knack is in learning to move on, Katie...'

Their faces were very close and he was staring at her intently. 'Rigo...'

'What?' he murmured, drawing her gaze to his lips.

'You could stay here at the *palazzo* and make things right for everyone...' She couldn't forget the faces of the servants waiting hopefully for news.

'Delaying tactics,' he breathed with his mouth only a whisper from her lips.

Perhaps, Katie admitted silently, though her concerns for the people who lived here were real enough. And now they had reached the point she had longed for she was frightened—frightened she would disappoint him. How could she not when Rigo was perfection—when he had taken one look at the flawed *palazzo* and turned his back on it? 'You don't strike me as the sort of man who walks away from problems.'

The mood changed as she spoke. The heavy, erotic beat fell silent and was replaced by humour, at least in Rigo's eyes.

'I thought I told you, no counselling?' he said.

'Sorry…' She eased her neck as he stepped back. Would she ever forget his touch? 'I wouldn't dream of advising you—'

'I think you would,' he argued. 'I think you do a lot of dreaming, Signorina Bannister. I think you dream and want and need as much as anyone else.'

Breath shot from her lungs as Rigo seized hold of her.

He wanted her. Wanted her? He wanted to lose himself in Katie Bannister. He wanted to bask in her goodness and have it heal him. To begin with he'd been amused by the fact that Katie had worried about him enough to come and seek him out, but now he remembered that no one had ever done that for him before. And then he saw the hunger in her eyes matched his own and the time for restraint had passed.

There was no subtlety. As he slammed her against his hard warmth and his towel hit the floor he made no attempt to retrieve it.

Katie's senses had sharpened in the darkness to the point where she could smell the water on Rigo. She pressed against him, believing she was someone else—someone flawless, bold and hungry. She might be falling deeper into the rabbit hole and leaving reality behind—and maybe she should try to pull things back, but she didn't want to, and her body wouldn't cooperate, anyway. It was swollen with need, moist and ready, and so instead of pulling away from Rigo, she raised her face to his.

'Needs are nothing to be ashamed of, Katie. Even I have them. I understand you, Katie,' he assured her. 'I know everything you feel.'

In that case he'd be ready to catch her when her legs buckled. Did he have any idea how hungry she was for this—how desperate for his touch? Did he know where and exactly how she wanted him to touch her? Her eyes were shut. She was barely breathing. She was suspended in an erotic net, and was totally unprepared when he pulled away.

The ache morphed into real physical pain. It took her a moment to realise Rigo's actions were so fluid he hadn't left her, but was kneeling on the hard tiles in front of her.

'No.' Her voice clearly said yes. As he lifted her skirt she clutched his shoulders for support.

'Yes,' Rigo murmured, burying his face.

An excited whimper ripped the silence as she unashamedly edged her legs apart. She was greedy for sensation, for experience, for him. Having taken the first step, she was ready to fly.

'Relax, worried *signorina*,' Rigo murmured, 'there's no rush.'

She could hear him smiling in the darkness.

CHAPTER FOURTEEN

HER heart was pounding so hard she couldn't breathe. Her wildest fantasy was coming true. Held firmly by Rigo, she was trapped, not by his grasp, but by her own overwhelming need. She didn't move, couldn't move, because she didn't want to. She craved fulfilment and satisfaction and a door into that world that had always been closed to her. She wanted everything Rigo was prepared to give her. She wanted to climax—and not once, but many times. She wanted this erotic dream to last forever and for reality to fade away. Closing her eyes, she bathed in darkness where there were no scars and only sensation registered. Consequences? What were they?

She sighed with disappointment as he started to stand up but he took his time as if imbibing her scent on the way up It thrilled her—aroused her even more. His face was only mil limetres distant from her own, and her body was crying ou for more contact between them. Swinging her into his arms he lowered her down onto one of the recliners facing the pool where silence enveloped them.

She blinked as he switched on the lamp by the chair.

'I want to see you come—'

'No.' She wasn't ready for that.

'Yes,' he argued steadily.

She was painfully self-conscious as he pressed her back against the cushions.

'Relax,' he said.

She was out of the dream and back to reality. This was embarrassing and wrong. She would regret it in the morning.

In the time it took to think that, he had pushed her skirt back to her waist, removed her underwear and lifted her legs to rest them on his shoulders.

She was completely exposed. Cool air brushed her most heated self as Rigo cupped her bottom in warm, strong hands, and instead of pulling away she settled down. Moments later he found her with his tongue and with his lips and with his fingers, rough stubble scratching the insides of her thighs, pleasure and pain intermingling. She hit a wall of pleasure and that wall gave way, drawing her deeper into a world of the senses where reality could not intrude. She bucked wildly. He held her in place. She screamed with abandon as he tipped her into the abyss, and while she was moaning with amazed contentment he kept her safe in his arms until the last flicker of sensation had subsided.

'Greedy girl,' he murmured.

With some satisfied sounds she was ready to fall silent. Language was a civilised pursuit and there was nothing civilised about her feelings for him. She was spent, exhausted, satiated—

And then she noticed the fire in Rigo's eyes. He was neither spent, exhausted nor satiated.

She jerked away as a hot stream of panic filled her. He didn't attempt to follow as she clambered awkwardly away from him. 'I'm sorry—'

'So am I. What are you ashamed of, Katie?'

'Nothing.' She spoke too fast and Rigo's eyes narrowed with suspicion. 'Sorry,' she said again, backing away. 'I don't now what I was thinking—'

'That we were two consenting adults, maybe?' he suggested in a voice that was calm while the expression in his eyes was anything but.

And who could blame him? Katie thought. She had led him to this point and then pulled away. 'I know what you must think of me—'

'You have no idea,' he assured her. Springing lightly to his feet, he collected his robe from the back of a chair and shrugged it on, belting it securely. 'So, Signorina Prim?' His voice had lost all warmth. 'What do you hope to get out of this?'

Rigo's expression frightened her. 'Nothing.'

'Nothing? So you haven't been leading me on in the hope of landing a greater prize?'

He wasn't talking to her, she felt instinctively, but to the woman who had taken his father from him, and to the many women who saw Rigo as the ultimate prize. 'No, of course I haven't been leading you on. Rigo, you're upset—you're not thinking straight—'

'Don't mistake me for one of your hard-luck causes—' dipping down, he scooped up her underwear from the floor. '—and don't forget these.'

He threw them at her, only for her to fumble and drop the dainty briefs she had bought in Rome.

'Pick them up,' he snarled. 'You might need them when you identify your next target.'

And with that he turned his back on her and stalked away.

He took the private staircase from the leisure suite to his rooms. The episode with Katie Bannister had sickened him. He knew who and what she was, just as he knew himself. This will, this so-called legacy, had undermined the man he had become and had left him feeling tainted by everything he had vowed to leave behind. Seeing his childhood home desecrated had done exactly what Katie said. It had rocked his world and he wasn't thinking straight.

Shouldering his way through the door, he entered his room pacing and didn't stop until he had reasoned his motives through on every point. He had encountered just about every ruse to capture his interest and reel him in and was always on his guard. Katie had reaped the whirlwind. Her appetite was undeniable, but when he weighed that appetite against her naïvety, or the shock on her face when she realised the road they were on led to penetrative sex, he knew she was innocent. So she had splurged on some decorative underwear. Did he begrudge her even that small luxury?

Anger, regret and frustration had coagulated into one ugly mass, he concluded. Seeing the *palazzo* brought to ruin hadn't just shaken him to his foundations, it had filled him with unnatural energy—or just plain fury, maybe. Whatever the cause, he had needed an outlet for that energy and had chosen badly. He should have stuck to swimming, he mused, smiling bleakly. He could never give Katie Bannister what she wanted and deserved, which was a loving husband and babies, a home, romance, a happy-ever-after ending. Thanks to him she had lost her innocence tonight. But perhaps it would keep her safe from men with fewer scruples than he.

Stripping off his clothes, he took a long, cold shower before swinging naked into bed. He wasn't going anywhere. He was staying until this mess was sorted out. As Katie hoped, he had embraced his legacy. He would take a negative and make it positive. He would drink from Carlo's poisoned chalice—but Principe Arrigo Ruggiero Farnese would not be making any more mistakes.

He woke at dawn after a restless night. One face had held sway in his mind, but she would hate him now. He turned his thoughts to practical matters he could do something about and went straight to examine the north tower, where he found the roof caved in. But it could be fixed. Having survived centuries, the old place would stand a few more knocks before it surrendered.

It wouldn't be easy to restore the *palazzo*, he concluded after further investigation, and it would take many years and a lot of money. Money he had, and he had the determination to set it right. He would oversee this project personally. He'd handled many major building works in the past, but they had been investments for his money rather than his heart. He consulted with architects who sent teams in, but he wasn't prepared to do that here. He would be the main point of contact. He couldn't allow anyone to interfere with the *palazzo* who didn't remember it as he did.

Swinging across a beam, he dropped lightly to the floor. It was time to persuade Katie Bannister to stay. He needed her clear thinking and organisational skills. She could coordinate the various teams—if she had the courage to stay after what had happened last night.

He went to the window in his room and pushed the rotten frame with the heel of his hand until it yielded. He had to breathe some fresh air. He looked down, searching for Katie. Something told him she'd be outside. Birds were singing— the sun was shining; it was Katie's kind of morning. Resting his hands on the cool stone, he looked in vain. Pulling back, he felt the wear of time. Like everything else the stonework required expert attention. He would ask her to find the best team of stonemasons to begin work right away—if she still worked for him.

She must work for him.

Last night he had been infected by a maelstrom of emotion, but today he could see clearly that it was an assistant he needed, not a lover. And if Signorina Bannister didn't work out he could always sack her like the rest. Meanwhile, he'd take a shower and get rid of this dust.

Last night the choice had seemed clear. She was going home. She had proved conclusively she wasn't cut out for this any more than she was cut out for her dead-end job in Yorkshire. Her encounter with Rigo had proved to be the worst humiliation of her life.

But the best sex.

Better than anything she could dream up, Katie conceded. But deeply humiliating; she'd never get past it. And as for Rigo? Trying to imagine what he must think of her made her shudder.

But, when she came down to breakfast and discovered a new mood of optimism sweeping the staff, she immediately put her own feelings on the back burner.

'You have to stay,' the housekeeper protested when Katie explained she was leaving. 'It's such a lovely morning,' the older woman pressed her. 'The best of the year so far.' And then the clincher. 'We have cleaned the outdoor swimming pool especially for you.'

Bare skin. Scars. More humiliation. 'But I don't—'

One of the maids stepped forward. 'We are about the same size, *signorina*,' she said shyly, 'and I have a new swimming costume I have never worn.'

As the young girl held it out to her Katie knew she couldn't refuse.

'You'd be quite alone, *signorina*,' the housekeeper quickly reassured her. 'I'll make sure everyone is kept away—'

'You're very kind—'

'And you're the first person to come here and give us hope,' the woman told her frankly.

Was she going to show her weakness now? She had to be strong for these people all the time, not just selectively.

'It would be such a shame to waste the day,' the maid said as the housekeeper nodded agreement.

The damaged skin on Katie's back tightened, but she would feel more than shame if she refused this kind gesture. 'If…if I was alone—'

'You have my word on it,' the housekeeper assured her.

* * *

The cool water felt like satin on her heated skin, and as sunshine warmed her shoulders any remaining cares she had floated away. This was the first time since the fire that she had stripped off outside the privacy of her own home and she was surprised to find the costume the young maid had lent her fitted her so well. She had Rigo's staff to thank for making this possible.

Submerging her face in the fresh, clean water, Katie basked in the unaccustomed luxury of having a whole swimming pool to herself. And what a swimming pool it was—if she had thought the *palazzo*'s leisure complex was like something out of a film, this outdoor pool was far more beautiful. Stern Doric columns marked the perimeter, while mosaics tempted her to look beneath the water to where a kaleidoscope of images told a story of ancient Rome, complete with gladiators and graceful beauties clad in flattering flowing robes. I want one of those glorious gowns, Katie thought, buying into the dream. She was beginning to believe she could forget anything swimming here.

The housekeeper had opened the shutters and folded them back, allowing him a clear view of the gardens and swimming pool. Drawn by the particular brilliance of the sunlight that day, he walked over to the window after his shower and stared out. His gaze was immediately drawn to the activity in the pool, where someone was preparing to dive in...

Katie...

She had already been swimming and her hair was slicked back. Her honey-blush skin gleamed like an impossibly perfect sculpture in the brilliant light. She had surprised him once again. He had always suspected she was concealing a stunning figure beneath her dowdy clothes—just how stunning had eluded him, he realised now. He already knew her legs were beautiful, but... A whisper from last night intruded on his thoughts. Could he forget? He had to forget—he had a pressing need for a PA and she'd make a great PA. But with her hair drawn back and her elegant profile raised towards the sky, there was no doubt she was one of the loveliest sights he had ever seen. He remembered their first telephone conversation, when her sexy voice had revealed so much about her. You could hear beauty in a voice. Why she dressed down almost to the point of disguise was Katie's business, but he couldn't deny he was curious. Pulling away from the window, he stretched his limbs. Even an hour without activity was an hour too long for him. He was restless with last night playing on his mind again. Katie's responses to him…her soft whimpers…her tremulous, yet passionate plunge into abandonment and pleasure—

Maybe a swim was what he needed too.

'No, Rigo, no…'

He stopped dead in his tracks. He had only walked halfway down the pool, but she was recoiling from him as if he meant her harm. The last thing he had intended was to frighten Katie, but the moment she caught sight of him she had catapulted out of the pool and now she was stumbling backwards with a towel clutched tightly to her chest.

'I didn't see you, Rigo,' she gasped.

Was he such a terrifying sight? It was certainly terror in her eyes. He took a step back with his hands raised, signalling his intention to come no closer. Still she backed away. If she didn't stop soon she'd fall over the sunbed—

He breathed a sigh of relief when she felt the bed behind her knees and stopped, but now she was feeling awkwardly behind her for a wrap she'd left there earlier, and only he could see she was in real danger of tumbling into the pool.

'No! Stay back!' she shouted in alarm when he moved to save her.

'What the hell's wrong with you? I'm not going to touch you.'

Ever again, he added silently. If this was Katie Bannister's reaction to him, imagine if they'd had sex.

None of this made sense. She'd seen him naked. She'd held him. He'd let her go without once trying to stop her. He was respectably attired this morning in swimming shorts with a towel slung around his neck. He couldn't understand her bizarre behaviour and was growing increasingly resentful. But still her safety was uppermost in his mind. 'Stay where you are before you fall in. I'm going to reach for your robe,' he told her firmly, 'while you don't move a single muscle. Do you understand me?'

He wasn't even sure she could hear him, so he put his promise into action, moving slowly and deliberately. 'And now I'm going to hand it to you.'

Part of him said this was ridiculous, while another part of him was too busy seeking an answer to the mystery to walk away. Katie, meanwhile, remained stock-still, staring at him in wide-eyed dread.

He held out her wrap at arm's length. She took it from him. Dragging it on, she belted it tightly, tweaking the edges as if not a single part of her could be on view.

Had last night done this to her? He would never forgive himself if that was the case, though he could fathom no reason why it should. She had been a willing partner all along, up to the point where a natural conclusion was facing them both, and then, because she for whatever reason had drawn back, he had let her go.

'When you've showered and dressed I'd like to see you in the library,' he said evenly. 'Anyone will tell you where that is. Say, twenty minutes—half an hour?' His look also added, if you still work for me? But he didn't labour the point.

He didn't stop walking until he reached the entrance to the *palazzo*, when he turned to see Katie still standing where he'd left her. He wondered if he would ever forget the look on her face. You would have thought she had been in danger of her life.

CHAPTER FIFTEEN

WHEN Rigo left her at the poolside it took her a long time to settle, mentally and physically. Since the fire she had longed to be invisible and had almost achieved that goal—until this trip to Rome, when Rigo had forced her to face reality again. Deep down, she was grateful to him. There was still such a lot of life to be lived. Even before the fire her appearance had placed her in the pigeonhole marked good girl, plain girl, quiet girl, studious girl, which did nothing to douse the fires inside her. Last night Rigo had been right to point out she had needs like everyone else. Her needs were exactly the same as all the pretty, vivacious girls with great figures and unblemished skin.

There had been one short interlude when she had found an outlet for her passion in training to be an opera singer. Music had given her a means of expression until the fire stole her voice away. She had never thought to experience passion again until Rigo proved her wrong. And now she was at another crossroads, Katie realised. She could go back to Yorkshire and pick up her old life, or she could stay on in Italy as Rigo's PA.

When she had buried her face in the hospital pillows and cried the first time she saw the scars on her back the doctor had told her she would have to be brave. Take it one step at time, they had advised. Life was a series of steps, she had discovered since then. You could take them bravely, or you could refuse to take them at all.

So the past had got the better of her?

She wouldn't let it.

Twenty minutes after leaving Katie at the pool, he was tapping a pen on the table, wondering if she was going to turn up—and if she did, was he about to make the biggest mistake of his life? He hadn't imagined taking Katie out of her comfort zone would throw her so badly. Forget the sex—that was never going to happen. But where the job was concerned he had to know if she was up to working alongside him in Italy.

The door opened and he put down his pen as she walked in.

'I know this is a business meeting,' she said when his face registered surprise, 'but I thought—if we needed to scramble round the building…'

His surprise that she had come at all was instantly replaced by relief and admiration. It took some guts to climb back to a position of composure and responsibility when you had lowered your guard to the point where you appeared a gibbering wreck. 'Sensible outfit,' he agreed, wishing she wouldn't always wear everything so big.

Camouflage, he realised, remembering the voluptuous figure she'd revealed at the pool. But why did Katie always feel this overwhelming need to cover up? The plain tailored trousers and simple jumper were a great improvement on the boxy suit, but they were hardly flattering. Thinking of the PAs he'd hired in the past made him want to shake his head in bemusement—when he would have preferred them to keep their clothes on they couldn't wait to whip them off. 'Don't you have any other clothes with you? Jeans?' he suggested.

'Just one pair I bought when I went shopping with Antonia. I didn't want to spoil them.'

He curbed a smile. That simple comment touched him somewhere deep. He'd become a stranger to having one of anything years ago. He turned determinedly back to business. He was already dressed in off-duty jeans and a casual top and was ready for the dirty work ahead of them. 'So you're ready to start work?'

'Yes, I am,' she said, staring straight into his eyes.

He came around the desk to shake her hand. 'Welcome to the team.'

She liked the way Rigo could be strong and unemotional. She also didn't like it—and for his sake more than anything else. A man so easily divorced from emotion could end up lonely. But she wanted this job and Rigo's grip was firm and compelling. She wished with all her heart things could have been different between them, but they weren't different. She had to hold her nerve now so he would understand she had drawn a line under everything that had happened between them. 'I hope I don't disappoint you,' she said, noting that Rigo held her hand for precisely the right length of time an employer should hold the hand of an employee.

He smiled slightly. 'I don't think there's the slightest danger of that.'

When roused, don't stand in his way. Rigo waited for no one, Katie concluded as he strode off. Even her embarrassment had been refused time to ferment. He was out of the library and across the hall before she had pulled a pen out of her bag, and now her heels were rattling across the floor in hot pursuit. They were surrounded by priceless antiques and frescoes that wouldn't have looked out of place in the Sistine Chapel, and the scent of history competed with the strong smell of disinfectant from the recently cleaned floor and was a dizzying combination. Or was that the Rigo effect? She was going to work for him. She did work for him. She ran faster and almost collided with him at the foot of the stairs. He gave her no time to recover. Seizing her shoulders, he swung her around. 'Tell me what you make of this.'

Breath shot out of her lungs in a gasp as she followed his gaze up the stairs to take in the garish stair carpet. Truth? Or diplomatic lie?

'Come on, come on,' he pressed. 'I want a reaction—'

'It stinks.'

'That's what I think. What should we put in its place?'

A runner at most. Or, depending on what they found underneath, the naked steps. She told him. He agreed.

'Make a note.'

She did so.

Oh, this job was fun. She raced after him. Who else had a boss so big and hard and sexy, a boss who only had to look at her to fill her body with the zest for life—along with other things? She didn't mind running to keep up with Rigo's easy, loping stride, because if he stopped suddenly she had discovered that crashing into him was like crashing into a padded wall—and who wouldn't want to rest against that, and even writhe a little, given half a chance?

'Well?' he demanded, thumping the wall with his meaty fist. 'What do you think of this?'

'They've plastered over stone that might have been better left exposed.' She pressed her lips together as their eyes met briefly. Images of other things—more interesting, but just as hard as stone—made her cheeks blaze.

'Exactly,' he rapped, striding off again.

She sucked in a breath and refocused determinedly before hurrying after him.

'This is a recent addition too.' He disdainfully flicked a hand at some dismal curtains and strode on again.

She made a note to replace the hangings.

'This is a disgrace,' he snapped, moving her aside to examine a sleazy mural more closely.

'Sandblast it?'

He almost smiled.

'We'll need a historical architect to advise us on renovations,' he said, walking on. 'Take a note.'

Something in the tone of that voice doused her enthusiasm. He was beginning to take her for granted. '*You'll* need one,' she said. 'I don't know how long I'm going to be here—trial period,' she reminded him, chasing after him down some stairs. This wasn't turning out as she had expected. She wanted more out of life than taking notes. She wanted to be listened to, at the very least, even if her thoughts were later discarded. But had Rigo even heard her?

She was ready to renege on their deal, Katie realised. She had been invited to become part of a team, not a dictatorship. She would stay until Rigo found a replacement for her, but then she would go home and find some other, safer way to spread her wings.

'This is more like a casino than a valuable historical site,' he remarked, opening one door and slamming it shut with a bang. 'Make a note—'

'You make a note.' She shoved her notebook in his hand. 'You know what you want. Presumably you can write it down.'

She'd never thrown a temper tantrum in her life. Rigo paused to look at her. He let one beat pass, and then another. He made no attempt to take the pen and paper she was offering him. 'What do you think of the room?' he said mildly then.

She gritted her teeth. 'I think it looks more like a casino than a site of historical importance,' she ground out.

His lips tugged. Her body yearned. They walked on.

'This used to be a slate floor,' he observed, sounding more relaxed.

The mood was catching and, in spite of her reservations,

she relaxed too; enough to carry out her own investigations. They had entered a second, dimly lit corridor leading off from the first and once again it was lavishly carpeted in hotel style. 'I think we'd better add a stone-floor specialist to the list.'

'I agree,' he murmured in her ear. There was humour in his gaze that did considerable damage to her composure. He walked on. 'It wouldn't surprise me to find a nightclub and a spa down here.'

'Could this be it?' Katie wondered, peering into a stale-smelling cavern. Judging by the heaped ashtrays and the litter of drinks, this was the room in which Carlo's friends had chosen to wait for them. 'I'll get round to clearing it up as soon as I can—'

'*You'll* get round to it?' He swung towards her. 'That's not your problem. Katie.'

Signorina Prim, Signorina Dull, had had enough. The demon temper had been roused and was still very close to the surface. She only had to remember working alongside Rigo's staff the previous evening for that temper to erupt into words. 'I might not be stylish and rich like you, but if there's one thing I do know about, it's cleanliness and order. Who do you think cleaned the hall? You have a wonderful staff if you chose to notice them.'

To her surprise Rigo didn't respond to her attack, and instead granted her a mocking bow. 'I can assure you my wonderful staff has already told me what you did here yesterday.'

'They did most of it—'

'You claim no credit?'

'Why should I?'

He gave her a look. 'Why didn't you ask me to help?'

Her only thought had been to start getting things in a better state for him. 'I didn't want to trouble you last night.' Blushing now, she quickly changed the subject, having convinced herself she neither needed nor wanted Rigo's praise. 'You were upset and so—'

'You're making excuses for me?' he suggested mildly.

There was that flash of humour again in his intense green gaze and she hungered for more of it. There was silence while they studied each other's faces with new understanding. It was no longer Rigo Ruggiero, infamous playboy confronting Katie Bannister, poorly paid messenger girl with a hopeless taste in suits, but a man and a woman who each had the same goal.

But don't get too carried away, Katie warned herself, breaking eye contact first. A leopard doesn't change its spots that easily. A maxim that could apply to both of them, she conceded as Rigo resumed his inspection.

'This room will have to be gutted…'

And with that the spell that had so briefly held them was broken.

'In fact,' he added, 'all the rooms will have to be gutted—make a note.'

She did so, but this time there was a smile hovering round her lips. No wonder he couldn't keep his staff. 'It's only cleaning and redecoration,' she pointed out, but by the time she looked up from her notebook Rigo was out of sight.

Had he forgotten she was with him? Katie wondered when she found Rigo examining an electrical circuit box. 'Electrician?'

'Full check,' he confirmed. 'Our first goal must be safety for everyone, and then we must concentrate on bringing the *palazzo* back to its authentic state.'

'No earth closets, I hope?' she couldn't resist murmuring as he cast an eye over her notes.

'State-of-the-art plumbing. There's nothing better than a long, hot shower.'

As he looked to her for agreement she blushed again.

Opening a door at the far end of the corridor, he stepped outside. She followed, desperate to be free of all the conflicting emotions bottled up indoors. Gulping in the fresh, clean air, she exclaimed with pleasure and relief.

Rigo turned to look at her. 'How do you like the job so far?' he demanded.

She saw the irony in his eyes. 'I'm only here until you find a replacement.'

'Or I sack you.'

There was another of those long moments where they stared into each other's eyes. A breeze had whipped Rigo's hair into a fury, but his eyes were full of laughter as he raked it back.

She'd asked for this and she'd got it. Mad for him or not, she was under no illusion: Rigo wanted someone with an organised mind to take notes for him, just as he said. He needed her—not for all the reasons she'd like, but because she could keep life organised. She was a convenient choice, Katie reasoned as he dropped onto one hip. 'Are you coming or not?' he said.

'I'm right here.'

'Of course, you do realise if you prove satisfactory this could become a permanent position.'

'*If* I decide I want it.' She looked away so he didn't see her disappointment. Her dreams extended further than being his PA in a suit.

They spent the rest of the morning checking and discussing and formulating an initial plan of action, while she filled her notebook with notes. By lunchtime Katie could only conclude Rigo had some magic dust that had wiped the previous night's debacle from her mind. The incident at the pool also appeared to have been forgotten. It was better this way for both of them, Katie concluded; no tension, no agenda, purely business.

They joined the staff for lunch, all of whom were keen to put Rigo's plan for them into action right away. 'But run everything past me,' Rigo reminded Katie as he left her in charge. 'I've had enough surprises for one visit.'

She didn't doubt it.

CHAPTER SIXTEEN

KATIE'S face burned as she saw knowing smiles exchanged between the staff. Rigo had come back into the kitchen to tell her that two teams of men were waiting and he needed her right away.

'To take notes?' she suggested, avoiding his gaze.

'You're quick,' he murmured, ushering her out. 'One team is here to start work on the heavy cleaning,' he explained, 'so we don't put unnecessary pressure on the staff.'

'Good idea. And the other?'

'They're here to sort you out—'

'Sort me out?' Katie exclaimed.

Taking the pad from her hand, Rigo stuck it in the back pocket of his jeans. 'You won't need to take notes for this.'

'For what?' Katie's heart leaped into her throat as Rigo took her by the hand.

'If you're going to be working for me you'll need a new wardrobe of clothes—'

'To go rooting round the cellars with mice and spiders?'

'Your clothes are giving me eye-ache.'

'Well, I'm sorry if I—'

'You might be in Italy, but you don't have to dress like a *nonna*.'

Katie was too shocked to speak. A maiden aunt was one

thing, but a grannie? Freeing her hand, she stood her ground. 'I'm hardly on show. And as I'm only here until you find a—'

'Think of it as your uniform,' Rigo interrupted, 'though, of course, I expect you to set a good example to the servants when you're off duty too—'

'And will you be buying them clothes?'

'I will, as it happens. It's about time they had something new, don't you think?'

He'd put her in an impossible position, but then Rigo was good at that.

'Rigo, wait—'

He stopped suddenly in the middle of the hall. Catching hold of her, he steadied her on her feet and stood back. Two groups of men were waiting at the far end of the hall—one team wearing overalls, the other in flamboyant suits. The overalls looked more appealing right now. She freed herself as discreetly as she could, conscious that even in a space as big as this sound travelled. As did sexual chemistry between two people. 'Even if I did work for you on a permanent basis, which I don't,' she told Rigo in an impassioned whisper, 'I have a perfectly serviceable suit—'

'That brown thing? Chuck it. Or, if I find it first, I'll chuck it out.'

'Fortunately it's already packed in my suitcase.'

'So you've decided not to stay?'

'I was ready to leave last night,' she admitted. 'I asked your driver if he would take me to the airport today.'

'Well, lucky for you I spoke to him too. And next time please do me the courtesy of speaking to me before you instruct my staff. Now, let's get on. None of these people want to be kept waiting. I can't think of a woman in the world who would turn down the chance to have the designers I have chosen create a look for her.'

'A mistress in the world, maybe.'

It was only a mutter but he heard her.

'Don't flatter yourself.'

Ouch.

'I'm merely extending the same courtesy to you I show to all the people who work for me—'

'And you can't keep any of them.'

She could always call a cab, Katie reasoned as Rigo's expression darkened.

'Those I don't want leave my employ.'

'So I have to earn the right to work for you?'

'You have to do the job you're paid for. That's reasonable, isn't it? There's a wonderful opportunity here if you want to be part of it. With the right team I can take Carlo's poisoned chalice and turn it into something wonderful—and that's all I'm prepared to say at the moment.'

'You're talking about something more than renovating the *palazzo*?'

'When my ideas are fully formed I'll let you know.'

'So you don't trust me, but you want me to work for you?'

'I'm saying confidentiality is an issue.'

'I'd need to know more.'

'When I'm ready.' And, when she still looked doubtful, his lips curved in a dangerous smile. 'Do you really need more time to get used to the thrill of working for me?'

Rigo's arrogance she could deal with, even his impossible behaviour she was getting used to, but when he played the humour card she was lost.

Just about. 'I can't afford to deal in riddles where my career is concerned,' she prompted, only to have Rigo close the matter with a decisive gesture. 'This will have to wait until you've seen your team. Come and show me when you've made your selection.'

'At most I need one plain and simple suit.'

Rigo shrugged. 'Your loss.'

And with that he left her to negotiate plain and simple with men for whom Katie guessed plain and simple was an abomination.

Katie was forced to admit she was wrong. As the designers discussed their ideas she realised their taste wasn't so far distant from her own—just in monetary terms. Unlike some men she could mention they were prepared to listen. When she asked for plain and simple they called it stylish and smiled. Once they had reassured her that all the measurements they needed could be taken over her clothes, she relaxed. They agreed on one tailored suit with both skirt and trousers to ring the changes, as well as three sharp shirts. They could dress her from stock, they admitted, to which she agreed immediately. It was both cheaper, and...well, truthfully, she couldn't wait to see what they had in mind.

So she did have a figure, Katie realised as she performed a twirl later in the privacy of her own room. It was a surprise to find she was a stock size and didn't even need an alteration, but then breasts were most definitely 'in' in Italy, where clothes made allowances for women with generous curves.

Left to her own devices she might have chosen something concealing, but the designers had insisted the jacket would hang off her shoulders if she chose a larger size. The elegant navy-blue tapered pencil skirt and matching short jacket with a sexy nipped-in waist made her look, well, if not glamorous—she could never be that—then, at least, something the right side of presentable. It was such a thrill to have some smart new clothes—and, as uniforms went, she conceded wryly, staring at the label in awe, this wasn't half bad.

The accommodation the housekeeper had chosen for her was another delight. It had survived the worst excesses of Rigo's brother and was the most beautiful suite of rooms Katie could imagine. The silks might be faded, as was the counterpane on the bed, but Katie had always loved shabby chic and this was the perfect example of it. She wouldn't change a thing in the room. Having everything pristine and new would take away from the *palazzo*'s charm. Any renovations would have to be carried out with the utmost sensitivity—though she had no doubt Rigo was more than capable of that. He was very different from his public face. The Press might think him a playboy, but that only showed how little they knew him.

She sighed as she gazed out across the formal gardens. She was more than a little in love with him even though much of Rigo was hidden behind whichever mask he had chosen to suit his purpose. She wondered what he was hiding and why—and what were these plans of his? He had decided to keep the *palazzo* and renovate it, but then he was going to use it for something he wouldn't tell her about. Would he ever trust her enough to tell her? And could she stay until he did?

He'd have to tell her if she was going to work for him, Katie reasoned, pulling back from the window. No employer could hide much from his PA. Was that why he'd sacked so many? Rigo was asking them to give blind loyalty to a man they knew to be ruthless and who would only tell them what he thought they should know. Would she put up with that?

Glancing at her watch, Katie realised it was time to show Rigo the outfits she had selected. Outfit, she corrected herself, smoothing the skirt of her new suit. So that shouldn't take up too much of his time—though what he would think of the sexy shoes the designers had insisted she must wear with the severely cut two-piece, she couldn't imagine. Well, she could. He would think her frivolous and extravagant and with very good reason. Lifting up a heel, she stared rapturously at the luscious crimson sole. The contrast with the black patent court shoe was both subtle and fabulous. She had never owned shoes like these in her life before and would have to pay Rigo back from her wages, which meant staying on—for a time. The shoes were worth it, Katie concluded.

Katie Bannister in high heels and designer labels—who'd have thought it? Katie Bannister, whose heart was beating like a jack-hammer, because she was going to see the man she loved, though Rigo must never guess how she felt about him.

He stood watching her as she walked across the hallway towards him. He noticed the way her hips swayed as if she had only recently become aware of her femininity. She loved her new suit. He loved to see her wearing it. He could tell she liked it by the way she moved. It was so good to see her standing straight, walking tall, hiding nothing.

He wanted her.

She hadn't seen him yet and so she knocked on the door of the library, where she expected to find him. Hearing no reply, she moved on towards the entrance to the leisure suite. He walked up behind her, hoping to surprise her, but something flashed between them and she turned. 'You look beautiful,' he murmured.

He heard her swift intake of breath. She remained quite still. 'Really beautiful…' He didn't touch her. He didn't want to spoil the moment as it shimmered between them. And then he noticed she was trembling.

'Do you really like it?' she said.

'More than you know…' He was sick of the pretence. He was sick of Katie's lack of self-belief. He wanted the chance to help her rebuild it. He wanted her in his bed. She wanted him. She couldn't have made it more obvious. Her honey-coloured eyes had darkened to sepia and her parted lips offered him a challenge he couldn't ignore. Katie Bannister was changing faster than any woman he had ever known and the look of question, of adventure in her eyes mirrored his own. 'Now you've got the uniform,' he teased her, 'be sure you obey all my commands.'

'Until you sack me?' She refused to see the joke. 'I'll work in a team as you first suggested, Rigo, but I refuse to be the next in a long line of disposable dollies dressed for your amusement—'

'Is that what you think this is?' He gave the suit ensemble an appreciative once-over. 'And I thought you'd like it.'

'I do,' she admitted. Her eyes were wide and innocent, but there was a riot of activity behind them.

'Rome *and* Tuscany,' he tempted, sure that was an offer she couldn't refuse.

'I'll stick with the trial period we agreed on, thank you.'

'I need your organised brain on board.'

'I'm flattered,' she said dryly.

'I mean it. You're quiet, organised, discreet, quick-witted—'

'Biddable, do you mean?' she interrupted. 'Or just plain dull?'

'Dull? Who said quick-witted was dull?' Had the definition changed since the last time he used it? 'Work *with* me,' he tempered, keeping the bigger picture at the forefront of his mind.

'As what, Rigo? The perfect back-room girl?'

'You want to run the show?' he demanded with exasperation, planting his fist on the door above her head.

'Before I agree to anything I'd have to know exactly what's involved. That's reasonable, isn't it?'

Their lips were inches apart and he was tempted to take advantage of that and then tell her everything. But he was still developing the idea and his kids' club wasn't up for negotiation. It was and always would remain confidential—not for his sake, but for theirs. He wouldn't go out on a limb where that was concerned and he wouldn't put unfair pressure on Katie. 'I can't tell you yet—'

'But you expect me to throw up everything I have in

England and move to Italy to work with you on a permanent basis on this…secret project?'

'I'm asking you to take a chance.'

'With you?'

He stared into her eyes and wondered how he had ever thought Katie Bannister a quiet little mouse. Passion lurked so close to the surface in both of them and her sweet wild-flower scent was driving him crazy.

But he was not as innocent as she was.

'No, you're quite right,' he said, 'this would never work. I can't imagine what I was thinking.'

Rigo enjoyed provoking her. She knew that. Even so she was tempted to go along with his plan. He had injected danger into her life and she was addicted to it now. But could she work for him and feel like this? Could she do anything with a clear head until he finished what he had started last night? Sexual desire did not play by the usual rules. Clear thinking could vanish in an instant, leaving only the danger of desire.

'Shall we take this somewhere more private?' Reaching past her, he opened the door.

The door swung to, enclosing them in the sensual cocoon of the luxury spa. Rigo locked the door and handed her the key. Neither of them spoke; they didn't need to. Heat spread through her body until it came to a pulsing halt. Her lips were parted and her eyelids were heavy. She was ready and so was he. She could feel Rigo's breath on her face, on her neck, on her ear, his lips only millimetres away. They stood facing each other, staring into each other's eyes. When she was certain she could stand it no longer he drew her close. The relief was such she cried with pleasure. Her body was pressed hard against his and she could feel his erection throb and thicken as it strained against the fabric of his jeans. The more she tried to fight this Katie registered dizzily, the more she wanted him.

'So what would it take to bend you to my will?' he suggested wickedly.

'A miracle?' she countered, deliberately provoking him.

'A miracle?' he murmured. 'Or this…'

He claimed her mouth, teasing her lips apart—punishing her with kisses. As she responded he cupped her bottom and memories of sensation came streaming back. Was it only last night? How could she be so hungry? This wasn't decent—she would go mad. She was composed of sensation and need, she was all hunger, all mindless, searching, craving, desire. 'Oh, please…'

Briefly, he lifted his head to stare down at her.

'Please, touch me…' She was so swollen and aching. Winding her fingers through his hair, she dragged him close, demanding more, demanding everything he had to give her.

'Is this any way to behave?' he whispered with amusement.

'Now…' She cried out with frustration. 'Don't tease me…' Edging her legs apart, she gave him the most brazen invitation yet. She had to have him. She had to draw him deep inside her. It was a primitive imperative she had no will to resist. Her inhibitions were cancelled out by the demands of a body that craved his touch. She needed more contact, more touching and stroking, more pleasure. Memories from last night were too vivid for her to ignore this opportunity.

'Tell me what you want,' he taunted her softly. 'Direct me…'

'I want all of you now…'

'Explain.' His voice was stern. He held back.

'I want you to touch me again.' She said this in a clear and lucid voice. 'I want you to touch me exactly as you did before…'

'Exactly?'

'But this time I don't want you to stop.'

There were no more words spoken between them. Rigo undid the fastening on her skirt and let it drop to the floor. Her new lace briefs followed. She closed her eyes as he enclosed the luscious swell between her legs. The touch of him there was indescribable.

'More,' she insisted in a groan, clinging helplessly to him. 'Give me more—'

'Like this?'

'Oh, yes…'

But he was teasing her with almost touches. He would stroke her deliberately the way she liked and then return to a touch that was far too light.

'Don't tease me,' she begged, and as her legs buckled he took her weight.

Somehow her legs were locked around his waist, and as he freed himself and protected them both, he insisted, 'Use me.'

She gasped with shock as if the idea had never occurred to her. Rigo had given her the key to a new world, and one she had been longing to open since the moment they met. Taking him in her hands while he supported her, she touched him to her swollen flesh.

'Again,' he commanded.

CHAPTER SEVENTEEN

SHE used Rigo for her pleasure, not once, but many times, although there came a point where using him that way wasn't enough. As her hunger rose Rigo backed her against the wall. 'Yes,' she groaned, clinging to him. 'Yes,' she husked gratefully on a long note of satisfaction as he eased inside her. Still cupping her buttocks with one hand, he added to her pleasure with the other and as he thrust deeper, faster, she arced towards him, urging him on with impassioned pleas. She had never thought, dreamed anything could feel so good, but this was more than a craving; for the first time in her life she felt complete.

He had never known sex like it. She was insatiable. She was passionate. She was perfect. But for him this was only the appetiser and now he wanted the feast. He wanted to take Katie to bed and make love to her all night.

He had lost count of how many times she had climaxed by the time he withdrew. He did so carefully, making sure she was steady on her feet when he lowered her to the ground. Embracing her, once, twice, his heart throbbed with unexplored feelings. The next step had to be bed, but to his astonishment when he suggested it she pushed him away. 'Not again.' He shook his head, refusing to believe she could do this a second time.

'I can't—'

'What do you mean, you can't?' Drawing her close, he kissed her passionately, tenderly, but she wouldn't or couldn't respond. It made no sense. Anger grew inside him. She wanted him for sex—for instant gratification, but when it came to something deeper, more meaningful…

He had been used. A surge of disgust swept over him. Had he misjudged this? Was it all an act? Was Katie Bannister in love with someone else? He stepped back. Seeing his expression change, she reached out to him. 'Rigo, please—you have to believe me when I say there's a very good reason—'

'For sating yourself and moving on?' He shook his head in disbelief. He had only felt this level of betrayal once before, as a child whose pure love had been wasted on a man whose lust for a woman had taken precedence over love for his only son. 'Give me the key.'

Fumbling through her pockets, she finally found the door key and gave it to him.

Clutching it in his fist, he left the spa without a second glance.

As the door slammed behind Rigo Katie slowly crumpled to the floor. Burying her head, she sobbed in a way she hadn't been able to cry since the fire. She had never grieved for what she'd lost. She had never let the feelings inside her come out. Only her love for Rigo could open those floodgates. She had never felt anything as life-changing as this before—or directed so much loathing at her scars. She was crying because they could never be together and because sometimes it was easier to be strong than to break down, because being strong meant putting on an act, but when the mask dropped and there was just Katie Bannister facing up to her new life Katie wondered if she was strong enough or if too much had been lost.

Strong enough? Dry your eyes this minute, Katie's inner voice commanded.

Picking herself up from the cold tiles, she rebuilt herself

breath by ragged breath. There was no reprieve, no easy way, because deep inside her was a determined little light that kept on shining however hard she tried to put it out. She would get over this. She would get over Rigo. She would go on living. Scarred or not, she knew there would always be problems. She could sit here on a hard floor in an empty spa, wailing for a past that had whistled away, or she could pick up her mental armour and go back into battle.

Which was it to be—wailing or winning?

She would do more than survive; she would make a difference.

'What's this?' Rigo stared at the letter Katie had just placed in his hand. They were in the library where she had found him pacing.

After what had happened in the spa she had no option but to do this. 'It's my resignation… You don't have to accept it, but I'll understand if you do.'

'That's very good of you.' He eyed her brown suit with distaste. 'So, are we right back where we started, Signorina Bannister?'

'Hardly.' She had barely finished the denial when Rigo's look communicated all he thought of her in wounding detail.

'I don't accept your resignation.' He handed the letter back. 'You agreed to stay until I could find a replacement.'

'That was before—'

'Before what?' he snapped.

She looked away, unable to meet his gaze.

'As you may be aware, I haven't had time to find a replacement for you yet. So I'd be grateful if you'd stay.'

He sounded so cold, so distant and, yes, so contemptuous. She flinched as he threw himself from his chair and stalked to the window, where he remained with his back turned to her, staring out. 'If I weren't so pushed…' he grated out, leaving Katie in no doubt that he would get rid of her the moment he could.

'I could resign. I still have my open ticket home—'

'You can do what the hell you want—and seem to do just that, from what I've observed.' Rigo's eyes were narrowed with fury and suspicion as he looked at her.

'I'm sorry—'

'Don't even go there.'

'You don't make it easy, Rigo.'

'I don't make it easy?' he demanded incredulously. 'You're guilty on that count too—and if it's easy you've come for you might as well leave now.'

Turn her back on him for ever? Face life with no possibility of seeing Rigo again? 'Is there any way we can work together now?'

'You tell me.'

Could he sound any more hostile? 'If we kept it on a strictly business footing?'

'Let me assure you right away there's no chance of anything else.'

Less than an hour ago there had been fire in those eyes. And now...

Digging her nails into her palms, she agreed to stay on. 'If you tell me what the job entails.'

'That's very good of you.'

'Rigo, please...I've said I'm sorry—'

'You're always sorry—maybe once too often.'

'I understand why you're angry with me—'

As she said this he made a sharp sound of disbelief. 'You understand nothing,' Rigo assured her. 'You're a child.'

And he, with all his Roman passion in full flood, was a formidable sight. She had never wanted him more or felt so distanced from him. Feet braced against the floor, fists planted on his tightly muscled hips, Rigo Ruggiero was a force she should run from as fast as she could before her heart was lost for good. 'If you won't accept my resignation—'

'Which I won't. We have an agreement,' he reminded her.

'Then will you tell me what you plan for the *palazzo*?'

'Do you really think I should trust you after what happened between us—not once, but twice?'

If they couldn't move past the sex there was no hope of a working relationship and if she was going to stay she had to do so with her head held high. The only way to do this was not to blush and shrink, but to challenge Rigo as he had challenged her. 'You threw down the gauntlet when you dared me to take a risk. I'm throwing that same gauntlet at your feet. Take a chance on me.'

Where had she come from, this female virago? Had he created her or were they equally guilty? Did they rouse such powerful feelings in each other that neither of them were capable of behaving as they should? He pointed to a chair. She sat while he paced. He was weighing up the potential of the *palazzo* for the scheme he had in mind—a scheme that would benefit his foundation—against his obligation to secrecy. Should he trust this woman? Could he trust her? What did his instinct tell him? 'I'm going to outline your contract,' he said, 'so if you would like to take a note...'

She hid a smile. He let it go. He dictated a letter to his legal team asking them to draw up a contract for Katie Bannister that gave her cast-iron guarantees.

She turned to look at him halfway through. 'I can't sign anything until I—'

He swore viciously in Italian. 'Must you argue every point? I want you to send the letter exactly as I have dictated it—'

'Don't I have any say in my own contract of employment?'

'Yes.' He was tired of playing softball. 'You can sign it or not. You can go back to Yorkshire and look for another job, if that's what you want, but I don't think it is. Am I right?'

She ground her jaw and came right back at him. 'I want a clause that allows for a time limit and fair notice to be given on either side—'

'A quick fix?' he suggested coldly. 'Is that the type of thing you deal in, Signorina Bannister?'

'Please don't turn me down out of hand. Try to see this from my point of view—'

His hackles stood on end. 'From your point of view? Isn't all this from your point of view? And what do you mean, don't turn you down out of hand? *Caro Dio*, what is this? I'm the one making the offer—'

'And making no allowance for my feelings—'

'You have too many feelings,' he roared, only to realise she was in tears. 'Don't play that card with me,' he warned, shaken to his core. 'I know your type—'

'My *type*?' she exploded, rallying faster than he could ever have expected. 'And what type would that be, Rigo?'

They were facing each other like combatants in a ring, but indignation gave way to amusement when it occurred to him that to any outsider Katie would appear by far the more dangerous of the two. With her hands balled into fists, her jaw jutting and mouth firm, her eyes blazing with the light of battle she was a magnificent sight, this woman of his—

His woman?

His woman.

The only woman he could ever want.

But his woman hadn't finished with him yet. Not by a long way.

'So I'm the type who can see you naked in a pool and make the mistake of thinking we could share something special—' She broke off. 'Oh, no, I forgot.' She held up her hand as if to silence him, though he had no intention of saying a word. He was content to let her continue this one-way argument with herself and by herself.

'I'm the woman who had sex up against a wall, and felt nothing, presumably? I'm a robot—an automaton.' Her voice was rising. 'I'm a frigid, sexless, boring spinster—'

'Hardly frigid,' he cut in mildly.

She made a sound like an angry bear, which made it all the harder for him to hide his smile.

Forget all things sexual? That had been her plan. She should have known Rigo would make this hard for her. His confidence was obvious in the way his lips tugged in anticipation of victory, as if nothing she could say would have the slightest effect on his arrogant assumption that she would sign his wretched contract without alteration or complaint. How dared he look at her and smile? How dared he use that look to stir erotic thoughts?

But—and it was a big but—he was offering her the chance to do something exciting and different. Living in Italy was that, even if she didn't know the precise detail yet. Had she come all this way in attitude and distance only to wimp out now? She'd pin him down and then she'd decide. Drawing herself up, which brought her—well, almost to his shoulder, she suggested, 'Can we sit down and talk?'

Could they? He kept his expression carefully neutral.

A negotiation beckoned. Now that he'd woken the tiger inside Katie Bannister, there was no way he wanted to see her vulnerable again. This was his type of woman. The type of woman he would like working alongside him, he amended. Katie Bannister had passed the interview process with flying colours and was definitely the type of feisty, focused individual his foundation needed on the board.

She was sitting at the desk, waiting for him. He leaned his hip against it and looked down. She looked too, but not into his eyes. Not that he was any measure of propriety and chaste thought. 'I'm going to tell you everything,' he said, reclaiming her attention. 'The club I run—'

'The club?' she interrupted, snapping into attack mode. 'I would never leave England for Italy to work in a club, Rigo. I'm sorry,' she said, standing up, 'but I really don't think there's any point in continuing this conversation—'

He cut her off at the door, one fist pressed against it. 'Now you listen to me.' His gaze dropped to her lips.

'And if I won't?'

He might kiss her?

Mild eyes flashed fire. 'Let me go, Rigo…' She rattled the door handle.

'Not until you tell me what you're hiding.'

'What I'm hiding?'

But her eyes told him clearly that she was. 'I know you're hiding something; you're not leaving here until I know what it is.'

'I'm your prisoner?'

He allowed himself a smile. 'If you like.'

Her jaw worked and then she said, 'All right—but not here, not now. Please, Rigo, let's sort out one thing at a time.'

He ground his jaw as she stared unflinchingly into his eyes. Questions competed in his mind. Why the pretence? Why had she pulled back, not once, but twice when they were so heavily into pleasure? Katie had no difficulty enjoying sex. It was anything deeper she shied away from. So what was Katie Bannister hiding from? Him? Men in general? Everyone? He had to remind himself how much she would benefit his foundation if he kept this rigidly confined to business. 'Please sit down again,' he said.

She still looked unsure. He could hear her thinking, work in a club? 'Before you jump ship you should make sure you're not jumping to conclusions. I'm going to tell you about my club and I'm asking you to hear me out. I think you'll be glad if you do—'

'So you trust me now?'

'As much as you trust me. Shall we?' He angled his chin towards the chair at the opposite side of the desk. He didn't turn to see if she was following; something told him she would be. Katie couldn't resist a challenge any more than he could and her curiosity was fully roused.

She walked towards him with her head held high until there was just the desk between them. Resting her fingertips on the edge, she remained standing. Leaning forward to make her point, she said, 'When I was a girl saving up to go to music college I checked coats and served drinks and I considered myself lucky to have a job in a club, but that was then and, at the risk of sounding ungrateful, I don't want to—'

'Pole dance?' he suggested dryly. 'Why don't you sit down, listen to what I have to say first and then give me the lecture?'

'On one condition—'

'Name it.'

'You take me seriously?'

'Believe me, I do take you seriously.' He would like to take her very seriously indeed and the only reason he hadn't taken the relationship to the next level was that Katie was holding him off.

Pulling out the chair, she sat down. 'I promise to hear you out.'

He ignored the rush of interest in his groin and concentrated on the scrapbook in front of him. He spun it round so it was facing her. 'This is my club…'

She went very still as she turned the pages and then she looked at him.

He shrugged. What could he say? This was his life's work, and had been the only thing he cared about and worked for…up to now. The fact that he had never forgotten his roots, or that by assisting these children he was not only helping them but also somehow healing the child he had once been, was his concern, and his alone. The fact that he was sharing this with Katie was a measure of his respect for her. She must stay, and not because revealing this had bared his soul. He knew his secret would be safe with her, but he wanted her to stay because he couldn't imagine life without her. She was a remarkable woman, this self-effacing, quiet, kind girl, and he knew he would never meet anyone like her again.

Katie studied the image on the first page. Rigo was standing in the middle of a small group of men dressed in motor-racing red. They all looked tanned and fit and wealthy, and they all had their arms casually draped across each other's shoulders. At that point she was still thinking the worst of him, but then she moved on to the second page and everything inside her went still. As misjudgements went, hers had been enormous. 'I don't understand...'

'What's to understand?' he said, frowning. 'How can you look at those photographs and tell me you don't want to become involved?'

Rigo's organisation fulfilled as many of the dreams of sick and disadvantaged children as it could. 'So that's why you were racing round the track when I arrived?' Each of the photographs was dated, and as she traced the image for that day lightly with her fingertips her heart filled with admiration and love for him. 'And your friend—the one who was in hospital having the life-saving operation...'

Rigo didn't answer and his expression didn't flicker. He took no credit for any of this, she realised, and even now he wouldn't reveal the identities of any of the families he helped. Now she understood that it wasn't his privacy he guarded so assiduously, but that of the children and their families and his friends.

'The children do occasionally make me late for appointments,' he admitted, smiling faintly.

One glance into Rigo's eyes told a world of stories and, while some of them were happy, many were sad.

'As far as I'm concerned,' he said, 'the children come first.

Well, Katie? Now I've explained why I need someone to help me with the expansion of the scheme, how do you feel?'

Rigo would stop at nothing to continue this work. Even his much vaunted pride counted for nothing in Rigo's mind compared to these children. How did that make her feel? Her heart was aching with love for him. She wanted the job. It was a job she could devote her life to willingly and without question. She could feel passion for the job, a passion that would never falter, but—

'I should warn you,' Rigo said, interrupting Katie's thoughts with a condemning glance at her dull brown suit, 'that everyone involved in the scheme is under orders to inject fun and colour into the lives of those we help—'

'And must embrace a more extensive palette than brown, I take it?' she suggested in the same dry tone.

A half-smile creased his face in the attractive way she loved. 'As you can see from the scrapbook,' he said, looking at it, 'you must wear whatever is appropriate for the activity you're taking part in.'

'I draw the line at a yellow jumpsuit.' She was remembering one of the most hair-raising photographs with one part of her brain, and longing for something that could never be with the other part.

'If you do a tandem parachute jump with me, Katie, the yellow jumpsuit is required equipment.'

Bizarrely, as he spoke a wedding dress flashed into her mind. She smiled it away, thinking of the children and the wonderful opportunity Rigo had put in front of her.

'We have to do anything that's asked of us.'

'I understand,' she said.

'Are you ready to give me your answer?' he said. 'Will you join us?'

CHAPTER EIGHTEEN

SHE would do anything for him right now.

Don't give up, Katie's inner voice begged, while common sense told her she could have the job of her dreams, but not the man. Maybe Rigo was playing with her in the sexual sense, Katie reasoned, but she knew he was wholly sincere about his scheme. Perhaps she should choose the security of home over the freedom and romance she had always longed for—at least if she did that her heart wouldn't ache constantly.

She smiled. She knew. There'd never been any doubt what she would do. 'I'll go and put on my new suit, shall I?'

Rigo relaxed. He understood the code. He had offered her the chance to make the difference she had longed to make and she was saying yes.

And now they were both on their feet.

'I can't tell you how pleased I am!' Rigo exclaimed as he came around the desk. 'Thank you so much for agreeing to join us, Katie. I'm going to turn Carlo's legacy into something wonderful. I've already decided I'll keep a small apartment here, but the Palazzo Farnese is going to become Carlo's Kids' Club—'

'So your stepbrother will be remembered for all the right reasons...'

'He will.'

'It's a great name—fun and friendly.' Could hearts explode? Katie wondered as hers pounded violently in her chest.

'I'm already talking to my team of doctors to make sure the centre is everything it needs to be and I'll build their suggestions into my plans—'

'I'll do anything you ask,' she interrupted. 'I mean it, Rigo. I want to be part of this.'

'Welcome to the team, Katie.'

He grasped her hand and let it go. 'This is a big ask.' He stared directly into her eyes. 'I need more than a personal assistant.'

She didn't breathe.

'I need someone like you to speak independently on the steering committee.'

She pulled herself together. 'Of course.'

This was so much more than she had hoped for, Katie told herself firmly. 'I only wish I'd understood all this from the start.'

'Would it have made a difference?'

Rigo's eyes searched hers relentlessly and they both knew he wasn't talking about business now. She knew she looked uncomfortable, but it couldn't be helped. She'd lost the art of masking her feelings the day Rigo had kissed her.

She was thankful when he let it go.

'People's lives are precious,' he said, referring to his scheme, 'and they are entitled to discretion from us.'

'You have my word,' she said, knowing Rigo's foundation was infinitely more important than her own small world of doubt and negative self-image issues.

'The last thing the families need is the media spotlight focused on them—and my friends aren't too happy about it either,' he confessed with a wry smile. 'It's better for everyone if we keep it low-profile.'

'Everything you have told me will remain between you and me,' she promised him. 'The details of your foundation are safe with me.'

'I never doubted it.'

But there was a question in his eyes. And that question was: why couldn't she be as open with him?

And then with an effortless switch of tempo, he became her boss again. 'I can't wait to get started. I'm so glad you're joining us, Katie.'

In his enthusiasm he caught hold of her arms and spun her round. They were both on a high. And Rigo was an impulsive man. Still, the last thing she had expected was that he would kiss her on the mouth...

The kiss was like no other they'd shared. The impulse and joy that caused it changed instantly to something more. Once reignited that fire raged unabated. She couldn't press herself close enough or hard enough. She had to taste him and feel him in every part of her. She could barely drag in enough air to sustain life...

Rigo swung her into his arms and strode out of the room. He didn't walk up the stairs, he ran.

Closing her eyes, she nuzzled her face into his chest. She was hiding from reality and intended doing so until the last bubble burst. Having mounted the stairs, he shouldered his way into his apartment. It was as shabby as her own, but to Katie's eyes it was equally charming and comfortable. Thanks to the attentions of a reinvigorated staff, it was also spotlessly clean, and as Rigo launched them both onto the super-sized bed she inhaled the faint scent of sunshine and lavender contained in crisp white bedlinen.

'Are you happy?' he demanded, drawing her into his arms.

She could never express how she felt. There was such joy in the air, such exuberance and laughter, and for every nanosecond left to her she was going to live this out to the full. While he was kissing her Rigo removed her jacket and tossed it away. 'Remind me to make a bonfire for that old suit,' he said, raising his head to look into her eyes, and while she was laughing her skirt followed the same trajectory. All that remained now between Rigo and her scars were her underwear and a blouse. The last bubble was about to be burst. She turned her face away. It was wrong to allow this. She would not cause him any more pain.

He searched for her lips with his.

She pushed him away. His eyes flickered and changed. She'd hurt him. There was no way not to hurt him. It broke her heart to do this, but it would destroy them both if she let him see her scars. Rigo would turn away from her in disgust, believing he'd been betrayed again.

But she should have known he wouldn't be so easily dissuaded. She let him kiss her one last time and felt her heart soar. When he released her she stared at him to imprint every atom of his features on her mind. Reaching up, she wove her fingers into his thick black hair, loving the way it sprang, glossy and strong, beneath her palm. She needed that sensation branded on her mind to sustain her in a future without him. In Katie's world love was a cause for concern. Whatever she felt for Rigo must be rigorously controlled so it never reached past the bedroom door.

Yes, and look where she was now…

Touching his fingers to her chin, Rigo made her look at him. 'What are you frightened of, Katie?'

Instead of answering, she traced the line of his beloved face with her fingertips until he captured her hands and kissed each fingertip in turn. Her skin was still prickling from contact with Rigo's sharp black stubble. Tears welled in her eyes as the thought, sharp and dark, like the end of this romance, rose in her mind; there could be no happy ending.

'So, *signorina*,' he murmured against her lips, 'have you no answer for me? Will you not tell me what is wrong, so I can help you?'

What is wrong? I love you with all my heart, she thought, and always will. My love for you fills every part of me with happiness… But she would never speak of this to Rigo. He was so confident and so happy. He was still at the top of the mountain, while she was rapidly slithering down it—though his sexy, slumberous eyes had begun to gain an edge of suspicion. In that brief moment she saw the same vulnerability everyone felt when they had bared their soul to another. And right on cue her scars stung a reminder of why this love for Rigo must go no further.

She pulled away. He dragged her close, kissing her until her soul was as bare as his. He tasted her tears and pulled back. 'What aren't you telling me? Is there someone else?'

'No!' she exclaimed; the idea was abhorrent to her. But Rigo's voice had turned cold and everything had changed. Their brief idyll was over.

'Katie?'

Someone else? No. Something else.

'I knew it.' He thrust her away. 'I can see it in your eyes.'

Could he? Could he see the ridged skin—the ugly, ruined skin? Those foul red shiny scars stood between them as surely as another person—

'Why don't you just admit it?' He launched himself from the bed.

Because she had wanted this too much.

But she had forgotten Rigo was not the tame, civilised man he appeared to the wider world, but a man who had survived life on the streets, fighting for every piece of bread he put in his mouth. Rigo had never stopped fighting, whether for his foundation or for his company and employees, or anyone else he believed needed someone to champion them, and he wasn't about to lose this fight. Whirling round, he seized her wrists and tumbled her back onto the pillows. Holding her firmly in place, he cursed viciously in her face. 'Not again! Do you understand me, Katie? Tell me the truth. Tell me why you have such a problem with commitment.'

'There's no one else—'

'And I should believe you?'

But his grip had loosened fractionally.

'I swear, Rigo—there's only you.'

He let her go and sank down on the bed with his head in his hands.

'You're my world,' she said. 'You fill my mind every waking moment and my dreams are full of you when I'm asleep—'

'Then I don't understand,' he said, looking up. 'What's standing between us? Tell me, Katie. I have to know. Maybe I can help you.'

This big, strong, powerful man, this man who was so confident he could make everything right for her if she only wanted it badly enough. But her voice would never come back and her scars would never go away. Could she burden him with that? Shaking her head, she clung to the edges of her blouse.

Rigo's gaze followed her movement. 'Oh, Katie,' he murmured and, gently disentangling her hands, he brought them to his lips. Letting her go at last, he stood in front of her, stripping off his clothes. When he was completely naked he lay on the bed and drew her into his arms. 'Why couldn't you tell me the truth? Do you think my feelings for you are so fragile?'

As understanding flooded her brain shame suffused her. 'It's not my breasts.'

'What, then?' He went still.

Moments passed and then Rigo drew her to him. 'You have to tell me, Katie. You can't live like this.'

He was right. Without him she was only half-alive.

'I'm going to take your blouse off.' He started unfastening it. He shared his courage, staring into her eyes. He lifted her up into a place he inhabited, a place where problems were dealt with and not pushed aside. He slid the blouse from her shoulders and embraced her back. His hands explored and his expression never wavered. 'Come to me, *cara*,' he said, drawing her closer. 'Trust me…'

And so at last she lay with her face pressed into the pillows while he looked at her back. Hot shame coursed through her. She felt dirty and ugly. She was repulsive. That was how she'd felt when she'd left the hospital and taken a long, hard look at herself in the mirror. Squeezing her eyes shut now, she pictured Rigo recoiling in horror. How could he not? He only had to measure his perfection against her flaws to know jokes didn't come this bad.

But she waited in vain for his exclamation of disgust, and felt the bed yield as he lay down at her side. And then, incredibly, she felt him kiss her back…all down the length of the scars. And when he'd finished, he said softly, 'Tell me— how do you think this changes you?'

'Isn't it obvious?' she mumbled, her voice muffled by the pillows.

'Not to me. Is this what you were hiding from me?'

She turned her head to look at him.

'I can't believe it,' Rigo murmured. 'I can't believe you would think me so shallow—'

'I don't. I think you're perfect—so perfect, how can you not be disgusted?'

'By you holding out on me, perhaps that might disgust me, but by these? You said you'd trained as an opera singer when we were at Gino's, and the letter of introduction sent to me by your firm mentioned it, but it said nothing about a fire—'

'I didn't put it on my CV. I didn't think it relevant to my new life.'

'So you shut it out and tried to forget you were in a fire that left you badly scarred and stole your voice away? And every day you were reminded of what you'd lost each time you spoke or when you took your clothes off.'

'It's not so bad—'

'Not so bad? You lost the future you'd planned. That's big—huge, Katie. Who did you confide in? No one!' he exclaimed when she remained silent. 'And you've been hiding your feelings ever since?'

'I had to hide my scars from you—'

'Because you thought I would throw up my hands in alarm?'

'Because I thought they would sicken you. I thought if you saw them they would take any feelings you might have for me and turn them sour and ugly.'

'So how do you feel now when I tell you that I love you?'

'You—'

'*Sì, ti amo*, Katie. I will always love you. I can't imagine life without you. You're my life now.'

He stopped her saying anything with a kiss so deep and tender, she felt cherished and knew the nightmare that had mastered her for so long didn't exist in Rigo's mind. Bottling things up, just as he had said, had allowed the consequences of the fire to ferment and expand in her imagination until they ruled her life. And now he was kissing her in a way that sealed the lid on those insecurities. There was no need for words; this was the ultimate reassurance.

Rigo made love to her all night and they woke in the morning with their limbs entwined, when he made love to her again while she was still half-asleep. To wake and be loved was the miracle she had always dreamed of, only it was so much better in reality. 'I love you, Rigo.' She said this, kneeling in front of him, naked. 'You've made me strong.'

'You've always been strong,' Rigo argued. Taking hold of her hands, he drew her to him. 'You just needed reminding how strong you are. If you weren't strong you wouldn't have chosen such a challenging path through life—first music, and now me.'

She laughed. How could she not? 'I love you so much,' she whispered, staring into his eyes.

'You're sure?'

'You made it possible for me to love.'

'So now the world is your oyster?' he teased in his sexy drawl.

'My world is you—'

'*Brava,*' he murmured with one of his killer smiles. Lowering her onto the bank of pillows beside him, he added, 'Just remember, I love every part of you—not just this leg, or that finger, or these ears. I love the whole Katie.'

And the fierce pledge in his eyes said that as far as Rigo was concerned her scars did not exist. 'I love every part of you that goes to make you the woman I love now and always.'

And to prove it he moved down the bed.

As she cried out with pleasure he took her again, and this time when they were one her heart sang.

They had a leisurely breakfast in bed, planning the future. They had already discussed the possibility of Katie seeing a plastic surgeon, should she want to, but for some reason the one thing that had obsessed her since the fire seemed unimportant to her now. Rigo had made it so. He had taken her internal compass and pointed it towards the future—a future they would enjoy together. 'But we will have to leave the room sometime,' she pointed out when Rigo's eyes darkened in a way she recognised.

'But not yet,' he insisted, drawing her down beside him.

'No, not yet,' she agreed.

And when he finally released her, she admitted, 'I fell in love with you the first hair-raising moment we met.'

'I was a brute.'

'You were challenging.'

'And you were very patient with me.'

'And just look at my reward…'

'Ah, there is that.'

Modest to the last, Katie thought, recognising the wicked smile.

'And, Katie—'

'Yes?' she whispered as Rigo drew her beneath him.

'Have you never considered singing again?'

'Now?'

'Later, perhaps,' he suggested, easing into her. 'But just think how the public would love your sexy, breathy voice. If I can fall in love with that voice over the phone—'

'But that's you…'

'Are you daring to suggest there's something wrong with my judgement?'

He was making it very hard to think at all. 'If I did that I would have to question your love for me,' she managed on a shaky breath.

'And you won't, so have some confidence, Katie. There is more than one popular style of music. You can still sing in tune, can't you?'

She was supposed to answer while he was making every part of her sing? 'Well, yes, but I can't sing as I used to—' She gasped as he moved up a gear.

'Your new public wouldn't want you to—'

'My? Oh…' She conceded defeat. No thought possible.

'Have you forgotten that one of my passions is making dreams come true? And I have a keen nose for business.'

She could only groan her agreement.

'You're going to record a track—an album—' he picked up pace '—and who knows? I might even make some money out of you.'

'Rigo, you're impossible,' she shrieked, recognising his game now. Rigo distracted himself while he concentrated on her pleasure.

'I try my very best,' he admitted, still moving as she quietened.

She had no doubt that he would.

CHAPTER NINETEEN

SUMMER came and went in a flurry of love and activity. It was almost Christmas before Katie knew it. The renovations to the *palazzo* were well under way, and she was fully involved in Carlo's Kids' Club. She had started this sunny December day in the kitchen at the Palazzo Farnese, where she was helping to prepare a special lunch for Antonia, who was travelling to see them on one of her regular visits from Rome. Katie was closer than ever to Antonia, having persuaded Rigo that, if she wanted to, his sister must play a full part in his scheme. She had pointed out that Antonia wasn't too young to face up to life and that, if Rigo insisted on shielding his little sister and sent her shopping all the time, Antonia would never grow up. Antonia had embraced this idea with the enthusiasm only Antonia could, and even Rigo had admitted then his sister had been brushed aside for far too long, both by his father and her mother, and then by him. Antonia had seized the opportunity to prove herself and had more than repaid Katie's faith in her, and now they were not just friends but soon to be sisters—

'Hey, *tesoro*.'

Katie's heart bounced with happiness as Rigo walked into the room. She would never lose the sense of excitement she felt each time she saw him.

Walking up to her, he swung her round to face the staff and, leaning his disreputable stubble-shaded chin on the top of the shiny tumble of hair she always wore down now, he announced, 'I have a surprise for you, *tesoro*—'

'Another surprise?' Katie exclaimed.

There had been nothing but surprises from Rigo since the day she moved in—not just to the *palazzo*, or the penthouse, but into Rigo's life. The wardrobe of clothes she had initially refused had miraculously appeared in her dressing room. And when she had asked him where they came from, he said, 'They must have been brought by fairies.' And when she finally stopped laughing, he admitted that he had given most of her measurements to the designers, and that her short audience with them when she first arrived had been a ruse.

'How did you do that?' she demanded.

'I have a good eye,' he admitted.

'Two good eyes,' she remembered telling him with a scolding look. Goodness knew where Rigo gained that sort of experience—and, frankly, she didn't want to know. 'You mentioned a surprise?' she reminded him now.

'Just a little something,' he said, delving into the pocket of his jeans. 'It's something for the wedding. See what you think. I got the colour scheme right, didn't I? White and ivory with a garnish of red roses…?'

Their wedding… She could hardly believe it. Two more days and they would be married at the cathedral in Farnese. 'You know you did,' she rebuked him playfully, wondering what could be in the beautifully wrapped box, with its iridescent ivory wrapping paper and rose-red ribbon.

'Well, open it,' Rigo prompted.

It must be a lacy garter, Katie thought, ripping the paper in her excitement. As the ribbon fluttered to the ground, Rigo caught it and handed it to her. 'Open the box,' he said.

She did so and gasped.

Everyone gasped.

Rigo affected a frown. 'Is blue-white straying too far from your original scheme?'

A huge blue-white diamond solitaire winked at her from its velvet nest.

Katie collected herself. 'Blue-white,' she said, lips pressing down as she pretended to think about it. 'I think it will tone quite nicely.' She turned to him, a smile blooming on her face.

'Is it big enough?' Rigo demanded.

Did Rigo ever do small? 'It's absolutely perfect,' she breathed, 'but you really didn't have to—'

'But I wanted to.'

'Then that's different.'

'Let me put it on your finger.'

He stared deep into her eyes as he did so, and all the staff gave them a round of applause.

'So you finally did it!'

Everyone turned as Antonia bounded into the room. A haze of vanilla and raspberry perfume accompanied her. Antonia's first hug was for Katie. 'My new sister!' she exclaimed. 'At least, you will be in two days' time.' She turned to Rigo. 'You took long enough,' she accused him. 'I thought you would never get round to asking Katie to marry you.'

'A week is too long?' He exchanged a glance with Katie.

'In my world it's forever!' Antonia exclaimed with a sigh. 'And now it's almost four months later, so you have no excuse—there's only me to sort out now—'

'Some day your prince will come,' Rigo interrupted, handing Antonia another box.

'I thought you didn't like shopping?' she accused him, staring at the gorgeous box with wide, excited eyes.

'For my wife-to-be and for my sister, I made an exception to that rule. I bought your gift with Katie along to guide me to thank you for being our chief bridesmaid.'

'There would have been trouble if I hadn't been your chief bridesmaid,' Antonia assured him.

Another amused glance was exchanged between Katie and Rigo. They didn't doubt it.

Antonia's fingers trembled as she held up the slim white-gold chain. 'Rigo, it's *favoloso*!' she exclaimed.

There were two charms hanging from Antonia's chain. The first was a diamond set into a sundial to remind them all to make time for each other, while the second charm was a tiny Cinderella slipper to remind Antonia that her prince would come one day—if she could only be a little patient.

'I love you, Katie!' Antonia exclaimed, throwing her arms around Katie's neck. 'And I have something for you.'

'For me?'

'I have bought you your own journal,' Antonia explained. 'Would you like to see what I wrote in mine that first day we met?'

'Only if you want to show it to me,' Katie said as Antonia delved into her industrial-sized bag.

Antonia extracted the small aqua leather-bound book with a flourish and opened it at the appropriate page. '"I want Katie to marry my brother,"' she announced. 'Well? Am I good at predictions or not?' she demanded, staring at Rigo.

'You're the best,' he admitted, 'and for once we were in absolute harmony, though I fell in love with Katie when I heard her voice on the phone before she even came to Italy. I heard the inner beauty when she spoke, and when I met her I fell in love with her all over again.'

Everyone sighed and it took a moment for life to take on its regular beat. When it did, Rigo turned to Katie. 'I have another surprise for you, *cara*, which will be revealed over lunch.'

Music was playing as they walked into the sun-drenched orangerie and it took Katie a good few moments to recognise her own husky voice. It sounded quite different when she was singing sultry love songs rather than opera.

'Your first album,' Rigo said, embracing her. 'I hope you like it…'

'As long as you love me, I don't need anything more.'

'Can I have your ring?' Antonia piped up.

'Find your own prince,' Rigo told her as they all laughed.

'I love you,' Katie whispered, staring into the eyes of the man without whom her life might have remained unrelieved brown.

'And I love you,' Rigo murmured, with a darkening look they both recognised, 'for…'

'For?' Katie prompted softly, her gaze slipping to his mouth.

'For allowing me to make a bonfire of that suit—'

'Yay!' Antonia exclaimed, discreetly leaving them to it. 'I love a happy ending…'

EPILOGUE

THE cathedral in Farnese was lit entirely by candlelight. The soft glow brought out the colours of the stained-glass windows and created jewel-coloured garlands on the white marble floor. The scent of the red roses Rigo had insisted on was everywhere, and the angelic voices of a children's choir provided the only fitting soundtrack for a bride and groom who had dedicated their lives not only to each other, but also to their children's foundation. Each ancient wooden pew was decorated with roses secured by a cascade of cream lace, which echoed the glorious floral arrangements throughout the cathedral supervised by the housekeeper and staff of the newly opened children's centre at the Palazzo Farnese. Guests had come from all over the world to celebrate this wedding, but the place of honour was given to Katie's friends from the office and to Gino and his wife from the pizzeria in Rome, while the young maid who had first lent Katie a swimming costume was now a bridesmaid.

Everyone applauded as the Principe and Principessa Farnese walked down the aisle. Rigo had never looked sexier in the dark, full dress uniform of a prince of the line, with a wide crimson sash across his powerful chest, while his bride wore a cream velvet cloak lined with ivory silk satin and, beneath that, a fitted guipure lace dress, frosted with diamonds. There were more diamonds in Katie's hair and on the diaphanous veil that billowed behind her. In fact, there was only one anomaly in Katie's modest outfit—her crimson shoes. 'It doesn't do to be too predictable,' she warned Rigo, smiling when he spotted them.

'I love your shoes,' he murmured, bringing Katie into the sunlight so the crowd could see their new princess. 'Life could be so bland and boring without any surprises—though something tells me life will never be that with you around, Signorina Prim.'

As he spoke the cathedral organ swelled with uplifting chords and mellow tonal resolutions in celebration of a true love story between Prince Arrigo Ruggiero Farnese and Katie Bannister, and as the crowd cheered them to their horse-drawn carriage Rigo squeezed Katie's hand and asked her, 'Happy?'

'How could I not be happy?'

His face creased in his attractive curving smile as he helped her into the golden carriage. 'I guess you must like the fact that we Italians laugh, cry and make love on a grand scale.'

Amen to that, Katie thought as she embraced her new world.

* * * * *

The Italian's One-Night Love-Child

Cathy
WILLIAMS

Cathy Williams is originally from Trinidad, but has lived in England for a number of years. She currently has a house in Warwickshire, which she shares with her husband Richard, her three daughters, Charlotte, Olivia and Emma, and their pet cat, Salem. She adores writing romantic fiction, and would love one of her girls to become a writer—although at the moment she is happy enough if they do their homework and agree not to bicker with one another!

CHAPTER ONE

COCOONED in the pleasantly cold confines of his black Mercedes, Cristiano De Angelis surveyed the hustle and bustle of the scorchingly hot streets around him from behind a pair of dark designer sunglasses. This part of Rome was as familiar to him as his own penthouse apartment in London where he lived for most of the year, occasionally taking time out to visit his family in Italy. He had grown up here, had gone to school here, had enjoyed the gilded life of a member of the Italian elite, only spreading his wings when he had flown off to go to university in England. It was both comforting and a little claustrophobic to be back, even for a week, and it would be something of a relief to return to the relative anonymity granted him in the streets of London.

He frowned, thinking back to the conversation he had just had with his mother and his grandfather, who had conspired to remind him, over a sumptuous lunch served with unnecessary formality in the opulent dining room of his grandfather's house, of the passage of time, in so far as it affected him and the pitter patter of small De Angelis feet which they were both, it seemed, desperate to hear.

It had been a dual assault of military precision with his mother on the one side, virtually wringing her hands as she elaborated on her maternal desire that he settle down, be happy, stop playing the field, while his grandfather chipped in with guilt-inducing asides about his declining health and old age, as though he was a decrepit centenarian and not the sprightly seventy-eight-year-old man who could still command attention without uttering a word.

'There's a very nice girl…' his mother had begun, assessing whether that casual piece of information might have landed on fertile ground, but Cristiano had not been having it. While he acknowledged that he would, indeed, one day get married to someone suitable, that time had not quite arrived. He had been firm on the point and, of course, it had been regrettable that he had been forced to witness their crestfallen faces, but the pair of them, given half a chance, would have proved more unstoppable than a freight train at full speed. Any hint of softening on his part and they would have been lining up prospective candidates within minutes.

A reluctant smile of wry amusement curved his mouth and he removed his shades, dangling them from one finger as he looked at the hordes of shoppers who swarmed the elegant designer shop-lined streets, for all the world as though the words *credit crunch* were not part of their vocabulary.

Without giving himself time to change his mind, he tapped on the glass partition separating him from his driver and leaned forward to tell Enrico that he could let him out here.

'Take the car back to my place,' Cristiano said, grimacing at the prospect of having to brave the sweltering summer sun but recognising that if he didn't do it then he would be stuck in traffic for the foreseeable future and, comfortable though it was inside the Mercedes, he couldn't afford to waste time sitting in it for the next hour or so. 'I have to deliver this for my mother and it will be quicker for me to take to the back streets than for you to drive me there. I'll get a taxi back.'

'But sir, the sun…'

Enrico, who had been the family driver for as long as Cristiano could remember, looked faint at the thought of his passenger stepping out into the sweltering heat, and Cristiano grinned.

'I'm not a swooning Victorian maiden, Enrico,' he said drily. 'I think I'll be able to withstand half an hour out there. After all, look at the shoppers. No one seems to be collapsing from heat exhaustion.'

'But sir, those are women. They are built to shop in all weather without being affected…'

Cristiano was still grinning as he strode out into the blistering sun, sunglasses firmly back in place. He was aware, and chose to ignore, the sidelong glances of women as he walked past. He was pretty sure that if he slowed his pace it wouldn't be long before some long-legged, dark-haired, pedigreed beauty approached him. Even though he no longer resided in the city, his face was well known in certain circles. Visits to Rome were seldom free from glittering invitations from women who courted his company, usually without success because, despite his mother's accusations, he was discerning in his choices. Which, as he began leaving the crowded shopping quarter, brought him right back to thinking about her matchmaking designs. He had had no scarring emotional involvements with any woman. He had nothing against the institution of marriage, per se. Nor did he envisage a life without children, despite the manner in which he had earlier brushed aside the subject with an indolent wave of his hand. Cristiano could only think that he had been thoroughly ruined by his parents' happy marriage. Was that possible? Wasn't it supposed to work the other way around? They had been childhood sweethearts, perfectly matched in every way and, as if plucked from a fairy story, had lived perfectly happy lives until his father had died five years previously. His mother still wore black, carried pictures of him in her handbag and frequently referred to him in the present tense.

In an age of quickie divorces, money-grabbing gold-diggers and women with an eye to the main chance, what hope in hell did he have of a comparable marriage?

It took him a little over twenty minutes before he was standing in front of the gracious block of apartments where he had been instructed to hand deliver a very delicate orchid to one of the women who had helped out two weeks previously on a charity fund-raiser, a belated thank you present for her contribution. His mother was leaving for their country house and the orchid, she told him, *would not wait* until she returned. Nor would she trust any old courier service to deliver it because those *ragamuffin boys* were useless when it came to delivering anything *of a fragile nature*.

Privately, Cristiano figured that it was her way of expressing her pique at his casual dismissal of whatever suitable candidate she had had lined up her sleeve for his perusal, but running the errand had been a small price to pay for making good his escape.

Nor had the walk been half as uncomfortable as he had imagined. He very rarely *walked* anywhere, he realised. His life was cushioned by the luxury of a full-time driver in London and, besides, walking for the sake of walking was a time-consuming business in a life that seemed to have little spare time as it was.

The block of opulent apartments was portered and he was pointed in the direction of the lift without question. Even dressed in casual clothes, Cristiano exuded the sort of wealth, power and confidence that ensured entry anywhere. The porter had asked for no identification and Cristiano would have been outraged had his movements been questioned.

Rather than take the lift, though, he decided to climb the three flights up to the apartment. This was no dingy staircase. Rich turquoise carpeting ran its length and the wallpaper was cool and sophisticated. He assumed the apartment would be more of the same. In all events, several rings on the doorbell elicited no response. Nor did his mother's mobile when he called to inform her that his mission had been a waste of time.

What the hell was he to do, stranded with an overpriced hothouse plant in search of a home?

Cursing under his breath for having allowed himself to be virtually blackmailed into running the ridiculous errand, he finally resorted to banging on the door. Like every single mega-expensive apartment building on the face of the earth, there was an eerie silence in the hall. He knew from his own personal experience that rich people rarely emerged to chew the fat and pass the time of day with the people living in the apartments next to them. He, frankly, had no time for useless chatter on stairwells or in elevators and happily was spared such inconvenience by having a private lift to his penthouse apartment.

He banged on the door again, this time very loudly, and was rewarded with the sound of scurrying feet.

Under normal circumstances, Bethany, hearing those three *ridiculously loud and incredibly rude* bangs would have flown to the door, prepared to give her unwanted caller a piece of her mind, but as it was these weren't exactly normal circumstances.

In fact…

She glanced down at what she was wearing and broke out

in a fine film of nervous perspiration. The dress, which must have set its owner back the price of a small car, clung lovingly to her body, graceful, floaty and as utterly, utterly beautiful on as it had been hanging in the wardrobe fifteen minutes earlier.

Oh, God, why, why, *why* had she given in to the temptation to just *try it on*? What had possessed her? She had managed to resist the urge for the past three days, so why now? Because, she thought frantically, it had been so hot outside and she had come back to the apartment and had a long, luxurious bubbly bath in the splendid marbled bathroom and then she had strolled into the dressing room, which was three times the size of the poky room she had been renting at university, and she had run her hands along the magnificent gowns and dresses and jackets and coats and had stopped at this particular creation and had just not been able to resist the wicked impulse.

Now, having ignored the doorbell, there was some persistent visitor banging like mad on the door and she knew for a fact that it wouldn't be Amy, who had gone to Florence for the weekend with her boyfriend. Nor would it be a salesman because they weren't allowed to set foot into the hallowed halls of the building. Which just left…*a resident* or, worse yet, *a friend*.

The fourth bang snapped her out of her merciless daydream, which involved first and foremost losing her job as house-sitter, which was a laugh considering Amy should have been the one doing it, followed rapidly by angry Italian policemen and a stint in a cell somewhere.

She stood behind the door and opened it very, very slowly, making sure that none of her body in its borrowed garb was revealed. Her eyes travelled from the ground upwards. And upwards. From expensive tan loafers and cream trousers towards a similarly cream collared polo shirt, taking in the tanned arms, the dark hair curling round the dull silver of a very expensive make of watch, up to…the most amazing face she had ever set eyes on in her entire life. In fact, the stranger standing outside the front door was so sensationally handsome that, for a few seconds, Bethany felt literally winded.

Then reality kicked in and she remembered where she was. In an apartment that wasn't hers and decked out in clothes that weren't hers. She edged further behind the safety of the heavy door.

'Yes? May I help you?' She didn't want to stare, but she found that it was practically impossible not to. It wasn't just the man's height, and he must be over six foot, nor was it the perfection of his features or the sculpted muscularity of his body. It was the aura of power and incredible self-assurance that invested him with a potent, suffocating sex appeal.

Cristiano, initially taken aback by the woman who had answered the door, a girl when he had been expecting an ageing dowager, was now busy taking in the delicate lines of her heart-shaped face, the full mouth, the slanting green eyes and the mass of copper hair that tumbled down, almost to her waist.

'Are you *hiding*?' he asked and was fascinated as a tide of pale pink coloured her cheeks. Nor was she responding as women usually did at his presence, with smiles and lowered lashes and all those coy signals that indicated interest.

'Hiding?' His voice matched his looks. Deep, lazy, confident. 'I'm not hiding.' Bethany sidled a little further along so that the wretched dress was not at all visible. She didn't know who this man was but if he lived here, if he was a friend, he would know that she certainly wasn't the Amelia Doni who owned the apartment and who was in her mid forties. He might, however, know that the outrageously expensive dress would not belong to a twenty-one-year-old girl who happened to be house-sitting. 'I'm just a little surprised…to have a visitor…I'm sorry, I don't know your name…'

'Cristiano De Angelis.' He waited for a glimmer of recognition because any woman who owned this apartment would have heard of the De Angelis family. He wondered how it was that he had not met her before at one of the high society events that he invariably attended when he came to Rome to spend time with his family. This was a face he certainly would have remembered. She was not the usual Italian beauty, although her Italian was fluent. She looked…It suddenly dawned on him why he might not have met her in the past and he smiled slowly, switching effortlessly from Italian to English.

'And now that I have introduced myself, perhaps you'd like to tell me if I'm at the right apartment…Signora Doni?'

'I'm sorry. You haven't told me what you're doing here.'

Cristiano produced the orchid, the existence of which he had temporarily forgotten. 'From my mother.'

Bethany stared blankly at him and, as the cogs in her brain began whirring back into life, she realised that he didn't know who she was. He was a man on an errand and had no idea what Amelia Doni looked like. Ergo, he would not be rounding on her for having sneakily taken advantage of her second-hand house-sitting to don some fancy clothing. She relaxed slightly and stuck her hand out for the plant.

'Great. Thanks.'

Great? Thanks? Shouldn't she be inviting him in? At least showing some semblance of interest in getting to know who he was?

'It's a little ridiculous to be having a conversation like this,' Cristiano drawled. 'Why don't you invite me in? After all, I've just spent the past twenty-five minutes in baking sun to walk over here and deliver a potted plant. I could really do with something cold to drink.' He was a little incredulous that she actually spent a few seconds mentally debating whether or not she should open the door and let him in.

'You may not have heard of me, but let me assure you that the De Angelis are a well known family in Italy. There's no need to fear for your life or your possessions.' Since when did he give long spiels about his background to anyone? In fact, when was the last time he had ever found himself in the company of a woman who looked at him as though he might leap out and attack her at any moment? In a word, never.

'I don't.' She breathed a little easier. 'I've been brought up never to talk to strangers.'

'I introduced myself. I'm therefore no longer a stranger. You also know my mother, if only casually…' He smiled and Bethany's entire nervous system seemed to go into immediate meltdown. Her skin tingled, her throat went dry and her breasts felt suddenly hypersensitive, her nipples hardening and aching at the same time.

This was not a familiar response for Bethany. In fact, she had always been comfortable around the opposite sex. She could chat with them, tease them, even assess them without this sensation of drowning. Sandwiched between her intellectually gifted older sister and a younger sister whose radiant beauty had had boys banging on the front door from the age of eleven, Bethany had happily occupied the middle ground, content with being reasonably clever and averagely, in her eyes, attractive. From her comfortable background position, she had been able to watch Shania, wrapped up in her elitist world of books and heavily intellectual boyfriends, and Melanie, prancing from one dishy guy to another and changing them with the sort of regularity that other women changed outfits. She had learnt to chat to both sets of boy-friends without treading on either of her sisters' toes. She was therefore a little shocked and taken aback by the way this tall, dark, lean and staggeringly good-looking stranger was managing to throw her into turmoil.

'Okay. I guess you can come in for a moment,' she conceded nervously. 'It's really hot out there. I can get you a glass of water, if you like…' She pulled open the door and stood aside to let him sweep past her. Looking down, she spied the dainty strappy sandals on her feet. It now seemed highly unfortunate that the absentee owner of the apartment was roughly her size.

'Nice place.' Cristiano gave the apartment a cursory once-over. He had been brought up in palatial surroundings. Other people's displays of wealth had always failed to impress him. 'How long have you lived here?' He had swivelled back round to look at her and her impact on him was such that for a millisecond time seemed to stand still. Her eyes had to be the clearest green he had ever seen and her tumble of copper hair was a stunning contrast to the creamy paleness of her skin. The sprinkling of freckles, paradoxically, added a freshness to her beauty, rescued her from being just another attractive face. And he had no idea why she had been so keen to hide away behind the door when she had first opened it. Her body was magnificent. Slender but full breasted and, judging from the dress, this was a lady who had taste.

'How long have I lived here?' Bethany repeated, parrot fashion. 'Not long.' Literally. 'I'll get you some water. If you just want to…um…stay right here. Won't be long…'

'You look as though you're dressed to go out. Have I caught you at a bad time?' He looked at her with gleaming eyes, sidelining his curiosity at her bizarre behaviour in favour of playing with the thought that he might be tempted to turn this casual meeting into something a little more rewarding. It wasn't often that he was put in the position of pursuit. It was even less often that his initial response to a woman was so immediate. He found that he was enjoying both experiences.

'Dressed to go out?' Bethany made a big effort and dragged her eyes away from him so that she could teeter in her borrowed heels towards the kitchen.

'Are you always this jumpy?'

Bethany, in the process of getting some bottled water from the fridge, invested his passing remark with bullseye accuracy as she, on cue, jumped, because she hadn't been aware of him following her into the kitchen.

'Would you mind not creeping around like that?' she said tersely. 'Here. Water.' She shoved the glass out to him and, once relieved of it, folded her arms.

'Do you have a first name, Miss Doni?' Getting anything out of this woman was like pulling teeth. His own white ones gritted together with irritation.

'Why would you want to know my name?' A trail of possible consequences crawled into her mind with poisonous clarity. The house-sitting job had originally fallen to one of the owner's relatives, who happened to be a friend of Amy's. Bethany wasn't too sure why the girl had handed over the responsibility to Amy, but Amy had then delegated it to Bethany because she had landed herself a boyfriend and wasn't happy about committing a month of her summer holiday to being cooped up in Rome. Bethany had been overjoyed at the arrangement. She would get to practise her Italian in the most beautiful city in the world and, furthermore, would have free accommodation in the sort of place she would never have clapped eyes on, never mind *lived in*, in a million years. *And* she would be paid for her trouble! Revealing her identity would be step one to landing her in a great deal of difficulty and, worse than that, would land Amy and her friend in even more trouble. She felt faint and half closed her eyes and leaned heavily against the kitchen counter.

'Are you all right?'

Bethany opened her eyes to find him standing disconcertingly close to her, which made her feel flustered and breathless, but she kept her voice even when she replied. 'Fine. I'm fine.' She shifted a bit and Cristiano frowned, irritated by that small gesture of flight.

'You don't look fine. Your colour's up. Maybe it's the heat out there. You're very fair. Italian women are accustomed to the heat in Rome over the summer months, but then you're not Italian, are you? Despite the fact that you speak the language fluently. Is this...' he looked around at the superbly kitted kitchen, which bore all the hallmarks of somewhere that was underused '...a holiday place?'

Bethany could only stare. Did people have *holiday places* that looked like this? Marble everywhere? Paintings on the walls that cost the earth? A dressing room stuffed to overflowing with fabulous designer clothes?

He settled that score by adding, 'I myself have several.'

'Do you?' She sidestepped the question and was relieved when he broke the hold he had on her with his eyes by tipping his head back to swallow some water.

Cristiano shrugged. 'Here. Paris. New York. Barbados. Of course, Paris and New York are largely used when I'm over there on business. It's useful not having to book hotels whenever I'm abroad.' He dumped the glass on the counter, determined to bring the conversation back to *her*. 'So your name...'

'Amelia,' Bethany told him miserably, crossing her fingers behind her back.

'And where do you permanently reside, Amelia Doni?'

'London.'

'You're not a very forthcoming person, are you, Miss Amelia Doni? I take it you *are* a miss...? I don't notice a wedding ring on your hand.'

'If you're finished with that water...'

Far from sounding flattered at his interest, she seemed even more keen to shepherd him out of the apartment, and it set his teeth on edge with rampant irritation.

'How long are you over here?' Cristiano asked because, perversely, the more disinterested she seemed, the more determined he became to break through her invisible silent barrier.

Bethany shrugged and muttered something along the lines of *not very long*.

'But presumably you were here long enough to get involved in the charity fund-raiser?'

'Charity fund-raiser?'

'The orchid? The one currently languishing on a table in the hall? It's a thank you present from my mother. You must know how much she contributes to charity and I gather the last fund-raiser was particularly successful. She would have delivered it to you herself but she's leaving for the country this evening and won't be back for a while.'

'Leaving for the country...' Bethany repeated, aware that she was beginning to sound like someone mentally challenged.

'We have a country house,' Cristiano elaborated, bemused by her complete lack of interest in anything he had to say. 'It's far cooler in the hills than it is in the city...'

'Yes, yes, I expect it would be. You must thank her for the...um...plant...'

'What was your role in the fund-raiser?'

'Ah…well…actually, I prefer not to hark back to things that have happened in the past. I'm a *live for today* kind of person…'

'My kind of woman. I'm not scheduled to return to London until tomorrow. Have dinner with me tonight.'

'What? No! No, no, no…!' Bethany was alternately appalled at the thought of being caught out and stunned by the realisation that *she wanted to accept his invitation*. She didn't know whether it was because she was in Italy and removed from her familiar comfort zone, but everything she was feeling and doing was horrendously out of character. 'You have to go,' she said in an agony of urgency.

'Why? Are you expecting someone? A man? Are you involved with anyone?'

'No.' She began walking towards the front door. Lying did not come naturally to her and she knew that it would be just a matter of time before she tripped herself up.

'So let's get this straight. You're not involved with anyone. You're not waiting for anyone. Why the reluctance to have dinner with me?'

'I…I…um…I think it's a bit rude for you to come here on an errand and then ask me out to dinner…'

'You mean you're not flattered?'

'I mean I don't know you…'

'So dinner would be the perfect opportunity to rectify that situation!' He noticed that he had somehow been manoeuvred towards the front door and her small, pale hand was very firmly round the door handle. He watched in disbelief as she began turning the knob. He had, literally, been shown the door!

'I don't think so, but thanks for the invitation anyway. And…for the plant as well. I'll make sure that I look after it, although I've never been very good with plants.'

'Funny. Nor have I.' He leaned indolently against the door, making it impossible for her to open it. 'Already we have one thing in common.'

'Do you do this a lot?' Bethany asked, heart beating like a hammer inside her because something about him was sending her nervous system into overdrive. 'Pop in to random strangers' houses and ask them out to dinner? Okay, so it's not *rude* as such, but you have to admit that it's a bit *strange*. I mean...' she tested the water '...you don't know me from Adam. Goodness, I could be *anyone*!'

'Yes,' Cristiano said thoughtfully, 'you could be anyone. Axe-murderer, psychopath...' He shot her a curling smile that made her catch her breath. 'Worse than that, scheming gold-digger after my money...However, you do have certain credentials, namely your connection with my mother and...' he looked briefly around him, then back to her '...the fact that you own a place like this. Axe-murderers, psychopaths and gold-diggers probably wouldn't be into charity fund-raising or have holiday apartments in one of the best post-codes in Rome. So my fears are put to rest.'

Bethany was beginning to feel giddy from the torrent of misconceptions swimming around her. *Credentials? Knowing his mother? Owning the apartment?*

'And, admit it, you have to eat.'

'I...I actually don't like eating out. I prefer eating in. Cooking. So many wonderful fresh ingredients over here. It's fun to experiment.'

'Fine. I'll come here.'

'But you can't.' She stared up at the dangerously good-looking face gazing right back down at her and was overcome with the unusual sensation of walking on the very edge of a precipice. The view was tremendous, but falling was a real possibility.

'Of course I can.' Cristiano shrugged. Blessed with a lethal combination of looks, brains and wealth, he had yet to come across a member of the opposite sex who could resist him, and he refused to credit that the woman standing in front of him would prove to be the exception. 'I can either come here or I can pick you up at eight.'

'Why? Why do you want to take me out to dinner? Did your mother ask you to?'

'Why should she do that?' Cristiano's brows knitted into a perplexed frown. 'My mother has no involvement in my personal life and, in fact, she'll be very firmly ensconced in the country by the time I come over here later.' He pushed himself away from the door, not taking his eyes off her face. She really had the most marvellous skin. Translucent. Even without make-up. Not at all like the sultry brunettes he normally favoured. His mother had said very little about her but, then again, why should she have? It would seem that the woman was merely a friend of a friend of a friend who had been sequestered to help out for the charity bash, hence the orchid, which was an expensive but fairly impersonal way of demonstrating appreciation. Anyway, it was a good thing that nothing had been said because it would have been a sure-fire way of turning him off.

'All mothers have involvement in their children's lives,' Bethany was distracted enough to point out, thinking of her own mother who clucked and fussed and still sent food parcels in the post from Ireland just to make sure that she wasn't on the brink of starvation.

'When it comes to women, I keep things strictly to myself.' He opened the door, not allowing her the chance to become embroiled in a debate on a non-subject which would give her the opportunity to remember that she was busily trying to turn him down. He'd never been turned down.

Furthermore, he had highly sensitised antennae and they were picking up her interest in him. He couldn't understand why she would try and fight something as innocent as a dinner date but, whatever her reasons, that wide-eyed way she kept backing away intrigued him. Of course, she could just be playing hard to get, but he seriously doubted that. She had a face that spoke volumes. In fact, he hadn't seen such an openly expressive face since…frankly, he couldn't remember. 'I should warn you that I usually get what I want,' he inserted without vanity.

'And you want dinner with me. Before you leave to-morrow.'

'Finally!' He gave her another of those amazing, toe-curling smiles. 'We have lift-off.' He took her hand, catching her by surprise, and turned it palm up so that he could press a brief kiss against her soft skin in a gesture that seemed purely, wickedly Italian and thrilled her to the bone.

'I suppose so. But…but it'll have to be an early night…' she said anxiously.

'You mean back home before the stroke of midnight when you revert to being a pumpkin?'

Bethany went bright red. She honestly couldn't say what had propelled her to accept the dinner invitation, but there was a trail of treacherous excitement curling inside her, starting at the tips of her toes, going right through her body to her dazed green eyes, which were locked onto his face with nervous fascination. Not even his quip about the pumpkin and midnight could wrench her from her foolhardy fascination and she was still feeling shell-shocked after he had gone.

It was only when she caught sight of herself in the floor to ceiling mirror in the bedroom that reality assaulted her with merciless clarity and she dialled Amy on her mobile phone.

She had to contain an impatient moan of pure frustration as Amy's excitable voice greeted her on the other end of the line with an enthusiastic rundown of her latest conquest and the fabulous Florentine sights, which they had yet to see because the bed was proving too alluring.

Bethany waited until she had run out of steam and then said hesitantly, 'Little problem on this end.' The floaty dress was still in evidence, witness to her moment of madness.

'Oh, God! Tell me the apartment hasn't burnt down!'

'Still in one piece. But there's been a visitor…and here's the thing…' The dress, which had seemed so temptingly beautiful, now stared balefully back at her from the mirror as she proceeded to tell her friend what had recently transpired. She kept getting muddled up because, in her head, all she could see was the stranger's lean, dark, outrageously sexy face looking at her in a way that was both intrusive and scarily exciting and nothing at all like the way other boys back home had ever looked at her.

'So you're going out with him for dinner…Oh, God, let me think…okay, okay…might be for the best…'

'Because…?'

Half an hour later, Bethany removed the offending dress, laid it on the bed because it would have to be dry-cleaned in the morning, and thought that there was a lot of truth about webs and lies and getting entangled. Catrina, the original house-sitter and cherished godchild of the hapless Amelia Doni, who was on a cruise a thousand miles away from Rome, was in London. In rehab. Very hush-hush, and all hell would break loose should loaded and doting godmother find out. So the task of house-sitting had fallen to Amy, with a code red level of secrecy but, Amy being Amy, Love had reared its head and her house-sitting mission had fallen quickly by the wayside. Thankfully, Bethany had been there, ever reliable and immune to being led astray. The sort of girl who enjoyed reading Italian books at night and thought that three glasses of wine qualified as a binge-drinking fest.

Now, as she stared down at the dress on the bed, Bethany wondered what had happened to Little Miss Reliability. The most daring thing she had done in ages had been to try that wretched dress on because yes, she really *did* enjoy curling up with a good book most nights and sometimes she even fulfilled that dreariest of clichés by curling up with a good book *and* a mug of hot chocolate.

But now she had accepted a dinner invitation from a guy who was sinfully sexy *and* ultra-sophisticated. Moreover, it was just going to be a one-night affair, and if, *for once*, she acted out of character, if she behaved like the kind of person who might conceivably have a holiday apartment dripping with designer clothes, the kind of woman who thought nothing of hanging around in a dress that cost a small fortune, then why not? She would be helping Amy out because no one, but *no one*, could get a *whiff* of Catrina drying out in a clinic in the UK and the *last thing* anyone needed was for some connected Italian guy to start asking questions.

Bethany felt a kick of excitement stir inside her. Of course, whatever she wore that night she would have dry-cleaned. She wasn't *that irresponsible*. She was just going to have a couple of hours of fun…no harm there…

CHAPTER TWO

'So...TELL me about yourself...'

It was an inevitable question but it still made Bethany's nerves jangle because after the initial crazy euphoria of wondering what it would be like to step into someone else's shoes for a night had come the shattering reality that she was, in actual fact, going to spend a few hours in the company of a sex god under false pretences. Between Cristiano's departure from the apartment and the sound of his voice four hours later on the intercom when he arrived to collect her, she had had ample time to concede that a man like him— sleek, sophisticated, extraordinarily handsome—would never have looked at a girl like her under normal circumstances. In fact, they would never even have *met* under normal circumstances.

Bethany, who had managed to fall back on most of her own clothes because leaving the house in someone else's wardrobe seemed a bit rich, all things considered, wondered how best to answer his question.

She finally settled on a vague, nonsensical answer along the lines of being a *free spirit*.

'What does that mean?' Cristiano looked across at her. She intrigued him and he had found himself looking forward to their dinner more than he had looked forward to any date with a woman in a long time. Nor had she disappointed. When the elevator doors had pinged open and she had walked across the marbled foyer towards him, he had literally been stopped in his tracks. She might have had all the money she wanted at her disposal, but she had foregone the diamonds and pearls, the little black dress that screamed *designer* and the killer stilettos, and instead had dressed down in a pair of jeans and some flat tan loafers with a pale blue wrap over her shoulders. Cristiano liked it. It took a confident woman to go for comfort and it took a sexy one to pull it off.

'What does that *mean*?' Bethany's natural warmth came out in her smile. Now that she was talking and not just gawping like a star-struck teenager, she could begin to relax a little and to enjoy the stolen moment in time. 'You sound like someone who's spent a lifetime living in a bubble.'

'Living in a bubble…' Cristiano looked at her thoughtfully. 'I suppose I *did* grow up in a bubble of sorts. Coming from a privileged background can have that effect. You're naturally supposed to do certain things…'

Bethany could only imagine. 'Like what?'

'Don't tell me you haven't experienced the same sort of thing. A certain lifestyle to which you conform, more or less, from an early age.'

Bethany thought of her own riotous Irish upbringing, the house always full of friends and family, boyfriends in and out, their two dogs and three cats and the general happy chaos that had made up her formative years. Conforming to anything from an early age was an alien concept.

'I'm more of a non-conformist,' she said truthfully. 'I mean, I'm not a wild child or anything like that, but I was never told that I had to be a certain way or do certain things.'

'Perhaps things work a little differently in your part of the world,' Cristiano murmured. 'Here, in Italy, I have always known what my future held in store for me.' They had drifted outside into a balmy summer evening.

'That must have been tough.'

'Tough? Why?' He was fascinated by the thought of any woman who could apply the adjective *tough* to any aspect of his life. Even the richest of women he had dated in the past had been impressed to death by the breadth of his power and privilege. 'Since when is it tough to have the world at your disposal?'

'No one has the world at their disposal!' Bethany laughed, as they began walking slowly towards his car, which he had parked, he had explained, in the only free space at the very end of the long road.

'You'd be surprised.'

Underneath the lazy, sexy timbre of his voice, she could detect the ruthless patina of a man accustomed to getting exactly what he wanted and she shivered. 'You just think you have the world at your disposal because everyone around you is primed to agree with everything you say,' she felt compelled to point out. 'I think it must be one of the downfalls of having too much money…'

'*Too much money?* I don't believe I've ever heard that expression cross a woman's lips.' He was privately amused that someone of presumably substantial private means could wax lyrical about *the pitfalls of wealth* but it was refreshing, for once, to find himself in the company of a woman who seemed to have a social conscience.

Bethany decided that if he was a learning curve for her, then why shouldn't she be a learning curve for him? What did she have to lose? She guessed instinctively that he wasn't a man who had much experience when it came to having his opinions questioned. The way he had asked her out to dinner, refused to concede that she might turn him down, indicated someone whose belief in the *whole world being at his disposal* was absolute.

'What type of women do you mix with?' Bethany asked, fascinated beyond belief by the wildly exotic creature looking lazily at her. His eyes were as dark as molasses, fringed by the most ridiculously long lashes imaginable, and the way his dark hair curled against the collar of his shirt, a little too long to be entirely conventional but not so long that he looked unkempt, brought her out in goosebumps.

Cristiano laughed and reached out to curl one finger into a strand of her copper hair. 'Always brunettes,' he murmured, 'although I'm beginning to wonder why. Is this the real colour of your hair?'

'Of course it is!' Excitement leapt inside her at his casual touch and her green eyes widened. 'Not *everyone* gets their hair colour from a bottle!'

'But quite a few do.' Her hair felt like silk between his fingers.

'So, in other words, you only go out with brunettes who dye their hair?'

'They tend to have other characteristics aside from the dyed hair.' He had an insane desire to yank her towards him and do what came naturally. Very unlike him. He reluctantly released the strands of hair and stood back just in case primitive instinct got the better of him. 'Long legs. Exquisite faces. Right background.'

'Right background?'

Cristiano shrugged. 'It's important,' he admitted. 'Life can be stressful enough without the added hassle of wondering whether the woman sharing your bed is more interested in your bank balance than in your company.'

Bethany's stomach gave a nervous flutter but she was re-assured by the fact that she knew she definitely wasn't after his money. 'Maybe you're a little insecure.'

'*A little insecure?*' Cristiano looked at her with rampant incredulity. 'No. Insecurity has never been a problem for me,' he told her with satisfaction. 'And please tell me that you aren't going to spend the evening trying to analyse me.'

'Where are we going to eat?' Bethany changed the subject and when he named a restaurant which was as famous for its inflated prices as it was for the quality of its fare she gazed down at her jeans with dismay. Lesson one in how the super-rich operate. With a complete disregard for social convention. Cristiano clearly couldn't care less whether she was dressed for an expensive night out or not. He, himself, was casually attired in a pair of dark trousers and a white shirt which would have looked average on any other man on the planet but which looked ridiculously sexy on him.

'I'd rather not go there in a pair of jeans, flat shoes and a wrap,' Bethany told him tersely. She also suspected that walking into a place like that on the arm of a man like him would make her the cynosure of all eyes and she had never enjoyed basking in the limelight, particularly now, when the limelight would have a very dubious tinge. And what if he introduced her to someone? The rarefied world of the rich and famous was notoriously small. In Rome, it was probably the size of a tennis ball. She would be revealed for the imposter she was in seconds flat.

'You look…charming.'

'Not charming enough to go to that particular restaurant.' Bethany was feverishly cursing herself, yet again, for having succumbed to his invitation to dinner.

'Don't worry. I know the owner. Believe me when I tell you

that he won't mind if I bring along a woman dressed in a bin bag.'

'Because you can get away with something doesn't give you the right to go ahead and do it,' Bethany said, making sense to herself though not to him if his expression of bemusement was anything to go by.

'Why not?'

'Because it's important to have respect for other people,' she told him, repeating the oft held mantra with which she and her sisters had grown up.

Cristiano was looking at her as though she was slowly mutating into a being from another planet and Bethany blushed uncomfortably. She was well aware that she was probably in the process of contravening yet another unspoken dictum of the unbelievably rich, namely that she shouldn't be blushing like a kid.

'A socialite with principles,' he murmured with a slashing smile that made her breath catch in her throat and put paid to all her niggling qualms about what she was doing. 'I like it. It's rare in my world to meet a woman who's prepared to be vocal about her beliefs...' In truth, the women he went out with generally didn't give a hoot about what happened outside their own orbits. They were rich, had led, for the most part, pampered lives and their birthright was to accept the adulation of males and the subservience of everyone else.

Not that they would ever have dreamt of setting one foot into Chez Nico unless they were dressed to kill. In actual fact, he doubted whether very many would have dreamt of going anywhere unless dressed to kill because appearance was all.

'I'm not a socialite,' Bethany said uncomfortably.

'No? You just own a monstrously big apartment in the centre of Rome which you use as a holiday pad. You do fundraisers. You're under thirty. Hate to tell you this, but that pretty much qualifies you as a socialite.'

'I told you, things don't work quite that way in… um…where I come from.'

'And where's that?'

'Oh, you wouldn't have heard of it,' Bethany told him truthfully. 'It's a little place in Ireland…um…in the middle of nowhere…'

'A little place with a large ancestral manor house, by any chance?'

'Yes, there's a large ancestral manor house…' Years ago, she could remember her mother doing a cleaning stint there to get some extra cash for Christmas. It was a great grey mansion with turrets and a forbidding, desolate appearance.

'So you must be half Italian…Which half?'

Bethany gave a self-conscious laugh. 'Are you always so interested in dinner companions you ask out on the spur of the moment?'

'No. But, then again, I don't usually have to drag information out of my dinner companions. It's a fact that most women love nothing more than talking about themselves.'

'You mean they try to impress you.'

'Do you want the truth or shall I treat you to a phoney spectacle of false modesty?'

'You have a very big ego, don't you?'

'I prefer to call it a keen sense of reality.' Cristiano was enjoying this banter. He had had to work to get her to this place, on a date with him and, having got her here, was discovering her to be skittish and unpredictable company. It made a change from the doe-eyed beauties who were always eager to oblige his every whim. 'Don't you feel the need to impress me?' he murmured, his words cloaked in a languorous, sexy intimacy that sent shivers racing up and down her spine.

'Why should I?' A frisson of danger rippled through her. This was no simple, exciting night out with a stranger. She felt as though he was walking round her soul, opening doors she hadn't known existed.

'Because I feel the weirdest desire to impress *you*.' He also had the weirdest desire to find out more about her. Weird because *getting to know her* had not been remotely on the agenda when he had asked her out to dinner. He had seen her, had been curiously attracted to her, had thought nothing of entertaining himself with a one-night stand. It wasn't usually his scene but, then again, he would have been a complete hypocrite if he had tried to dredge up a bunch of reasons why he should not indulge in a night of passion with a woman he would probably never see again. It wasn't as though his goal in life, thus far, was to recruit a love interest for a permanent place in his life.

'Why don't you tell me what it would take…?'

His voice was like a caress, as was the lazy, amused, speculative expression in his eyes, although she noticed that he was keeping his distance, half leaning against the door, his long legs eating into the free space between them. She had not started the evening in the anticipation that it would end up in bed and had he tried to invade her space she would have pulled back at a rate of knots, but there was something wildly erotic about his self-restraint. It was a sobering thought to know that he would probably be repelled had he known her modest background. He might consider himself a man of the world, and he undoubtedly *was* a man of the world, a sleek, highly groomed, fantastically sophisticated animal who was the master of all he surveyed. Except there was quite a bit that he *didn't* survey, wasn't there?

'We could walk…' she said. 'Rome is full of so many exciting, wonderful sights. And then we could go somewhere simple and cheerful to eat. A pizzeria. I happen to know an excellent one not a million miles away from the Colosseum.'

'Sure. Why not? I haven't eaten in that part of the city since I was a teenager. In fact, I think I know the place you're talking about. Red and white striped awning outside? Dark interior? Empty wine bottles on the tables with candles, sixties style? Overweight proprietor with a handlebar moustache?'

'He must have lost weight over the years—' Bethany laughed '—but the moustache is still there. You used to go there? With your friends?'

'Before real life took over,' Cristiano said wryly.

'What do you mean by *real life*?'

'University and then stepping into my father's shoes. Pizzerias don't have much of a role to play in the life of an empire-builder.' He grinned, enjoying her forthright manner. It was refreshing to meet a woman so upfront. Those games women played could get a little tiresome after a while.

'So now you only go to fancy restaurants.'

'Where pizza is never on the menu.'

'Poor Cristiano.' Bethany laughed and their eyes tangled. She felt a rush of blood to her head because she could sense the sexual invitation in his slumberous, amused dark gaze.

'I know—' he sighed piteously, his eyes never leaving her face for a second '—condemned to a life without pizzas. No wonder you feel sorry for me. Okay, here's the deal. I'll do the pizza but I'll pass on the scenic walking. Enrico is paid far too much, as I keep telling him. What's the point of paying someone for doing nothing?'

'Who's Enrico?'

'My mother's driver, of course. Don't tell me you don't have one in London.'

'Several,' Bethany said, thinking of the numerous bus

drivers who serviced the buses between her flat and the university.

'Good. Then that's settled.'

Bethany felt like a princess as she slid into the back seat of the sleek black Mercedes. A princess whose clothes didn't quite match the luxurious leather and gleaming walnut of the car, but what the heck? She had to restrain herself from running her hands along the seat. Presumably she would be accustomed to these levels of mega-luxury.

Seen from this angle, through the windows of a car that drew glances and had people swivelling around to try and glimpse who was inside, the city felt like her possession. No wonder that sense of *ownership* sat on this man's shoulders like an invisible mantle! Fifteen minutes in his car and she was already beginning to feel like royalty!

Even when they were installed at a table at the back of the buzzing, lively pizzeria, she was still hyper-sensitive to the reality that women were still sneaking sidelong glances at them, trying to figure out who the sexy guy was and his much drabber companion. Cristiano appeared to notice none of it.

He was busily delivering his verdict on the lack of changes to the pizzeria since he had last been there, which was nearly two decades ago, and she contented herself with arguing with everything he said, finally concluding that he was a snob for daring to inform her that the least the proprietor could have done was change the dated gingham tablecloths which loudly proclaimed a stubborn refusal to move with the times.

'Me? *A snob*?' He had been pleasantly invigorated by her arguing, because women didn't argue with him, and was now vastly amused at her one word summary of his character. She was laughing when she said it, her crystal clear green eyes throwing out all sorts of invitations that had him aching for her.

'Yes, you!' A bottle of wine had been brought for them and she had already finished one glass. 'Loads of people flock to this place because the food is simple and hearty and very, very good…'

'And would be improved by a shake up in the decor…'

'*You* like white linen and fawning waiters, but that doesn't mean that *everyone* shares your taste…'

'But most would, given half the chance.'

'*I* happen to prefer the rustic ambience…'

'How rustic? I'm sure I recognise a couple of those wine bottles stuffed with candles from when I was last here a hundred years ago.'

'I'm having dinner with an old man!' Bethany groaned in mock despair while he refilled her glass with some more wine and grinned in open appreciation of her teasing.

'You'd be surprised at what this old man is still capable of doing,' Cristiano intoned softly, the smile still playing on his lips as he savoured her flushed face with indolent thoroughness.

'Such as…?' Bethany questioned breathlessly. Her skin prickled and she felt quite unlike herself, as if she had stepped into another life, one where the normal rules of behaviour didn't apply. Which, she admitted to herself, she had. Kind of.

'Oh, running a business empire that has branches in most major cities in the world. Takes a lot of stamina to do that. Then there are my sporting interests. The usual gym routine, not to mention skiing, polo and very vigorous games of squash once a week.'

'Yes, that *is* impressive for a geriatric…' she said nonchalantly—at least she was aiming for nonchalance; inside, she was anything but as she experienced a sexual longing she had never felt before with any man. Nor had she ever indulged in sexual banter before. In fact, she had never indulged in sexual *anything*—at least nothing beyond kissing and the occasional groping. She had never seen the point of tossing her virginity out of the window for no better reason than because *everyone else her age had done it*. The temptation to do so now, with this man, curled inside her and made her feel as if she was no longer in complete possession of her own body.

'Then there's the sex...' His eyes never left hers. 'I've never had any complaints...'

'Aargh...' Colour flamed into her cheeks and she nervously grabbed her glass of wine and downed the contents. 'We were talking about the fact that you're a snob...' she reminded him shakily and he lowered his eyes, obliging her with a tactical retreat.

'And I was protesting my innocence of any such thing. A less snobbish person it would be hard to find!' he declared.

Bethany's nervous system settled a little now that she wasn't skewered by the naked hunger in his fabulous eyes, which he had made no attempt to conceal.

'Okay. So do you ever go *anywhere* inexpensive to eat?'

'You mean like one of those disgusting fast food places where people eat reconstituted meat drowning in sauce? No.'

'Cinema?'

Cristiano frowned. 'Not recently,' he admitted, surprised to find that it had been literally years since he had been inside one. Surely the last time couldn't have been at university?

'But you *do* go to the theatre? The opera?'

'Okay.' He held both hands up in surrender. 'I'm a

crashing snob.' Their food had been brought to them and he hadn't even noticed. Nor had she. In fact, although the big bowl of pasta smelled amazing, the food still seemed like an unwelcome intrusion into a conversation that was unexpectedly energising.

'But, on a serious note—' he tucked in to the spaghetti, which was nothing like the dainty little portions served in expensive restaurants, usually as an accompaniment to the main dish, but a massively generous helping liberally covered in the finest seafood sauce he had tasted in a long time '—are you telling me that it isn't easy for you to be a feisty left wing radical when you have the comfort of money to support your ideals?'

'What do you mean?' For a second there, Bethany had almost forgotten the charade she was meant to be playing. She was reminded of it soon enough when he began to expound.

'Well, it's easy to relish the role of the free spirit, not tied to the shallow world of the rich and privileged, when you must know, at the back of your mind, that you could move between the two any time you wanted to. Yes, you come to pizzerias like this but, if you get a little bored, then it's well within your means to jump into a taxi and head for the nearest Michelin starred restaurant. And let's not forget the little matter of your apartment. Money can buy you the luxury of pretending to be one of the normal little people without any of the reality that goes with it.'

Bethany opened her mouth to contradict him and closed it just as fast. She could understand the irony of his observation and was powerless to refute it given the circumstances, so she made do with saying lamely, 'I'm not a left wing radical. Believe me.'

'And I'm not a snob. Believe me.' He gave her one of

those toe-curling smiles that made her tummy flip over. 'Good food.' He raised his fork in appreciative acknowledgement. 'I might very well come back here again.'

'Are you sure the type of women you date would be up for this sort of place?' She found that she didn't care for the thought of him returning to her favourite haunt in the company of another woman. One of the leggy, glamorous brunettes with the dyed hair which he had previously mentioned. In fact, one of those women to whom he was much more suited, if only he knew it.

'Maybe not,' Cristiano conceded. 'Which makes you so unique.'

'Hardly. You should see this place some evenings. There's a queue a mile long to get inside. If I'm unique, then so are the hundreds of people who flock here every day of the year.'

'You know what I'm talking about.'

She did. 'You say that you're not a snob,' she heard herself say, 'but would you be sitting here opposite me if I weren't *unique*?'

'Meaning what?'

'Let's just say that I was…um…the genuine article. A pretty average girl from a working class background, just like all the girls in here…would you still be sitting where you are?'

It seemed a strange hypothesis but Cristiano was willing to go along for the ride because he had, quite frankly, never met anyone like her before. She was amazingly untouched by her wealth and if her conversation was unpredictable then it was just something else about her that he found so impossibly alluring.

Also, no one had ever raised the issue with him before and he frowned, giving her question thought.

'Probably not, if I'm to be honest.'

'Because…?'

'Because, like I said, a wealthy man can't be too careful. I would never allow myself to get tied up with a woman who wasn't financially independent in her own right. Marry in haste and repent at leisure and if you don't fancy doing the repentance bit, then you might just find yourself dragged through the courts and parting with a sizeable chunk of cash you've spent years working hard to attain. But hell, why waste valuable time talking about a situation that's not relevant?'

'I can't agree more,' Bethany agreed fervently because she had stepped into a princess's shoes and she wasn't going to spoil this one glittering night getting embroiled in an argument that was never going to go anywhere. She was Cinderella at the ball and why start beckoning to the pumpkin to come fetch her when it wasn't yet midnight?

He was entitled to his own opinions and he was entitled to protect his wealth however he saw fit, even if he *was* cutting himself off from so many experiences.

'So…' he kept his eyes on her while he beckoned to a waiter for the bill '…are we finished with the soul-searching conversations? Can we move on to something a little lighter? Or, failing that, why don't we just move on…?'

'To what? I don't know any clubs in Rome.' *And probably wouldn't have the cash to fund a visit even if I did.*

'I was thinking of somewhere a little…cosier. My place is less than ten minutes away.'

His scrutiny was hot and hungry and left her in no doubt that the outcome of the evening would finish in bed. *A one-night stand.* Her sisters would be shocked. Her parents would be mortified. Her friends would think that she had been taken over by an alien being who looked like her, spoke like her, but lived life in a different lane. Everything she took for granted about herself would be shattered and yet the pull to surrender to this new being was almost irresistible.

He made her feel sexy. Was making her feel sexy now, the way he was staring at her as if she were the only woman on the face of the planet. Her nipples nudged the white lace of her bra.

'Of course, I can just get Enrico to deliver you back to your apartment,' Cristiano told her, because he wasn't into forcing himself upon a reluctant woman, even if all the signals had been in place from the moment he'd picked her up from her apartment.

'Would you be very angry?'

'I would be in need of a very cold shower.'

Bethany had an image of him showering, his big, muscular body naked under the fine spray, his beautiful face raised, eyes closed, to the running water. It was an effort to keep her breathing even just thinking about it.

'Don't you want to get an early night?' she ventured tentatively and Cristiano laughed.

'I don't do early nights. I need very little sleep, as it happens.'

And that, in turn, made her think of them making love over and over, languishing on some great king-sized bed which probably had sheets of the finest, coolest Egyptian cotton and not the bargain basement stuff she was accustomed to. From calmly standing on the sidelines, she seemed to have morphed into a sexual creature in the space of a few hours. She had never had to fight off urges when it came to the opposite sex so it had been easy to put her celibacy down to her high-minded principles.

'Well…there's just one small thing…'

Cristiano could smell polite rejection in the making and, while he acknowledged that it would hardly be the end of the world, he was still surprised to find that his disappoint-ment was much sharper than he had expected. But, then again, the evening had been much more pleasurable than he had anticipated. Usually, female conversation was a dullish background noise to which he paid lip service but essentially little in-depth attention. Tonight, he had found himself taking the time to really talk to her, to enjoy the unexpected pleasure of having a sparring partner who could make him laugh and pepper him with questions which had made him think.

'I'm all ears.' He settled the bill, brushing aside her offer to go Dutch, and sat back in the chair, giving her his full, un-divided attention. The evening seemed to have been full of firsts, starting with the bizarre way he had invited her to dinner. Being turned down would also be a first.

'I…I'm not the most…um…you know….experienced person in the world…'

Cristiano sat forward, bewildered by this deviation from what he had been expecting. 'I don't get you.'

'What don't you get?' Bethany bristled defensively.

'I don't get what you're trying to tell me.'

'That's because you're not listening hard enough.' Embarrassment gave a sharp edge to her voice and she sighed. 'Okay. I know you have a certain idea of the person you think I am…' *expensive apartment in Rome, country house in Ireland, a string of drivers who presumably do nothing else but wait around in fancy cars for me to snap my fingers* '…but I'm not like all those other women you dated.' She took a deep breath and for a few seconds contemplated telling him the whole truth. The mix-up with the clothes, the silly little white lie…Would he laugh? Forgive her? No. The answer came before she could voice what was in her head. He would be horrified. He didn't go near girls like her, girls who didn't inhabit the same privileged background that he did. And she didn't want this moment with him to pass her by. She wasn't sure why she felt so strongly about it, but she did and she wasn't going to mess up her one snatched night with this guy. He had managed to crawl under her skin and she wanted him there.

'Here's the thing,' she said, spelling it out in black and white. 'I'm a virgin.'

CHAPTER THREE

'I'M A virgin...'

Possibly the only three truthful words she had uttered to him as she had played him for a complete and utter fool.

Cristiano, parked in a dark green Land Rover he had rented in Limerick, coldly surveyed his quarry, which was a picture postcard thatched cottage at the end of the road.

It was five months since she had walked out on him without warning and five weeks since he had discovered that she had strung him along with a pack of lies. Amelia Doni was no fresh-faced, copper-haired girl with green eyes and a knack for teasing him that had proved so addictive that he had cancelled his return to London and ended up whisking her off in his private jet to Barbados for two weeks. Amelia Doni, when he'd accidentally bumped into her over Christmas at his mother's house, was a blonde in her forties who, she'd told him in mind-numbing detail, had been on an extended cruise because she was recovering from a broken heart. She was the epitome of the wealthy owner of a slice of Rome's most prestigious apartment block and had bored him to death within two minutes. She had also stoked the fires of his simmering anger into a conflagration when he'd learned about her house-sitting arrangement with her darkly beautiful Italian god-daughter and realised the woman he had met had been an imposter. Not only had he been summarily dumped, he had also been well and truly taken on a scenic route up a very winding garden path.

It had taken him a mere week to track down the address of one Bethany Maguire, and a couple more had passed as he sat on the information, telling himself to let it go before finally realising that he wouldn't rest until he had confronted the woman and given voice to his consuming rage.

He had no idea what he hoped to gain by confronting her and it went absolutely and utterly against the grain of the person he was, a man who had always been able to keep his emotions in check with ease, a man who prided himself on his ferocious self-control. A man, it had to be said, who had never found himself in the position of being left high and dry by any woman or, for that matter, being told barefaced lies and gullibly eating them up.

Without the engine running, it was beginning to get cold in the car and the January light was beginning to fade. Give it ten more minutes and the line of picturesque thatched houses that jostled for space along the broad road with colourfully painted cottages and shop fronts would fade into an indistinct grey blur. There was still time, he knew, to drive right back to the hotel, grab a meal and head back to London first thing in the morning. On the other hand, would that put paid to the bitter, toxic knot that sat in the pit of his stomach like a tumour?

He stepped out of the car and began walking along the pavement, cursorily taking in the fairy tale village setting. Not to his taste. The place looked as though it had been designed by a kid who had been given a blank canvas and told to go mad. He almost expected to bump into a gingerbread house at any moment.

The house at the end of the road was no exception. The trees were bare of leaves and the front garden lacked colour, but he imagined that in summer it would be filled with all the stereotypical stuff straight out of a children's book. Apple trees out back, flowers running rampant everywhere, the prerequisite stone wall over which neighbours would chat while, presumably, hanging out their washing and whistling a merry tune. He scowled and banked down the rise of bile in his throat as he ignored the doorbell to bang heavily on the front door instead.

Bethany, in the middle of foraging in the fridge for ingredients to make a meal for her parents which she had enthusiastically promised three hours earlier, cursed under her breath because she had left everything to the absolute last minute and couldn't afford to take time out for a chat. Having spent the past two years in London, she had forgotten how life worked in the small village where she had lived all her life. People stopped by. They chatted. They drank interminable cups of tea. It had been worse in the first couple of months after she had arrived back but, even now, old neighbours would drop in and would be offended if she didn't sit and chat over tea and biscuits.

She wondered if she could pretend to be out, perhaps duck down under the kitchen table and wait until the coast was clear, but then dismissed the idea because half the village would know that her parents were at the village fund-raiser and would also know that she had skipped it because she had felt ill that morning. That was just life around here, and she was going to have to make the best of it for the foreseeable future.

She dumped her handful of random ingredients on the kitchen counter and raced to the front door to intercept another bang.

In her head, she played over the possibilities of who it could be. Several of her old school friends, ones who had never left the little village in which they had grown up, who had settled down at ridiculously young ages to marry and have families, had looked her up. She had been grateful for their support and had tried very hard not to feel hemmed in and claustrophobic. She missed Shania and Melanie, who had both returned to their respective lives in Dublin after a two week family break over Christmas. Perhaps it was old Mrs Kelly a few houses along, who had become a frequent visitor and was prone to extended visits.

Bethany stifled a groan of near despair as she pulled open the front door and then stared at her visitor in frozen, nauseating disbelief.

She blinked, thinking that she must be hallucinating, but when she opened her eyes he was still there and this was no crazy illusion.

'*You!*' she squeaked in a high-pitched voice which she hardly recognised as her own. 'What are *you doing here?*' She clutched her mouth and swayed.

'No way are you going to faint on me,' Cristiano said through gritted teeth. He insinuated his foot over the threshold and pushed the door open wide, letting himself in while she was still gasping in shock and as pliable as a rag doll. Her eyes were as wide as saucers and she looked as though she was on the verge of collapse. Good.

Bethany heard the slam of the front door as he closed it and it resonated with the sound of the executioner's blade. She was busy trying to get her thoughts together but the sight of him, all six foot two of cold aggression towering in the hallway, had slowed her thought processes down to an unhelpful standstill.

'Cristiano,' she finally threaded unevenly. 'What a surprise.'

Only the wall, against which she had pressed herself, was keeping her from sinking to the ground in an unlovely heap.

'Life is full of them. As I've discovered for myself, first-hand.'

'What are you doing here?' she stammered, choosing not to pursue that particular avenue of conversation.

'Oh, I was just driving by and I thought I'd take time out to pass the time of day with you...*Amelia*. But it's not Amelia, is it, *Bethany*?'

'I feel faint. I honestly do.' She put her hand to her head and took a few deep breaths. 'I think I'm going to be sick.'

'Feel free. I'll be waiting right here for you when you've recovered.' He closed the gap between them and with each passing step Bethany felt her heart rate rocket.

'How did...did you f...find me?'

'Now, now,' Cristiano said with sibilant menace, 'isn't it a little rude for you not to have offered me a cup of coffee? For us to be standing here in a hallway playing catch up when we could be chatting over old times somewhere a little more comfortable...? And after I've travelled all this way to see you...'

The man was in no hurry to go. And he was stifling her by standing so close, sending her frayed nervous system into even more acute disarray.

Belatedly, she remembered that she might be in the house on her own *at the moment* but her parents would be returning in under an hour, by which time he would need to have disappeared. The longer she remained in a state of shock, the longer he would be around, and she just couldn't afford to have him meet her parents.

Another wave of nausea threatened to have her rushing to the bathroom, but she quelled it and cleared her throat.

'Okay. I'll get you a cup of coffee, but if you've come to

bludgeon me into saying sorry then I'll spare you the effort. I'm sorry. Satisfied?'

'Not by a long chalk. So why don't we start with the coffee and then we can have a really good chat about everything. By the way, did you know that impersonating someone can be prosecuted as a criminal offence?'

Bethany paled and Cristiano, who had only thought of that on the spur of the moment, shot her a smile of pure threat.

'What else did you get up to while you were staying at the Doni apartment? Aside from shamelessly raiding her wardrobe? How light were your fingers? If I recall, the place was stuffed full of valuables.'

'How dare you?'

'I know. Nasty of me, isn't it? But I'd think twice before I start reaching for the moral high ground if I were you.' He had expected her to be taken aback by his appearance on her doorstep. No, he thought, scratch that. He had expected her to be shocked and defensive, but he hadn't bargained on the panicky apprehension in her eyes. Then again, she was a lady of unexpected responses and definitely not one whose words and actions could be taken at face value.

Bethany felt like a mouse pinned to the ground by a predator whose aim was to smack her around for a while before ripping her to shreds. When she had walked away from him, admittedly with a finality which stemmed more from cowardice than anything else, the last thing she had expected was to be hunted down. She hadn't taken him for a man who would lower himself to chasing after a woman who had dumped him without explanation. His pride would have seen to that. Unfortunately, she hadn't thought ahead to what he might do if he discovered that the woman who had dumped him had also been as genuine as a three pound note. At least as far as outward appearances went. Now she knew. He went on the attack.

'I wasn't trying to reach for any moral high ground.' Bethany shifted, crablike, against the wall because he was so close to her that she could feel his warm, angry breath on her face. 'I was just trying to say that I'm *not a thief.*'

'Now, I wonder why I'm finding it hard to believe anything you have to say…'.

Since there was no arguing with that and trying to plead her innocence on that front was just going to be met with scathing disbelief, she decided that it was time for the cup of coffee. She deserved his anger and she would sit through it with lowered head and genuine repentance. Then he would leave and her life could return to its hollow routine.

'The coffee…I'll make you a cup…if…if you want to wait in the sitting room…it's just through there…'

'And have you out of my sight? Not a chance. I don't know whether you'll do a disappearing act through the back window. You seem to be pretty good at that.'

'I'm…sorry. I told you that.' She stared down at the ground but there was no escaping his presence because she could see the dull burnished leather of his shoes. Even when he stepped away to fall in behind her, she was horribly, horribly aware of him and it felt as though she was holding her body in agonising tension just to stop herself from shaking like a leaf in a high wind.

'Nice house,' he said conversationally, which didn't fool her for a minute into thinking that he had dropped his anger in favour of a more reasonable approach to having his questions answered. He was just enjoying the moment, toying with her. 'Funny, you told me that you lived in London.'

'I did.' She had her back to him as she filled the kettle with water and fetched down one of the mugs from the mug tree by the sink. Sadly, she couldn't take refuge in the task of making his coffee for ever and eventually she was obliged to turn around, albeit reluctantly, to find that he had taken up residence on one of the pine chairs at the kitchen table. It was a reasonably big kitchen, big enough to fit a generously proportioned table, but he still managed to reduce the space to the size of a prison cell.

She shoved the mug of coffee in front of him and sat on the chair furthest away. This cold-eyed stranger staring at her with biting antagonism was as far away from the sexy, amusing, highly intelligent charmer who had swept her off her feet sufficiently for her to extend her *one night of fun* into a two week, mind-blowingly idyllic trip to paradise as chalk was from cheese.

Playing at the back of her mind was his casual insinuation that she could be prosecuted for impersonation. Was that true? Could that really happen? She couldn't even begin thinking about that, so she shut the horror of it away and focused instead on the humiliation awaiting her at his hands.

Of course she deserved it. She had meant so many times to confess the truth to him, but every time she'd got to within striking distance of doing so she had pulled back because she hadn't wanted their affair to end. Instead, she had laughingly sidestepped awkward questions, glazed over the truth and generally done such a good job of dancing round anything remotely incriminating that she could have had a career as an escape artiste. Houdini would have been proud of her.

In the process, he had stolen her heart and if he had asked her to stay on in sunny Barbados for another fortnight she knew she would have jumped at the chance and postponed the inevitable again.

Her punishment was as deadly as it was conclusive. He had taken up residence inside her and not a single day had gone by when she hadn't thought about him and about the fact that she would never be entitled to have him in her life again. Ever.

'Stop looking at me like that,' she muttered mutinously.

'Like what? How do you expect me to look at a liar, a cheat and a thief?'

'I told you *I didn't steal anything from Amelia Doni!*'

'But you certainly managed to rip me off for quite a bit when you count the dinners, the wardrobe, the first class ticket to the other side of the world…'

'You don't understand…'

'Enlighten me.' He sat forward and Bethany instinctively cringed back, licking her lips nervously, with one eye on the clock behind him over the kitchen door.

'I meant to tell you the truth…'

'The road to hell is paved with good intentions.' He intoned the age-old motto with icy grimness. 'When did the good intentions disappear? When you realised that it would be a hell of a lot more rewarding to hop on the gravy train and take advantage of my generosity? Sex with all expenses paid?'

'Don't be crude!'

'When did you decide to leave London?'

'Wha…?' Confused by the abrupt change of subject, Bethany looked at him in bewilderment before her brain clanked back into gear and she caught on to what he was doing. Instead of going for the kill, he was nipping away at her, pulling back before he could draw blood, only to home back in again just when she had managed to recover. He was getting under her defences and making sure that she had no time to rebuild them.

'London. When did you decide to leave? Ditch the university course? Fly back over here, to the middle of nowhere? Did you think that London was too small for the both of us? Was your conscience acting up too much for you to stay put and risk running into me at some unspecified point in time?'

Bethany paled as his carelessly tossed question found its unintentional target.

'How…how did you find me, Cristiano?' She fell back on her original query. 'And why did you bother?'

Cristiano shrugged elegantly. Even at the height of his anger, when his face was a cold mask of freezing disdain, she couldn't help but register his magnetic pull. Everything about him was unbearably graceful, unbearably and unfairly masculine, and her memory had not begun to do justice to his shamefully abundant sex appeal. She was ashamed to find that she was lapping it up, shoving it into some storage compartment in her brain from whence she knew she would retrieve it over and over again in the future. The man who had once told her that he had never felt what she made him feel with any other woman now loathed her and still she was helplessly feeding off his beauty like a brainless leech.

'Why did I bother?' Cristiano drawled in a voice that sent shivers running up and down her spine. 'Good question. I didn't. You might have done a midnight flit but, hell, I'm man enough to cope with a bit of dented pride…' It felt good to let her know straight off the bat that she had left no lasting impact on him whatsoever. Okay, so the image of her had been annoyingly intrusive, had made him lose concentration in the occasional meeting, but he would have stuck it out and he was sure he would have forgotten about her in a couple of months. And if he had felt no inclination to look at another woman since her, then that made sense. In fact, it pointed to a certain amount of wisdom because only a fool would have jumped back into the water so soon after having been attacked by a shark. 'Easy come, easy go,' he additionally pointed out. 'But now, here's the thing…There's a difference between a woman walking out and a woman who's played me for a fool.'

Bethany greeted this with silence because she had said sorry enough to make her realise that apologies weren't denting his implacable anger.

Another thought crept into her fevered mind and took root. What if he had come for more than just an explanation? What if he had come to recover all the money he had spent on her? Yes, there were the meals and then the wardrobe. She had taken over her own clothes, claiming to have shoved things into a suitcase at the very last minute because the trip to Barbados had been so unexpected. This had left her in the awkward position of arriving at his spectacular beach house without a swimsuit to her name and when he had offered to go on a shopping trip with her she had guiltily agreed and only half-heartedly offered to pay.

Sex with all expenses paid. His words reverberated in her head like acid and made her feel cheaper than a common tart. Of course she had bagged up all the clothes the minute she had returned to London and given the lot to charity, but she doubted he would believe that and how could she protest her innocence in that small, insignificant matter when she was so palpably guilty of a much larger fraud? Regret attacked her on all fronts.

Then there was the small matter of those flights. First class. She had no idea how much that ran to but she knew it wouldn't be hundreds.

She paled at the thought of how much she would owe him. God, she hadn't even got a job yet. In two weeks' time she would be starting work at the local school, covering for someone on maternity leave, but that would be nowhere near the kind of money she would need. The cash register in her head pinged with such force that she buried her face in her hands and emitted a soft moan of pure despair.

'Yes, I know,' Cristiano said without a trace of sympathy. 'Our sins usually *do* end up catching up with us.'

'I don't understand how you knew where I lived…'

'Because you made sure to keep it a secret? I happened to meet the *real* Amelia Doni at my mother's house. Imagine my surprise when I discovered that she was a forty-something blonde with an axe to grind about the male sex.'

'What did you tell her?' Bethany immediately thought of Amy and her hapless friend who was now on the road to recovery. She looked at him, wide-eyed and nervous.

'Nothing. Of course. I explain myself to no one. I did manage to find out, however, who *should* have been house-sitting and it was just a matter of time before I got my people to link the connections and find out the person at the end of the chain.'

'*Your people?*'

'You'd be surprised at how efficient they can be at finding me the answers I need. Like bloodhounds.'

'Amy asked me to house-sit,' Bethany told him immediately. 'Catrina had asked her because she was over in London…'

'In rehab. Yes, I know.'

'She didn't want her godmother to find out. Look, there was no harm in anything we did.'

'Do you really think I give a damn about some dippy girl with an addiction?'

'No, but I'm just trying to tell you that…well…'

'Let's cut to the chase, shall we? When I showed up at the apartment, why didn't you tell me immediately who you were…?'

Her subterfuge rose in his head like a mist of red rage as

he remembered how conclusively he had been taken in by her, like a gullible teenager falling for the prom queen who told him that he was the centre of her world while fooling around with a hundred other guys.

'You caught me at a bad time…' Bethany whispered miserably. 'I was…I was…'

'Let me help you here. Playing at being the lady of the manor? In borrowed garb? Faking it?'

'Don't!'

'Don't *what*? Oh, yes, I forgot you had a problem with the truth.'

'I…Okay, I had been out in the sun, I had come back to the apartment and had a really long bath and I thought it might be fun to try on one of the dresses in the wardrobe. I've never owned anything expensive. I was tempted. Haven't *you* ever been tempted to do something you know you shouldn't?'

'Strangely enough, I have some notion of the difference between right and wrong!'

'It didn't seem *wrong* at the time!'

'No? So tell me…*when* did it start *seeming wrong*? Or didn't it?'

'I wasn't expecting anyone to come by,' Bethany muttered. 'And then you invited yourself in…'

'Don't even *think* of trying to palm off the blame for your deception onto me!'

'I wasn't!' Bethany backtracked hurriedly. A glance at the kitchen clock told her that although, over the past few months, time had seemed to go by at a numbingly slow pace, it was now speeding past.

'Going somewhere?' Cristiano drawled, not missing a thing. 'Hot new date with some hapless guy who thinks you're someone you're not?'

Bethany clasped her dampened hands together and ignored

the thickly sarcastic interruption. 'I was just trying to explain…you came in and I couldn't very well start babbling about trying on someone else's clothes. I wasn't even *supposed* to be in the apartment in the first place! I didn't want to land my friend Amy in trouble and I don't know Catrina, but I gathered that finding out she was in rehab would have blown her relationship with her godmother out of the sky…'

'So, because you're such a *thoughtful* and *considerate* human being, you thought it wise to keep mum…'

'I never expected that things would end up where they did,' Bethany said in a burst of defensiveness. Another five minutes had been gobbled up since she had last looked at the clock. And he'd only taken a couple of sips of the coffee which he had made a point of demanding!

'You mean…*in bed*…?'

'Yes!'

'By which time, it naturally didn't occur to you that I might have been entitled to learn the real identity of the woman I was sharing my bed with…'

'I wasn't putting on an act when I was with you.'

'Run that by me again?'

'I'm really sorry…You *were* entitled to know everything, but I was scared that…that…'

'That you might lose out on a *real* taste of the high life?'

'No! I'm not like that!'

'Forgive me if I'm struggling to think otherwise.'

'I was a…a virgin!' Bethany whispered shakily.

'Meaning…? What, exactly?' It angered him that all his logical thought processes were veering away from the stark black and white attack and shame route he had envisaged. She was a scheming, lying bitch but she was still managing to get under his skin with her wobbly voice and her shaking hands. 'Is your virginity supposed to be a blanket excuse for the fact that you lied to me for two weeks? Maybe the simple truth is that trading in your virginity for fun and frolics with a wealthy man seemed like a pretty good exchange.'

'You don't know me at all if you can say that!'

'Events would seem to suggest otherwise. Why didn't you just come clean when the holiday was finished?' Cristiano demanded. 'Why do the vanishing act?'

Bethany opened and shut her mouth. How could she tell him that she might have confessed everything if he had been the simple fling that she had anticipated? If she had been capable of walking away and relegating him to the role of some amusing escapade which didn't have the ability to touch her, she might have come clean because his reaction wouldn't have mattered to her, not really. But she had fallen in love and his reaction *would* have mattered. Either way, she would have been walking away but she just hadn't been able to face walking away with the image of his shock and hatred in her head. How on earth would she ever have been able to rid herself of it?

So instead she had done the midnight flit. Literally. They had returned to Italy and, over their last meal, back to the pizzeria where they had had their first, he had held her hand across the table, playing with her fingers, threatening that he would be looking her up in London and then later, after he had returned to his own place, she had quietly packed up her paltry belongings—she couldn't really stay as Amy had reluctantly returned to take up her house-sitting duties when Bethany had taken a leaf out of her book and flitted off to Barbados—and she had left. It had been pretty close to midnight, as it happened.

'I should have left a note,' Bethany now said miserably. 'I should have explained everything in a note.'

Cristiano felt a surge of anger. 'Because, of course, telling me to my face would have been just a little too much like hard work,' he said scathingly, and she flinched.

'I knew how you'd react. Like this.'

'Tell me. I'm curious. How much of your personality did you have to edit to accommodate your charade?'

'I didn't edit *any* of my personality!'

'You just fine-tuned it to fit in with the deceit.'

'No!'

'So you really *are*…sweet, genuine, easy to laugh… Hmm, finding it a tad tricky to believe that…'

'Oh, this isn't getting either of us anywhere.' She stood up and swept her hands across her forehead wearily. The ingredients for the promised dinner lay forgotten on the counter top. 'It was all a terrible mistake and I can't say much more than *I'm sorry* and I understand why you're angry with me.' A tear threatened to squeeze itself out and she pressed her fingers against her eyes, sending it right back from whence it was trying to come.

This was a nightmare. She had never expected him to descend on her in the one small corner of the planet where she had taken refuge.

'Why do you keep looking at the clock?' Cristiano said suddenly. 'This is the fourth time in the past fifteen minutes.' He wondered if his crack earlier on about her having a hot date had been nearer the mark than he had intended. Never one to indulge in wild flights of imagination, and certainly never in connection with a woman, he now found himself gritting his teeth furiously together at the thought of her with a new plaything. Some local village lad who had doubtless been waiting in the wings for her to return. Someone who, at least, had the luxury of knowing the woman he was dealing with, instead of some fictitious person fabricated from a mixture of lies and play acting.

'Am I? I didn't think I was.'

'And who is the food for?' He jerked his head at the unprepossessing pile of vegetables. 'Entertaining? Is this why you jacked in the university course and hotfooted it back here? Does he know about us?'

'What are you talking about?' But there was a nervous stutter in her voice that sabotaged any attempt at sounding genuinely innocent of a hidden agenda and his eyes narrowed suspiciously on her face.

An ugly, insidious thought crept into his head like poison. Never lacking in the confidence stakes when it came to women, he wondered now whether his eager little virgin hadn't used him as an unsuspecting trial run for someone else. A rampant flare of jealousy forced aside the nonsensical idiocy of the supposition, leaving him with a series of graphic images of her offering her body for another man's pleasure.

'Now, I wonder what your local sweetheart would say about a woman who spends two weeks in another man's company and at another man's bidding…before hightailing it back home to him…? Hmm…? Not many men would be forgiving on that score. In fact, I would say roughly *none*. So have you told him about your overseas romp? Or were you using me so that you could take your newly found sexual experience into his bed?'

'Don't be ridiculous!' Bethany spluttered, her face scarlet as much from his far-fetched accusations as from the evocative pictures he was unwittingly creating in her head. Pictures of *them* together on *their* overseas romp. She had gone to him a virgin, but at the end of two weeks she had become a recklessly wanton woman who had had every inch of her body slowly and meticulously explored and had tasted the delight of exploring every inch of *his* body. In fact, there had not been a night since when she hadn't recreated those memories in her head.

'Am I being ridiculous? Why else would you have come back here? Left London and your university degree? If not for a man?'

The silence that greeted this question stretched between them like a piece of elastic being pulled to its absolute limit. 'Not everything a woman does is because of a man.' Bethany struggled to sound as normal and natural as she could, which was not very as her voice was a weak croak.

'But most of the time it is. At least, that's always been my experience.'

She resisted looking at the clock. Again. Although it was difficult.

'Okay, if you must know, I promised I'd cook something for my parents. They've gone to the village hall...some sort of do to raise money for an orphanage in Africa. They'll be back soon. I'm sure you don't want to be here when they arrive...'

He didn't leap from his seat. She didn't even know if he believed a word of what she had said. In any case, it didn't matter because the sound of the front door opening impacted like a bullet through her panicky thoughts and she heard her mother's familiar voice calling, 'Honey? Bethany? We're home!'

CHAPTER FOUR

FOR the space of a few desperate seconds Bethany wondered if she could reasonably hide Cristiano, who had risen to his feet and was adding to her feeling of suffocation. Stuff him away in a cupboard somewhere or else shove him into the back garden and lock the door on his harsh, beautiful face, now alive with curiosity.

The only upside was that at least she had proved him wrong on his fanciful idea that she was inviting some man back to the house.

She raced out to intercept her parents and found them in the act of removing their coats and making noises about the weather, which had apparently taken a turn for the worse. Snow predicted.

'But the fund-raiser was an enormous success.' Eileen Maguire smiled at her daughter. 'Raised well over five hundred euro. Doesn't sound like a lot, but every little helps. There was a very interesting chap there, Bethany. Gave a talk about where the money would be going. Wasn't he interesting, John? I was tempted to ask him back here for supper; poor man is having to make do with sandwiches at the B&B because Maura's gone to visit her daught...'

Her mother stopped in mid-sentence, which was a phenomenon that seldom occurred, and Bethany didn't have to look around to know why. She could *feel* Cristiano's presence in the hall behind her. Why on earth couldn't he have stayed in the kitchen just a tiny bit longer? Given her time to warn her parents of the unexpected arrival?

'Mum…Dad…' She turned round reluctantly as Cristiano moved smoothly towards her. So she hadn't been lying. There was no man hovering on the scene, as he had mistakenly suspected. At least not at this moment in time. He just couldn't figure out why all the drama when she could just have told him that her parents would be heading back. Would that have been his cue to leave? He wasn't sure. Having been reeled in by an expert liar, he might have been curious to meet her parents. As it stood, he could not have been in the company of two more normal people. Both appeared to be in their late fifties, possibly a bit older.

'I'm…'

'We know who you are, son, and I'm just glad we've finally met you. Aren't we, Eileen? She's glad too,' John Maguire said, smiling with his hand outstretched, 'and will tell you so herself just as soon as she stops gaping like a goldfish. Mind you…' he shook Cristiano's hand warmly and winked at his daughter, who was standing to one side, her face ablaze with hot colour '…perhaps we should relish seeing her lost for words. As Beth probably told you, it's a rare sight.'

Not, Bethany thought with an agonising sense of doom, as rare a sight as it was to witness Cristiano lost for words, which he clearly was and she couldn't blame him. Nor could she begin to imagine what was going through his head, although he seemed to gather his wits with insufferable speed, returning her father's handshake before moving on to, of all things, raise her mother's hand to his lips in a purely

Italian gesture of chivalry, which had her mother blushing like a teenager.

'Oh, my,' she said, glancing over to Bethany. 'You said that he was dashing, darling, but you didn't let on just how *much of the gentleman he was*!'

'Dashing?' Cristiano slanted a look across at her that might have seemed innocent enough to her gullible parents but was loaded with questions of a highly uncomfortable nature as far as Bethany was concerned.

'I'm afraid I didn't quite get round to making that meal…' Bethany changed the subject to a general chorus of *Never mind* and *We understand perfectly* from her parents.

'You should have called us, darling!' Eileen was smoothing down her grey skirt, moving forward to warmly take both of Cristiano's hands in hers. 'We would have hurried back! No. That wouldn't have been such a good idea, would it, John?' She glanced at her husband as though he had been the one to make the silly suggestion and he raised both his shoulders with an air of indulgent resignation. 'I guess you two young things had so much to catch up on! Now, Bethany, you stay here with Cristiano…*such* a lovely name…no, better still, why don't you take Cristiano into the sitting room…John, darling, will you get the fire going…? And…'

'Good idea, Mum!' No. There was no way that she could bear to face Cristiano.

'And don't you worry about the food, Beth…' John turned to the other man and grinned. 'I've told this young lady a thousand times that…'

'Dad! *Please.* I'm sure Cristiano doesn't want to hear all sorts of boring stuff…'

'Boring stuff? If there's one thing I've discovered about your daughter, John, it's that the word *boring* can never be applied to her. Can it, Bethany?' His voice was silky smooth and was it her imagination but did it also sound as menacing as the slash of a knife ripping through paper? Or maybe, she thought with a sick feeling in her stomach, flesh. Hers.

'We'll just take ourselves off to the sitting room now and why don't you and Mum…er…go and change…and then we can…'

'Get to know one another!' Her father was beaming and Bethany smiled back weakly.

'And I'll just rustle up something for us all to eat. It'll have to be simple fare, mind…' She looked at Cristiano, who scored another few Brownie points by immediately offering to take them all out to dinner. Snow, he was told, was on the way. Best stay put.

'In that case, I couldn't want for anything nicer than a simple meal. Your daughter must have told you that I'm a man of uncomplicated tastes.'

That earned him a friendly pat on the shoulder from the older man who said, to Bethany's horror, although how much more horrible could the situation get? 'Guess that's the way it plays with the kind of risks you take on with what you do, eh?'

Cristiano greeted this bewildering statement with a non-committal smile and said nothing. His life, until he had met the woman hovering slightly behind him, had been an ordered affair. Work. Women. Everything in its place. He was a man who had always believed that by wielding firm control he could successfully limit unpleasant surprises and thus far he had never had occasion to doubt the philosophy. So he was ill prepared for the sensation of walking on quicksand, which was what he felt he was doing now. Risks? Sure, he took risks in his line of work, but somehow he had got the impression that the risks to which Bethany's father had referred did not apply to those associated with high finance, mergers and acquisitions. So what the hell had the man been talking about? And how, for that matter, had they known his identity before the usual round of introductions?

Behind him, Bethany cleared her throat and he spun around to face her as her parents disappeared up the stairs, talking in low, excited voices.

It grated on his nerves, but even in her own territory, a modest thatched cottage a million miles away from glamorous designer shops and sexy wine bars, she still had the look of a woman who could reel in any unsuspecting man with the pretence of being born to privilege. She didn't have the air of someone who looked down on anyone they considered their inferior, which was just one of the things he found so insanely irritating about many of the women he had dated in the past. Bethany, instead, just looked refined. Something about the way she was put together. Maybe the vibrant, rich colour of her hair tumbling down past her shoulders. Or the perfect clarity of her eyes. Or maybe it was the silky smoothness of her skin with its dusting of freckles, untouched by the make-up mask so many women used to camouflage less than flawless complexions. Or perhaps the manner in which she held herself. Poised, proud and assertive but in a very muted way.

Angry with himself for even bothering to register her as anything more than a woman who had had the temerity to play games with him, Cristiano looked at her with grim, unsmiling menace. As always, silence proved to be his ally and Bethany stumbled into speech, her eyes shifting away from his as she led him towards the sitting room. He listened without saying a word as she rambled on about her parents, apparently pillars of the community, involved in all sorts of charitable causes, virtual saints if her eulogy was anything to go by.

As he listened, he took in everything around him, from the profusion of family photos to the gleaming ornaments collected over a lifetime and obviously cherished. Although just a cottage, it was an extremely spacious one and the downstairs was comprised of a honeycomb of little rooms which quaintly interconnected with one another. On one of the chairs in a room which had been kitted out as a study, a fat, contented tabby cat was snoozing. This couldn't be further removed from the ancestral manor she had given him to believe was her family home and Cristiano hung on to the thought, which provided just the right spur for the aggression with which he had earlier confronted her.

'So,' he said conversationally, once they were in the sitting room and he was installed on one of the sprawling comfy chairs, 'what a charming place your parents have. So different from the turreted mansion you described...'

Bethany blushed. She hadn't been treated to Cristiano's brutally cold side, although she had known it was there because men of power were invariably ruthless, and she was finding it hard to marry the two personas. The gorgeous, sexy man who had whisked her away to a tropical idyll and the icy stranger looking at her with shuttered eyes and a cruel curl on his lips. She had to remind herself that she would never have glimpsed the gorgeous, sexy man if he had met her as Bethany Maguire. She might not have met the icy stranger, but she would bet her limited savings that Mr Indifferent would have been in ample supply.

'I never said that the turreted mansion belonged to my parents,' she told him. 'I only said that there was certainly one in my home town and there is.'

'I'm afraid I find it hard to appreciate the fine line of distinction between an outright lie and an economical use of the truth.'

'You're only finding it hard because you don't even want to try.'

'And why should I? But you were right when you said that there was no point going over old ground. It's not going to get either of us anywhere. So let's move on to another topic, shall we?' He delivered an icy smile that sent flutters of real fear racing through her body. Cristiano, seeing that, broadened his smile and relaxed. He had wondered why he had bothered to make the trip but now he knew. Yes, he had needed to see her face to face so that he could exorcise some of his built up fury with her for lying to him and with himself for being taken in by her deception. He had also, he now realised, felt the urge to close what he considered unfinished business because what they had *was* unfinished.

The two weeks they had spent in Barbados had been tantamount to a complete, reckless breakdown of his self-control. He had been like a straight A student who had decided to play truant. Naturally, she had been blissfully unaware of that, had not known that that was the first time in his life when he had breached his own rigidly self-imposed boundaries. Cristiano wasn't quite sure how she had managed to achieve that feat but achieve it she had and, by the time they had returned to Italy, he was by no means ready for her to vanish from his life. Seeing her again here had had the negative effect of reminding him why he was still so damned hot for her. He had expected to feel nothing for her but derision and contempt. And sure, she was little more than a cheap liar, but the knowledge hadn't gone very far to extinguishing the flare of attraction he had neither sought nor courted but which was, it seemed, still there and very firmly alight.

Even looking at her now across the width of the sitting room, folded into the chair like a kid with the long sleeves of her oversized jumper pulled right down so that she could catch the ends between her slender fingers, was alternately rousing and enraging him.

Like a mathematician addressing a convoluted problem, Cristiano brought his finely tuned and coolly logical brain to bear on the illogical situation. How better to put an end to his anger and frustration than by just taking what had been summarily denied him? Could he *pretend* to overlook the little matter of her outrageous deception until he got her into bed and sated his hunger for her, which was still running through his veins and sabotaging all his efforts to get his life back on track?

He'd have to think about that one but he relaxed for the first time since he had set foot in the house. Just having a solution to hand, even if he decided not to put it to use, went some way to re-establishing his control over proceedings which, with the appearance of her parents, had taken a definite knock.

Also, he quite liked the nature of his solution. He hadn't been able to shake the memory of her face from his head, or the memory of her moaning under him, on top of him, in the massive circular bath at his house in Barbados, in the pool, in various parts of the house and several times on his private stretch of beach where only the moon and the stars had witnessed their inexhaustible passion. It would be sweet revenge, not that he applied such a primitive description to his wandering thoughts, to take her again and then leave her, but when the time was right and at his say-so.

He surfaced from his unexpectedly pleasant thoughts to see her perched forward on the edge of her chair, staring at him intently.

'Did you hear me?'

Cristiano frowned. 'Repeat,' he commanded. 'My mind was elsewhere.'

Bethany could only assume that having given her the full force of his fury he was already thinking about leaving, getting back to his wonderful, privileged life—the same wonderful, privileged life he had mistakenly assumed she knew all about.

And, God, she was so tempted to let him walk out of the door but then…how would she explain that to her parents? The web of deceit which she had begun weaving the minute she had accepted his dinner invitation all those months ago wrapped a little tighter around her.

She was also discovering that the thought of seeing him for the last time *again* was already beginning to dig its claws in. She mentally stuck that inappropriate reaction into a box in her head and firmly taped it down.

'I was *saying* that there are one or two things that I need to tell you before Mum and Dad come back down.'

Cristiano's antennae immediately went onto red alert.

'You mean aside from explaining how it is that your parents seemed to know who I was without any introductions having to be made?'

'I…um…told them about you.'

'Really. And what exactly did you say? I'm keen to know, considering your amazing capacity for stretching the truth.' His eyes drifted lazily from her flushed face down to her breasts—breasts which he had known intimately, had tasted and luxuriated in. It made no difference that they were well hidden under the capacious jumper. His memory was more than up to supplying an image of the luscious body beneath it.

Bethany's brain threatened to shut down. 'I told them…you know…that we met while I was out in Italy…'

'Oh, so they *knew* that you were in Italy. That's a promising start. Did they know that you were house-sitting for a random stranger whom you had decided to impersonate?'

'Yes, they knew that I was house-sitting!'

'Lose the pious tone, Bethany. It doesn't suit you. And I take it that you didn't breathe a word about your charade of being one Ms Amelia Doni…? Hmm…?'

Bethany could feel the slight dampness of perspiration on the palms of her hands, but she kept them well covered in the sleeves of her jumper. 'No,' she admitted.

'Didn't think so. Your parents didn't strike me as the sort of people who would find it an amusing anecdote. So what exactly did you tell them about me?'

'Right. Okay.' Bethany cleared her throat and braced herself. 'I know you probably think it a bit peculiar that I would even mention you, considering things didn't exactly end well.'

'Understatement of the year, don't you think?'

'But they're very moral people. Great believers in the sanctity of relationships…'

'Obviously a trait that they didn't pass on to you, then.'

'You're not going to make this easy for me, are you?'

'Any reason why I should?'

'I just don't think that this is such a great time for us to be arguing.' Her eyes flicked towards the door but her parents were still safely upstairs. Knowing them as well as she did, they would be taking their time, giving her time to be alone with Cristiano. She felt faint when she thought about the length, breadth and width of her crazy deception.

'What have the moral values of your parents got to do with anything?' Cristiano suddenly asked. Astute at reading all situations, two and two in this case was not adding up to four. Even for Bethany, downright liar, possible thief, massive opportunist and altogether unpredictable entity, there were strands of her conversation that were just not adding up to anything he could catch hold of.

'Can I just say that I never, ever expected you to turn up here out of the blue?' Bethany could feel her heart thudding in her chest as though it was about to explode. 'I mean you're a sophisticated guy. I guess I thought that you'd look back at what we had as nothing more than a pleasant interlude. I didn't think ahead how you would react if you ever found out about…you know…'

Cristiano could smell a dodge a mile off but he was willing to let the cross-examination ride because, sooner or later, she would get down to answering all the questions flying around in his head. The ones which she was ostensibly dancing around at the moment.

'Dashing.'

'I beg your pardon?'

'*Dashing*. Wasn't that the word your mother used to describe me?'

'Right. Yes. Dashing. And adventurous.'

'Dashing and *adventurous*?'

Bethany nodded miserably.

'Why am I beginning to find this all a little surreal?' He stood up and began pacing the room, pausing to look at the happy photos in frames on the mantelpiece, on the bookcase in the corner, on the small round table by the window. Here were parents who were immensely proud of their offspring. Within a five metre radius, a lifetime of joyful memories was played out in a succession of pictures.

'I know it must seem a bit crazy…'

'A *bit*?' He swung round to look at her, pinning her to the chair with an intensity that brought her out in goosebumps. She had thought it difficult dealing with the remembered version of Cristiano. She now knew that *difficult* took on a whole new meaning when it came to dealing with the real thing.

While she struggled to put her thoughts into order and find a way of explaining *the surreal situation*, Cristiano strolled over to her chair and then leaned down, supporting himself on the sides of her chair and instantly bringing every nerve in her body to attention.

His clean, masculine scent filled her nostrils and inflamed her senses and her eyes fluttered, riveted to his striking face. *Dashing* didn't even begin to do justice to his strikingly handsome, lean, bronzed face. Awash with fear and panic, she was still aware of her body reacting to his proximity, her nipples tightening with remembered pleasure and her mouth softening. She looked down quickly but not so quickly that Cristiano didn't see her unconscious reaction to him.

He felt a kick of satisfaction. So *something* had been real. She might have lied about everything under the sun because a trip to sunny Barbados had been just too good an opportunity to pass up, but she hadn't lied about wanting him. When she had fallen into his arms, it had been the real thing. Furthermore, if he still wanted her, and it was a big *if*, then she was his for the taking.

'So I'm dashing,' he prompted, his voice smooth and cool, 'and adventurous…'

'Could you please…stop looming over me?' Bethany squeaked in response, and Cristiano anchored himself even more firmly to her chair.

'Why? Does it make you feel uncomfortable? Does your guilty conscience bother you when I'm up this close and personal? Or maybe…' he felt a burst of savage, unwelcome desire as his libido went into overdrive '…you're terrified that what you really want is for your *dashing, adventurous* ex-lover to get even more up close and personal…' He was rewarded by a fleeting look in her eyes that gave him the answer he had already suspected. Satisfied, he stood up and sauntered back to his own chair. If this were a game, which it most definitely was not, he figured he had scored the first point.

'So...you were telling me why you had an insane desire to spill the beans about our little fling to your parents...'

This time it was Bethany's turn to stand up. She walked towards the door, which was slightly ajar, and shut it completely. Her parents would be tactfully keeping out of the way but sooner rather than later they would head down for a bit of family bonding and the last thing she needed was to have her conversation eavesdropped.

When she sat back down, it was on the sofa next to his chair, close enough to talk without having to raise her voice, even though her body was still humming from the dangerous thrill of being so close to him. She didn't want to dwell on the mortifying fact that he had seen right through her, deep down to the helpless longing she had felt then and now. Had he also seen how *bone deep* it was? Like a stubborn weed, it fought through everything, including his hostility, condemnation and glacial contempt. She could hardly blame him, given the circumstances, that he would use her own weakness for him against her. If he had tried to kiss her just then, she didn't think that she would have been able to resist. The fact that he had brought her to that point only to pull back would have satisfied just a bit of his wounded pride and dented ego and she tried very hard to look at it from his point of view. Fair was fair, after all.

Which didn't mean that she wasn't still smarting from his rejection.

'Yes. Right.'

'And, by the way, *how* adventurous am I? Exactly?'

Bethany drew in a shaky breath. 'You wouldn't believe,' she said.

'I'm surprised you wanted to paint a picture of our sex life with your parents,' Cristiano remarked sardonically.

'Sorry?'

'Well…' he shrugged, still on a high from having irrefutable proof that she was as hot for him as he was for her and from successfully exerting his will-power and turning her down '…if your parents are as moralistic as you tell me, then I'm a little surprised that you would discuss our sex life with them. Or was it more in the nature of a cosy mother and daughter chat?'

'Of course I haven't discussed our sex life with my mum! She'd be mortified!'

'Then what the hell are you talking about?'

'I'm talking about what you do!'

This time it was Cristiano's turn to look at her in pure bewilderment. Even for him, this was a leap too far. 'What do I do?'

'You make loads of money,' Bethany said feverishly. 'Running that empire of yours, but obviously that wasn't, you know, enough.'

'Wasn't it?' His clogged up brain was refusing to clear. He also didn't like the shifty way she was refusing to look him in the eye. She might have lied through her teeth the entire time they'd been together but she had never been one to avoid eye contact. She was avoiding it like crazy now.

'Well, no.' She sighed and a sense of inevitability gave her the courage to carry on in a more normal voice. 'You weren't satisfied building empires so you decided to embark on a programme of good deeds.'

'A *programme of good deeds*? Sorry, but you're losing me here.'

'I know. I guessed I might. And I know you're not going to like what you're about to hear, but it can't be helped. Well, it probably *could* have…'

'Just get on with it, Bethany!'

Bethany looked at him for a few seconds. She wanted to imprint this image of him in her head. It wasn't a great image because he was as angry as hell with her, although not quite as angry as when he had first arrived. However, it would prove to be a far more comforting image of him than the one which would be presented after she had fully explained herself.

'I told my parents that you were involved in building all sorts of stuff in...well...in dangerous places...places where there are no amenities...for example in the depth of Africa and in war-torn zones...you know, doing your bit to help ease the suffering of helpless victims all over the world...'

Cristiano shook his head as though that simple gesture would sort out her confusing babble. Then he ran his fingers through his hair before staring at her with a perplexed frown.

'I *build all sorts of stuff in dangerous places*? What sort of stuff?'

'I don't know! Stuff. Schools! Community centres! Medical facilities!'

'In the *depths of Africa*?'

'Some of them, yes. And other areas where there's conflict, so to speak.'

'I don't get it. Have you lost your mind? I realise that you must be a compulsive liar, but what the hell did you think you were playing at?'

'You weren't supposed to find out!'

'I must be missing something here, but what exactly was the *point* of turning me into some kind of do-gooder? No, let me ask you something even more fundamental. What was the point of telling your parents about me in the first place? It wasn't as though they were ever going to find out and, even if they had, it's the twenty-first century. However moralistic your parents are, surely they're up to speed with the fact that men and women have relationships, some of which don't last for ever! You have two sisters! Are you going to tell me that both of them have spent a lifetime saving themselves for the right guy and have never been on a date with a man in the meanwhile?'

'No, of course not!'

'Then why the elaborate confession to two people who could happily have remained in the dark? And why not just stick to the facts? You met a guy. You had fun for a couple of weeks. The end.' A brief silence greeted this clearly rational observation, during which Bethany's colour went from shell-pink to scarlet as she prayed for the ground to open and swallow her up or, even more unlikely, for her to open her eyes, blink twice, stretch and realise that the past few months had been nothing more than a weirdly convoluted dream.

'Is your obsession with lying so rampantly out of control?' Cristiano looked at her with narrowed eyes as he tried to get his head round her bizarre admission. 'If so, then you need to seek help.' He stood up. 'And I refuse to go along with this deception.'

Bethany scrambled to her feet and grabbed his hand. The physical contact sent a sharp burst of red-hot awareness rushing through her at speed and she immediately dropped her hand.

'Wait! I'm not finished!'

'No?' Cristiano's mouth curled into a derisive smile. 'More to come? Aside from the missionary service to parts of the world I've never so much as visited? I'm struggling to think of what more you can add to my glowing recommendations.'

'Can we sit back down? Please? I realise you probably

think that you've entered a mad house…but there are some other things you…you need to know…'

Only because she looks particularly fetching with that desperate, wide-eyed look on her face…and, hell, the woman was born to be a roller coaster ride, so where was the harm in giving her another few minutes…?

Bethany was relieved that he had listened to her. Having watched the clock like a hawk before her parents had arrived, she was now watching it again in anticipation of them coming down the stairs and making a straight line for the sitting room, where the conversation would go who knew where. Time suddenly seemed a commodity in very limited supply.

'I said all those things because…what we had was rather more involved as far as my parents are concerned. And before I tell you what I mean by that…' She half wished that he would interrupt with something nasty and accusatory instead of just looking at her in silence waiting for her to carry on. Her hands, still tucked protectively in the long sleeves of her baggy jumper, were clammy.

'Before I tell you what I mean by that…' she repeated, stretching that one harmless sentence out for as long as she possibly could, 'I just want you to know that I sent you to all those places…'

'Central Africa, you mean? War-torn zones?'

Bethany nodded. 'I sent you there because it would have been easy for you to disappear…'

'Easy. For. Me. To. Disappear.'

'I mean I could have sent you to New York or Tokyo or even the other side of the planet…New Zealand, maybe, but it would have made things more complicated…'

Cristiano nearly choked at the notion that things could get more complicated than they already were. Bethany, staring off into the distance, relieved that she was unburdening herself because she had known that it would come to this the second he had walked through the front door, hardly noticed his staggered expression.

'But if you were based in say…*the Congo*…then our relationship could just have drifted. I mean, how easy would it be for an engaged couple to keep up their relationship across such a hefty distance?'

'*Engaged couple?*'

Bethany, once again looking at him, nodded and slowly extended her hand to reveal a very discreet engagement ring. 'It's not real, of course, but I had to have something to show Mum and Dad.'

He hadn't noticed the ring, but then he hadn't been paying much attention to her hands and he realised now that she had kept them out of sight as much as she could, tucked up in those long sleeves of hers. Cristiano stared at her in utter disbelief.

'You think I'm nuts, don't you?'

'Nuts? That's putting it mildly.'

'Okay. Hear me out. I know you might be a bit angry…' Her keen ears detected the sounds of approaching parents. It was now or never and never wasn't an option. 'I had to tell this little white lie…'

'*Little white lie?* Please, do me a favour and define *big*!'

'Because, like I said, Mum and Dad are pretty old fashioned and they would have been bitterly disappointed if they had known that their daughter had had a two week fling with a guy abroad and returned home pregnant.'

CHAPTER FIVE

CRISTIANO finally discovered what it felt like to have a bomb detonate in the epicentre of his life. He stared at her in stunned silence and he could feel the colour draining away from his face. He looked, Bethany thought, like a man who had leapt out of a plane only to find that he'd forgotten his parachute. He was in shocked free fall and she could understand why. From being a carefree, single guy he was now an engaged man with a kid on the way. All in the space of a couple of hours and, worse than that, he was engaged to a woman whom he considered a scheming liar with an eye to the main chance. Did it get any worse?

With impeccable timing, her parents arrived on the scene, postponing the inevitable showdown, for which Bethany was grateful, although it might have been better for her to have just got it out of the way. As it was, they were both at the mercy of both her parents, who had innumerable tales to tell of their dearest daughter and her fabulously loving childhood where money was stretched to its limit, what with three children and their menagerie of pets. And then, when her mother had disappeared to rustle up something to eat, at the mercy of her father who immediately installed a drink in Cristiano's hand and called him to account on his many varied travels.

'Africa,' he mused, settling down on the sofa for the long haul. 'Never been there myself. Must have been a hell of an experience for you. Great to know that there are still young people out there who care enough, though, son.'

Bethany groaned to herself as her father tilted his head to one side and looked at Cristiano with keen interest.

'Cristiano…' She cleared her throat and smiled weakly at her dad. 'He…er…doesn't really like to talk about his good works out in…um…Africa…and other places…He's very modest…you know…' She hazarded a laugh, which fizzled out into silence. Thanks to her parents' happy belief that they were really engaged, she had found herself stuck next to Cristiano on the sofa, which was richly ironic, she felt, considering the only reason he would choose to be this close would be to strangle her. Now, he reached across and gathered her hand in his and gave it a little squeeze.

'That's very sweet of you to say that, Bethany…' He turned to her profile and was gratified to see that she was as jumpy as a cat on a hot tin roof. Doubtless her poor innocent father would put all that blushing and trembling down to her delight at her so called fiancé's unexpected arrival but he knew better. 'But don't you remember all those pictures I showed you…?'

'Pictures?' She turned to look at him and tried, uselessly, to wriggle her hand out of his grasp.

'You know the pictures…the ones in my album, *my Africa album.*'

'Oh, yes, right.'

'So why don't *you* give your dad the gist of what I did over there…?' He gave her hand another squeeze and felt her dig her nails into his palm, at which point he promptly released her fingers, only to insinuate his hand on her thigh, a gesture of demonstrable affection, except to her. His smile of encouragement earned him a thinly concealed glare and it was all he could do not to tell her how much he was going to enjoy watching her dig herself out of her lies.

Bethany read all of that in his fleeting look and that warm smile on his lips was anything *but* encouraging. She took a deep breath and crossed her fingers behind her back as she launched into a flowery description of a community centre which was one hundred per cent lifted from something she had recently seen on television. As she finally came to a stop, she heard Cristiano say softly, 'Now *that* deserves a round of applause.' He looked at John. 'Your daughter has a very persuasive way with words. She could sell snow to the Eskimos…couldn't you, *darling*?'

Bethany braved his eyes, which were coolly at odds with the smiling mouth. She forced herself to smile back. At least in the company of her parents she would have to try to look enraptured or, if not enraptured, at least pleased that her gallivanting fiancé had turned up.

Seen from another angle, she guessed that the farce being enacted might have seemed hysterically funny. Unfortunately, caught in the middle of it, it was more tragedy than comedy.

'I don't know about that,' Bethany muttered, but Cristiano was undeterred.

'I mean—' he turned to face her father but his hand remained firmly glued to her thigh, a gentle reminder that he was right here on the sofa next to her and was not going to let her out of his reach until he was good and ready '—when she described her house here, in Ireland, I almost got the impression that she was talking about a castle!'

'Couldn't be further from the truth, as you can see!' John shook his head, smiling at his daughter. 'But you're right. I know she's going to pull a face when I say this, but our Bethany was always top of the class in her English!'

'I can well imagine.'

'But now that circumsta…'

From the kitchen, Bethany heard her mother carolling them in for dinner and she breathed a small sigh of relief. Her father preceded them and it gave her a vital chance to move out of Cristiano's reach as they both stood up.

'Stop it!' she hissed at him under her breath.

'Stop…what?'

'Stop touching me!'

'Now why would you say that?' Cristiano's voice was as hard as nails. 'You're a conscienceless liar and I'm supposed to play the part of the lucky husband-to-be. Surely a bit of touching is only to be expected? And, correct me if I'm wrong, but nothing's been mentioned of any so-called *pregnancy*. Funny, that, wouldn't you say?'

'What are you getting at?'

She was spared an answer to her question by her parents beaming at them as they entered the kitchen. Hand in hand. The loving and now united couple. Bethany reminded herself never to trust appearances. She felt pretty sure that the man standing next to her was thinking the very same thing.

'Just fetched some chicken casserole I had in the freezer,' Eileen confided as they all settled at the long pine table in the kitchen, the surface of which bore the hallmarks of homework past. 'Tell me what you think, Cristiano…' She looked at him expectantly and puffed up with delight when he went into profuse compliment mode while next to him Bethany tortured herself by wondering what he had meant when he had said that it was *funny that her parents hadn't mentioned a word about the pregnancy*. Had he thought that she'd been lying? Made the whole thing up? What if he let slip some killer remark about *never wanting kids?* She racked her brain to remember if he'd ever mentioned anything of the sort. Never had she felt more need for something alcoholic, if only to survive her mother's questions about *where they had met, how they had met*. No amount of attempts to drag the conversation onto neutral territory could derail the older woman from her curiosity. Bethany was only thankful that her father was no longer quizzing him on all those wonderful things he had done in darkest Africa.

What had seemed a good idea at the time, a way of saving her parents from the anguish and disappointment of their daughter turning up on their doorstep pregnant and single, had returned to bite her.

Almost worse was the reality that Cristiano was charming the socks off them. He drew on amusing anecdotes like a magician pulling rabbits out of a hat and it was only when they were clearing away the dishes that Bethany found a sudden spark of inspiration and, while she was loading the dishwasher with her mother, she managed to insert in a casual voice, 'Now you understand what I meant when I told you that he was dashing!'

'Oh, darling. I'm so happy for you. Of course, it's such a shame that you've had to put your university course on hold, but he seems such a lovely guy. I don't think he'd mind one bit if you resumed your studies in due course, do you?'

Bethany leaned against the kitchen counter, ears alert for the sound of any approaching feet from the dashing man in question, who had been taken to the sitting room with her father. 'Well, I might have to…'

'What do you mean?' Eileen paused to look at her daughter with concern.

'I mean…' The sound of yet another lie, piling up on top of the multitude she had already told, raced towards her like a galloping horse that was out of control and Bethany sighed.

'Nothing. I just meant that…it's always good to have a degree up your sleeve.'

'But don't forget that you have other duties now, darling.'

Bethany grimaced. 'Fat chance of me forgetting that.' In truth she had gradually become accustomed to the thought of having a baby. What had been an enormous shock to start with had levelled off to a calm acceptance that her pregnancy wasn't going to go away and she would have to deal with it. It was a blessing that she had had her parents to support her, for continuing with university had been out of the question and she had had no desire to remain in London as a single mother.

'I told your dad not to mention anything about the baby,' Eileen rattled on, as happy as a bunny in a field of carrots. 'I thought you might like to break it to Cristiano yourself and I wasn't sure if you had said anything…'

'Thanks, Mum.'

'You don't seem as thrilled at Cristiano's arrival as I might have expected, Beth,' her mother said anxiously. 'I know you thought that he might be stuck out there for months on end with his building project…'

'But here I am!'

From behind them, and latching on to that last pensive observation, came the all too familiar voice of Cristiano. He strolled across to Bethany and casually slung his arm over her shoulder, pulling her towards him. Reluctantly, Bethany extended her hand around his waist. Through his shirt, she could feel the rock hardness of his body and a convulsive shiver made her feel temporarily giddy.

'And, as I mentioned to John in the sitting room, the bearer of glad tidings, my darling.'

'What's that?' Bethany looked up at him, horribly aware that both her parents were watching them with eagle eyes.

She could almost *hear* her mother's breathless, expectant silence.

'No more projects…'

Bethany's jumble of thoughts lagged behind her mother's and it was only when her mother clapped her hands that it dawned on her exactly what he was saying.

'Yippee!' She tried to insert some enthusiasm into her voice as she watched the last glimmers of any excuse for his disappearance from her life take wing and fly through the window.

'That's right,' Cristiano expanded, just so that she was in no doubt as to what he was saying. 'My priorities are here now. Aren't they, sweetheart? Right here with you and…our baby.'

Suddenly the world was full of rainbows and angels. At least, as far as her parents were concerned. Her mother could barely contain her excitement and while the babble of voices resounded around her Bethany felt nothing but a dull aware-ness of a situation that was now no longer in her control. Had she thought that she might persuade him to disappear out of her life? He didn't love her. He never had. Yet he had found himself landed with the prospect of fatherhood in a little under four months, welded against his will to a woman he now loathed, a woman he considered an inveterate liar and heaven only knew what else. When had it ever been her dream to find herself expecting a baby by a man she loved who felt nothing but scorn towards her? Since when was that *any woman's* dream?

'I wasn't sure if Beth had mentioned it to you…'

'We were shocked when she broke the news to us…'

'But now that we've met you, we couldn't hope for a better son-in-law…'

'*Dad!*'

'Of course, we wouldn't dream of rushing you into anything,' Eileen hastened to add. 'You just have to excuse us because we're a little old-fashioned when it comes to things like that...'

'So, as it happens, is my own mother.' Had he really thought that she had been lying about the pregnancy? She had lied about pretty much everything else but, in that one area, she had been telling the truth. Her father had tactfully asked him whether he knew or whether he had already disappeared to Africa by the time Bethany had found out, and at that split moment in time Cristiano had kissed sweet goodbye to his freedom. Two weeks of fun in the sun and he would be paying the price for the rest of his life. What choice did he have? It was a mess but it was a mess from which he could not walk away. He tried to imagine how his mother and his grandfather would react and for a fleeting few seconds he could understand why she had fabricated this particular lie. His mother would have been devastated if he had shown up with a child in tow and no mother in sight.

'You'll have to tell us all about her...about your family... I'm afraid Bethany has been a bit economical on information...'

Your daughter, it was on the tip of his tongue to tell them, has been economical on a number of things.

'But right now—' John put his arm around his wife with affection '—Eileen and I are going to hit the sack.'

'And we may be old-fashioned—' Eileen gave Cristiano a warm smile '—but we're not so old-fashioned that we expect you two love birds to sleep in different rooms...'

'But *Mum*!' Bethany's voice bordered on a screech. 'You've *never* let Shania or Melanie bring their boyfriends home and share a bedroom!'

'Slightly different situation here, don't you think, pet?'

'Well, yes,' Bethany huffed, 'but that's no reason…I mean, I wouldn't want to disrespect…'

'Thank goodness we got rid of that single bed of yours a few years ago! Remember how upset you were at losing the headboard?' This to Cristiano. 'She had collected a range of stickers on it from when she was just knee high to a grasshopper! Can you believe it? Detached all of them and stuck them in a scrapbook!'

Bethany felt herself go crimson. Did her mother imagine that that somehow made her sound *sweet*? Couldn't she see that the flip side of *sweet* was *fruit loop*, which was what Cristiano was already thinking? No, she thought unhappily, why on earth should her mother think that her dearly beloved and only recently engaged daughter might not want to share a bedroom with her sexy, *dashing, adventurous* fiancé who couldn't wait to rip her to shreds?

With that parting shot her parents, still chatting and laughing with each other, headed off, leaving a brutal silence behind them.

'So…' Cristiano moved so that he was standing in front of her '…where to begin…'

'We can begin with the fact that *I won't be sharing my bedroom with you*. You can have Shania's room. Mum and Dad will never know if I get up early enough and smooth down the quilt.'

'I can think of a better place to start.' He walked towards the kitchen door and shut it. Then, making sure that she couldn't bolt, he remained standing in front of the closed door, six foot two of lethal determination. 'For instance, did you get pregnant on purpose?'

Bethany was horrified at the outrageous insult. She clenched her hands into tight fists and glared at him.

'That's the most idiotic thing I've ever heard!'

'Then you've led a very sheltered life,' Cristiano said cuttingly. 'From where I'm standing, I'm seeing someone who connived her way into my life…'

'*Connived my way? You* were the one who showed up on my doorstep, don't you remember?'

'Hardly *your* doorstep.'

'Okay, the doorstep!' She pushed her hair away from her face.

'…And, having found my bed, decided that I was just too good a catch to let go and what better way to hold a man than to get pregnant by him?'

Bethany laughed incredulously. 'You think I *planned this*? You really think that I *wanted* to abandon my degree, abandon my independence so that I could have a baby?' Her eyes filled up, her mouth wobbled; she felt like someone on the edge of a nervous breakdown. She was hardly showing her pregnancy but for the past few months it had been on her mind every waking minute. She had been living on a day to day basis, not daring to think beyond the very near future. The dream of finding her feet away from the little town in which she had grown up was in ruins around her and she couldn't face the thought of sitting down and really working out what happened next. It was as though Plan A, around which she had based her future, had devolved into some other plan and she no longer had the right tools to grapple with it. Where would she be in six months' time? A year? Where would she be living? She couldn't very well remain an indefinite lodger in her parents' house with a young baby, still sleeping in the bedroom she had slept in as a child herself. But where would she go? And how would she be able to earn a sufficiently good living to support two?

That he could stand there and coolly ask whether she had planned the pregnancy was just too much!

'Do you really imagine that you're that much of a dream catch?' She propelled herself angrily away from the counter against which she had been leaning. 'You're *arrogant*, you're *cruel* and you're a massive *snob*!' She poked one shaking finger at him. 'Do you honestly think that I would throw away my future so that I could hitch my wagon to a guy who hates my guts and thinks I'm a cheap liar?' She dashed an angry tear away from her face. 'How sad and…and *desperate* do you think I am?'

'Calm down. You're beginning to get hysterical.' *Arrogant? Cruel? A snob?* Shouldn't *she* be the one on the back foot? To the best of his memory, *he* had been totally upfront with her, so how was it that she was now hurling accusations at *him*?

'It's impossible talking to you.' Bethany was further enraged by the fact that Cristiano was as cool as a cucumber. She felt that if she didn't leave she would explode and the explosion would wake her parents, if not the entire town.

'You're not talking. You're being hysterical.'

'You make me *feel* hysterical!' Her green eyes clashed with his and she felt dizzy and off balance. How was it possible for him to do this to her? To shake her to the very core and make her feel giddy when all she wanted to feel was repulsion?

'You don't *look* pregnant.'

'What?'

'Shouldn't you be bigger?'

Bethany was thoroughly disconcerted by this abrupt change of topic. 'Some people don't show until quite late on and I'm one of those. Why are you changing the subject?'

'Because you shouldn't be getting so overwrought in your…condition.'

'How do you expect me to feel when you stand there like

a block of ice sneering at me and accusing me of plotting all of this?' Deep breaths, she thought. Hysteria was no way to deal with the situation. 'If I had been lunatic enough to get pregnant to trap you, then don't you think that I might just have contacted you the minute I found out?'

'Why didn't you?'

'For the same reason that…I took off. I wasn't the rich, worldly-wise woman you thought I was. I was a nobody, the sort of person you wouldn't have looked at twice in the normal course of things.'

'Don't run yourself down,' Cristiano censured, frowning.

'I'm not running myself down, Cristiano. I'm telling it like it is. You told me yourself that you would never date any woman who didn't come from a similar background to you because you would never be sure that she wasn't after you for your money.'

'I never said that!' The conversation seemed to have run away from him and he couldn't figure out where or when he had relinquished control.

'Yes, you did!'

'Okay. Maybe I did, although I'm not convinced.'

'So when I discovered that I was pregnant, I knew that I couldn't contact you. How would you have felt if I'd shown up on your doorstep, one Bethany Macguire, pregnant and average, with nowhere to go and barely a dime to her name? Don't tell me that you would have fallen over yourself with joy and rapture!'

'That's hardly the point.'

'Then what is?'

'I deserved to know. When it comes to a child, it's not about how I would feel or how you would feel, it's about the child. Had you any intention at all of ever contacting me to tell me that I had fathered a child?'

Bethany looked away, reddening. Put like that, she sounded like a selfish cow, but at the time the thought of telephoning him, explaining herself, explaining that she was going to have a baby, had left her mind almost as quickly as it had entered it.

'I would have. In due course. Most probably.'

Cristiano stamped on his immediate response to that. There was little point in pursuing that line of attack, but in his mind he envisaged a scenario in which his child grew up without him around, became the stepson or stepdaughter of some other man who would have entered her life at some point in time. The thought outraged him. Just thinking of her in the arms of someone else outraged him. He put that thought out of his head and resolved to approach the situation from a practical direction.

He also found himself reluctantly believing her reasons for lying to him in the first place. Which, naturally, didn't excuse her opportunistic manipulation of the truth, but he would overlook that because there were now far bigger things in the mix and that was a reality he couldn't afford to forget.

'I'm surprised you didn't kill me off,' he mused and Bethany looked up at him, again sidetracked by his change of tone. From icy-cold and enraged, his voice was now low and husky and mildly amused. It made the hairs on the back of her neck stand on end and something inside her uncurled, making her feel vulnerable and exposed.

'I'm not *that* horrible,' she stuttered breathlessly. 'Besides, it's just as well that I didn't, considering you've appeared here. Explaining the sudden appearance of an absent fiancé is enough of a nightmare. Explaining one who had come back to life would have been impossible.' With some of her anger defused, she was belatedly aware of just how close she was to him. Practically touching and it was beginning to get to her. She took a couple of steps back and told him that she was going to bed.

'Where are your clothes, anyway?' she asked. Her parents wouldn't have noticed his lack of a suitcase and she only had now.

'A certain large hotel a few miles away, as it happens.'

'Oh, right. The converted manor.' She would have suggested that he drive right back there but what was the point? Her parents would think it bizarre for the newly reunited couple to spend their first night apart, especially when they had shown such remarkable twenty-first century liberalism in allowing them to share the same bedroom. 'So you have no clothes with you. Well, what are you going to sleep in, just out of interest.'

'Tut, tut. Don't tell me that your memory's *that* short.'

A stirring, heady drumbeat started deep inside her, bringing hectic colour to her cheeks as she remembered their nights together. No clothes. For her, that had been a novelty. She had *never* slept in the nude before and the first time she had done so she had been incredibly shy because it was almost more intimate than making love. But Cristiano, on the other hand, didn't even possess a pair of pyjamas.

'No way. And, furthermore, could you please move. I want to go upstairs now.'

Cristiano didn't hesitate to step aside. He wasn't quite sure what the conclusion of their conversation had been. Whether she was Bethany Maguire or Amelia Doni or the Queen of England, she was still as feisty, argumentative and unpredictable as he had remembered and, as usual, he was left feeling as though he had been stuffed in a washing machine and spun at full speed.

Besides, he was interested to see what was going to

happen when they made it to her bedroom. He watched her small, rounded derrière with appreciative eyes as she walked ahead of him. One thing he had not forgotten was her delicacy. She was like spun glass and she moved with the grace of a dancer, even though she most likely had never been to a ballet class in her entire life. It was difficult to judge whether she had any kind of bump at all underneath the baggy jumper, but from behind her shape had certainly stayed the same.

For the first time, Cristiano considered the baby she was carrying as opposed to the pregnancy with which he had been presented and decided that it was a great credit to his talent for flexibility and his strength of character that he hadn't immediately felt bitter or trapped. His mother and his grandfather would be over the moon, of that he was sure. It might not have happened in the perfect way, as they would have ideally liked, but the end result would be welcomed with open arms.

They had reached the top of the stairs and Bethany turned to him and pointed down the corridor.

'My bedroom's the last on the right,' she said in a hushed voice. 'I'll be in in a minute and you'd better make sure that you've made yourself a bed on the floor. I'll bring you a spare quilt and you can use one of my pillows.'

Cristiano didn't say anything. He headed for her bedroom, taking his time to have a look at the other rooms he walked past, which were undoubtedly her sisters' rooms, and he was even able to tell which room belonged to which sister. The one with the shelves and shelves of books would be Shania's, and the one with pots of make-up and creams would be Melanie's. Something else, he half mused, that she had not lied about. Her own room was, at the end of the corridor, the biggest, with sprawling windows on two walls and decorated in neutral shades of creams and oatmeal. The furniture was old and heavy and not at all to his taste, but it seemed to suit the feel of the room and the bed was big. Four fluffy pillows, none of which would be going anywhere near the floor, if only she knew.

Cristiano kicked off his shoes, got rid of his socks and then settled down on the feather mattress with satisfaction, his hands clasped behind his head, his mind pleasantly involved in imagining her reaction when she returned with her spare quilt to find him lying on her bed.

He didn't have very long to wait. Literally five minutes later she tiptoed into the room, pausing by the door to get her bearings because he hadn't bothered to switch on the light. It was something she remedied straight away, banging on the switch and then pulsating as she looked at him sprawled out on her bed. She wanted to slam the door hard but resisted the impulse and closed it with a decisive click.

'What are you doing?' She flung the quilt at him and he fielded it expertly onto the floor.

'I'm enjoying the luxury of this great feather mattress of yours. Much more comfortable than the one at the hotel, which shows that money doesn't always buy the best.'

'Well, now that you've enjoyed it, you can get up and start doing something about your sleeping arrangements.' The intimacy of their surroundings was choking her and she had to force her legs into action. 'And these are some of Dad's pyjamas. Put them on.'

'Why? You've already seen me naked.'

'That was then and this is now!'

'Something about horses and stable doors springs to mind here.'

'I don't *care* what springs to mind!' Bethany almost wept with frustration. 'Just go and…and get into the pyjamas…' She breathed deeply. 'The bathroom's next door…'

'Sure.' Cristiano stood up and stretched. 'But I'm not sleeping on the floor.'

'Then *I will*!'

'Oh, no, you won't.' He wasn't smiling as he walked slowly towards her. 'You're going to get into that bed and so am I. I won't have you sleeping on the floor, pregnant.'

'Then *you* sleep on the floor.' Her eyes locked with his and her breathing became shallow and laboured.

'Neither of us is going to be sleeping on the floor and if I come back in here to find that you've done something with that quilt other than stuff it away in the wardrobe then I'm not going to be happy.'

'Oh, and *your* happiness is paramount, naturally!'

He shot her a lazy smile and wondered if he'd actually forgotten how fetching she looked when her eyes were blazing and her colour was up. 'So we agree on something. It's a start.'

Bethany spent three seconds fuming as he unhurriedly left the room, grabbing the towel she had brought in with her and stuck on a chair by the door in passing. Then she moved as though propelled by a rocket. Having already washed her face and brushed her teeth, she flung on her old pyjamas, tartan plaid flannelette that any granny would have been proud of, and got into the bed, making sure to draw the covers up to her chin and position one of the pillows as a barrier between them. She then turned her back to the door and squeezed her eyes tightly shut. Neither protected her from the way her skin tingled as she heard the bedroom door quietly open and shut ten minutes later. He moved so silently that she was only aware of him getting into the bed when it was depressed, almost causing her rigid body to topple over the side.

'I know you're not asleep,' Cristiano said conversationally, 'and, whilst I appreciate that you finally accepted the fact that neither of us was going to sleep on the floor like teenagers at a rock festival, I still don't like the pillow between us, so…' he took the pillow and chucked it on the floor '…that's much better. And now we need to talk.' He rolled over onto his side and Bethany stifled a squeak as she felt the brush of bare skin against her. She was over on her side in a shot and facing him, although she could hardly make out his face.

'Where are Dad's pyjamas?'

'On the floor. I'm in my boxers, though, so there's no need to get your reinforced knickers in a twist.'

The silence settled between them and, with each passing second, Bethany could feel her nerves straining harder.

'You do realise that we need to have a proper conversation, don't you?' Cristiano said calmly. 'By which I mean a conversation without the hysterics.' Fully aware of the full impact barrier she had erected between them by way of her pyjamas and determined not to be distracted, Cristiano was nevertheless aware that his body was riding roughshod over his intentions.

'This isn't a good place to have a conversation.'

'No…? I thought that's where all couples talked. In bed.'

'We're not a couple.'

'Then define what we are, not forgetting that we're engaged.'

Now that her eyes had fully adjusted to the lack of light in the bedroom, Bethany could see him more clearly and she could feel her whole body aching from the torture of being within inches of him. Her double bed might be big for one but it was reduced to the size of a handkerchief with Cristiano taking up more than half of it.

'I wish you wouldn't keep reminding me of that,' she whispered.

'Fine. Then I'll change the topic. After all, I wouldn't want to damage that fragile conscience of yours…so how do you feel about me asking you this…? How has your body changed?'

'I beg your pardon?'

'Your body,' Cristiano murmured huskily. 'How's it changed? I want to feel your stomach. I want to feel my baby.' He reached out and slipped his hand underneath the unflattering checked long-sleeved top which was way too hot to wear to bed. 'I think you'll agree that I have a right…'

CHAPTER SIX

'WHAT are you doing?' Bethany emitted a little squeak of protest and tried to wriggle away from those long fingers but there was limited room to manoeuvre so she had to content herself with a pointless tussle with his hand.

'You hide it well,' Cristiano conceded as he felt the smooth, rounded swell of her stomach. He couldn't believe that he hadn't noticed before she had told him but, then again, he hadn't been looking.

'Don't…' Bethany drew in a shaky lungful of air, her body red-hot and aching as he continued to rub her stomach with the flat of his hand.

'Don't? But I have every right, wouldn't you agree? I am, after all, the prodigal daddy-to-be, just returned from his dangerous stint in the depths of Africa.'

'That's not funny.'

'No, you're right. It's not. Twenty-four hours ago, I was a man with no responsibility to anyone but himself…' He removed his hand from her rounded belly, assailed by the magnitude of the situation.

'Twenty-four hours ago you were a man who was speeding up here to lay into me for deceiving you!'

'Little did I know the depth of the deceit.'

'But you would never have sought me out if you hadn't found out, would you, Cristiano?' Was she hoping that he would contradict her? Her cheeks flamed angrily at the realisation that, yes, fool that she was, she *still* wanted to hear *something* that might indicate that she had been more than just a two week interlude in his busy schedule.

'Did you expect me to?'

'Of course not! So can you blame me for coming back here when I found out that I was pregnant? Can you blame me for not getting in touch with you to tell you the good news?'

'I have no intention of being your accomplice in justifying yourself.'

'You are so…*so superior*!' She balled her hands into fists and gritted her teeth together to stop herself from shouting and bringing her parents flying into the bedroom.

'If by that you mean that I'm upfront with people, then yes, I am.'

'Haven't you ever done something you shouldn't have, Cristiano?'

'Yes, I spent two weeks in Barbados with a woman I barely knew. In retrospect, you might say that that was one of my more spectacular mistakes.'

'That's a horrible thing to say!'

And Cristiano knew it. He also knew that it was a lie but damned if he was going to be the sort of loser who would ever confess that those stolen two weeks had been two of the best he could remember in a long time. Damned if he would give oxygen to that niggling voice in his head that was telling him that yes, he might very well have tried to contact her, *whatever the circumstances of her flight*. What sort of sad man would pursue a woman who had walked out on him? He absolutely refused to admit himself into that category.

'I apologise. Unreservedly.'

'Oh, well, that's all right then.' Bethany gave a strangled laugh under her breath. She lay on her back and stared up at the ceiling, acutely aware of his steady breathing and the fact that his arm was only a couple of inches away from hers.

In the thick, dark silence Cristiano grudgingly smiled at her sniping response. Okay, so his life had been turned on its head. So had hers. Any other woman, faced with an enraged ex-lover, a man who had the wealth and power to move mountains, a man who had been tricked and conned, would have at least had the decency to be suitably humble. None of that with Bethany. Typically, she was fighting fire with fire and no amount of fighting was going to do any good.

'So now that I have shown up on the scene, none the worse for malaria, famine or curare-tipped arrows, what do you intend to do with me?'

As he expected, a stunning silence greeted that question and he allowed that silence to stretch between them until he could *smell* her tension rising in waves.

'Fortunately, I am prepared to do the decent thing.'

Bethany swung round to look at him in surprise. 'Do the decent thing? What are you talking about?'

'You are pregnant with my baby and I am a man of honour, a man who takes his responsibilities seriously. Naturally, I have no other option but to marry you.'

'*Marry me? Have you completely lost your mind?*' Bethany gave a snort of laughter. Did he really expect her to leap at his generous offer because he was *a man of honour*, who *took his responsibilities seriously* and, boxed in as he now found himself, would therefore rise to the occasion by *putting a ring on her finger because there was no option*?

'What are you saying?' With one hand, Cristiano reached

to the side of the bed and flipped on the light. Immediately the tiny area around them was thrown into relief. He hoisted himself up on one elbow and looked down at her with a cold frown of incomprehension.

'I'm *saying*…' Bethany sat upright because it felt too weird conducting this conversation when she was horizontal '…that I'm not going to marry you! This isn't the nineteenth century, Cristiano!'

'Well, it's not far off, considering you felt obliged to fabricate an imaginary fiancé for your parents so that you could return here, pregnant!' He was finding it hard to credit that she had just thrown his proposal back in his face! As far as he was concerned, he was one in a million!

'Fabricating an imaginary fiancé is a far cry from walking down the aisle with a man who doesn't even like me!'

'It is pointless bringing emotions into this.'

'What do you mean, *pointless*?'

'Keep your voice down or your parents will be running in here to see what the hell is going on!'

Bethany counted to ten, very slowly. 'Okay. I'm going to keep my voice down because I don't want to create a scene and have Mum and Dad worrying, but I'm not going to marry you, Cristiano. Not in a million years. It might have been stupid for us…not to have been as careful as we should have been, but it would be even more stupid for us to sacrifice our lives for the sake of this baby.'

Eyes blazing, Cristiano flung himself out of the bed and walked across to the window, a vision of semi-naked masculine beauty which drew Bethany's eyes like a magnet.

'I have no idea why you're so taken aback,' she informed his erect back. 'Most women would have leapt at your offer and where would that have left you? Trapped in a marriage which would become a cage for you…for both of us…' He was a man with a strong libido and it didn't take a genius to work out that two and two would inevitably lead to four. He had no feelings for her and it wouldn't be long before he would stray. She would be no more than the mother of his child, to whom fidelity would hold no outstanding advantages.

'So what,' Cristiano said in a soft voice, 'do you suggest?' He felt it was important to maintain a practical note to the conversation but it was taking every ounce of self discipline not to give way to his temper. Virtually as soon as he had known of the situation, he had been aware of what had to be done and he was shocked that his offer of marriage had met with a negative response. She obviously wasn't thinking straight and, whilst he might have been inclined to put that down to hormones, which apparently affected some women during pregnancy, he was forced to conclude that her mind did not work in the same way as his. Nor, for that matter, did it work in the same way as most of the human race, or at least most of the female contingent. She had been spot on when she had remarked that most women would have leapt at his offer.

Bethany couldn't help it. She felt a thread of disappointment snake through her at his ready acceptance of an alternative plan. Had he only proposed marriage as a way of clearing his conscience? Decent guy, duty done, offer rejected so time to move on. She could practically hear his sigh of relief whipping through the air between them.

'Well, you'll have to stay a day or two, I guess. Or it might look a bit odd…'

Cristiano folded his arms and inclined his head to one side. It was in his nature to contradict the stupidity of what she was saying but he was also sharp enough to know that jumping in with his opinions would only provoke yet another bout of high drama and her immediate stubborn retreat.

Bethany licked her lips and looked to him for some verbal encouragement. Finding none, she continued slowly, 'Then you'd have to return to London…you know, because you can't very well stay here for ever…My parents know that you're a businessman, first and foremost…'

'And where do you fit in to this neat little picture?'

'I'd stay here, of course.'

'Why of course? Wouldn't your parents think it a bit strange that you remain behind?' There were more holes in her story than a colander and he had to fight down the sarcasm which threatened to spill out.

'I could always tell them that it would just be more…reassuring for me to have them around, seeing that your business takes you all over the world. At a moment's notice.'

'I thought I'd already made it clear that there were no more *projects*?'

'Well, you *do* travel, don't you?' Bethany said irritably. 'Why can't you help me out here? Can't you see that I'm just trying to do what's right for both of us?'

'I think it's time we both got some sleep.'

He began walking back towards the bed and she followed his movements with restless, anxious eyes.

'But we haven't sorted out anything.'

'I'm tired. I'm going to sleep. Feel free to let that fertile little imagination of yours run riot with suggestions as to what the next step should be.' He got into the bed, turned on his side with his back to her and ignored her frantic scrabbling movements as she tried to wrest some of the quilt for herself.

Five minutes later and Bethany could hear the soft breathing of a man who had succumbed to sleep. It took her an hour before she felt her own eyelids begin to droop, during which time she had developed serious stiffness in her arms and legs from trying to remain as still as she possibly could.

The next time she opened her eyes, it was to find herself face to face with Cristiano, their noses practically touching. In the course of sleep, they had somehow become entwined. Her leg had managed to insert itself between his thighs and his arm was flung round her.

His eyes were closed and his face was all hard angles barely visible in the darkness. Like a thief, she stole the opportunity to look at him. He couldn't see her. She could linger on his face, allow herself to express her feelings with her guard down.

She wanted to reach out and trace the contours of his mouth and eyes and nose. She used to do that when they were lovers. He had found it amusing, the way she would stare at him as though he was the most riveting man on the face of the earth. She had never, ever seen anyone as beautiful as him.

She was going through a mental checklist of all the things she found so attractive about the way he was put together when he opened his eyes. Fast asleep one minute. Wide-eyed and alert the next. Bethany gave a little gasp and tried to pull away but he snuggled up against her, drawing her against his body.

'You're awake!' she whispered accusingly and Cristiano grinned.

He laced his fingers through her tumbled hair and brought her closer against him. She was no longer making a show of trying to wriggle away, he noticed. He hadn't realised how quiet it was out here in the depths of the countryside. He was accustomed to the constant undercurrent of noise, even in the early hours of the morning. It was so still that he could hear her jerky breathing.

His arousal was fast and hard and he knew the very instant she became aware of it by her soft whimper. Even though he had only spent a little over a fortnight in her company, it had been an intense experience and he seemed to be able to read her tiniest little reactions. Like the way she had shifted her body fractionally, getting just a tiny bit closer to him. He was surprised to find that he was holding his breath, not wanting to splinter the moment.

'I missed you,' he confessed roughly. 'You left and I couldn't get you out of my head.'

Bethany felt as though a gust of air had whipped her up and carried her off to cloud nine. She sighed and squirmed and closed her eyes and threw her head back with a little moan as his hand circled her stomach, retracing the gentle, tentative exploration he had begun earlier but this time extending it to include her breasts.

'I thought about touching you a thousand times.' Cristiano cupped one of her breasts in his hand, feeling its enlarged weight. 'Your breasts have grown.'

'Yes,' Bethany said in a strangled voice.

'Your nipples will have grown too. Have they? Become larger?'

'Cristiano…' His words made her pulses race. She felt like someone caught in the grip of a fever. No, caught in a raging inferno, one that had been sparked the minute he had walked through the front door.

'Shh…' He leant over her and her mouth parted to receive his questing tongue. His kiss became deeper, more urgent and, as she felt him throb against her, she frantically wanted to rid herself of the crazy toe to neck barrier of her flannelette pyjamas, which she had worn in an attempt to stifle her sexuality.

'I want to see you,' Cristiano told her in a hoarse voice. He didn't give her time to answer. She was soft and compliant and he didn't want to give her the slightest opportunity to gather herself into attack mode. He pushed up the long sleeved top and lost himself in wordless appreciation of her breasts.

He wondered how he could have deluded himself into thinking that his life would slot back to normality the minute he returned to London. *This* had been on his mind for months and he couldn't get enough of her. What was it with this woman? She made him lose control and he abandoned the struggle to resurrect it.

Instead, he grazed his tongue over her pouting nipples, bigger and darker than before. Her body was preparing itself for the birth of their baby and the thought of that was a massive turn-on. His mouth replaced his tongue as he sucked on one nipple, pulling it into his mouth and enjoying the way she was shivering and shuddering underneath him. One hand cupped her breast and the other wandered down, curving over her stomach, which had been practically invisible when she had been decked out in her oversized camouflage gear but was decidedly round and plump when bared. He slipped his hand beneath the elasticated waistband of the pyjamas, moving lower still.

Bombarded by sensation, Bethany arched back and the rasp of his mouth suckling on her nipple became unbearably exquisite. She curled her fingers into his thick, dark hair, steering him towards her other breast. She literally felt as if she couldn't get enough of him. When he raised his head to ask her whether it was safe, whether it was all right, she found herself nodding and telling him *not to stop*.

He made a running commentary on her body, on its changes, and the low velvety words were as erotic as his hands running along her. She was panting as he licked his way along her stomach and then his tongue was in her, flicking and squirming until she was bucking under the exquisite torment. He had teased her like this before, bringing her to the brink and then waiting for her to subside, but now there was no lull in his hunger and, before she could pull back, he had taken her over the edge. Wave upon wave of pleasure sent convulsive shudders through her body and, when she finally stilled, he heaved himself over her and grinned.

'Felt good?'

Bethany said something that emerged as a breathy whimper, which made him grin some more.

'We shouldn't have done that,' she said weakly.

'Why are you using the past tense?'

There was no way that he was going to let her gather her thoughts. She had already done way too much thinking as far as he was concerned. He silenced her with his mouth, kissing her with lingering thoroughness.

'You're very sexy, pregnant,' he whispered.

'No, I'm not.'

'You are to me.' He parted her thighs with his hand, taking time to feel the moisture between her legs that was an indication of how aroused she was. 'We men are simple creatures,' he murmured, teasing her with his erection, which had her moving against him so that his hard shaft rubbed against her sensitised clitoris. 'Evidence of our virility can't help but prove satisfying. Call it a weird macho thing.' Never before had he felt so liberated as he thrust into her, gently at first, then deeper and harder as their rhythm picked up speed. From the very first time they had made love, their bodies had been extraordinarily attuned and nothing had been lost in the months between the last time they had been together. They moved as one. Maybe that was why making love to her had always been such an amazing experience.

Spent from a climax that ranked right up there as one of

the best experiences of his life, Cristiano rolled onto his back, content that things had been sorted between them.

'That was a mistake.'

Her words, crashing through his good mood, took a few seconds to register, then he turned to her, half thinking that he might not have heard her correctly.

'What are you talking about?'

'We shouldn't have made love. And now I'm going to have a shower and I'm going to freeze to death in the process because the central heating's gone off.' She made as if to slip out of the bed and the restraining hand that reached out to circle her wrist was as quick as a whip, dragging her back to him.

'Not so fast,' Cristiano grated. 'You're not ducking out of this conversation. What the hell do you mean by *we shouldn't have made love*? I didn't hear you complaining five minutes ago.'

'I'm not saying that I'm not attracted to you,' Bethany whispered, not daring to look him in the face. 'But that doesn't mean anything.'

'You have no idea what you're talking about.'

'Don't pretend to know me better than I know myself!' she said fiercely, deeply ashamed at the ease with which she had fallen back into his arms. When a clear head had been needed, she had abandoned hers and leapt right back on to the emotional roller coaster ride, as if she hadn't been battered enough by it.

'But I *do* know you better than you know yourself,' Cristiano purred with lethal assurance. 'I know, for instance, that you haven't got a clue how to handle this situation.'

'How dare you?'

'Because I need to do the thinking for both of us,' he told her calmly. 'And spare me another of your hissy fits. I've listened to everything you've had to say and now you're going to lie back and listen to the voice of reason and common sense.'

'I don't believe I'm hearing this.'

'Well, start believing it. And I'll keep it simple. You're pregnant and, whether you like it or not, I'm not about to disappear on an extended trip to anywhere. I'm not going to be conveniently vanishing to Afghanistan to set up a medical centre. I won't be revisiting Central Africa to see how that non-existent community centre's doing. Nor will I become the callous ex-lover who thinks nothing of leaving his pregnant fiancée for months on end to cope on her own, giving her a handy excuse for the relationship to fizzle out because who can be expected to stay with a complete bastard? Face up to those facts and then we might be getting somewhere.'

'Okay. So maybe you don't *have* to disappear. I'm willing for you to have some involvement…'

'Oh, now, that's remarkably generous of you,' Cristiano told her with biting sarcasm. 'Do you suggest I travel over here once a month to see how things are coming along?'

'It's not that difficult. The air and road links are very efficient.'

'Not efficient enough. I live in London and London is where you will be, like it or loathe it.' He raked his fingers through his hair and sighed in sheer frustration. What was her problem? Why was she so intent on fighting him every inch of the way when he had risen to the occasion in such a superb fashion?

'Do you think you can win me over by trying to force my hand, Cristiano?'

'*Trying to force your hand?* I offered you marriage and you turned me down, even though it is the only reasonable solution and a pretty good one from where I'm standing. It isn't as though we aren't attracted to one another. We are. You can say what you want about it being a mistake that we made love but we were only doing what two people do when they want one another.'

'And, as far as you're concerned, good sex and a sense of duty is enough for a marriage?' She dispelled the lump in her throat and snapped her hand out of his grip. 'So if you had, say, accidentally got another woman pregnant, would your solution have been the same? A marriage of convenience for the sake of the baby?'

'That's a hypothetical question and I'm not into answering hypothetical questions.' But it lodged somewhere in his brain and, although he was not accustomed to ever going down the road of self-indulgent, pointless introspection, he was a little shaken to realise he harboured doubts about whether in similar circumstances he would have committed to marriage with any of the women he had dated in the past, however fine their credentials had been. Maybe it was because none of them had ever been so challenging, maybe it was because this relationship had not had time to run its natural course. He decided that nothing was to be gained from thinking about it. They were in a unique situation, end of story. 'You attack me for asking you to marry me. Have you stopped to think that the child would benefit from having both parents? I come from an extremely conventional family. I had the benefit of both a mother and a father on the scene. I find it inconceivable for you to blithely assume that the absence of one parent is a good thing.'

'I never said that it was a *good thing*. You're putting words into my mouth…'

'I'm putting sensible ideas into your head…'

Bethany found herself thinking about what it might have

been like to have grown up without her dad and she resented the fact that he was trying to imply that she was selfish. Selfish for wanting a life that didn't involve her being married to a man who neither liked nor respected her, a man who saw her as an obligation that had to be taken on. He casually accepted that the sex was good, and maybe he saw that as a kind of temporary bonus, and maybe, if she wasn't in love with him, she could have gone along with the proposition. But she *did* love him and to trade herself in as a suitable business deal so that his traditionalism could be satisfied would be like opening a wound and pouring salt in.

'It's not sensible to sign away your life for the sake of convention. Two unhappy people don't add up to a healthy environment for a child. Yes, two parents on the scene is ideal, but two *happy* parents.'

'We were both pretty happy ten minutes ago,' Cristiano pointed out, 'and I'm pretty sure that, given half a chance, we could both be pretty happy again.'

'No, we could *have sex* again! Which isn't going to happen, by the way. It was a moment of madness and…'

'…we had many of those when we were in Barbados, if I recall. All things come with a price.'

'And I'm willing for us to be…friends…' Lying in bed with him, telling him that she was willing to be *friends*, after they had made love, almost brought on a fit of hysterical laughter. 'I'm willing for you to have…whatever input you need to satisfy your conscience…'

Cristiano gritted his teeth but didn't say a word. Her emotional, highly feminine thinking did nothing for him. They had been presented with a problem. He had the solution to it and he didn't see why she couldn't accept it without digging her heels in and stubbornly putting forward a list of arguments that made no sense. And what was with the *friend-*

ship talk? The fact that she was as physically attracted to him as he was to her made a nonsense of that.

Bethany waited for him to try and demolish her suggestion, but he didn't and she continued hesitantly, 'I mean…we shouldn't deny ourselves a chance of happiness with someone else…' She made a valiant effort to try and imagine someone else with whom she could be happy but she couldn't get past Cristiano's forceful, darkly handsome face.

'What does that mean?'

'There could be a guy out there for me, a guy who wants to marry me for who I am, and not because he's duty bound…!'

Cristiano felt a smouldering aggression overwhelm his ability to think rationally. It was an effort to remain lying on the bed next to her, his eyes fixed on the ceiling, his hands loosely linked behind his head. The thought of her with another man was beyond unacceptable. It was outrageous.

'What sort of guy? Someone from around here?'

'Maybe…' Bethany tried the thought on for size. She still knew quite a few of the guys with whom she had gone to school, guys who had remained in the town or close by. They would run a mile from a woman with another man's baby in tow, which was a depressing enough thought, but even more depressing was the certainty that she would not have looked at any of them in a million years, even if they were to give her a second glance. Why bother with minnows when there was a predatorial shark cruising in the waters? Why bother with being sensible when she knew that it only ran skin-deep?

'It would take a saint to commit to a relationship with a woman who was pregnant with another man's baby.' Cristiano subdued his mounting rage to keep his voice level. 'Especially another man who had no intention of leaving an open field.' Now more than ever, it seemed imperative to nail the marriage suggestion. He was not going to idly sit by and watch someone else usurp his role as father. Jealousy and possessiveness, two emotions which were anathema to him, rose up like bile in his throat but he knew, with the instincts of someone adept at reading situations and people, that trying to impose his forceful personality on her would have her running for cover. She might have rosy ideas of some gormless local lad who would tiptoe round her and pander to her every need but she was mistaken on every single count, the foremost one being that he would simply not allow that situation to happen. He had to restrain himself from pointing out what, to him, was an inescapable truth. She was headstrong, stubborn and explosively unpredictable. She would eat most men up and it was very fortunate for her that he wasn't most men.

But she wasn't going to listen to the voice of reason and that being the case, he would just have to adopt a different voice. Same result but a different approach. He felt smugly proud at the level of tolerance which he was—unusually—exhibiting.

'But...' he shrugged in the darkness and shifted away from her '...I'm willing to go along with the friendship card. Like it or not, we are going to be parents and I will not allow us to be parents at war. Now, I think I'm going to get some sleep.' He settled himself further, felt the brush of her leg against his back and briefly contemplated how admirably swift his turnaround had been. From the bottom of his world dropping out, he had rapidly regrouped and seen the advantages of the institution of marriage in which he had previously harboured next to no interest.

Firstly, it would provide the ideal environment in which his child could be raised, happy and well balanced.

Secondly, it would satisfy every member of his family, not least his mother, who would greet the news with enthusiasm, of that he was one hundred per cent sure.

Thirdly, he would have her. This last seemed vitally important to him and he assumed it was because his hunting instinct had been sharpened by her refusal to have him as her husband. With a long history of women who would do anything for him, he had at last met his match in a woman who, seemingly, would put herself out to do absolutely nothing for him. Except in bed, where she lost all her control. Just thinking about that loss of control threatened to undo his calm frame of mind.

All things considered, Cristiano was feeling pretty good by the time he finally fell asleep.

He awoke to a heavy grey light which could barely manage to filter through the thick curtains, and an empty bed. He had slept like the proverbial log and felt all the better for it. Accustomed to rarely venturing out without his laptop computer, BlackBerry and generally complete access to the outside world, he realised that he was now cut off from civilisation, at least until he got back to the hotel later in the morning and, surprisingly, he was okay with the situation.

He rolled over onto his back and then heaved himself onto his elbows at the sight of Bethany framed in the doorway, fully dressed in a full skirt and another baggy sweater, this time in a different colour. He absent-mindedly wondered how she managed to make such a shapeless outfit look so tempting. He had a vivid and instant recall of the feel of her swollen breasts in his hands and the taste of her nipples on his tongue and his body responded with alacrity.

'I see you're up.' She entered the room and shut the door quietly behind her because, from personal experience, walls in her parents' house tended to have ears.

She had postponed going back into the bedroom until the last possible moment. In fact, until her mother had more or less demanded that she wake Cristiano so that he could partake of the full Irish breakfast which she had made especially.

Cristiano refrained from making the obvious quip about being up in more than one sense. Instead, he informed her that he had not had such a good night's sleep in a long time. Bethany, who felt punch-drunk from her restless night, scowled and was disgruntled when he grinned broadly in return.

'You have no clothes,' she said, eyeing his bronzed torso, which he was making little attempt to conceal. 'What are you going to wear?'

'Oh, I can go back to the hotel and get them.'

'Have you looked outside the window?'

Cristiano obliged, slipping out of bed, glimpsing her rise in colour as he did so. It had snowed and it was a spectacular sight. The fields which fell away from the back of the house were a landscape of pristine, virgin white. The sky was a yellow grey, dull and threatening and still releasing its heavy load. He dropped the curtain and turned to her.

'So…' he spread his arms wide, unperturbed by the uninviting expression on her face '…tell me what you want me to do…You call the shots…'

CHAPTER SEVEN

CRISTIANO found out soon enough. After a hearty breakfast, the like of which he had not tasted since he had been a teenager with an insatiable appetite and an abundance of free time that could be apportioned to satisfying it, he found himself with a checklist of things to do, which he was pretty sure Bethany had compiled with a great deal of satisfaction. Most of the chores necessitated him being outside and, since he had not a stitch of clothing with him, aside from what he had arrived in, which were in the process of being washed, he was obliged to brace near blizzard conditions in some of her father's clothes, which were too short in the arms and legs and too large in the waist.

'Clear drive...and salt...chop wood for logs...milk and bread from corner shop...' He lounged against the door-frame and looked up from the list. 'Sure this is all? There must be a few *more* outdoor duties you need me to fulfil...' She was busying herself by the kitchen sink, the picture of domesticity were it not for the smirk on her face. She saun-tered up to him, took the list, read it slowly with a thought-ful frown and then returned it to him.

'Nope. That's all *for the moment*. Why? Do you think the Mr Perfect image might come a bit unglued by all the heavy outdoor work?' It still rankled that his charm offensive had been relentless and highly successful over breakfast. He had made himself useful in the kitchen, despite her mother's protests that she was fine, and had won her father over with his ridiculous knowledge of Irish politics, horse racing and tips on investments for pension funds, which seemed to be her father's most recent area of concern.

In the process, he had practically ignored her and she had had to remind herself that that was all to the good, considering they were now just *friends*. He had listened to what she had said, had backed off and the situation was now perfect. Fabulous. Of course, she would have to think about her story when it came to letting her parents down with the wedding that would never be, but she would cross that bridge when she came to it. In the meantime, she decided that satisfaction was the order of the day. She had got exactly what she had wanted! His respect! He had understood the situation and would no longer think that he could subject her to his unwanted attentions. She was uncomfortably aware that she had to gloss over that last thought but the end result was the same. He was keeping his distance and if her parents were blissfully unaware of the slight shift in the atmosphere, then *she* was very much aware of it. There had been no more of those suggestive looks or accidental brushing of hands or innuendo.

'My *Mr Perfect* image…Now, should I take that as a compliment, I wonder?'

Bethany had a moment of wishing that her parents were around like chaperones because the lazy gleam in his eyes was mesmerising. She had to pull herself back down to earth and slam the door shut on a mind that wanted to play with the taboo images of running her fingers over his shirt, undoing the buttons, slipping her hand underneath to feel his warm skin.

The outfit which she had chosen for him, having told her parents that he had left his clothes at the hotel into which he had booked *just in case she had not been at home when he had arrived*, should have reduced his sex appeal to zero. It was one of her father's oldest shirts. Something he used to wear for gardening a thousand years ago, a checked flannel number with two buttons missing, frayed cuffs and faded to the point that the original colour was no longer obvious. The very opposite of the handmade Italian shirts Cristiano favoured. The trousers were of a similar age and needed a belt. His handstitched leather shoes had been exchanged for green wellies, and the waterproof anorak she had supplied was heavy and shapeless. She had also insisted, under cover of the caring girlfriend, that he wear a woollen hat to combat the thickly falling snow and deep, penetrating cold.

'Wouldn't want you catching your death out there,' she had said, smiling smugly when she had handed him the bundle of clothes. 'We wrap up warm in this part of the world. No time for silly designer clothes...'

'Understood,' Cristiano had said, leaning in to her so that his warm breath had fanned against her cheek. 'I would know all about the pointlessness of designer clothes, having spent so much time in Central Africa on that project, wouldn't I?'

Bethany looked at him now and folded her arms. 'I know you've probably never done a day's hard work in your entire life—' she began and he cut her short before she had time to finish her sentence.

'And your assumptions would be based on...what, exactly?'

'You're a company man, Cristiano,' she stammered, sticking her chin up. 'You sit behind a desk...'

'Every summer when I was at university I worked on a

building site,' he informed her succinctly. He straightened up and pushed himself away from the door. 'I've always thought that work that stretches the body is good for the brain and excellent for maintaining a healthy balance. Even now, I make sure that my trips to the gym are as physically gruelling as possible. So do me a favour and try not to pigeonhole me.' He slung on the borrowed anorak which, Bethany thought sourly, had never looked like that on her father. 'In fact, when I'm done with this list of things, I might just join your father in the fields and help out with the cattle. Now, why don't you be a good little girl and run along and make sure that my clothes are nicely laundered…?'

'How dare you…?'

'What?' Cristiano threw her a mocking smile over his shoulder as he headed out. 'Pigeonhole you?'

She was still smarting from the way he had neatly turned the verbal tables on her when, a couple of hours later, she indeed found herself fishing his clothes out of the tumble dryer and setting up the ironing board so that she could iron his shirt.

'Women don't do this stuff any more,' she complained to her mother, who had taken it as a given that Cristiano's clothes, once washed, would be returned to him in the sort of pristine condition in which they had originally been bought from the shop, or tailor or wherever he stocked up on his mega-expensive outfits.

'If you're tired, I don't mind running the iron over them,' her mother said placidly, taking time out from the stew she was in the middle of making.

'I'm fine,' Bethany muttered in a driven tone. 'I was just saying that the days of toiling over an ironing board, ironing a man's shirt and trousers are over.'

'Oh, I don't think it's asking too much for Cristiano to

come back here to some nice, clean, pressed clothing, do you? Not when he's been making himself so helpful around the house when he's probably exhausted and in need of a rest himself after everything he's been through. And your dad said that he's had the best advice off him about what to do with his savings, better than that accountant in Limerick he's been using.'

Bethany's teeth snapped together on the tart retort to her mother's eulogy. She debated letting the sizzling iron sit on the pristine white shirt just long enough for it to leave a hideous indelible stain.

'He's certainly a gem when it comes to finances,' she managed. Shirt and trousers finished, she switched off the iron and stood it upright on the ironing board for it to cool.

'The man seems to be a gem when it comes to most things,' her mother mused with a smile. 'A rare find. I'd be more than pleased if your sisters decided to bring home a couple of those for my prospective sons-in-law.'

In a minute she would start making noises about weddings and honeymoons. Bethany could feel it hovering in the warm, aromatic air between them and she sighed.

'Mum...I've been having some doubts about...you know...marrying Cristiano...' She felt awkward colour seep into her face, intensifying as her mother stopped stirring the pot and looked at her, open-mouthed.

'I really wasn't going to say anything...' It had to be done. The longer the charade continued, the more difficult it would be to back out of an impossible situation and also, what on earth was she going to do when Cristiano returned to London? Go back with him? Live where? In his apartment? Where they would work on their *friendship*, while she fell deeper and harder for the man? Would she have to sit around and watch as he went out with other women? Pretend that none of it mattered? Because the only thing that did was the child they had accidentally created together?

'Sit down, Beth. I'm going to make you a cup of tea. In fact, I think I'll make us both a cup of tea.'

'I've been thinking,' she said, hands round the mug of sweet tea, 'that everything happened really quickly with Cristiano. I know you're going to tell me that it was like that with you and Dad but things are different these days. Marriage isn't the immediate option. I just don't feel I know him well enough to tie the knot…' Her mother's expression was altering from concerned and anxious to disappointed but valiant with it.

'But you love each other…'

Bethany opted to evade that statement. 'I just think that it's important not to get swept up by the fact that I'm having a baby…'

'But Cristiano's the father…What could be more natural than…?'

'I know, I know and I would never deny him his rights as a father, but we've spent so little time truly getting to know one another and it's better to stand back now than get into a situation I…*we*…end up regretting…I'm really sorry if I've disappointed you and Dad…' She shrugged her shoulders helplessly. She had spoken her piece. Without the figment of an impending marriage, Cristiano would return to London because he would have no choice and he would no longer be in a position to blackmail her into going with him *to satisfy her parents' misconceptions*. She should have been feeling the light-headed relief of a great weight being removed from her shoulders, but Bethany was assailed by a sensation of corrosive emptiness. Her success at out-manoeuvring him was a lot less satisfying than it should have been.

Furthermore, her mother couldn't understand how she could have doubts about someone who was so spectacularly perfect. Bethany could see it on her face. Cristiano had put his best foot forward and won her over and it was horribly upsetting to think that her mother, whilst not saying anything, might actually *blame her* for being picky and un-reasonable.

The atmosphere was strained by the time the front door opened and her father and Cristiano came in on a gust of sharp cold air and thick falling snow.

Bethany was ready and waiting. She had stuck on her thickest jumper, which hung down past the waist of her full gypsy skirt, her woolly hat and her fur-lined boots and hijacked Cristiano before he could make it into the kitchen, where the delicious smell of the stew was wafting out into the hallway.

'I need to talk to you,' she said, putting on her gloves and resting her small hand lightly on his arm.

'Can it wait? I need to have a shower.'

'No, it can't.' There was a vitality about him that struck her like a bolt of electricity. He might not have anticipated everything that had happened but, in fairness, he had adapted well. His world had been turned upside down and he had risen to the occasion with admirable speed. He had come up with a solution that might be inappropriate as far as *she* was concerned but it was more than a lot of men would have done under similar circumstances. And he had wormed his way into her parents' affections through a cunning combination of the gift of the gab, which always found an appreciative audience in Ireland, and a willingness to muck in.

Lord only knew how he had managed to familiarize himself with the chainsaw, but he had succeeded in chopping enough logs to last a couple of weeks and, although the snow was already piling up onto the drive, he had still managed to clear the majority of it, leaving a gritted path that was safe to walk on.

Cristiano frowned. The past few hours spent outdoors had felt good. The challenge of the land was more immediate and rewarding than he might have expected and, trudging back with John, he had allowed himself to ponder the hitherto unexplored notion that there was something deeply satisfying about the old caveman approach to life…returning to the hearth after a day of solid hard work. Big, open fire, dutiful wife, kids. Naturally, he had had to grin at his own misconception there because the last thing Bethany could be described as was dutiful.

However, he hadn't banked on returning to find her positioned by the front door like a pitbull on patrol and wearing an expression that promised a difficult end to the morning.

'The log shed's at the back of the house. I'll help you carry the logs in and we can talk.'

'Why do I get the feeling that this *talk* of yours doesn't revolve around you wanting to find out how my morning's been?' The shed which housed the logs and Ireland's trademark fuel of turf was surprisingly big and leant at an angle against the back of the house. Cristiano was only aware of the size when the final trip had been completed in silence and the last log dumped on the stack at the side. A naked overhanging lightbulb was the only form of illumination but it was enough for him to pick up the determined set of her jaw.

'Have I successfully jumped through the first set of hoops?' His mouth curled derisively. 'Or have you thought of a few more? To prove my worth?'

'You don't have to prove anything.'

'No, you're right. I don't. I'm glad you've finally reached

that conclusion.' She was leaning against the side of the shed, hands behind her back, swamped in far too many clothes that were way too big for her. She looked small and defenceless and vulnerable but looks, Cristiano reminded himself, were deceiving. This was the woman who had lied to him, had lied to her parents about him, had kept her pregnancy a secret, something which he had unearthed purely by chance. She had fought him tooth and nail ever since he had arrived on the scene and even her compliance when she had fallen into bed with him had been short-lived. Still basking in the afterglow of their lovemaking, she had jolted him out of his warm, pleasant drowsiness with recriminations and rubbish about wanting to be friends. He'd offered her a solution to her problems, was big enough to overlook the enormity of her deception and she threw it back in his face. He said one thing and she immediately made sure to say the opposite. He went in one direction, she hived off in the other.

'I've had a long chat with my mother.' Bethany broke the silence. It would have been more comfortable to have had this chat in the house but she imagined that her parents were having a little chat of their own and she wanted to be out of the house to give them time to absorb what she had said earlier. The log shed was the least intimate place in the world, if you discounted its size which now, full of fuel, placed him way too close to her for comfort but, even so, she felt her eyes skittering over him, drinking him in. She would have loved to have known how he'd found his morning, was seduced by the thought of them pottering in the kitchen, her making him tea while he regaled her with anecdotes of battling through the frozen fields, but she pursed her lips and, instead, said abruptly, 'I've said that there isn't going to be any wedding.'

Cristiano had not been expecting this. He had been so

focused on a successful outcome that he hadn't appreciated that time might not have been on his side.

'And why would you do that?' He kept his voice low and soft and mildly interested, which annoyed Bethany because, under the insufferably calm exterior, she felt she could read the mindset of someone who wanted to sweep all her considerations under the carpet.

'You know why. I've already explained to you that having a baby together isn't the right reason for two people to get married.'

'And your mother wasn't curious as to the sudden decision?'

'I explained that…that we might have made a mistake, that we got involved too quickly…'

'Ah. So you stopped short of the full, undiluted truth, in other words.'

'You have to return to London, Cristiano, and it would be madness for me to go with you, but how could I stay behind if my parents believed that everything was sunshine and roses between us? I had to set them straight, so…'

He didn't say anything. Playing it cool wasn't going to work. Nor was reminding her that he had no intention of abandoning his child to an uncertain future and sporadic visits while she got on with *trying to find the right guy*.

He strolled slowly towards her and Bethany felt the fine hairs at the back of her neck begin to prickle in alarmed response.

'What…what are you doing?'

'Not fighting with you.' She might make a big deal of denying what she felt, but he could sense the desire throbbing in her, coming at him in waves. He braced himself against the back of the shed, leaning on the flats of his hands so that he was staring down at her. His anorak, unzipped at the front, hung open like two heavy curtains around her slight frame.

Bethany feverishly wondered how he could manage to make her feel so jittery and racked with nerves when he *wasn't fighting* with her. She drew in a ragged lungful of air.

'So you agree that we…we can…discuss this…um…like adults…? Now that there's no need to pretend that we're going to live out the…um…happy ever after fairy tale to my parents…?' She barely recognised her own voice.

'Sure we can…if you want.'

The clean, masculine outdoor scent of him filled her nostrils and she closed her eyes for a few seconds, breathing him in until she felt her head swimming.

His eyes were slumberous, veiled behind his thick dark eyelashes. He had a way of screening his gaze that had used to give her goosebumps because there was something outrageously erotic about it and he was looking at her like that now. Her body responded on cue. Her breasts felt heavy and the memory of how her sensitised nipples had felt the night before when he had touched them, sucked them, instantly heated her from the inside out, despite the cold weather. She wanted to back away but there was no place to back up *to*.

'Of course I…want to discuss it…you know…' She could hear herself gabbling and took a few deep breaths, which did absolutely nothing to steady her wildly beating pulse.

'Okay.'

'So…when you decide to return to London…'

'With this snow falling, it's a little hard for me to think about that just yet.' He rubbed the back of his neck and stood back. 'Tell me when exactly you want me to leave,' he said conversationally.

Faced with that direct remark, Bethany blushed and stared down at her feet. He was done fighting for the baby. She had got what she had wanted all along. He was airbrushing himself out of the picture.

'You must be keen to be on your way,' she hedged and he looked away for a few seconds with a crooked half smile.

'You haven't answered my question.'

'Well…it'd be lunacy to try and go now. The snow…when it snows here…it's difficult to predict how long it'll last…' She was horrified to find that, having engineered his disappearance, she was now thrown into a panicky tailspin at the thought of him leaving for good. Sure, he'd return now and again, definitely to start with, and he would be brilliant with maintenance, that she knew for sure, but…

'You *do* want me to leave, don't you…?' As she hesitated on the brink of asserting her control, Cristiano placed his hands on her waist. He ignored her sharp intake of breath. He had tried being Mr Nice Guy, had chosen to give her time to come round and he was done trying now. If she wasn't going to admit to how she felt about him, then he would just have to remind her. But, this time around, he wasn't going to give her any bolt-holes. No way was she going to get the chance to erect any more barriers against him.

'Yes…you know I do…'

'Then you can creep back into your tidy little world here…' As he spoke, his hands eased under her jumper, under her shirt, found the thin stretchy fabric of her thermals. How many layers did she have on? he wondered.

Bethany emitted a noise that was halfway between a sigh and a moan. Just so long as he was standing well away from her, she could keep him at bay with reason and logic and good common sense, but the minute he touched her she went up in flames like tinder and he was touching her now. He had managed to work his way under all her protective layers and his fingers against her skin were warm and insistent, stroking her ribcage and under her breasts. She wasn't wearing a bra—her old ones were now slightly too small and she hadn't bothered to buy replacement ones.

'We're supposed…to…to be friends…' she gasped as his thumbs found the tight, firm buds of her nipples and began rubbing them in little circling movements.

'I'm finding that the friendship card doesn't work for me. I start thinking about being *friends* but I can't get the thought of you, naked and aroused, out of my head. I burn for you…' To emphasise his point, he pushed up the offending layers of clothes and cupped her swollen breasts in his hands, still rubbing her nipples and sending her into a frenzy of passion and longing.

'Stop…' Bethany pleaded shakily. 'You're not being fair…'

'I know…' Cristiano pressed her back and began kissing her neck as she arched up to meet his urgent mouth. 'That's something else that hasn't been working very well for me recently.'

Bethany whimpered softly and searched out his mouth with her eyes closed, collapsing back as he began really kissing her, his tongue moving sinuously against hers. He barely gave her time to surface and she didn't want to. She could barely keep still and her hands were tangled in his hair, pulling him down to her.

He was whispering stuff to her, snatched Italian words that were unbearably sexy, even though his voice was so low-pitched and rough that she could barely make them out.

When he paused in his hungry ministrations, a voice which she hardly recognised as her own pleaded for him to carry on.

Just this one last time, she was thinking, but even as the thought entered her head it was reduced to splinters by the bitter realisation that she would succumb over and over again. He drained her of her strength and her willpower. He, clearly, could separate lust from emotion, just as he could separate emotion from duty, but for her everything was too entwined and she hated herself for not being able to stay away from his dangerous appeal, even though she knew that it was bad for her.

'What was that?' Cristiano asked. His mouth curved into the smile of the all conquering hero.

'I don't want you to stop and I hate you for…making me say that…'

'You don't hate me. I challenge you and you feel that you need to fight against the challenge but you don't. If it's any consolation,' he continued roughly, 'you challenge me too and I've discovered that trying to fight it is no good. Why don't we stop trying to deny what we want?'

'You don't know what I want,' Bethany protested weakly.

'I know exactly what you want. Trust me.' He pulled off her woolly hat and buried his face in the abundance of her luxuriant copper hair. She always smelled of flowers, fresh and clean and somehow innocent, and he could happily lose himself just in the aroma of her.

With one hand behind her head, he set about the delicious task of plundering her mouth and with his other hand he re-acquainted himself with the soft feminine curves of her body, reaching under her skirt to smooth her thighs and then to push down beneath her thick tights so that he could slip his fingers into her.

He couldn't understand what power she had over him but, from the very first time they had made love, she had made him feel like a starved man suddenly confronted with a banquet. Touching her felt *right*.

'Cristiano…no…please…' Bethany quivered as his fingers

delved into the very core of her, stroking and rubbing and sending all sorts of wonderful sensations racing round her body. She had her eyes closed and her head flung back and her mouth slightly open. 'Don't stop...'

In one fluid movement, he was on his knees, her suppliant. Bethany stared slumberously at him, curled her fingers into his hair and then groaned in anticipation of what he was going to do. She felt him pull down her tights and panties and then raise her skirt. She parted her legs to accommodate him and then shuddered compulsively as his tongue replaced his deft, exploring fingers.

Her breathing sounded laboured and she wanted to cry out but couldn't. Instead, she gave little grunts of encouragement and satisfaction and twisted feverishly against his mouth as he continued to tease her with a stop/start rhythm that took her so close to the edge only to pull her back down to earth at the very last minute.

She gave a groan of utter frustration when he stood up and pressed himself against her, all the better for her to feel his hardness but, just in case she was in any doubt whatsoever, he pushed her hand against his trousers and had to clench his teeth as she felt the shape of his erection and squeezed it.

'I need *all of you*,' he growled, stilling her as she clumsily attempted to undo the zip of the trousers. 'And not here. Don't get me wrong, I've never been the sort of guy who's averse to a little kinkiness, but taking you in a shed is going a little too far...'

'We *can't go in*...!' An unseemly giggle threatened to emerge. 'Mum and Dad are in there and I...we...'

'I don't think we have much choice, my darling. We can't strip down to our birthday suits in here and I, for one, *need* this...need *you*...' He didn't give her time to start getting her thoughts in order. Instead, he laid it on heavy by reminding her of what he wanted and needed—what they *both* wanted and needed—by closing one big hand over her breast and feathering his finger over her nipple.

He knew that he was resorting to slightly underhand tactics but he didn't really care. Nor did he stop to question the astounding fact that he was *having to resort to tactics, underhand or not.*

'We can go through the back door…I don't even know why…we're not supposed to be *doing this*…' Her hands were shaking as she straightened herself up and there was a thread of excitement uncoiling inside her. Like a teenager making use of the parents' house while they were out, she wanted to tear inside and hotfoot it to the nearest empty room. She wanted to rip his clothes off…She felt faint just thinking about it and even fainter at the thought that this was *the last thing they should be doing*. She had regaled her mother with a long speech about *reconsidering the whole marriage deal*, she had lectured him about the idiocy of sacrificing themselves for the sake of a baby, she had *positively waxed lyrical* about the fact that the best they could aim for was friendship. Since when did friends make out like a couple of sex-starved adolescents?

None of this stopped her from leaving her hand in his as they scuttled back out into the driving snow and tiptoed back into the house via the utility room door, which was always kept unlocked for easy and quick access to the log shed in the depths of winter.

In fact, the feel of his fingers curling around hers felt amazing.

They could hear the distant sound of voices emerging from the sitting room and, having removed their boots at the door, they were soundless as they hurried up the stairs, barely making it to the bedroom and shutting the door before they were on each other. Clothes, tights, underwear—everything hit the floor and was trampled underfoot as they found the bed.

'Don't go under the covers,' he growled before she could take refuge under the duvet.

'I'm fat!'

'You're beautiful.' She was. She moved him. Lying there, with her pale arms outstretched and her hair trailing across the pillow. He took his time looking at her, told her to look at him. Her stomach was decidedly rounder, her breasts fuller, her nipples bigger and darker. He could appreciate it so much better when she lay like this. It was the most erotic experience of his life. When he thought about the baby growing inside her he felt giddy. How could a man who had never given a moment's passing thought to fathering a child *feel giddy* at the thought of his baby inside her?

'So are you,' Bethany admitted unsteadily.

'A compliment…' He shot her a sexy half smile that made her toes curl. 'I like it. A lot.'

'That's because you have an ego the size of a house.' Her eyes widened, her breathing thickened as she watched him cross the shadowy room towards the bed.

'Now,' he drawled, sinking onto the bed, 'remind me where we were…Oh, yes…How could I forget…?' He parted her legs, positioned himself between them, hoisted them over his shoulders so that he was surrounded by her and, when he breathed, he breathed in the honeyed sweetness of her femininity. The way she gasped softly, as if she couldn't help the little noises emanating from her, as if she had no control over them, was a massive turn-on for him. How could she try and push him away when they both knew that this was what they both craved?

He tasted her thoroughly and then, temporarily sated, he made his way up her body until she couldn't stand it any longer and pushed his head to her breasts, which were heavy and aching.

She had to stuff her dainty little bed cushion over her mouth to stop herself from crying out as he drew one tender nipple into his mouth and began suckling on it, tugging it tenderly, then resuming his suckling. When she reached out to touch her other nipple, he pushed her hand away so that he could switch breasts. Gazing down with hot, drowsy eyes, she could see the glistening trail his mouth left across her breasts and she closed her eyes again, luxuriating wantonly as he devoted his undivided attention to her other swollen nipple while teasing the dampness between her legs with his fingers.

'Feel good?' He looked up and his smouldering eyes locked on hers. Bethany nodded like a puppet obeying its master's controlling hand. Worse, she had no qualms of conscience about what she was doing.

She just wanted him on her, in her and with her.

He pulled her up to him when his body could no longer be restrained and then she was on top of him. Cristiano, relinquishing control, grunted as she began moving restlessly on his erection. Her breasts swayed as she moved faster and harder, driving down on him until he could bear it no longer and he groaned with a long shuddering release. He could feel her body stiffening and arching as the waves of her orgasm carried her away. Looking at her during her moment of release, the way the colour flooded her face and her eyes fluttered tightly, was enough to have him stir again in her and she sagged onto him, smiling.

'Aren't you *ever* satisfied?' she asked, stroking his chest with one finger.

'When it comes to you, it would appear not. Do you feel the same way?' His voice was lazy but his eyes were sharp as he looked down at her face against his chest.

When she nodded his satisfaction was like a shot of adrenalin.

'Good. I'm glad because this is the way it should be. Once you stop fighting me, you can start enjoying the fact that I'm going to be a permanent fixture in your life. If you don't want to marry me, then I'll respect that but know that we are still going to be together.'

'Your pregnant mistress?' There was a lump in her throat which she swallowed down.

'I prefer not to use labels when it comes to relationships,' Cristiano said, kissing her unruly hair. 'Especially when the label is *friend*. That's the one label I think you'll agree is now totally irrelevant…'

CHAPTER EIGHT

CRISTIANO had never, personally, involved himself in the tedious pastime of buying presents for women. Firstly, he didn't have time to waste dithering in shops, peering at items of jewellery and asking sales assistants for help. Secondly, he could think of nothing more soul-destroying than trying to rack his brains and come up with a suitable present for any woman. No, this was where his faithful PA had always come into her own. A woman buying for another woman. Made sense.

For the past six weeks, however, he had ditched the PA in favour of the personal touch and had found the exercise a lot less arduous than he had expected. In fact…he had discovered that there was a great deal of enjoyment to be had browsing in the shops for things that would put a smile on Bethany's face. She had quirky tastes. Having made the initial mistake of buying her jewellery, which all women presumably loved, incredibly expensive jewellery with super-watt diamonds, only to find his present politely accepted and then equally politely returned, he had revised his ideas. She didn't care for jewellery, she said, especially expensive jewellery.

'I just bet this is the sort of stuff you're accustomed to

giving your girlfriends,' she had shrewdly remarked, and then had given a snort of disgust when he had defended himself on the grounds that he had never had anything returned to sender.

'Why is it,' she had asked, 'that rich men never feel the need to be imaginative?'

Cristiano, who had never failed to rise to a challenge, had become imaginative.

He had taken her to weird plays in fringe theatres, had bought her a first edition book by an Italian author which was over five hundred pages long, although he had asserted himself sufficiently to tell her that there was no way he was going to be reading it, even if he *did* speak Italian fluently, because if he couldn't get to sleep then he'd rather try his luck with a sleeping pill. But she had loved it and it had thrilled him to watch her face warm with pleasure.

He had given in to her ridiculous infatuation with a stuffed dog the size of a sofa which she had seen in Harrods and hadn't been offended when she had laughed at his scepticism and told him that he was a grumpy old man.

It seemed that there was very little she could do that offended him except for one little thing. That one tiny bump in the satisfactory progress of their relationship, namely the fact that she refused point-blank to marry him. Indeed, she had refused to move in with him, even though he had enumerated all the reasons, yet again, why it made sense, throwing into the mix the fact that they were now sleeping together; at least there was no more talk of *just being friends*. Cristiano couldn't understand it. If he was prepared to make the sacrifice, then why couldn't she? The more he had argued, the more she had dug her dainty little heels in but he had not given up. He simply resolved to get what he wanted via a more circuitous route.

Having never had to woo a woman, his attempts had not always met with resounding success. A constant conveyor belt of expensive meals out had met with a brick wall. So staying in had become the preferred option. And the kitchen, she had informed him, was a shared domain. She had bought him a recipe book and he had clumsily found himself cooking the occasional meal while he had wondered what his mother would have made of the arrangement.

Details such as those he had tactfully omitted when he had broken the news to his family. He had glossed over the lack of marriage, vaguely hinting at it as something that would happen *down the line*. He may even have let slip that Bethany was keen to walk down the aisle *after* she had given birth, when she had regained her figure. His mother had bought it but he still hoped to avoid learning what Bethany would make of that little white lie. It made no difference that the size and volume of her own lies would have put his tiny insignificant one in the shade.

Cristiano put this level of concern about her down to the fact that she was carrying his child. Under normal circumstances there was no question that things would have turned out very differently. He would have confronted her, as befitting any man who didn't like being duped. Had she not been pregnant, she would never have been able to gain the luxury of the moral high ground. The pregnancy had been the ace up her sleeve. Without it, she would doubtless have been duly repentant, would probably have thrown herself at his mercy and from that point, who knew what would have happened? It was highly likely that he would have exorcised her out of his system and returned to life as he had always known it.

As it stood, memories of his previous life seemed to belong in a very distant place.

He shopped. He was fascinated by her rapidly expanding stomach and the football games that seemed to take place inside it. He had read, cover to cover, a book on what to expect when you were expecting, which had a lot more allure, much to his bemusement, than his usual evening pastime of working. He thought about her when she wasn't with him. It seemed unnatural but he had grown to accept it.

Despite the cataclysmic change to his lifestyle, Cristiano was proud of the way he had handled the situation.

He rang the doorbell of her apartment. It was more and more ludicrous with each passing day that this was the arrangement that existed between them. Although he had settled her into the closest apartment to his that he could lay his hands on, the fact that she not only refused to marry him, for reasons which defied logic and which he couldn't begin to fathom, but insisted on separate living arrangements was a constant source of low-level dissatisfaction.

No one could tell him that she didn't enjoy sleeping with him, in positions that were frankly ingenious, taking into account her advancing pregnancy, and with penetration not always on the cards. He knew women and she wasn't faking it.

He had tactfully stopped trying to bludgeon her into an answer that made sense to him, but it still played on his mind constantly. Was this her way of keeping her options open? Was she deluded enough to think that she wasn't tied to him now? Did she really think that she could temporarily appease him, have the baby and then resume her hunt for Mr Perfect?

He was so busy scowling at the train of his thoughts that it was a few seconds before he realised that she hadn't answered the door and, at a little after seven, he couldn't think of any reason why she should be out.

He had been away for the past two days but he had spoken to her several times on the phone and she knew that he was coming over. So where the hell was she? He buzzed the bell again, this time more insistently, and at the lack of response immediately dialled her mobile. It was the most up to the minute mobile and one he had bought for her when she had moved down to London with him because he had been worried that her ancient cellphone might cut out at any given time when he might need to get in touch with her or vice versa.

He let it ring a few times, killed the connection and tried again. Worry was beginning to kick in. He raked his fingers through his hair. His instinct to break down the door was swiftly replaced by the realisation that there wasn't a hope in hell of him achieving that. The door was as solid as a slab of lead. In fact, he had had a new, exceptionally robust one put in to replace the flimsier original because, in London, you just never knew. He cursed his foresight, tried her phone again and was about to hit Plan B, which involved a locksmith, when she answered in a voice he barely recognised.

'Where are you?' was his opening demand.

'I'm here!' Bethany croaked. The doorbell had failed to wake her but the shrill ringing of her mobile had done the job. She glanced at her bedside clock and realised that she had been sleeping off and on for most of the day and into the evening.

'Where's *here*?'

'Here! In the apartment!'

'Then why the hell haven't you answered the door? And what's the matter with your voice?' He was aware of the locks being turned as he finished asking his questions and the worry which had come from nowhere and which had been dispelled the minute she had picked up her mobile slammed back into him as he took in her deathly white pallor, the shadows under her eyes and her tousled hair.

He stared down at her and panic, an emotion that was alien to him, hit him like a freight train at full speed.

'I don't feel very well.' Bethany stated the obvious as she turned and began heading back to the bedroom.

Having come straight from the airport, Cristiano grabbed his overnight bag and followed her, dumping his stuff on the ground. His heart was beating fast—too fast.

'I just need to sleep.' Bethany flopped down onto the bed and curled up under the quilt, pulling it over her head so that only her bright copper hair was visible on the pillow.

'Forget sleep. You need a doctor.' Cristiano flipped open his phone while he gently pulled down the covers so that he could feel her face. 'You're burning up. Why the hell didn't you get in touch with me?' He paused briefly to say something rapidly down the phone in Italian before snapping shut his cellphone so that he could devote one hundred per cent of his attention to her.

'You were fine when I spoke to you last night!' he told her accusingly and Bethany shot him a baleful look.

'I don't need a doctor, Cristiano.'

'Let *me* do the deciding on this one.'

'It's just a cold! A twenty-four hour bug.' She groaned and tried to submerge herself back into her warm cocoon under the duvet but he was having none of it. 'I just need to rest. And I was fine yesterday. I just got up this morning feeling a bit off-colour…'

'I spoke to you this morning and you didn't say anything.'

'You were in New York, Cristiano. What could you have done? You might think that you're capable of everything but you're not Superman. You couldn't have put on a red cape and flown across the Atlantic.'

'That's not the point.'

Bethany grunted indistinctly.

'I deserve to be kept abreast of your health at all times.' The thought of her alone in this apartment, too ill to drag herself out of bed, engendered a feeling of sick anxiety that bordered on the physical. 'You're pregnant,' he finished, standing up so that he could pace the room while cursing his friend for not already having arrived. Hadn't he told the man to get over to the apartment *immediately*?

The warm glow that had filled her at Cristiano's obvious concern dissipated like mist on a summer day. Of course he was concerned! He was concerned because she was pregnant, because she was carrying his precious cargo. The past few weeks had lulled her into a false sense of security, had seduced her into thinking that his solicitousness had been about *her*. Now those two words were a timely reminder that Cristiano only ever acted with an agenda and the agenda was about coaxing her into his way of thinking, about getting her to the point where she agreed to every proposition he ventured. She had stuck it out with insisting on having her own place, thinking that the formality of the arrangement would ensure a certain amount of essential emotional distance between them. She hadn't banked on the way he had managed to creep under all her defences.

He went shopping at the supermarket with her and he didn't complain. He bought her little things and she knew that thought had gone into the purchases. Twice he had cooked with the aid of the recipe book she had bought for him and, although the end results had borne no resemblance to the colourful, glossy pictures on the pages, he had tried. Again, without complaint. Most noticeably, he had *just been around*. She had no point of comparison on that score, but she would have put money on him being the sort of guy who always, but always, put his work ahead of everything and everyone. But he had been as regular as clockwork with her, there at the apartment by early evening, except on the occasions when he had been abroad for a couple of days and when he *had* been abroad he had called with unnerving regularity.

It had taken Herculean efforts to maintain her defences in the face of this aggressively silent onslaught but she had managed to convince herself that she had succeeded. What a fool she had been! Her crushing disappointment at the realisation that everything he had said and done had been because of their situation rather than because of *her* was ample proof that there was nothing reasonable or containable about her love.

She peeped at him from under her lashes. The sight of him literally took her breath away. It was shameful to admit, but he brought out the driven and the obsessed in her. In the middle of staring at him, he paused in his restless pacing to lock gleaming eyes on her.

'I can see that my trips abroad are going to have to be put on hold until the baby's born.' Cristiano never thought he'd see the day when his working life would take a back seat to a woman, but it appeared that that day had come. He needed to know that she was all right at all times and he knew that if he set foot out of the country then it would play at the back of his mind, like a record stuck in a groove, that some catastrophe or other might have happened about which she was keeping silent to spare him the inconvenience.

She was so obstinate and independent, despite the fact that he had managed to coerce her into moving back to London and for a few disconcerting seconds it occurred to Cristiano that those traits in her were less than ideal.

He didn't want her obstinacy, nor did he value her independence. He had always abhorred clingy, needy women but right at that moment he couldn't think of anything more rewarding than having her in a position where she would automatically turn to him for support in any crisis.

'Don't be ridiculous.'

In less than two strides, Cristiano was by the side of the bed. He didn't want to stress her out but it was suddenly imperative that he made her aware of his concerns, his *very reasonable* concerns.

'I'm not being ridiculous, Bethany. I'm being sensible. One of us has to be.'

Bethany gave an elaborate sigh that turned into a yawn. 'And naturally that role falls to you.'

Cristiano gave her a slashing smile and sat on the side of the bed so that he could half lean over her. He smoothed some of her damp hair away from her face. 'Two minutes out of the country and look what happens.'

Bethany reminded herself that this touching outpouring of concern for her welfare was just gift-wrapping around the more basic reality that he was only concerned for her because she was carrying his child but, lacking the energy for a fight, she contented herself with saying sourly, 'Like I told you, Cristiano, you're not Superman and you're not a miracle worker either. I would have got this cold whether you'd been in the country or not. I think I caught it when we were at the supermarket a couple of days ago. I stopped to chat to that little girl and she had a streaming nose. It happens.'

'You should be staying as far away as possible from anyone carrying germs!'

'What do you suggest? Maybe you could keep me locked up for the next couple of months.'

Cristiano was interrupted from informing her that it was

not an unreasonable idea by the sound of the doorbell and the arrival of his friend, who he introduced as Dr Giorgio Tommasso, a man in his late thirties who, Bethany translated from the rapidly spoken Italian, was then unfairly subjected to an irate cross-examination on the lateness of his arrival.

'Just ignore him,' Bethany murmured as he sat on the bed next to her, which elicited a grin of wicked delight.

'At last,' Dr. Tommasso said, 'a woman who is capable of standing up to this brute of a friend of mine. Now, I'm going to have a listen to the baby, make sure that everything is all right…'

Like a brooding sentinel, Cristiano stood by the door and watched as his friend asked questions in a low voice, said something apparently amusing because Bethany smiled, which nearly made him remind the good doctor that he was here to examine her and not play the stand-up comic and, finally, when the examination was over, he walked towards the bed.

'Well? Diagnosis?'

'The baby's fine, Cristiano.' Dr Tommasso smiled and patted his friend gently on the arm. 'No need to get frantic.'

'I think you're confusing *being concerned* with *getting frantic*,' Cristiano said coldly. It was obvious that, even in a state of pregnancy, she was still able to charm the birds from the trees. Giorgio had a grin on his face a mile wide. What the hell was so hilarious?

'My mistake, in that case.' He struggled not to laugh as they moved towards the door. 'Bethany's got a simple case of a miserable cold. She'll feel rough for a couple of days but she's young, she's strong and she'll be fine. Her blood pressure is good and the baby's heartbeat is strong. Nothing to worry about. How are you at making soup?' His eyebrows shot up in astonishment at Cristiano's grudging reply that he saw no reason why he couldn't do that, considering his skills in the kitchen were getting better by the day.

'I might be tempted to relay that back to your mother, Cristiano. She won't believe that her son is finally becoming domesticated!'

Spoken in jest but a salutary wake-up call for Cristiano. One step forward had, without him really noticing, entailed two steps back as far as Bethany was concerned. No more.

He found her in the bedroom sitting up, having just taken some mild medication which Giorgio had told her would make her feel better and would not affect the baby.

'Didn't I tell you?' she said, setting the glass of water down and folding her arms. 'A simple cold. Bed rest for a couple of days. Everything back to normal.'

Cristiano didn't reply. Instead, he went across to her wardrobe, opened it up and cast his eye over the range of clothes hanging up. On a shelf at the top of the wardrobe, she had stashed her suitcase and he proceeded to remove it in silence while Bethany watched him, open-mouthed.

'What are you doing?'

'What does it look like I'm doing?' He looked at her briefly over his shoulder. 'Don't even think of getting up. Bed rest.'

'You can't just start packing my case!'

'Watch me.' He strolled over to her chest of drawers and scooped up a handful of underwear, which he proceeded to pile on top of the clothes in the suitcase. This was followed by some random jars from her dressing table and unidentifiable make-up, not that there was much as she used precious little of the stuff. Task completed, he turned around and faced her with folded arms.

'Now listen to me very carefully,' Cristiano said in a voice as hard as granite. 'I've given this arrangement a go and it's not working.'

'It's not *my fault* that I picked up a cold!' Either the tablets she had taken had begun working with supersonic speed or else the adrenaline rushing through her body was powerful enough to disperse all her aches and pains.

Cristiano ignored her interruption. 'First and foremost, whether you like it or not, you're in no fit state to look after yourself here. You could barely make it to the front door earlier on. What if you had collapsed here on your own? Think about the consequences.'

'I would never...never do anything...' Bethany spluttered, but she paled at the picture he had cleverly painted. He had no key to her front door. She had stubbornly refused to give him one because she wanted to maintain her independence, but what if something *had* happened and he had been unable to enter the apartment? Was she so busy fighting him and fighting herself that she would risk jeopardising this baby? Was she really protecting herself or was she just punishing him because he didn't love her?

'I can't take your word on that.' He slammed shut the suitcase and yanked the zip around. 'Instead of getting in touch with me the minute you began feeling ill, you took to bed, pulled the duvet over your head and pretended that the outside world didn't exist. If you'd called, sure, I might not have been able to get here from New York in minutes, but I would have called Giorgio and he would have come over at a point when you would have been up and able to let him in. Do you see where I'm going with this? Am I spelling it out loudly and clearly enough?'

'I hate you!' Tears of bitter frustration filled her eyes. Gone was the warm man who had been worming his way through her defences. Back in his place was the cold-eyed stranger who had showed up on her parents' doorstep with a truckload of accusations.

'That's not the feeling I get when we're in bed together.'

'Is sex the only thing that matters to you?'

'It tells me that you don't hate me.' Cristiano shrugged and took out his cellphone.

He was calling his driver. Bethany listened as he directed him to collect them and from there on she would be staying at his apartment. She told herself that her stay was going to be of the minimum duration but not even that bracing thought could still the nerve-racking sensation of a net closing in around her.

'My driver will be here in an hour. Now, I think you should have a bath. It'll make you feel better.'

'I don't want a bath.'

'And you can quit sulking. It's not going to change anything.' He sauntered off in the direction of the en suite bathroom and Bethany ground her teeth together in frustration as she heard the sound of running water.

He returned a few minutes later and unceremoniously lifted her from the bed, ignoring her angry protests and carried her into the bathroom.

She liked big bathrooms. It was a legacy, she had told him in passing, from having to grow up sharing a bathroom with her sisters which had always seemed to be occupied whenever she had needed it. He had accordingly got her an apartment that had a ridiculously big bathroom, big enough to house a deep padded chair on which he proceeded to sit her down.

'Your fever's going and your colour's returned,' he said approvingly. 'But I still don't trust you to make it to the bath without falling over.'

'Don't be ridiculous!' Bethany, still smarting from his appropriation of the decision-making process and his snide reminder that she couldn't possibly hate him because they were lovers, eyed him with resentment. He ignored it.

Her head was beginning to spin. She squeezed her eyes tightly shut as he began to undo the buttons of her voluminous nightie, one of two she possessed which still fit her comfortably. She could smell the fragrance of the lavender bubble bath but she wasn't going to admit that yes, she really did want a long soak in the bath.

She also told herself that it was crazy to start being coy about her body when he was so intimately acquainted with it. Who would she be kidding? Nevertheless, as he helped her to the bath with a gentleness that was incongruous in a man as big and powerful as he was, she was acutely conscious of the weight of her breasts and the sensitivity of her nipples.

She slid into the beautifully warm water with her eyes still shut and was aware of him pulling the chair across so that he could sit alongside her.

'I'm fine now,' Bethany informed him.

'Thanks, but I'm not willing to take the chance.' Furthermore, Cristiano was enjoying her acquiescence. With no options on the table, she had been backed into a corner and he felt absolutely no guilt about that because, as far as he was concerned, he was just doing what had to be done.

Her stomach protruded above the level of the water, wet and shiny and unimaginably sexy, and so did the pouting peaks of her nipples, although he was pretty sure that she wasn't aware of that, with her eyes stubbornly closed and her mouth pursed into a tight line.

She might exude all the outward signs of frosty disapproval and maidenly outrage, but that, he knew, was only skin-deep. He would bet his vast fortune that if he bent over and took one of those tempting pink crests into his mouth she would melt faster than a candle over an open fire.

'How does that feel?' he asked, reining in his wayward

thoughts when he felt his body hardening at the delectable sight of her in the bath. She did, after all, have a cold.

'I'm not going to be staying with you at your place once I'm back on my feet,' Bethany was constrained to point out and, as she opened her eyes and looked at him, he gave an elegant shrug that signified precisely nothing.

'Let me soap you. My driver will be here in a minute.'

'I'd rather not.'

'Why? Because you don't like being told what to do? Even though it's for your own good? Sit up.'

Bethany looked at him with flashing, angry eyes and he raised his eyebrows in mild amusement and reached for the soap. 'Enjoy the experience,' he drawled as she dutifully and sulkily sat up, 'because the next time I soap you it'll just be a prelude to taking you.' Did he have time for a cold shower? Probably not, but he would damn well have to have one the minute he got back to his place.

He began soaping her, taking his time as his hands slid over her shoulders and around and under her breasts.

'That's the most arrogant thing I've...I've ever heard in my life...' Her nostrils flared as his tactile fingers brushed against her nipples, which hardened in immediate response, thereby making a nonsense of her insult.

'Is it?' Cristiano murmured, reluctantly surrendering the soap back to its rightful place and standing up so that he could reach for a towel. 'Don't you like being taken care of?' His voice, as he began drying her, was like oozing, melted honey, tempting her senses and turning her brain to mush. 'I may be a dinosaur but isn't that most women's dream?'

'I don't know about most women's dream. I just know about my own and this isn't it.' She reached for the large fluffy towel which he had put by the side of the bath and wrapped it securely and protectively around herself, still keeping her eyes firmly away from him.

Was she being greedy in wanting the dream of being loved for herself? Was that asking too much? She felt that if she released that dream then she would have nothing. Yes, he would be a responsible husband and a diligent father but, for her, it would be a sham. She didn't want a marriage based on duty or a man who would sooner or later see her as a burden.

'I refuse to rise to the bait, Bethany.' Cristiano called upon all his reserves of restraint and reminded himself that she was not feeling well, that her thoughts were probably all over the place. Yet he could feel the frustrated anger rising inside him, wanting to find a way out.

'Whatever.' She allowed herself to be helped out of the bath, which was daily becoming more of a chore for her.

'You,' he said through even, gritted teeth, 'can be the most infuriating woman on the face of the earth. I have been accommodating to the point of insanity with you, and yet you insist on throwing it back in my face.'

Bethany felt a twinge of guilt but overriding that was the thought that she didn't want an *accommodating* guy; she wanted a *doting, adoring guy who would climb the highest mountains and forge the deepest canyons for her*.

But arguing would get neither of them anywhere and she didn't want to fight with him so she kept her thoughts to herself.

'Why do you want to marry me if I'm that infuriating?' she pointed out with, Cristiano thought, an utterly feminine lack of logic. He watched in simmering silence as she dressed with her back to him and then turned and faced him with a defiant expression on her face. 'Well?' she pressed, hating herself for persisting in this and yet not wanting to let it go just yet.

'How are you feeling?'

'You haven't answered my question.'

'And I don't intend to.'

'Why not?'

'Because it doesn't deserve an answer.' He picked up her suitcase as though it weighed little more than a feather and walked towards the front door. Then he waited for her and gently held her by the arm as they headed down to his waiting driver.

'Doesn't it bother you that you're not my dream come true?' Bethany felt the sting of tears at the back of her eyes. It was a pointless exercise but she wanted to hurt him the way he was, without even knowing it, hurting her.

'Call me prosaic, but getting hyped up and emotional over romantic dreams has never been my thing.' He ushered her along to where his car was parked on a double yellow line outside her apartment block. 'We are faced with situations in life and we deal with them. End of story.' So who the hell *was* her dream guy? he wondered viciously. He was finding it hard to credit the depth of rage her wholly unjustified criticisms were arousing in him.

And he had dealt with this particular one with grace and consideration, Bethany grudgingly conceded.

'I'm beginning to feel tired.' She could feel herself wilting in the back seat of his car, drained of all her reservoirs of energy, which she had uselessly poured into arguing with him.

'My shoulder is right here,' Cristiano said gruffly. 'Lean on it.'

She did. Closing her eyes and then falling into another of her light dozes. Her brain felt muddled and tired. He wanted her to lean on him and she so badly wanted to do just that and for a few confused moments, before she drifted off, she wondered why she was bothering to fight him every inch of the way.

Was her way any more valuable than his when it came to dealing with their *situation*? He was offering her two parents for their baby and a stable arrangement. As he had reminded her on more than one occasion, they were brilliant in bed. How long that would last, she had no idea but wasn't it better to have a slice of bread rather than shout and scream because the whole loaf wasn't on offer?

The confused thoughts were still with her when the car finally came to a stop and she was lightly shaken out of her uncomfortable sleep.

She blinked sleepily and gazed up into his unswerving gaze. For a few seconds, she felt her breath catch in her throat and she straightened up and looked around her with a stifled yawn.

'You were mumbling in your sleep,' Cristiano told her. 'Care to tell me what that was all about?'

Bethany went beetroot-red but remained silent as the door was opened for her and she was helped out of the car by Cristiano's attentive driver.

All the questions which she had been asking herself when she had finally drifted to sleep were still there, nagging away at her convictions. Alongside them now, arranged like an uninvited supporting cast, was the thought of her parents, who would be over the moon if she just gave in and married the man they had welcomed and accepted like their own son…the thought of his mother who, she knew from what he had told her, would be likewise in the queue of happy people…to be joined by both her sisters, who had met and been charmed by Cristiano and flatly disparaging about her decision to wait in hope rather than marry a man who might not be the perfect guy for her…

'We need to talk,' she whispered uncertainly.

'The four least welcome words in the English vocabulary,' Cristiano remarked grimly. His hand was still around her as they rode the lift to his penthouse at the top.

'I'm thinking you won't find this talk too bad…'

CHAPTER NINE

'NO TALKING until you're in bed,' Cristiano told her, preceding her into his penthouse, which made her own sizeable apartment look like a doll's house in comparison.

The cool, imported Italian tiles, which ran through the entire floor, were liberally interrupted by the warm, vibrant colours of luxuriously expensive rugs. With virtually no doors to break the clean sweep of the sprawling apartment, the illusion of acres of space was breathtaking.

Even feeling as miserable as she was, Bethany paused, as she always did, to absorb the impact of his place.

She had never failed to marvel at the casual way with which he accepted this level of opulence. He could very well have been blind to the excruciatingly expensive originals hanging on the walls, all of which were independently worth more than most people could hope to make in a lifetime of hard graft.

He wasn't snobbish. His fabulous wealth was just an accepted fact of his privileged background and a powerful learning curve for her in understanding why he had always chosen to protect himself by knowing the pedigrees of the women he had dated. Until she had come along and blown his well thought out control measures to smithereens.

His bedroom was as impressive as the rest of the pent-house. Dark wooden shutters kept the rest of the world at bay and dominating the room was his bed, handmade because he had wanted something larger than a normal king-size. Every stitch of linen was tailored specifically to fit and the creams and chocolates imbued the space with an utterly masculine stamp.

As she obediently slid under the duvet, she noticed that the little bunch of flowers which she had impulsively bought him three days previously as a tongue-in-cheek present because his penthouse, she had told him, was just a little too relent-lessly alpha male, had found their way to his bedroom and were in the process of wilting in a vase on his chest of drawers.

The sight of the flowers focused her mind and brought her tangle of thoughts together.

She had fought long and hard for her independence. She had stoutly refused to be browbeaten into marrying him because his traditionalism demanded it and she had actually thought that she had made headway because he had stopped mentioning it, but now she was tired and doubtful as to the validity of her arguments.

She had missed him when he had been away, even though she would have died rather than admit it. She had also missed his reassuring presence when she had started feeling unwell, missed the way he took control and made her feel safe. It was a joke, really, when *safe* should have been the last thing she felt around him. She had scoffed at his pig-headed insistence that marriage was the only way of dealing with their circum-stances but, in truth, when she thought about him agreeing to her terms and backing out of her life, she was assaulted by a sense of driving blind panic.

The flowers gave her hope that if he didn't love her then he might just have it in him to care enough to treat her with respect when the novelty of their sexual relationship petered out for him. She held on to this fragile hope as he left, to return a couple of minutes later with a glass of water because dehydration, he informed her, was the last thing she needed. The truth was, and she couldn't make herself stifle it, maybe, just maybe, there was a chance that he could grow to feel some kind of love for her. Surely that happened! But, if it didn't happen for them, then the banquet which should have been her married life would be a plate of crumbs and she would learn to deal with it.

'So…' Cristiano sat on the bed next to her and braced himself for one of those conversations which would have him gritting his teeth in frustration and clamping down on his inclination to shout at her until she saw things his way '…you said you wanted to talk.'

'You kept my flowers.'

Cristiano followed her eyes to the chest of drawers and he flushed. 'I can't remember any woman ever buying me flowers,' he said with a shrug.

'But I bet you've bought dozens of roses for women in the past.'

'Was this what you wanted to talk to me about? Because, if it is, then it can definitely wait.'

'I…I wanted to thank you for…looking after me. If I seemed ungrateful then…'

'You're deeply sorry? Apology accepted.'

He realised how unusual it was for her to apologise. Of course, she had in the past, when he had first shown up on her doorstep and exposed her deceit, but even then her apology had bordered on challenging. Right now, she sounded sincere. He liked it. In fact, he liked it so much that he decided to work the conversation to his benefit. Ever the opportunist, he considered it a crime were he to fail to.

'It's tough always having to stand on your own,' he murmured persuasively, taking one of her limp hands in his and distractedly playing with her fingers while he tried to mentally work out how to turn this brief moment in time, when her defences were well and truly down, to his advantage.

'Let's take tonight,' he continued softly, his dark, sexy voice rolling over her like waves lapping on sand. 'You were unwell and yes, I admit that calling a doctor might not have been strictly necessary, but isn't it reassuring to know that I care enough to do so?'

'I'm not dependent on you...'

'Of course you're not! And I would never ask you to be...' The idea, however, was an alluring one but one not to be mentioned at this juncture. 'Which isn't to say that accepting a helping hand is a sign of weakness.' The conversation seemed to be meandering and Cristiano decided to take the reins a little more firmly. No way was he going to be getting back to the value of friends rubbish she had been fond of spouting. 'We've been down this road before, Beth, but I really think it's time for you to acknowledge that it's just a hell of a lot easier dealing with this as a couple.'

He was encouraged by her lack of fighting talk. This, he thought, was more like it. He swept aside the discomforting thought that he, a man who was used to having the world at his fingertips, needed to use every trick in the book to get this woman down the aisle.

How severely he had underestimated the impact impending fatherhood would have on him!

'And think about our child.' His voice was grave. 'Should we not be man and wife, what would he think if he found out that he had been denied the privilege of both his parents because you wanted no part of it?'

Bethany frowned. 'I can't speculate that far into the future.'

'You don't have to. I can.'

She had the unnerving sensation of being under siege when, after ten minutes, he had managed to paint a picture from which she emerged as inconsiderate, thoughtless and selfish. This time round, however, she was not inclined to fight the tacit accusations, delivered by his honeyed tongue.

'Nothing to say?' Cristiano asked into the silence.

'I'm tired.'

'You should be resting,' he said immediately. He was sharp enough to know when to leave well alone. He had planted the seed and this time it appeared to have fallen on slightly more fertile ground. In due course, he would water it and he was pretty sure that it would reap its harvest eventually. Indeed, sooner rather than later. 'I'll have some food ordered in. What do you fancy?'

'Is this your way of reminding me how necessary it is to have you around, Cristiano?'

He looked suitably affronted and stood up. 'I'm only trying to do what's best and, anyway, I'm hungry if you're not. Even if you're not,' he was obliged to point out, 'you have to eat. You've probably had a lousy diet while I've been away. So what do you want? Chinese? Indian? I could get my driver to bring something from the Savoy Grill. In fact, I'll do that. You don't need greasy food. Soup and some fresh bread sound okay?'

'You don't have to.'

'Don't have to what?' Cristiano stilled, something in her voice making him feel uneasy.

'Send out for food. I'm fine with whatever you have in your fridge.'

'I've been away for two days and, before that, have only

touched base with this place. I wouldn't want to compromise your health by attempting to feed you with the contents of my fridge.'

There he went again, she thought sadly—all about the baby.

'Actually, what I meant, what I *mean*…is that you're right and you don't have to pander to my needs to get the point across. I've got it. Getting married is the sensible thing to do, so if your offer still stands, then…'

Having shamelessly manoeuvred for just this occurrence, Cristiano was reduced to a few seconds of complete and utter shock.

'In other words…' Bethany shrugged, making sure he didn't miss her concession '…you win.'

Considering he was the victor, Cristiano found that he didn't care for her phraseology, although he didn't pause to question why that might be.

'I'm glad.' In fact, ridiculously so and that was perfectly understandable, bearing in mind that he was a man who didn't like any situation that frayed at the edges. He strolled back towards her, smiling. 'In fact, I'm more than glad.'

'I'm surprised you haven't said something along the lines of knowing that I'd come to my senses in the end.'

'I knew you'd come to your senses in the end.' For someone who had been wrapped up in a million and one emotional, illogical reasons as to why she couldn't possibly commit to marriage with him, Cristiano was oddly disconcerted by her sudden change of mind. He knew that it was a conversation best left alone but he found himself sitting on the bed next to her, frowning as he tried to harness his thoughts.

'What brought about this change of heart?'

'Does it matter?'

'Possibly not, but why don't you satisfy my curiosity?'

Bethany shrugged. Now was her opportunity to show him that she could be as level-headed and downright cold as he was when addressing the delicate situation between them.

'Maybe I realised when I got ill that I'm more vulnerable than I like to think. Maybe I've just reached the point when it's time to put crazy notions aside. This is my life. I'm pregnant, for better or for worse. You've done the honourable thing by proposing marriage to me. It's the most sensible course of action, so…'

She was repeating everything he had said to her in the past, virtually word for word, but Cristiano felt unsettled and disproportionately angry at her resigned acquiescence.

'All true.' His voice was clipped and matter-of-fact. 'I just wonder what happened to all the romantic notions of not wanting to be tied down with the wrong guy.' *The wrong guy*. Never had three words left a more bitter taste in his mouth.

He also couldn't work out why he wasn't more upbeat about this. He had spent long enough canvassing for such a result, after all. Yet, in possession of the spoils, he now perversely thought that the least she could do was show a bit more enthusiasm. He'd spent weeks bending over backwards to accommodate her and yet none of that appeared to have been taken into account.

Bethany worried her lower lip. Cristiano, whose strong, aggressive personality had been predictable in one area only, and that was in his desire to have her firmly wedded to his side to fulfil his prehistoric notions of conventionality, was now responding in a way that brought her out in a fine film of nervous perspiration. He had told her that he was glad, that he was *more than glad*. But he wasn't looking very glad.

The thought that he might have changed his mind, that he

might, actually, have come round to *her* way of thinking, despite everything he had said in the past, made her feel sick. Had he just been going through the motions of presenting the marriage option as the one and only solution to what he saw as a shared problem, in the vague expectation that she would continue rejecting his offer, giving him the chance to claim the pious moral high ground in the years to come? He had insisted on her moving in with him. Maybe he saw that as a necessary step at a time in her pregnancy when she needed to have him around. Maybe, without even realising it, he had already accepted that the move would be temporary, until the baby was born, at which point he would, of course, remain a dutiful and generous presence in the life of his child and probably to her as well, but perhaps her insistence on maintaining their respective freedom had begun its gentle process of eroding his convictions that a child required both parents on site.

She wanted to backtrack, to tell him that if he'd changed his mind then that was *perfectly all right*.

Instead, she said coolly, 'I wasn't thinking in a practical way. If you're still interested in marriage, then I'm willing to submit but with a few provisions of my own.'

Willing to submit? Provisions? Anyone would think that he had threatened torture instead of a lifetime of having anything she could possibly want!

'And what, exactly, might these provisions be?' Cristiano asked blandly.

'I realise that it'll be a marriage of convenience, but... but...' She fiddled with the duvet and then stared down fixedly at her fingers while she tried to catch her breath and sound as normal as possible. Two adults being sensible. 'I don't expect you to...start playing the field the second you get tired of playing Happy Families...'

Cristiano's eyes iced over. He walked over to the window, buying himself a bit more time so that he could control the volcanic fury rising in him. 'What sort of person do you think I am?' he asked in a voice as smooth and as sharp as a razor blade. 'How sleazy do you think I am?'

'I don't think you're sleazy.' Bethany stuck her chin up and glared at him. 'I think you're a man who has…needs… and, when you get bored with me, then you might be tempted to stray…'

'Then you'll have to make sure that life never gets boring, won't you?' It was a pretty sleazy remark, considering he had professed outrage at the description, but Cristiano wasn't ashamed of himself. This wasn't what he had expected when he had envisaged his plans for them both finally coming to fruition.

'Is that a threat?' Bethany asked tautly. 'Do whatever you want or else you find someone else?'

'You're putting words into my mouth and I don't appreciate it.'

'Well, *excuse me* for just trying to lay down some boundaries here, in so far as they'll affect my life!'

'You're not laying down boundaries. You're bracing yourself for failure.'

'That's not the way I see it and if you won't agree to this small thing then it's probably better that we do the best we can with a custody arrangement.'

Cristiano wondered how it was that she had such a knack of saying precisely what he didn't want to hear. Just the words *custody arrangement* ratcheted up his outrage, bringing to mind as it did visions of her with another man. He made a Herculean effort to control his temper. She had agreed to marry him, albeit gracelessly, and he would work with that.

'We marry,' Cristiano stated flatly. 'I won't fool around and neither will you. Moreover, you will throw everything you have into making our marriage work. I will not tolerate anything that reeks of being a sham.'

Bethany took that to read that, as far as the outside world was concerned, they would present the image of the perfect couple. She knew that it was now or never. Agree and her fate was sealed. Object and he would no longer bother trying to convince her to walk down that road with him. He would see her through the pregnancy and then he would step back. Not from his child, but from her.

It angered her to finally admit to herself that she didn't want him to be with any other woman. She couldn't bear the thought of him looking at anyone else, speculating about what it might be like to have sex with them.

Bethany nodded and didn't say anything. When she next sneaked a look at him, he appeared more relaxed. He pulled out his mobile phone, dialled into it and handed it over to her.

'Your parents. Time to break the good news to them. I will then let my mother know.'

'Already?' Her voice was high-pitched and nervous but she could feel a treacherous thread of excitement fluttering through her. Her hands were shaking as she took the phone from him.

Fifteen minutes later, she returned the phone to him. He had remained in the bedroom, standing with his legs slightly apart, his arms folded and giving the impression that he was making sure that she didn't chicken out at the last minute.

'Your turn.'

Cristiano scowled. She had complied with his wishes but there was a tension between them that had been absent since she had moved back to London. He felt as though she had given in, accepted the unacceptable and the mere fact of it now stuck in her throat. Thanks to him, she had been forced to relinquish her romantic dreams and bow to practicality. The notion that they might actually *be happy* did not seem to figure anywhere on her horizon, never mind that they had been perfectly happy before, in bed and out of it, for that matter.

'I will call later. And there's no need to look so miserable about the prospect of marrying me. I'm going to be giving you all the security you could possibly hope for.' He looked at her with brooding frustration.

'I know.' *Security!* When marriage should have been a joyful exchange of love, he offered her security. She hated herself for loving him so much that she was willing to compromise the principles she held dear. She hated herself for knowing that, however inadequate any marriage to Cristiano might be, it would still be better than living apart from him, seeing him on appointed days, watching from the sidelines while he inevitably hooked up with another woman, maybe one who he went on to fall in love with. And she hated the unpalatable truth that if she didn't marry him he would get bored with her sooner or later, at which point she would have no hold whatsoever over him and, without him in her life, she would be rudderless.

She would always be faithful to him because she had no choice. She was a prisoner of her own ungovernable emotions. He, on the other hand, whilst professing to be insulted that she would even think of confining him to a life of fidelity, would have no such emotional ties. She would be condemned to a life of never really trusting that he wouldn't stray. How many men, with a libido as powerful as his and the sort of sexy, magnetic pull that had women swinging round for a second look, would embrace monogamy once the novelty of a wife who had been forced on him began to fade? He wanted her *now*, he found her pregnancy sexy *now* but, when it came to calendars, *now* was over in the blink of an eye.

And there he was, frowning at her and ordering her to look happy!

Worse than that, she wanted to smooth the frown from his face and she had to fight against the temptation to beat herself up for putting it there.

'You were happy.' Cristiano issued that as a statement of fact.

Bethany flushed because yes, she *had been*. Happy in the little bubble they had created since their return from Ireland. She had had the one hundred per cent attention of a very devoted Cristiano. Now she felt oddly confused instead of at peace with her decision.

'What's changed?' he asked. He was finding it difficult to comprehend her new mood. They had good sex, she had accepted his proposal of marriage. So why the hell did she look as though she had found a penny and lost a pound? He raked his fingers through his hair and began pacing the room.

'Nothing,' Bethany whispered miserably. She lay back and closed her eyes, shutting him out because it tore her heart in two just to look at him.

After a while, she forced herself to open her eyes and give him a wobbly smile. 'What about that soup and bread you were talking about?'

Cristiano was oddly reluctant to let go of their conversation although he didn't know where he expected to get by pursuing it. He had forced her to marry him, of that he was in little doubt, had laid down one or two ground rules of his own, which was important. If he had come across as tyrannical, then it was for her own good, as she would discover in the fullness of time. Of that he was certain. Any thought that he might have behaved differently was not allowed to surface because the more time he had spent with her, the more convinced he had become that he wanted her exclusively to himself. He permitted himself to return her smile because there was no sense in dragging out an uncomfortable situation. He had already got a grudging admission that she had been happy with him. He saw no reason why she wouldn't be happy again.

'I will set things in motion,' he said softly, content to have reasoned himself out of his peculiar mood. 'A small wedding, I think…Wouldn't you agree? Although, of course, if you feel strongly about having the whole big traditional thing, then I will be more than happy to oblige.'

'Dress in white and about to give birth…It doesn't work, does it?'

'It would work for me,' Cristiano said roughly. 'But then so would pretty much anything else.'

Bethany's face suffused with colour. The black cloud that had been hanging over him had been shrugged off. He was back to his normal self. Did that mean that he was really happy that they were getting married? He was so much better at concealing his emotions than she was.

'Now,' he said, before his eyes began drifting and his body began following suit, which it always seemed to do whenever he was around her. 'Food and then sleep.'

Bethany sipped her coffee and stared out idly at a scene of London in the throes of Friday lunchtime shoppers and workers making the most of their hour away from the desk. She, herself, with only a couple of weeks left of her pregnancy to go, was far too big to do anything as dramatic as shopping. She was still determined to walk as much as was comfortable, which got her as far as the patisserie in the square just off the King's Road, and she had developed the pleasant habit of having a cup of coffee and her lunch there. From her vantage point behind glass, she could muse on her impending wedding, due to take place three months after the baby was born, while the rest of the world went about its business.

Cristiano, who preferred to have things done slightly faster than the speed of light, had peremptorily assumed that they would be married just as soon as he could arrange someone to physically marry them, but Bethany had stood firm. She only intended to be married once and she wasn't going to submit to a rush job even though the marriage might be one of convenience. She wanted to pretend to herself that it was the real deal. Since when was that a crime?

A couple in front of one of the high end shops were arguing with one another and Bethany followed their angry hand gestures while she lost herself in her thoughts.

She had pretty much given up trying to hang on to any defence system with Cristiano. With the single-minded focus that was so much a part of his driven, assertive personality, he had set about proving himself indispensable. He was attentive, he was supportive, he was everything she could have hoped for and if he never, ever, not once told her that he loved her, then it was a telling omission to which she never alluded. In return, she kept her feelings to herself and quietly gave in to the crazy hope that he would, suddenly and miraculously, decide that he was in love with her.

To the outside world, he certainly gave every impression of it. The weekend spent in Ireland with her parents only recently had seen him the very embodiment of the devoted husband-to-be and she was pretty certain that when she met his relatives in two weeks' time he would project the same image.

Bethany, however, did not want to go down this particular road. The minute she started thinking about the stark reality of their situation she could feel herself begin to flounder and panic and she had become adept at shoving all her uncomfortable thoughts to the back of her mind.

The arguing couple had moved off. Bethany glanced down at her watch, thinking of the wall to wall meetings that Cristiano would be facing today while she loitered with her savoury pastry and her hot chocolate. He would be back late, he had told her, because his schedule was packed tighter than sardines in a tin.

She looked up, half smiling because just thinking of him made her feel like a giddy teenager and, as her eyes focused, she blinked and leaned forward, dropping the pastry back onto the plate.

Her heart began to thud as she recognised Cristiano, so impossibly distinctive in his impeccably tailored Italian suit, one hand thrust into his trouser pocket where he would be idly jangling whatever loose change happened to be there because that was one of his little habits. He was laughing, leaning into the petite blonde woman standing in front of him and he was concentrating on whatever she was saying with every fibre of his being. Because that, too, was just something that he did.

Bethany felt her breathing become laboured. Her eyes slid away from him to look at the woman he was with. She had a gamine face, big eyes and her blonde hair was cut close to her head. It was a style she could pull off. She looked like a very pretty tomboy with her saddle style bag slung over one shoulder and her sneakers and combats.

Cristiano was supposed to be at meetings all day. He didn't have a window, he had told her. Some big deals were on the brink of coming to fruition, he had told her. He had kissed her on her nose and drawled, with lazy amusement because he knew that his remark would be provocative, that she shouldn't worry her pretty little head about any of it, then he had transferred the kiss to her mouth and told her how tempted he was to ditch the deals and climb back into bed with her.

Clearly whatever deals he had had were wrapped up in attractive little packages, which was a little technicality he had omitted to mention.

She was so focused on the tableau taking place where the couple had earlier argued that she only realised how tightly her fists were clenched when the soft palms of her hands began to hurt from the pressure of her fingernails. She came close to passing out as he took the blonde's arm with what looked to her as way too much familiarity and then strode off, still smiling, still looking *bloody pleased with himself*.

The monster that she had become accustomed to thrusting to the back of the cupboard jumped out and grabbed her by her throat. This was what she had feared. Having got her in the position he had wanted from the very beginning, he was already beginning to appreciate that the world was full of women. Did the girl work with him? For him? It didn't matter. All that mattered was that he had lied to her and the lie was loaded with significance. What sort of meeting took place close to the chic cafés off the King's Road? What sort of businesswoman dressed in combats? The secretive sort, it would seem, that he couldn't tell her about.

She spent the next few hours in a state of emotional meltdown and when, at a little after ten, she heard the sound of the front door opening and slamming shut, her entire body tensed.

He was tugging off his tie as he strolled into the bedroom. He walked straight across to her, for all the world as if absolutely nothing was wrong, as if it had all been just another day at the office and shot her one of those trademark sexy smiles that made every bone in her body go to liquid.

'You're up.' He stated the obvious. He leant over the bed, where her book was resting comically on her protruding stomach, and deposited a kiss on her mouth.

The smell of him was so intensely satisfying, so uniquely *him*, that she almost returned the kiss.

'Good day?'

'Busy. I'm going to have a shower. Don't move a muscle. I'll be out in fifteen minutes.'

He didn't close the door to the adjoining bathroom, nor was he modest when it came to disrobing in front of her and her eyes lingered on him with sickening hunger until she looked down and lay on her side, the only comfortable position for her now.

Cristiano, shower finished, exited the bathroom with his towel slung low round his waist and paused by the door. He was acutely attuned to her every mood and right now his antennae were telling him that something was wrong. He didn't like it. His days of fundamental indifference to how women interpreted his behaviour was a thing of the past.

He walked slowly towards the bed and circled so that he was in her reluctant line of vision.

Bethany stared at the unnerving sight of his legs in front of her and the bottom of the white towel which only paid lip service to the task of concealing his impressive manhood.

She had had a few hours to work out how she was going to deal with what she had seen. She had contemplated saying nothing and had rejected that option because the *not knowing for sure* would eat away at her like a cancer. But she wasn't going to get hysterical. Cristiano didn't do drama. She rolled over onto her back and heaved herself up into a semi-sitting position.

'Have you eaten?' she asked, her eyes fluttering away from the magnificent sight of him which, she realised with dismay, could still make her feel weak and gooey inside, even though that was a sensation she desperately wanted to suppress.

'There were sandwiches tonight round the conference table.' Cristiano stared down at her taut frame, the way her eyes were skittering away from him. 'You're tiptoeing round something. Why don't you just come right out and tell me instead of working yourself up into a lather?'

'How did you spend your day?'

Cristiano shook his head impatiently and walked towards his chest of drawers, dropping the towel en route and shrugging on a pair of boxers. 'I worked. That's what I do. I sat opposite boring men in suits poring over reports, checking legal documents and signing off on deals. In between I kept my eye on the shares index so that I could head off any potential investment crises. At eight-thirty one of the secretaries went out to buy some sandwiches. I ate two. I came home. You were upbeat when I left you this morning. I did not envisage returning to find you in a mood.'

'I'm not in a mood. I'm just trying to find out how you spent your day.'

'And now you have. Unless you'd like me to elaborate on some of the more tedious details.'

'Maybe just one,' Bethany told him, taking in a deep, steadying lungful of air.

Cristiano sighed and looked at her wryly. He had no idea where she was going with this but he would humour her. She was big with his child and she was his wife-to-be. All normal rules of play were suspended.

'Can't wait to hear.'

'What were you doing at lunchtime with another woman? And don't try to deny it. I saw you.'

CHAPTER TEN

CRISTIANO stilled. He was hanging on to his temper with restraint because he didn't want to stress her out, but no one had ever questioned his movements before.

'I don't have to deny anything,' he said. Habit born from a lifetime of being unanswerable to anyone slammed into place. He wasn't going to be cross-examined by *anyone*. It smacked of being under the thumb and yes, he had altered a lot for this woman but enough was enough. Lines had to drawn, essential boundaries established.

His words shattered every fragile hope that there would be a perfectly reasonable explanation for what she had seen and Bethany felt as though she had been delivered a physical blow.

'You're too much, Cristiano,' Bethany whispered. 'You're just too much.'

'What is *that* supposed to mean?'

'It means that I can't go through with this marriage with you.'

'This is ridiculous.' He was keeping his voice low and reasonable but it was a feat of willpower. 'And you don't need to get worked up at this point in time.'

'I'll get worked up if I want to get worked up!' Everything

came down to her health because she was carrying his baby! Tears of bitterness and disappointment and frustration trembled on her lashes and she pursed her lips to avoid the disadvantage of becoming emotional.

Cristiano gritted his teeth together. 'Is this it, Bethany? Am I to be subjected to a change of mind every single time you get a little down over something?'

'I'm not *getting a little down*, Cristiano! I'm just asking you to explain why you lied to me about where you were today. Is that asking too much?'

'It's telling me that you don't trust me,' Cristiano said quietly. 'You're accusing me of having an affair and I'm telling you that I'm not. I don't see why there should be anything further said on the matter.'

So why, Bethany wondered, wouldn't he tell her exactly what he had been up to with the woman she had seen him with? If he was as innocent and as pure as the driven snow, why the secrecy? Maybe he was *technically* telling the truth. Maybe he wasn't involved in some kind of rampant sexual situation with the woman but what if he was *playing with the idea*? Maybe he didn't count *flirting* as infidelity, but *she* did. She didn't want him to even *look* at another woman. Ever.

Her thoughts clamoured in her head like a thousand squabbling voices. She tried to get hold of a little reason and common sense. She knew that he was right in so far as she couldn't chop and change her mind about marrying him like a leaf blown about in a high wind. But he didn't love her so how could she, ultimately, trust him?

'Fine,' Bethany muttered miserably.

She had retracted her claws, Cristiano acknowledged, but not for long. He knew this woman like none other, knew her well enough to recognise her determination when it came to getting answers. Indeed, she was very much like him in that respect. But he wasn't going to be browbeaten in this instance. He bracingly told himself that however much he was responsible for her well-being and however honourable a man he was when it came to doing his duty, he was not about to be emasculated by anyone demanding detailed reports on him to satisfy her feverish imagination.

He had done nothing wrong, end of story.

Arriving at this irrefutable truth should have instantly restored his mood, but Cristiano found that he was still weirdly out of sorts.

'It's late,' he said abruptly. 'And arguing into the early hours of the morning isn't going to do you any good. You need your sleep.'

'Stop telling me what I need and what I don't need.'

'Why? I'm right.' He said that as though it was a truth written in stone.

'For *right*, read *arrogant*.' How could he stand there and treat her like a child throwing a temper tantrum over nothing? Would that be the way he intended to treat her in the future? To every concern she might voice, would he just always say, *Trust me, I'm right*?

She had made her bed and she knew that she would lie in it, but she couldn't stop herself from thinking about the woman who had been smiling up at him. If she had been dressed in a suit, if she had looked the part of the business-woman, then Bethany might not have had such a hard time believing him, but what businesswoman dressed in combat trousers?

Like a record stuck in a groove, she kept replaying the scene in her head until she wanted to burst into tears.

Cristiano was watching her carefully. Her body was as rigid as a piece of board. He couldn't understand why she was making such a fuss over nothing but, driven into a corner, he refused to unbend. Instead, he said in a conciliatory voice, 'I'm going to go to the study and work for a while. Leave you to calm down.'

'I don't *want* to calm down! I want to talk.'

'You either trust me or you don't. Yes, I met a woman at lunchtime. No, I am not sleeping with her. Now, I'm going to leave you on your own to get some sleep. Don't be concerned if you wake and I'm not here. I think I might sleep in one of the spare rooms tonight.'

As soon as he had left the room, Bethany succumbed to a flood of hot tears.

Had she been wrong? She had wanted answers and no one could say that that had been unreasonable, but if she had been right, then how was it that she now felt as though the bottom of her world had dropped out?

She resisted the temptation to follow him to his study and pick up where they had left off, but pride glued her to the bed and, besides, would he say anything different from what he had already said? Cristiano was fiercely independent and ran his life according to his own personal laws, which were always fair. He had conceded much on her behalf. She remembered his revised timetable which had seen him with her at times that would have surely gone against every workaholic gene in his body. He had accused her of mistrust and her brain had shrieked that mistrust was always going to be an issue when he didn't love her, but she couldn't imagine Cristiano sneaking around behind her back. Which, in turn, brought her back to the same old questions and the same old fears.

Added to this horrible mix was an element of doubt. When had Cristiano ever lied to her? In fact, when it came to that particular trait, it was fair to say that *she* was the main culprit. Yet she had not hesitated to accuse him of lying or at least of concealment.

She finally fell asleep, disquieted by the fact that some-how, somewhere, the conversation had turned and she had been left feeling the guilty party.

She surfaced the following morning at the ungodly hour of seven-thirty to find that his side of the bed had not been slept in.

Panic gripped her and she stumbled through her ablu-tions, which now took much, much longer because of her unwieldy girth.

Where was Cristiano? Despite her troubled thoughts, she had slept like a baby, despite her awkwardness lying down. She had not heard him enter the room at any point. Had he been true to his word and slept in the guest room? There was no sign of him in any of the guest rooms. Perhaps he had gone to work early.

She was dialling his number with trembling fingers as she walked out of the bedroom and she almost fainted in relief when he picked up on practically the first ring.

'Where are you?'

Cristiano heard the urgency in her voice with a deep sense of satisfaction. Direct inquisition had disagreed with him, but he had felt no better having stood firm on his resolve not to have his movements questioned. In fact, he had spent the night feeling as though he had been punched in the gut. At some ridiculous hour in the morning he had sneaked into the bedroom and looked at her. It felt all wrong not to slide into the bed next to her, but he hadn't wanted to risk waking her up. Hadn't wanted to take the chance that she might surface to resume her argument with him.

'You're up.'

'Where are you? You haven't answered me.'

'Give me a minute.'

Bethany heard the dull burr of a phone that had gone dead and she snapped shut the lid of her cellphone. Her heart was beating like a hammer. She glanced down at the cellphone in her hand and, when she looked up, it was to see him standing in the kitchen. She hadn't heard him but he must have been working in the study at the end of the apartment. Relief at just *seeing him* nearly blew her off her feet. She wanted to race over to him, fling herself into his arms, tell him how much she loved him.

'Sleep well?' she asked instead, looking at him cautiously as he strolled towards her. He was absolutely gorgeous. She wondered whether, one day, she might become accustomed to the immense physical impact he always contrived to have on her. He wasn't smiling, which made her nervously wonder if he was still brooding on their argument of the night before. Right or wrong, she realised that she didn't want that.

How far would she go, she wondered, in accepting whatever Cristiano chucked at her? Because she loved him? Experience was fast telling her *very far indeed*.

'No.'

That single word jolted her out of her painful musings. 'You don't look like a man who's had a restless night.'

'I scrub up well.'

'What…were you doing?' She hated herself for asking the question but she unhappily heard herself ask it anyway.

'I worked for the better part of the night. Right here, to forestall your next question. On my own.' Cristiano had had hours to think about their argument. He had had hours to analyse his initial response to her questioning and minutes to conclude that really, far from being driven into a corner, which was a place he didn't care for, he had *liked* it. He had *liked* the fact that she had been jealous because from jealousy came need and need was a very good thing in her. Habit had conditioned his initial response. It was time to say goodbye to habits, even the old ones that took the longest to die.

'Come and sit down,' he said, urging her into the kitchen. 'I'll make you some breakfast.'

'Why?'

'Aren't you hungry?'

'I mean why aren't you mad at me?' She wondered if he thought that she might suddenly go into premature labour if she became too stressed out. His concern usually centred on making sure that she was in tip-top shape with the pregnancy.

'Why should I be?'

'Because…because…' She found herself seated at one of the bar stools in the kitchen, watching as he deftly whipped up some scrambled egg on toast for her. She wasn't entirely sure how she had got there.

'You had every right to ask me what I was doing in the company of another woman.' Cristiano placed the plate of toast and egg in front of her and pulled one of the chairs around so that he could sit on it facing her as she dabbled with her fork, ostensibly not meeting his eyes, until he gently tilted her face up.

'You either have to eat or else look at me. You don't have the option of doing neither.'

Bethany chose to concentrate on her food. He had become a dab hand at cooking certain basic dishes. Scrambled eggs was one of them.

'I *do* trust you,' Bethany mumbled between mouthfuls, her face burning. 'It's just that I was…' While she racked her brain to think of an adjective that wouldn't reveal the level of her obsession with him, he jumped in to supply it.

'Jealous?'

There was a whisper of silence and she put down her

fork, staring down at her plate, which seemed the only safe point on which to focus. His hand covered hers and she risked a glance at his face.

'I'd be jealous of you too,' he admitted roughly.

'You…would?'

'Hell, yes.'

'That's because you're the kind of guy who sees women as possessions.' She made her excuses for his confession lest she begin playing with the seductive fantasy that it meant more than he intended.

'You couldn't be further from the truth, in actual fact.' He stood up abruptly and removed the plate, which seemed to have acquired mesmerising qualities for her. He didn't want her mesmerised by anything or anyone but him.

'I won't pretend that I haven't had my fair share of women,' he began, his back to her as he roughly washed the plate followed by the saucepan and pieces of cutlery. Then he turned round so that he was looking directly at her, leaning against the counter, his feet loosely crossed at the ankles. He shrugged as her eyes flickered towards him and he noted that glint of jealousy again. However hard she tried to hide it, it seeped out of her and she was obviously innocently unaware of how intoxicating he found it.

'And I've never allowed any woman to dictate terms and conditions to me.'

'I wasn't dict…'

'Shh. Let me finish.' He nodded towards the sitting room and waited until she was settled comfortably on the sofa before sitting next to her to continue. 'I've always led a life conducted on *my* terms. Women had the choice. Abide by my rules or quit. My rules were simple. Work came first and there were to be no scenes. No hissy fits, no possessiveness, no wanting more than I was prepared to give.'

Totting up the number of rules she had broken on his magical list made Bethany feel a bit faint. She had also *got* onto his list, in the first instance, by breaking the cardinal rule number one, which had to be *no deception*. He had shown remarkable resilience in the circumstances but had he now run out of patience with her?

Cristiano leaned forward, his elbows resting on his knees. He raked his fingers through his hair and shot her a baffled sideways glance that had her nerves frantically racing.

'Okay. So maybe I broke one or two of your…'

'Forgot another rule. No interrupting. Not when I'm trying to figure out how to say what I have to say.'

'Which is…?' Bethany's voice was a shade above a whisper.

'Which is…' Cristiano looked at her. There was a strange, swooping sensation inside him. It alternately made him feel terrified, exhilarated and absolutely convinced that this was where he was finally destined to be. 'Which is…that you are allowed to break every rule in my book. In fact, if I'm not mistaken, you've already ridden roughshod over most of them and I've discovered that I don't care.'

'You don't have to say stuff like that.'

'What do you mean?'

'I mean, I know that you don't want to upset me because I'm pregnant, but that doesn't mean that you have to…have to…'

Cristiano gave a smile of such immense warmth and tenderness that Bethany drew in her breath unsteadily.

'You're beautiful. Have I told you that? You pulled me in hook, line and sinker from the very first minute I laid eyes on you. Even when I stormed over to Ireland to confront you, you were irresistible.'

Bethany didn't say anything. Actually, she didn't want to

breathe for fear of disturbing this frank outpouring of emotion. She never wanted this moment to end. She wondered if it would destroy the mood if she told him that he was beautiful too.

'I should have been gutted when you told me that you were pregnant. I had never anticipated my lifestyle changing. On the few occasions I thought about marriage and children, I foolishly imagined that my life would carry on without major interruptions. A suitably docile wife would hover somewhere in the background, doing whatever needed doing on the home front, leaving me free to remain exactly the way I'd always been.'

Bethany was fascinated by the vulnerability she saw on Cristiano's face. She reached out to touch him and he clasped her hand tightly in his.

'When you offered me the uninterrupted choice, however, I found that there was no way I was going to take it. I wanted all of you.' He looked at her steadily. 'I didn't want to be a part-time father and I definitely didn't want to be a part time fixture in your life. Okay, this is really hard for me to say and I've never said it before, but I love you. I think I fell in love with you over those two weeks in Barbados but hell, how was I supposed to know that? I'd never felt that way before and, to tell you the truth, I didn't figure that love could be wrapped up in such a bloody unpredictable, turbulent package. I called it lust and thought it was a passing affliction. Then I called it duty. I gave it every name under the sun but the right one.'

'You *love me*?'

'Don't sound so shocked,' Cristiano told her defensively. 'Everything I've done over the past few months has proved it.'

And it had. Bethany threw her arms around him and

would have told him a thousand times over that she loved him too if he hadn't stopped her, laughing.

'I am sorry I didn't explain about Anita,' he said eventually.

'You felt cornered,' Bethany mused slowly. 'I wasn't trying to be a horrible, nagging shrew.'

'You have every right to be a nagging shrew. I'd rather that than thinking that you wouldn't care if you saw me with another woman because if I ever saw you with another guy I'd grind him to a pulp.'

Still on cloud nine, Bethany learned that Anita, the wearer of the combat trousers who had given rise to such drama and soul-searching, was a coordinator for charity work in Africa.

'I wanted to surprise you when I told you. I'm now involved in building a community village centre in Central Africa. It's to be the first of many.' He grinned at her open-mouthed expression of surprise. 'Don't look so stunned,' he told her, holding her close and depositing a loving kiss on her mouth. 'Didn't you tell your parents, after all, that I'm involved in charity work all over the world...? You can help me decide where my next project will be...considering you're the instigator...And, by the way, you have nothing to fear from Anita. She's gay.'

Cristiano and Bethany's baby daughter was born without any drama two weeks later. Cristiano announced, with an earnest sincerity that made Bethany laugh, that he had fallen in love all over again. Helena Grace was plump, with her mother's copper hair and her father's lustrous dark eyes and those amazing eyelashes. Grandparents descended and fussed over the first grandchild for both lines, wedding plans were discussed in detail, with Cristiano and Bethany watching on with amusement and contributing as required and neither could wait until they found their bed at night.

With their baby often between them, before she was gently transferred to her Moses basket at the side of the bed, her tiny fists curled tightly as she slept, they softly discussed leaving London for somewhere with commuting distance but less hectic.

'I never thought,' Cristiano mused more than once, 'that I would live to see the day when I would want to escape the frantic pace of working life in London. This is your fault, my darling witch…'

Bethany was all too happy to take the blame.

Happy ever after is only the beginning!

Callie Grey has got a great job, a great man and, fingers crossed, a whopping great diamond—then her boss/boyfriend gives her dream and her sparkly ring to someone else...

She's spent her life reaching for the moon. Now Callie's let go and, falling among the stars, who will be there to catch her?

www.millsandboon.co.uk